The Incorruptibles

John Hornor Jacobs

The right of John Hornor Jacobs to be identified as the author
of this work has been asserted by him in accordance with
the Copyright, Designs and Patents Act 1988.

First published in Great Britain in 2014
by Gollancz
An imprint of the Orion Publishing Group
Carmelite House, 50 Victoria Embankment, London EC4Y 0DZ
An Hachette UK Company

This edition published in 2015 by Gollancz

1 3 5 7 9 10 8 6 4 2

A CIP catalogue record for this book is available
from the British Library

ISBN 978 0 575 12346 5

Typeset at The Spartan Press Ltd,
Lymington, Hants

Printed in Great Britain by
Clays Ltd Elcograf S.p.A.

The Orion Publishing Group's policy is to use papers that
are natural, renewable and recyclable products and made
from wood grown in sustainable forests. The logging and
manufacturing processes are expected to conform to the
environmental regulations of the country of origin.

www.johnhornorjacobs.com
www.orionbooks.co.uk
www.gollancz.co.uk

'I wish more books were as fresh and brave as this'

Patrick Rothfuss

'An exceptionally well written book'   Mark Lawrence

'Fantasy needs writers who push the envelope, and Jacobs finds the edge and tears right through it. If you want original, you've picked up the right book'   Myke Cole

'*The Incorruptibles* is a rare thing: a clever story *and* an action-packed one'   *SFX*

'*The Incorruptibles* blends cowboys, the Roman Empire and high fantasy and not only get away with this unusual mix but pulls it off with such aplomb that you're left wondering why no one has attempted it before'   *Financial Times*

90710 000 461 172

For John Ronald Reuel, George, Elmore, Colleen,
and Larry
Strange bedfellows

In girum imus nocte et consumimur igni

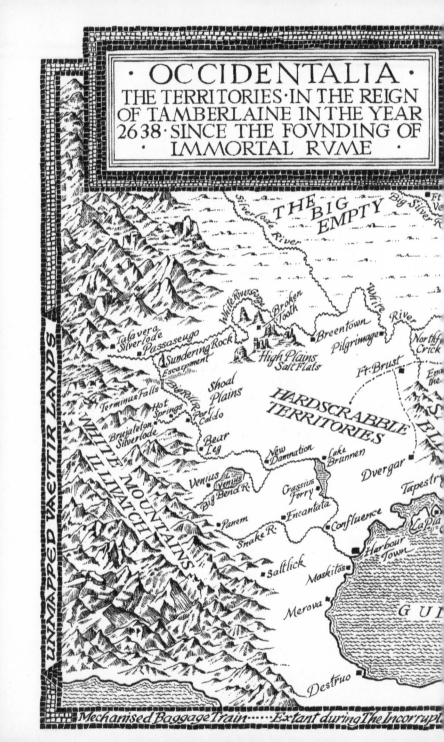

IMPERIAL
RESERVE PROTECTORATE
NOVORUM
(NOVO RUMA)
Center Spike
Bloody Spur
Greenway
formerly
Verde Fields
BLACK IRON MTS.
Weald
SULLA
THOUSAND
ACRE WOOD
Mammon R.
Argenta
NOVO
LUGDUM
Alexandria
Novo
Ciprea
NOVO
LATINUM
Big Rock
Covenant
Aurelia
OCCIDENS OCEAN
FT. LUCULLUS
OF MAGERAS
MEDIERAN BLOCKADE
Chiba
(New Mediera)
N
Mechanised Baggage Train
Proposed Lines 2643

ONE

W E RODE THROUGH fields burning like the plains of Hell –
Fisk on the black, Banty on the roan bay, and me on Bess,
the mule, leading a string of ponies. We came up from the delta
and the lush watershed of the Big Rill through the edge of the
farmlands. Settlers worked the fields, shovels in hand, throwing
dirt on fallow fires. The farmhands looked lean and scrappy; poor
folk, eking a living off the land.

'The praefect orders another hunting expedition, they'll be
floating his body back to New Damnation,' Banty said, low and
through his teeth.

Fisk sniffed, glanced at the smoke billowing above us and then
back out over the Big Rill's sun-hammered silver. No one moves
the way Fisk does. Slow and deliberate, each gesture languid and
relaxed. Until it isn't.

The *Cornelian* churned the wide waters of the Big Rill, brag-
rags whipping in the wind, steaming upriver, while we kept pace.
Fisk and I had picked up the escort contract from Marcellus out
of New Damnation, but the proconsul's tribune had saddled us
with Banty, the greenhorn, who was good for nothing, except big
talk and no action. The tribune wasn't a bad fellow, but even good
folks make mistakes.

Fisk watched the *Cornelian*, the sky, the land. He remained still

1

but his gaze never stopped roving, his grey eyes bleached by sun and years in the elements. We'd been partners for the last decade and I still didn't know anything about the man, other than scraps and pieces. Had a family once. Could shoot out the eye of a sparrow on the wing. Feared no man or *vaettir*. There would be no rest for Fisk until the stretchers were gone from the earth. He hated them with a passion wronged men reserve for gods, dangerous women, and whiskey.

Head-count conscripts milled about on the boat's galleries, staring out into the West, no doubt scanning the horizon for stretchers, terrified. Up on the top deck, in the shadow of the pilot's roost, stood an umbrella sheltering patrician women. The stacks, *daemon*-fired, blew ash and cinder skyward as if answering the flames of the fields.

Fire calls to fire, they say. I believe that.

From where I sat on Bess, I watched the other scouts – Sharbo, Ellis, and Jimson – riding the western shore, stirrup-high in fallow growth. No farms that side of the river, so close to the mountains. Stretchers come down, raiding.

Fisk said, slowly, 'How d'ya come to figure that, Mr Bantam?'

Banty put a hand on his pistol, a Hellfire six-gun with *imp* rounds. Sure to sully his soul, but deadly.

'I'll kill him.'

Fisk glanced at the young man, taking in the rumpled uniform, the tight grip on his pistol.

'You might be stupid enough, at that.'

I laughed at the pup's posturing and watched as his face went through a series of expressions, from shame to embarrassment. Maybe some anger in there as well. When they're as young and full of juice as Banty, you never know which way they'll jump.

At the sound of my laughter, Bess showed gum and green teeth and turned her head to nip at my leg, but I swatted her with my hat. There isn't anyone, anything, any animal, like Bess. Stout, indomitable, with feet that never slip, not on mountain trail or riverbed. She was the lead mule, the fountainhead, immovable and cantankerous and full of mirth. Behind us followed the string of ponies, bays and roans, dappled and skewbald. None would challenge her lead.

Except maybe Fisk's black. That bitch was fierce.

Then Banty laughed too, barking a forced, childish sound, and said, 'I almost had you there, Fisk.'

He was quiet, my partner, holding the black's reins lightly in his big, rawboned hands. He watched the sky to the east of us, up high in the heavens, as turkey buzzards circled slowly above the plains.

He didn't even turn when he said to Banty, 'That's right.' He slowed the black and took a Medieran cigarette from his vest pocket. 'You almost had me, Mr Bantam.'

There wasn't any warmth in Fisk's voice. But there was never any warmth in it, except maybe when he cooed to his horse and nuzzled the beast's canescent neck, or rubbed down her flanks. She was a bitch and a brute, but his and his alone and valuable. Never could understand why he didn't name her.

Banty kept talking. 'He's a devil for the hunt, Cornelius is. When we hit that thicket of quail, Fisk, you shoulda seen the look on his face. Like Ia'd done forgave him all his sins and he'd gone straight to Heaven.'

Fisk's expression hardened. He wouldn't shoot the boy, not now, not for foolishness alone. But Fisk's a killer, natural born. I didn't know much about the man after a decade, but I knew that much. With every bit of idiocy issuing from Banty's mouth, he put his life in jeopardy.

Banty slapped his knee and laughed again. 'Nice gun he's got, though, ain't he?'

'It's a nice piece,' I said. 'Real nice.'

'Now that you're with us, maybe things'll be different,' Banty said.

'Possible,' said Fisk. 'Contract is to escort the *Cornelian* and to scout the territories she'll be passing through. Doesn't say nothing about hunting.'

Fisk had joined us at the confluence of the Big Rill and the Snake. He'd been south in Harbor Town to restock his ammunition from an engineer there. I don't have no truck with engineers, for fear of the final disposition of my eternal soul, Ia help me, but Fisk and Banty – and it seems like every other able bodied man in the Hardscrabble Territories – does. Which means I have to be polite, and small, and humble as a saint. Show no aggression or some pistolero will give me extra breathing holes, which ain't high on my list of priorities. Hellfire pistols – their upkeep and ammunition – are expensive, and men who're moneyed well enough to afford them are usually prickly in their honor, or the appearance of it.

But I keep various sharp, pointy metal things on my person, and I'm good with a blade, and I can bring down a running rabbit at fifty feet with a sling. But there aren't enough good deeds in the world that can counter-balance the taint you do your soul once you pick up a Hellfire pistol. Each bullet takes a bit of you with it.

Fisk thumbed a match into fire and lit his cigarette, which smelled of spice and brimstone and brown ladies on a tropical shore. Smoke is a vice that sullies your body, not your soul, so I'm not finnicky about it and enjoy a puff every now and then myself, Ia forgive me.

'He's highborn. A senator, with proconsular imperium. That's big. And acting governor of the Territories, so I'll remind you to watch yourself. But, it's true, he's mad for the hunt,' I said. 'With his cohort behind him, if he wants to hunt, he'll hunt.'

Fisk did this thing with his eyebrow as he looked at me. Hard to tell what the man was thinking, other than he *was* thinking.

He turned the black to the east and rode out a fair distance.

'There's his private engineer to think about,' Fisk said over his shoulder. He took a long draw off the cigarette, held it, and expelled the smoke that whisked away on the breeze. He spat loose tobacco into the dry grasses at his feet. 'Shoestring?'

'Yeah?' I answered.

'Believe I'll outride a bit. Take a gander there.' He nodded at the pinwheel of turkey buzzards, hanging in the sky like dead cinders on the wind.

'Huh. Might be something. Might be just a lame shoal auroch.'

He nodded again and pulled his hat tighter on his head. Everything about him was weathered. The grey hat, the faded riding leathers and vest, his gunbelt.

He squinted at me and said, 'There's stretchers about.' And then he looked back to the grey-washed plain. 'I'll catch up with you,' he added, and rode off. We watched him go, up the far rise, over the slope and into the east where the buzzards wheeled under a big sky.

'What's stuck in his craw?' Banty asked. Always talking, that one.

'He's just hard.'

'There's always hard men. Garrison's full of them.'

'Yep. You're right there.' I touched my forehead, my lips, my heart. 'Ia save us from hard men.'

'You believe that shit?'

'Yes. Matter of fact, I do.'

Banty grinned then, and placed his hand on his six-gun. 'Can't deny you Ia. But if he gives a shit about us, he sure is doing a good job hiding his concern.'

Just a boy, playing at being a man. There's nothing to do in the company of the faithless. Or the addle-brained. 'Ia *will* keep us from hard men, stretchers, shoal beasties, and *daemon*-born. Never you worry.'

'I'll give you a full gold denarius if you can tell me how.'

'Ia sends us our *own* hard men.'

Banty looked puzzled; then his expression clouded as he looked after Fisk.

We'd come out of the farmlands, into the dry flat plains before the foothills of the White Mountains, a wide expanse of wind-whipped shallow hillocks wreathed in grass. The *Cornelian* churned the waters, silvering its wake, while lascars in johnboats paddled ahead to plumb depth and search for rocky shoals and sandbars. The Big Rill was wide here, and shallow. The boat's *daemon*-fired engine pumped a tilted column of ash and smoke into the brittle sky, and gunfire, like the crackle of cooking pig fat, echoed across the open spaces. The Senator was shooting again.

Ignoring that Banty had opened his mouth to speak, I threw him the ponies' lead rein.

'Watch for the skewbald mare. She balks at streams.'

I turned Bess to the east and followed Fisk.

TWO

HE DIDN'T LOOK at me when I brought Bess abreast his black, though she chucked her head and nickered and tried to pull ahead.

'Thought I might tag along.'

He nodded, keeping his eyes on the buzzards.

It's a big country, and the vast expanse of it calls for silence, at least from humankind, though I'm not quite human. Got enough *dvergar* blood for folks in New Damnation or Passasuego to look at me twice. To rough me up maybe, spit on me, if they've a mind to. Lynch me if I look funny at their women. Might be different if I carried Hellfire with me, if I was willing to tarnish that immortal part of me, but I won't do that. Not for pride, or station. Not for rudeness.

Fire calls to fire.

Fisk seemed to sense what I was thinking because he tugged his carbine out of the long holster on the black's flank and began feeding *imps* into it. He popped each one off his belt, thumbed the intricate wards to make sure of the round's integrity, and slipped it into the chamber. The silver of the bullets was tarnished and black, but the warding was bright where it caught the light. When Fisk was done, he levered the action and unloaded and reloaded his pistol.

We rode, trotting through the long plains grasses. After an hour or so, we came upon a tangle of scrub brush and fragrant but stunted sumac trees. Fisk dismounted, and I followed suit.

He gave the black a small nosebag of oats, and I let Bess forage the sumac berries. She's sure got an iron belly. Found her chomping brambles once, and I had to tug her away.

I tossed Fisk a hunk of jerked auroch tongue and some hardtack, and we both ate a little underneath the unbroken sky, watching those damned turkey buzzards circle and bank.

'There's something dead there, I think,' he said.

I didn't argue. 'Most likely a lame calf or cow.'

'Seems like.'

He dropped the hobble rein, pulled the carbine, and looked at me expectantly. 'We walk the rest of the way?'

'Yep.'

We strolled under the big sky, up a shallow rise, through the long shoal grass. Occasionally Fisk slowed and let me catch up, but before we reached the peak and could look down on the carnage there he'd broken into a run – a big ungainly lope, his spurs jangling with each footfall, his arms pumping even with the carbine clutched in his fist.

Fifteen or twenty of the shoal auroch sprawled in a disarray of lumps on the plain; woolly little hillocks. But that's wasn't what Fisk ran to. When I caught up, I saw the remains of the settlers.

At our approach, the buzzards erupted in a flurry of black wings and a stench of blood. But the corpses were pretty fresh. Probably no more than a day old. Hours maybe. The carrionfowl had only had time to take their eyes, lips, and other soft bits.

There was a boy, no more than eleven, a shattered rifle in his lap, an arrow through his throat, whose shocked, eyeless face was turned to the low, gunmetal grey clouds. There was a man, nearby, leaning against the carcass of an auroch, his mouth gaping wide in a frozen scream, his stomach split open. Wasn't until I got closer that I saw he was holding his own tongue and liver.

Fisk hissed air through his teeth. 'And this one.'

A man, spread-eagled over an auroch, his back flayed open.

He pointed. 'They took his backstraps.'

Stretchers are many things, but I'd never heard of them eating a man. At least I'd never imagined they would. The man was skinny, though. Not much tenderloin on him.

'Buzzards probably snatched up the straps. There's a bloody mark on the ground over here.'

Fisk remained silent, his grey eyes scanning the bodies. There was a tenseness about him. At times like these I felt there was some doom waiting for us just beyond the next hill, and nothing Ia or the old gods or Hellfire pistols and *daemonlore* could do about it.

Still get that feeling, sometimes. There ain't no bottom to the well.

Fisk squatted on his hams by the boy, looking at him, maybe trying to fix his image into memory, or maybe trying to get an idea of how the boy might have looked before he died, putting the puzzle of his face back together to honour him.

He reached out and snapped off the end of the arrow with the fletching.

'It was Berith, I think.'

'Who?'

'That big red son of a whore.'

He turned the arrow in his hands, ruffled the feathers that'd been daubed with paint in a triangular pattern.

'What, the stretcher from Broken Tooth last year? That his name?'

'No. Just what I call him. Nobody understands their Ia-damned gibberish anyway.'

'I'm curious. Why Berith?'

'Just seemed like the sort of name a murderous arsehole would have.' He stuffed the arrow haft in his belt. 'And there was a big red-haired tussler at Fort Verrier by that name. This stuff reminds me of that son of a bitch.'

The sun broke through the cloud cover, sending a bright column of slanted light sweeping across the carnage. Fisk stood upright and raised his rifle.

The creature on the rise seemed to have just coalesced out of air, or risen up from the earth, a thing of dirt and grass, wind and sky, and the blood of settlers. He stood there, impossibly tall, long red hair whipping in the wind. All pointy ears and sharpened teeth. *Vaettir*.

Everything was silent but I could tell he laughed at us. And when he moved, it was a blur so damned fast I recognised an arrow in the air before even registering that the stretcher had moved. The first arrow stuck out of Fisk's thigh, and then another drove into the ground at his feet. A figure appearing beside the *vaettir* Fisk called Berith, also impossibly tall, cradled something over his shoulder.

Even with the pierced leg, Fisk didn't fall. He had the carbine up and firing.

The gun belched Hellfire, and there was a boom as the *daemon* was released inside the chamber, behind the bullet. In the half-lit, grey world of the plains, the muzzle-fire left an after-image of a winged horror, expanding and rising, loosed into the world. An *imp*.

You can't hear their screams of joy at freedom, the *imps*, but you can feel them, and every shot tears at the air, beats at your ears and exposed skin – as damaging as lying in the too-hot sun. It's an invisible pressure. The pressure of damnation.

And Fisk loosed them. If the stretchers were fast, Fisk was their equal, like light moving across water even while arrow-struck.

One shot after another, he levered the rounds, his hands moving blindingly fast.

He stopped firing only when it was clear they were gone. Disappeared into the grasses, subsumed by sky, eaten by earth. Who knows how they move? They appear and disappear. They're beyond man. Beyond *dvergar*.

'Ia-damn. Ia-damn.' He said it over and over. He was pale then, and I couldn't tell if it was from the arrow wound or the after-effects of gunwork. I'd felt each of those rounds as they loosed. I didn't like to imagine their effect on him. 'Got to follow ...'

'No, you're struck.'

'You see that other one?' Fisk tried to push me away. 'Carrying something. Maybe a settler. Ia dammit, he took a settler.'

'Nothing you can do about it. Here.' I grabbed his arm and laid him down. He still clutched the carbine. No telling how many bullets were left or how much damage he'd done his immortal soul.

There wasn't much blood coming from his leg, so it didn't look as if he was going to expire from blood loss.

'We gotta get back to the *Cornelian*. We'll get this out.'

He groaned, pushed himself up off the ground and hobbled west, toward the White Mountains and our horses.

He stopped and turned to me. 'Don't let all this auroch meat go to waste, Shoestring.'

Opening my oiled satchel and withdrawing my longknife, I went to the nearest auroch, still warm to the touch. I took its tongue and liver and, moving to the next animal did the same. I harvested the carcasses until my satchel was full of meat, bloody, still warm.

Then I jogged to catch up with Fisk, the eyes and breath of the plains upon me.

THREE

Banty was wet and miserable by the time we returned to the *Cornelian* and the gurgling waters of the Big Rill.

The leaden clouds had opened up, the sun slipped behind the mountains, and the land was dark and rainswept.

Banty'd managed to start a fire and set up a lean-to in the lee of a bank break. The ponies, still tethered together, stood stamping and steaming on the sand. A johnboat lay on the shore, while a legionary and two lascars moved among the ponies with a feedbag.

We came into the firelight and Cimbri, the legion prefect, raised his whiskered head. He wore his oiled greatcloak and uniform. His phalerae from old campaigns, those brass and golden gilt plates indicating his rank and accomplishments, peeked from the open flaps of his coat – small, but conspicuous, and absolutely necessary to enforce his command, given his low birth. Cimbri's wide-brimmed hat bore the crossed spears – two pila – of the classic Ruman legionary of old, before Hellfire and artillery had been introduced. A bragging stick was jammed into his belt alongside his six-guns and longknife. Cimbri looked as irritated as Banty looked miserable.

'There you are, dwarf. Where's the pistolero?'

By then I was leading Fisk's black, who kept tugging at the reins and pulling away until I had to hobble her front legs. Fisk was awake, but he'd gone into some kind of muttering dream while his leg oozed blood. I keep a flask of cacique on my person for medicinal purposes – solely medicinal, on my honour. He had drained it the moment I'd handed it to him.

Cimbri noticed Fisk, slumped on the black, and raised his eyebrows.

'Trouble?'

I hopped off Bess, and moved to help Fisk down. Cimbri stood up, kicked at Banty, and said, 'Fool. Go help.'

We got Fisk under the lean-to and I retrieved the whiskey from the packhorse that carried what Bess wouldn't. Fisk was delirious, almost insensible, but not quite far enough gone not to take a swallow. A man's got to be pretty far gone not to swallow when whiskey is at hand.

I gathered up my barber's bag, scissors and clean linens, pliers and hacksaws, and spread out them out on a scrap of clean canvas. I split Fisk's britches from cuff to crotch and pulled the flaps out of the way. There was blood, but not too much of it, and it was doubtful he'd lose the leg. For a man doomed to perdition's flames, he had been granted luck by Ia, that's for damned sure.

A good amount of whiskey went into Fisk, and Cimbri and I both took long pulls from the bottle before I drenched his wound in liquor and pulled free the arrow shaft. He didn't yelp or make a sound, but his eyes were open, looking straight into my face. It wasn't an empty stare, but it wasn't altogether with us, either. His body jumped some when the shaft cleared flesh. I followed the removal with another dousing of liquor, and wrapped his thigh in clean linens.

'Those'll have to be changed in the morning,' Cimbri said. 'You want to bring him to the *Cornelian*? We can have Miss Livia look after him. She's schooled in bloodwork.'

'Let's just let him settle here before we get a highborn woman involved. Leave us a lascar and Banty.'

Cimbri nodded. 'I'll send back the lascar. Report?'

'Stretchers.'

'I figured that.'

'Murdered a group of settlers just about an hour distant. Took one of them to Ia knows where.'

Cimbri glanced at Banty. 'Take care of their mounts. Groom them, then half nosebags, each.'

Banty scowled, stood up, saluted. 'Sir, yes, sir.'

He waited until Banty had reached the horses before saying, 'That boy is a nuisance, and I'm sorry I saddled you with him. But he's the youngest son of a rich equite out of Harbor Town. It's my job to keep him out of trouble, and alive.'

'Might want to keep him on the boat, then, rather than riding scout in stretcher territory.'

'Hell, if he stayed on the boat, one of my legionaries would split him wide open in a matter of days.' He laughed and tilted his head toward the whiskey bottle. 'And the only thing he knows how to do is ride. And sulk.'

I gave him the bottle and dug around in Fisk's vest pockets until I located the tin of Medieran cigarettes. Cimbri and I shared them sitting by the fire.

'There's more.'

'What? The *vaettir*?'

'They left a dead boy alone, but they took a man's liver and tongue, and the backstraps of another settler.'

'Ia be. That's some gruesome shit. Why?'

'Can't be 'cause they give two damns about the shoal aurochs, I know that much. I've seen where they slaughtered thousands of the beasts, back when we were pushing west out of Fort Brust, nigh on a century past.'

14

Cimbri raised his eyebrows at that and looked me over. He knew my *dvergar* blood, but it was rare we talked about the differences between us.

He considered me for a while, smoking his cigarette. 'So, why now?'

'No idea. Fisk might know – he's so damned wrapped up with them. Think they killed his family. Whatever the case, they're getting more active. On the warpath.'

There was a groan. A cough. 'Bullshit.'

We looked back at Fisk, who was struggling upright. I clasped his hand and pulled him up.

He grabbed the whiskey, took a long pull, and then patted his vest.

'Ia-dammit, Shoestring. Gimme my smokes.'

I handed them over. He took out one and tamped down the loose tobacco on his wrist, very slow and deliberate, like he was drawing out his audience. Or it might have been that I'd dumped half a bottle of whiskey into him. And the cacique.

'Was a message.'

Cimbri snorted. 'They smart enough to deliver messages?'

Fisk nodded. 'Hell, yeah, they are. Smart as you. Or me.'

'That ain't saying much,' Cimbri replied.

Banty joined in. 'I hear tell they've got a *vaettir* whore at Pauline's in New Damnation.' We hadn't seen him come back, and now the pup's voice was loud and eager. 'Heard she's got the sweetest pussy known to man, but they gotta keep her bound.'

Cimbri snorted. But he didn't send the boy away.

Fisk lit his smoke from the fire and drank more whiskey. I hated it when the man went dissolute, but I imagine his leg hurt something fierce. 'Just what I heard,' Banty said. 'Cornelius himself was smitten with her.'

Cimbri raised a hand as if to cuff him. Then stopped and

lowered his hand. 'Mr Bantam.' His whiskers quivered with outrage. 'You don't talk about our charge in that manner.'

Banty ducked his head and covered his ears.

I felt a tad sorry for the boy, so ungainly and over-eager. A damned deadly pup with a Hellfire pistol. I said, 'I heard the same thing too, but that's just camp talk. If there was someone they were touting as stretcher pussy, must've been a tall whore they tricked out to look *vaettir*, but she weren't no *vaettir*.'

'How could you know that?'

'Don't argue with him, boy, green as you are,' Cimbri said.

'Just want to know how he could know that.'

Fisk shifted and stirred the fire with a branch, his leg sticking out at an angle. 'Ain't no *vaettir* woman gonna allow herself to be touched, not to mention fucked, by some Ruman. Highborn or not.'

'How do you know this?'

'Look around you, pup.' He took a long pull on the whiskey, then shoved it at the boy and waited until he'd taken a swallow. 'This is a big land. But it ain't big enough for man and stretcher to live side by side and never conflict.' He spat. 'They don't age, the stretchers. They don't change. They're proud. They'll skin you alive. They'll fuck their own sister, or mother, or brother. They ain't got no laws nor decency, as far as I can tell. When you're never gonna die except through violence, why worry about salvation or morality or whatnot? Huh? They'd spill your blood for pleasure, and slaughter your Ia-damned children ...' He stopped there, swallowed, and, passing a hand over his eyes, shook his head. I didn't have to guess what he was thinking.

I stood up, went to my saddlebags, and took the satchel of meat I'd sliced from the aurochs. I returned to the fire, opened the scorched piece of leather – my outrider's kitchen – and began prepping the livers and tongues for roasting. I had some salt I'd won in a card game, a small onion. Sweetgrass and winterfat grew thick in these parts, too. I crushed the sweetgrass, sliced the onion, and then flayed open two livers and stuffed them with the spice and herbs.

Finally, Fisk said, 'No. No *vaettir* woman would ever let you stick your cock in her and make a half-breed. She'd kill you first.'

'She might try.' Banty chuckled.

'She *would*. Stretcher women are as fearsome as the men. More, if you count their terrible beauty. You've never seen how they move. It's like light, or *daemonfire*. Wouldn't be no *trying*.'

Banty closed his mouth then.

I had the livers on spits and crackling in the fire. Cimbri stood up.

'You said it was a message.'

Fisk nodded, his face seemingly devoid of pain or drunkenness as he stared into the flames.

'What is it?'

'Pretty simple, really.' He took a last drag of his smoke and flicked it away, making a little red falling star which cut through the night. A lascar near the johnboats raised his head at the tracer, his breath pluming in the air. 'You harvest these aurochs, we'll harvest *you*. Not because they give a shit about the animals. But because they like games. They're bored. And tormenting is their favourite sport.'

Cimbri blinked, then stood there for a while, thinking. Finally, he snapped his fingers, and a lascar went to the johnboat to prepare for the ride back to the *Cornelian*.

'Might need you to talk to Cornelius. He's quite leathered right now and who knows what mischief he's up to. They spotted a mama bear on the western shore this afternoon and now he's a tad excited about his hunt tomorrow. Rest and we'll send a relief in the morning. Sharbo and Horehound, most like.'

He strode to the boat, hopped in, and the lascar shoved them into the waters of the Big Rill. The rain beaded and pattered on the sailors' oiled jackets, down their cowls. In the distance, lanterns lit the galleries of the *Cornelian*. Around us, the air had begun to mist and close in tight, but we could hear the sounds of revelry and the clatter and crash of bottles, the high-pitched laughter of women. And below it, the banked thrum of *daemon*-fired engines idling, pushing heated water through its innards.

Fisk hocked and spat into the fire. 'Get me my bedroll, Shoe. There's a saint.'

FOUR

IN THE MORNING we took a johnboat over to the *Cornelian*. It was a marvel, the steamer, frilled with intricate woodwork railings and littered with little fleur de lis and smiling *daemon* masks, festooned with copper piping and valves that intermittently erupted steam, and covered with doohickeys whose function I couldn't guess. From the lower deck Cimbri waved to us with his bragging stick and motioned to a soldier, who pulled a lever on a cluster of pipes near the outer rail – causing a mechanical ladder to extend from the boat and allowing us to come abeam and climb aboard.

Fisk disembarked the johnboat stiffly, and had some trouble mounting the clever mechanical ladder even with the lascar's help. He hadn't let me change his dressing before coming over. Only let me roughly sew his trouser leg shut so as not to offend the patricians with the sight of his manhood. Though they might have enjoyed it. Who knows what pleases the patricians?

Maybe forty legionaries were billeted on the bottom deck barracks. Soldiers aren't truly happy unless they're fighting or whoring, and the *Cornelian* didn't look like it offered much of either. So, to fill their time, maintenance. Many of them lolled near the railing, sharpening longknives and polishing their tall caligae, lovingly restaining the ornate greaves embossed into the leather, another remnant from the legions of old. They watched us with appraising eyes, thumbs crooked in their weapon-filled balteuses at their waists. Some grinned in the morning light as we climbed unsteadily onto the burnished wooden deck. But they were all close shaven, and their gear was well maintained.

'Morning, gents.' Cimbri looked Fisk up and down. 'You look like hammered shit.'

Fisk had self-medicated until deep in the night, Ia help him. I smiled.

'Fresh as daisies, prefect,' I said. 'Daisies blooming in the morning light.'

'More like black-eyed Susans.' He laughed at his own joke. 'But at least you're not still drunk. As it stands now, you'll be a match for the boss.'

He led us around the lower deck to the stairway, and up to a middle deck that smelled of incense and perfume and sulphur, to a dark tight hall of stained mahogany with golden filigree and scrollwork. Hard to get an idea of the theme, but it looked like forestry with mystical animals and distant mountains. Old country images that seemed exotic and foreign to someone like me, who had never left the colonies. Furthest I've travelled east was Mariopolis, though I did ride down into the hot lands to the south once, when I was just coming into manhood, to look for gold. Only found dissolution and got my heart broke. But that's a tale for another time.

In the hallway, we could hear the muffled sounds of women talking and the buzz of what sounded like large insects filtering through the air. Fisk stopped his limping walk and looked at a door.

I followed his gaze. A finely wrought silver sunburst of ward-work radiated outward from a knob in the centre of the door. My skin prickled at the sight of the silver, and the hairs stood at the back of my neck.

Cimbri glanced around, noticed our lack of forward movement, and clomped back down the tight hallway.

Fisk glanced at the opposite door. It, too, was laced in ward-work, but not as extensively as its neighbour.

'Ah. Yes.' Cimbri clicked his teeth. 'The engineer's chambers. Heavily protected.'

Reaching out, Fisk touched the knob.

'Nothing happened.'

'Doesn't need protection from your kind, Fisk.'

We moved on, out of the silver-webbed hall. I had begun to feel tight and a little itchy in the close confines of the passage. Silver does that to me.

Seen from the bank, the boat looked small, almost toylike, in the wide blue of the Big Rill. But now we were aboard and I couldn't help but be impressed by how large it was. The staterooms alone were, if not large, then spacious, and if the craftsmanship of the boat was any indication, well appointed.

At the end of the hall was a spiral wooden staircase, which we took, and we found ourselves on the topmost level of the *Cornelian*, above the hurricane deck. Higher still stood the main stack, and a pilot's roost, but on this deck was a gazebo, woven of wicker and bound with what looked like copper hasps and heavy ropes. Under it was a table with a large canvas umbrella rippling with the wind.

Three men and two women lounged on couches around this table, which was laden with foodstuff. The womenfolk had shawls wrapped around their shoulders, even though the sun was bright – a cold wind came down from the White Mountains. In an upright wicker chair, another woman sat with a book in her hand. She was long-necked, high-breasted. And beautiful.

'Ah, Cimbri! Are you ready for the hunt?' one of the men asked.

Cimbri grunted an acknowledgement, and the oldest man sat up on his couch and peered at us with bleary eyes. He was heavily whiskered and dressed in a linen outfit, rumpled and breezy, and he wore a pistol even when dining with what I could only assume was his family. He held a glass of wine.

'These the outriders, then?' He gestured with the glass, not spilling a drop.

Cimbri glanced at us and tossed his head at the older man, indicating we should step forward.

'Mr Fisk, Shoestring – this here's Mr Cornelius. And his family.'

Fisk took a step forward and inclined his head.

'So, Cimbri tells me you have information for us.'

Slowly, Fisk described the events at the auroch slaughter, no embellishment or flourishes. Just the facts – we rode west; we found dead things; spotted indigenes; fired upon them.

I watched the Cornelian children. The two men – the Senator's sons, I imagine – were sturdy and heavily muscled. As Fisk spoke of firing shots at the stretchers, one of the sons smirked and glanced at his brother before drawling, 'What did they look like, these indigenes?'

Fisk turned his gaze to the man. 'You ain't seen drawings of them in the papers? They're tall and deadly.'

'Please forgive my son,' Cornelius said. 'He forgets his place.'

'Father,' one of the women said, 'I want to see a *vaettir*.'

'Me, too.'

The thicker-set of the two sons sat upright and put his hands on his knees. He looked Fisk up and down. 'You ever bag one?'

Fisk ignored him.

'What kind of a name is "Fisk"?' This from the beautiful woman sitting in the wicker chair. Her gaze was cool, her eyes intelligent.

'Livia's going to make a pet of the commoner,' one of the other girls said, voice bright and full of mirth.

'Children,' Cornelius said, holding up his hands. 'This debriefing is getting—'

The same young man got to his feet. 'No, I want to know, scout. You ever kill a *vaettir*?'

'Is that all you can think about, Gnaeus? Trophies?' The girl picked up a slice of orange from her plate and popped it into her mouth. She spat the seeds onto a copper bowl. 'You've become as droll as Papa with his dragons.'

'Carnelia, there's no call for that kind of talk.' Cornelius bristled and swigged his wine.

'You haven't answered me, scout.' Gnaeus slapped his fist on the table, like a schoolteacher drawing the class's attention back to the lesson at hand.

'Oh. Gnaeus is going to throw a tantrum. How delightful. It's been *so* long.' Carnelia clapped her hands, lightly, mocking. She didn't smile. She was a lovely woman, much like the other two, but she had lean, narrow features and hawklike eyebrows that gave her face a rapacious aspect I didn't care for. But her arms were plump and her bosom ample enough to please most men, I'd wager.

'If you don't mind, I'd like to get back to my business and let you fine folks get back to yours.' Fisk pitched his voice up to cut through the banter.

The beautiful woman – Livia – arched an eyebrow at Fisk's words while Gnaeus purpled and spluttered.

'How dare you …?' Gnaeus patted at his waist for a gun that wasn't there and then glanced around, wildly, as though looking for something with which to beat Fisk to death.

Fisk watched him unperturbed, and Carnelia laughed.

'This one prickles your skin, does he, brother?'

Cornelius intervened. 'Gnaeus, stop your blustering at once.

This isn't a saloon in New Damnation. Secundus?' He gestured to the other young man, who put his hand on his brother's shoulder and pulled him back into the wicker couch.

The Cornelian children remained quiet for a moment, which, I imagine, was a rare occurence. There was one girl at the table who hadn't spoken, and she was darker, more delicate. She looked Medieran to my eyes, but there were no introductions forthcoming. A pretty little thing. Maybe the wife of one of the sons, or his mistress – but the patricians don't normally set them at the breakfast table. Could even have been the father's mistress, though she hardly looked out of her teens. But some like them young.

'So, Mr Fisk, what conclusions do you draw from the murder of the settlers?'

Fisk shifted his weight, relieving his injured leg. 'I reckon the *vaettir*'re gonna go on the warpath. Not because of some territorial nonsense regarding the aurochs. No. Most likely, just because they don't like humans and enjoy killing us.'

'I don't understand, Mr Fisk,' Livia said. 'These *vaettir* will go to war merely for thrills?'

He looked at her. 'No. Not really. But they're obscure, the stretchers are. You can't really use reasoning to figure them out because ...' He shifted again. 'Because they ain't human. Don't think like us.'

Cornelius sat forward and put down his wineglass. 'So how do *you* explain them?'

Fisk sniffed and glanced around, looked at the Cornelian sons. 'They're bored. It's easy getting bored when you're ageless and near indestructible.'

Gnaeus smiled and slapped Secundus' shoulder, a playful gesture appropriate for arenas and gymnasia. With these patricians emotions were as changeable as summer rainstorms sweeping across the plains. 'I can sympathise with that. This ship is Ia-damned deathly.'

Cornelius glared at him, then turned back to Fisk. 'Continue.'

'Not much more to say about it. Stretchers get bored and restless and here we come, moving into their land, little mice for them to play with. They like us because we're smart enough to be afraid.'

'But we have silver. We have holly.' Secundus pointed at the whipping brag-rags flying at the stern of the ship. One had a grey circle, and the other had a sprig of holly with crimson berries on a field of black.

Everybody knows that holly and silver are like poison to *vaettir*, while only silver is deadly to *daemonkind*. Rumans like to remind their enemies that they can hurt them. So they fly brag-rags to show their might.

Fisk said, 'Gotta hit the stretcher to kill him. Gotta get close enough for holly to work. You haven't seen how they move. And you scarcely can, they're that fast.'

Gnaeus smirked again, and Secundus looked incredulous.

Cornelius poured another glass of wine, lifted it, and drank. When he was done, he wiped his whiskers with a sleeve and said, 'Thank you, gentlemen. You are dismissed. Cimbri, we're ready for the hunt once you've allocated today's assignments.'

Livia rose from her chair saying, 'Come, Mr Fisk. I will tend your wound.'

'It's fine, ma'am. No need to trouble yourself.'

'Nonsense. I won't let you, our *vaettir* expert, die of a minor wound.' She smiled – truly smiled, changing the whole configuration of her face – and I could see the wrinkles at the corners deepen, showing her age, yet somehow only adding to her beauty. Strange how polite society fixates on youth, when age and experience bring so much more richness than unlined skin. Not a young woman, this Livia, but beautiful and a little fearsome. I think I might have fallen in love with her right then, a little at least. I've never learned if Fisk felt similarly at that moment, but I suspect it was so.

Secundus, his voice low but not entirely careless, said, 'You think that's a good idea, sis? Let the plebs take care of themselves.'

Livia slowly turned her head to look at her brothers, her father – a slowness that seemed to arise from struggling to hold back a multitude of thoughts and words. I don't know; I don't spend a lot of time with womenfolk. But she was a regal one, this Livia.

'I am the most accomplished healer on the boat, brother. As you know, every time you came to me with a cut or scraped knee.'

The young man blushed, blinking. For a moment I thought he might argue, but he tamped it down and nodded.

The wind picked up and ruffled the brag-rags. It was hard to tell if the temperature drop was due to the weather or Livia's stare.

'Come with me, Mr Fisk.' She walked from the table and didn't look back.

I glanced at Fisk, who returned my look, shrugging. We both followed.

Before we mounted the stairs, Gnaeus called out, 'Cimbri, have those two accompany us on the hunt, will you?'

Cimbri turned to Cornelius and waited. Cornelius tilted up his glass and finished his wine.

'Damn fine claret, Gnaeus. Damn fine. It was prescient of you to have those cases brought aboard at New Damnation.'

Gnaeus smiled and said, 'I had some in Pauline's and knew you'd be partial, father. It is quite good, but I prefer a good Tueton beer in the morning. Especially before a hunt. It won't throw off the aim.'

'Quite right.'

Cimbri cleared his throat. 'Sir?'

Cornelius waved a negligent hand. 'Do as he says, do as he says.'

Cimbri turned, frowned, and stomped toward us. The woman, Carnelia, erupted into peals of laughter and, after a moment, was joined by Secundus.

'Looks like you're going on a hunt, boys.'

FIVE

L IVIA'S FACE WAS stern as we descended the stairs; in the close space I could smell the spice of her perfume. Cimbri and Fisk must have been aware of it, too.

We reached the bottom of the stairwell and she announced, 'I'll tend to Mr Fisk in my chambers. For propriety's sake, it would be best if one of you remained with us.'

Cimbri's eyes grew large. He coughed, muttered something about the guard roster, and clomped off, boots loud on the dark panels.

She turned to me. 'Ah, so, Mr ...?'

'They call me Shoestring, ma'am.'

'Shoestring? That's your praenomen?'

'No, ma'am, just what they call me.'

She stopped, put a hand on my shoulder. 'What is your name, sir? I can't address you by that absurd nickname.'

Hell, I'd been Shoestring, solely, for fifty years by then and it took a bit to recollect my name.

'Dveng Ilys is what my momma named me. We don't have no cognomens, ma'am, like you Rumans, if you'll forgive my forwardness.'

'*Dvergar*, then – your mother or your father?'

'Mother, ma'am.'

28

'Ah. I see. Well, Mr Ilys, it is a pleasure to meet you. I'm sorry it couldn't be under more commodious circumstances.'

By Ia's beard if she didn't reach out and shake my hand. I don't think Fisk noticed my blush.

She led us on, down the hall to the door we'd examined before, across the hall from the engineer's room.

'So, all this wardwork is supposed to keep you safe from stretchers, then? The silver?' Fisk kept his voice even but I could hear the discomfort in it. He's a stoic one, Fisk is, but he can't fool me.

'Not quite,' Livia said, an amused smile teasing her lips. 'Engineers make their living summoning the infernal. Surely you must know that much?' She waited until Fisk gave a terse nod. 'The wardwork is to protect the ship should Beleth's negotiations turn ... troublesome.'

'Beleth's his name?'

'That's right.'

'He dabbles in munitions? Or only the big stuff?'

'You must ask him. While we all inhabit this same, very small space, our paths do not cross frequently; I suspect he is not on board very often.'

I was curious. 'What? The lascars put him ashore? Surely we'd have noticed that.'

'I am told there are other, distant shores, Mr Ilys, and Beleth knows other ways to ...' She paused, tucked an errant strand of hair behind her ear. A worried expression crossed her face. 'To disembark.'

Fisk and I thought about that for a bit while Livia withdrew a silver key on a chain from her bodice, unlocked the door and ushered us in.

It was a small berth, maybe six by ten feet, with a single bed, a desk – loaded with papers, quills and ink, and a built-in armoire fastened to the hull. Two Gallish doors, slatted with mahogany, opened up on a miniature gallery, large enough for one person to stand above the waters and look out on the shore. A small bookcase, near the armoire, was crammed with tomes of all sorts. Above, a strange wooden-bladed contraption hung – the centre wrought of copper, with a dangling cord. Livia tugged the line, the copper contraption hissed and belched a small puff of steam, and the wooden blades began to spin, generating a light breeze.

Amazing, really, what *daemonwork* can get you. But what does it get you, in the end? The damnation that threatens us all. Don't these conveniences just add to the staining of our souls? Hellfire pistols, bound *daemons* propelling the *Cornelian*, driving the steam through its innards, turning this bladed fan above our heads without even the faintest whiff of brimstone. Does it even matter? I figure it does, but even here, in the midst of so many *daemon* powered contraptions, I couldn't sense that sullying I felt every time Fisk fired his pistol.

'There is some baffling.' She pointed to a folded, lacquered enamel screen. 'Deploy it to protect your modesty, Mr Fisk.'

Fisk looked at the screen, then at me. He blinked once, but no surprise crossed his face. He unslung his gunbelt, carefully so as not to mar the warding on the ammunition, and then dropped his trousers.

Livia straightened, then coughed. 'Mr Fisk, allow me to get my medical kit. Please sit on the bed.'

He straightened his leg, and then sat.

She opened the armoire, withdrew a large wooden box – again filigreed in silver – and withdrew a phial and woven cotton bandages. 'Mr Ilys, there's a dry-bar there. I'm not normally one for raw spirits before afternoon, but, in this situation, we might all like a bit of port, or brandy ... My father was negligent in his duty as host.'

I looked to Fisk, who nodded and said, 'Brandy.' There was a crystal decanter of amber liquid, and another the colour of blood. Snifters and glasses sat upside-down on small, padded horns, so I removed three and poured the booze. I had never had port before that day. It was quite tasty, a bit of mellowed fire that burned the tongue. The brandy bottle housed less liquid, so I figured Miss Livia was partial to it, and I poured her one of those.

She had out her medical kit by the time I was through and waved me to set her glass down on the desk. The stained black leather box had a very clever hinged lid that she popped open, revealing neatly wound cotton cloths and various bottles. I saw needles, thread, a paraffin candle, and several bright steel cutting utensils. Much nicer than my barber's kit, and it had seen some bloodwork, for sure.

'Now, Mr Fisk, let's see that wound.'

As indifferent as he had seemed when he dropped his britches, he kept his hands over his privates while she cut away my bindings and then wiped the flesh around the wound. Fisk sucked air through clenched teeth.

'You're a lucky man, Mr Fisk. The *vaettir* narrowly missed a major sanguiduct ...'

She withdrew a vial of clear liquid from her kit, poured some over bleached cotton balls, and continued to wipe the blackened blood. Once she had the wound clean, she made him roll over – I saw him tug down his shirt tails to cover his nether regions – and she addressed the other side of his leg.

She threw away the dirty cotton, re-stoppered the clear liquid, and then drew out another phial, this one holding a dark, viscous fluid.

'What's that?' Fisk asked. As he looked over his shoulder at the vial, his face clouded.

'It's called *tersus incendia*, and it will clean the wound, but it will hurt – perhaps more than you imagine, Mr Fisk.'

He looked at her, blinked once, then nodded.

Livia poured the black liquid slowly, dribbling it like honey. When it touched the raw opening of the wound, which now oozed blood, it bubbled and hissed as though entering and fusing with his flesh. Fisk's body went rigid, his eyes growing large. Livia placed a hand lightly on his thigh. He remained frozen until the bubbles from the liquid died, and she covered the wound with a clean cotton cloth before gently urging Fisk to turn back over. He did so, but slowly.

'Again now, I'm sorry to say.'

'Hold on a moment, ma'am.' I brought Fisk his brandy, but he waved me away and nodded to her.

She poured the tersus incendia, and Fisk again went through the silent contortion of pain from the bubbling liquid. Only when she had bandaged his leg did he take the brandy from me and knock it back.

'I've never heard of that stuff before,' I said, pointing at the bottle she was stoppering.

'Ah, it's a discovery from the natural philosophers. It combats the numina animus – the evil motes that cause infection in wounds.'

'Motes?'

She smiled and fastened Fisk's linens. 'Invisible, infinitesimal creatures. Numina. Malicious and disease-causing spirits. Something in the tersus incendia combats their presence. The fire of it, maybe. I must admit, I don't understand all of the theory, but, in my experience, it certainly works.'

'I'm familiar with the numen of the world, the spirits of rock and tree and river. But I don't hold with the old religion.'

Livia smiled. 'I think the philosophers mean something a bit different from the old gods.' It wasn't said with any condescension or aloofness. Just a statement of fact.

She stood up, straightened her dress, and put away her kit. She tossed the soiled linens into a trash bin. In the corner of the room was a copper bowl fitted against a column of pipes with various levers and handles. She tugged one and the bowl began filling with water. She washed her hands. She dried them on a small hanging towel and turned back to us. When she saw my expression, she laughed.

'Mr Ilys, would you like to examine the basin?'

There were a few knobs that I couldn't figure out, but three open pipes protruded over the basin, each one topped by a handle. Each had a letter pressed into the metal. C, T, and F.

I put my hand on the handle labelled C and began to turn it. It hissed and sputtered and hot water poured forth into the bowl that had a hole in the bottom to carry away any superfluous liquid. For now a small bit of cork stoppered the hole.

'Careful. It gets quite hot. Hot enough to burn.'

I cupped my hands and felt the water. It was indeed hot, but my skin is very coarse – a gift from my mother and her kin – and a little hot water doesn't bother me. I brought it to my nose. I couldn't smell brimstone.

'Why, Mr Ilys, it's safe to drink.'

I let the water slip through my fingers, dried my hands, and moved toward the door. 'Yes, ma'am. This truly is a miraculous ship.'

She cocked her head and narrowed her eyes, and I was forcibly reminded that she wasn't some ignorant miller's daughter or farm matron. She was highborn, beautiful, and sharp.

'Well, I thank you, ma'am, for your care of my leg,' Fisk said. 'Thought I was like to die when you put that stuff on it.'

She looked at him, and smiled again.

'So, I asked before and you chose to ignore me: what kind of name is "Fisk"?'

He shifted his weight on the bed, leg sticking out at an angle, tugging his shirt over his nethers. Never thought I'd see the day that Fisk was bare-arsed in front of a highborn woman. I don't think he really cared if she saw, but rather seemed to cover himself because he thought he ought to.

'You think I might be able to find some britches?'

She laughed, went to the wall, and pulled a lever. Before she could resume talking, a knock sounded at the door and a female voice said, 'Mistress?'

Livia opened the door. The woman looked at Fisk, grinned, and then glanced at me, and her grin disappeared. She was short, too, and her *dvergar* blood was obvious in her face, the squareness of her shoulders, the strength of her hands. It was clear she had no love lost for me – perhaps because I reminded her of it.

'Go to Gnaeus' room and get a pair of his trousers. Mr Fisk's have been ruined in our service.'

The woman nodded and disappeared.

'So, where were we?' Livia stepped close to the desk, picked up her snifter, swirled the amber liquid around, smelled it, and then took a dainty sip. She sat down at her chair in a movement that struck me as curiously masculine, the ease and comfort she had sitting at the desk as if she'd spent countless hours there writing, or reading. She crossed her legs and arranged her dress.

'Now that I have you half-undressed and nearly alone in my quarters,' she turned and winked at me, 'tell me about your name.'

'Not much to tell, other than it's mine.'

'It's unusual. Is it short for anything?'

He looked at her sharply. 'Fiscelion.'

'Ah.' Her eyes brightened, and she clasped her hands. 'And you were born in Ciprea, if I'm not mistaken.'

He nodded.

'Well, that *is* very interesting. Cognomen?'

He looked at her fearlessly and said, 'My name is Hieronymous

Fiscelion Cantalan Iulii. But folks around these parts just call me Fisk, which is fine with me.'

She nodded again, her eyes never leaving his. 'Thank you for your confidence, Fisk. I won't betray it.'

Now, I'm not the sharpest tack, but I knew I had missed something and that was a tad irksome, that this woman – granted, this highborn, highly educated woman – could discern in moments something about my partner that I hadn't figured out in more than a decade. But there wasn't much to do about it then.

Another knock at the door and the serving woman entered, bearing some leather riding britches with intricate buckles and small silver doodads going down the side of legs. Fancy duds.

'I shall wait in the hall, Fisk, Mr Ilys, to give you privacy to dress. They'll be waiting for you on the lower deck.'

The moment the door shut Fisk yanked off his boots, whipped the trousers over his feet and stood up quickly. He glared at me, and I knew better than to make any jokes.

So I said, 'How's the leg?'

He looked down like he'd forgotten it.

'Feels like hell. But better than it was, that's for sure.'

'Well, at least that's something.'

'It's something.' He looked around the room wildly. 'That woman scares me silly.'

I'd never seen Fisk act like this before. He buckled on his gunbelt and went to her sink and washed his hands and face. When he walked back his face was dark – back to normal – and he was more composed.

'Let's take these fools on a hunt, Shoe,' he said, pulling open the warded door and limping out into the *Cornelian*'s hall.

SIX

AFTER THE LASCAR fetched my tack and Fisk's carbine – bringing back Banty, unfortunately – we rode out into the foothills of the White Mountains on the western shore. The eastern shore, for this scouting rotation, had been assigned to Fisk, Banty, and me. All of our tack and mounts were there, currently. Porting them across on a flatboat was a labour too great to do on a whim, even a senator's. So, Horehound and Sharbo rustled up some mounts and gave Fisk a feisty mare and me a stumpy but ornery spotted pony, maybe in jest but probably spite.

Gnaeus rode an enormous stallion, steel-shod and tufted at the hooves, rippling with leather and frilly silverwork, while Secundus rode a beaut of a mare, fine lines and even disposition and tacked sensibly, without frill or bangle. Cornelius himself rode a gelding, rough with the first of winter's growth but white-muzzled and temperate. It seemed Gnaeus was the showman of the family.

All of the Cornelius brood were accoutred like kings, leather hunting vests decorated with ammunition and each one holding a massive long-bore rifle. They bristled with Hellfire. A personal legionary in full uniform – Imperial blue jacket dotted with brass and gold phalerae, grey trousers tucked into leather caligae – toted Cornelius' rifle. The gun had a barrel half an arm longer than the others, with a series of curious ground glass reticules where the sightings were normally affixed to the barrel. They reminded me of the lenses of spectacles I'd seen a few shopkeeps wear in Covenant, so I had to assume Cornelius had poor eyesight, which the strange sighting glass assisted. He didn't act near-sighted, though; he constantly raised his hand to shade his eyes and stared toward the large, wooded gulley we fast approached.

I watched Banty as he rode among them, his eyes lingering on the weapons, their clothes. The pup would require constant guard.

We rode through the fallow growth up to the rise, with a view of the *Cornelian*. Sharbo accompanied us, having spotted the bear, and led us down, away from the Big Rill, his tall, lanky form swaying easily on horseback.

'What was all that about your name back there on the boat, pard?'

Fisk raised an eyebrow and shifted in his saddle to look at the Cornelian clan. When he was satisfied they were out of earshot, he said, 'She knows a little bit about my history.'

'What about your history?'

He looked at me sharply, narrowing his eyes. One of the reasons we're good partners is maybe because we've both been around long enough not to jabber away, to think before speaking, and to consider who we're speaking to.

'It's a long story, Shoe, and one I always meant to tell you. But I never saw any need.' He raised a hand and gestured out to the land, the sheer massiveness of the Hardscrabble Territories, the White Mountains. He reined in and pulled out his last two machine-rolled cigarettes and held one out to me. I brought the pony in close enough to take it. He lit his smoke with a match and then passed the cigarette over, and I lit mine from his. We smoked for a while and surveyed the foothills, wreathed in tall shoal grasses rippling with the wind coming down from the mountainside.

'But now ain't the time, and it don't matter anyway.' He drew on the smoke and expelled it harshly, as though it tasted foul even though it was spiced and fragrant. 'It's an Ia-damned monster of a world always ready to take what you love. Always hungry, this world.'

I nodded. It weren't nothing I didn't know from my mother's milk.

'This ain't gonna cause us problems, is it?' I asked.

He was quiet for a bit, but not too long. 'No. I don't think so. Depends on Livia. You think we can trust her?'

'As much as you can trust anybody. These Cornelians are high-born. Different breed of cat from you and me.'

He remained silent and watched the mountains.

Cornelius adjusted the sights on his massive rifle while Sharbo led the legionaries into the aspen break at the top of the gulley and we waited at the lower mouth.

'Banty, you go with the legionaries.'

Even though Fisk's voice sounded fierce, Banty said petulantly, 'Why? There're enough men with Sharbo. They don't need me.'

Fisk pulled the mare abreast Banty. The mare chuffed her head at the closeness of the other horse. Fisk leaned forward and patted her neck with a gloved hand. She stilled.

Watching Fisk was like watching a snake uncoil, striking. One moment his gloved hand was patting his black beast's neck, the next instant it lashed out and smacked Banty across the jaw, knocking off his hat and tumbling him arse over head off the rump of his mount. He landed in the dirt and gravel.

'Next time you question me, I'll put a hole in you. Get after those legionaries, understood?'

Banty found his knees and rose, hand going to his Hellfire. Hard to tell if he was smiling or if his mouth was pulled back in pain, but his teeth were bloody and his eyes wild.

I said, 'Don't kill him, Fisk,' knowing he wouldn't anyway, unless the boy drew. When Banty glanced at me, Fisk kicked his horse forward and Banty scrambled to get out of the way. Fisk didn't look back.

'If you want to keep breathing, I'd take my hand off that piece of damnation,' I said, low, softly, and as gently as I could.

Banty glanced at me and spat a clot into the dirt.

'No percentage in it, son.'

If looks could kill, Banty's gaze and expression would have done for us all. 'Not your son, dwarf.'

'Thank Ia for that.'

Cornelius and his sons watched from a fair piece away, no doubt wondering what the ruckus was all about.

'You better get on after them legionaries, Mr Bantam. You can tend to your honour later.'

He spat again in my direction and went after his horse.

We watched Banty scramble up the gulley's edges, after the men. Cornelius and his sons joined us and commenced fiddling with their gear and weapons. Gnaeus drank some sort of spirit from a leather bladder, handed it to his father, who swallowed a great draught. Secundus waved away the proffered refreshment with a scowl.

After a while, the echoes of hollers and beating of the small *dvergar*-crafted tambours came rattling over the wind as the beaters made their way through the gulley.

'We were grousing here, yesterday afternoon. Gnaeus bagged a brace of hens. Sharbo spied some movement in yon bramblewrack and called my attention to it.' Cornelius shifted the rifle in his hands. 'I made her out, dimly at first. But she appeared like a dream. A huge creature she was, easily fifteen hands high on her back feet, I swear. Her belly was loose with the slough of fat from suckling a cub at teat, and she had a wild rangy look, she did.'

I thought I should point out the obvious. 'Mr Cornelius, a mama bear with a cub is at her most vicious. I've seen a small bear maul a man to death. She gets in close, Ia save you.'

Gnaeus laughed. Secundus said, 'It's doubtful any creature could get within a hundred paces of our dear pater while he's holding that cannon.'

'If I might be so bold, Mr Cornelius,' I said, dismounting. 'We should take positions.'

The beating grew louder, and there came some excited shouting. And the bellow of something hairy and mighty pissed off.

Mama bear.

The highborns dismounted and arrayed themselves at three points in the mouth of the gulley. They might have been a tad too close, but it was too hard to tell – the brush and bramble-wrack stood dark and impenetrable before them. Fisk remained mounted, unsmiling, leaning forward, arms crossed and resting on the saddle-horn. The whiteness of his face reminded me that he'd been leg-shot only yesterday and must still be in considerable pain. Deep flesh wounds hurt more in the days following the injury than the time immediately after. At least that has been my experience, and I've lived through four knife fights and a gunfight that got me through the fat on the edge of my belly. But the shooting was down south in the hot lands and there was a woman there to soothe me. And knife fights are as common as schoolyard scuffles in the Hardscrabble Territories.

The bramblewrack rustled, shifted, and then parted. A bear cub caromed out of the mouth of the gulley, roused from its den, mewling and growling and making small pathetic sounds. I felt a moment of sadness for the small creature, having to live out its last moments in heart-shattering fear of man. Ia save us, we *are* fearsome beasts.

A grunt followed, deep as the voice of the mountains, and the she-bear ripped down the bramblewrack and stood like a great shadow behind her cub.

Gnaeus raised his rifle, but his father called, 'She's mine!' and, hoisting the cannon, sighted down the length of the barrel. He held it steady for a moment, squinting his left eye, and then there was a great boom and an incandescent flash of light. Whatever *daemon* was bound behind that great burst, it was unlike any I'd seen before and there was no afterimage of wings, or horns, only a writhing mass of *something*. What it was I couldn't tell – but I whispered a prayer to Ia, thankful that the *daemon* was without a host. But I felt weak, and I can admit here that had I not expected some horror my bowels might have loosed. As it was, my heart hammered in my chest and I felt like something very bad was going to happen.

Daemons. Damned things. Damn them, and damn guns, and Ia damn the men who wield them.

The mama bear roared, rearing back, but blood darkened her brown fur, flowed from her chest. It pumped, bright in the light streaming over the plains, and her muzzle, already frothed with white, began to fleck crimson.

She dropped to her paws and came forward, twisting her body and head, giving a roar that shook me like thunder. I was thinking, *What a magnificent beast—*, when I heard the snick of rifle-work and knew Cornelius was reloading his monstrosity of a gun.

'She's mine, Gnaeus! Do *not* fire!'

The massive bear surged forward toward Cornelius, closing the distance in a flash. The patriarch fell backward and the bear swiped with her paw, snagging his leg. There was a bright ripping sound as her long claws tore through leathers and into flesh. Cornelius screamed and dropped his fancy rifle, grabbing at the earth as the bear jerked him forward.

Then there was another brilliant flash, a sinking despair, and when the afterimage of the *daemon* died away I saw Secundus standing on the far side of the bear – the slumped bear. A pained expression was on his face, and I couldn't tell if it was due to killing such a magnificent creature or because of the effects of *daemon* gunplay. Maybe both. Or neither, and some other dark current washed his tarnished soul. You never can tell with highborn.

'Secundus,' said Gnaeus, through clenched teeth. 'By rights, that kill should have been mine.'

Secundus laughed. 'Brother, you can claim it, should you want. I care not one whit. I acted to preserve our father.'

Gnaeus sneered. 'You arse. You don't know your place. I have primacy, *little brother*.'

Again, Secundus laughed. 'And you can keep it.'

Cornelius cursed, loudly, in a variety of languages. It seemed he'd spent some time in Petrugal.

'Might want to tend your father, gents,' Fisk said as the bramblewrack rustled again and four legionaries emerged with Banty following close behind – a scowl darkening his features. I went to Cornelius and knelt by him. The mama bear had shredded his britches, ripped his black leather boot clean away. There was a lot of blood. Beaucoup blood.

'She got you good, sir. We gotta stop the bleeding.' I whipped off my belt and cinched it tight around his thigh.

I'd refilled my flask of cacique since Fisk's injury; I withdrew it and handed it to Cornelius. He twisted off the silver cap and swallowed, his throat working up and down.

While I tended the injured highborn, Gnaeus said, 'And the cub? Shall we take it as a pet?' He gave a laugh. Not a pleasant sound to my ears, and I'm no saint, Ia knows. But that one, he was sour.

'I don't know, Gnaeus. It's just a cub.'

I pulled my longknife and split Cornelius' britches – the second time I'd performed this action in two days – to get a better look.

He'd been hamstrung, surely, and would never walk right again. But when I moved his leg, and he screamed, I saw how bad the damage was.

'Banty! And, you ... soldier! What's your name?'

'Jim Orrin, sir.'

'Mr Orrin, take Banty here and a hatchet, and cut as many long saplings as you can. We've got to get Mr Cornelius back to the boat. And quick, boys.'

Banty came to Cornelius, a strange look upon his face, like he was innocent and eager all at once, and whipped off his hat. 'I'll make sure you have what you need, sir. On my honour.'

Cornelius looked from Banty to me, and back. I shrugged. If the boy wanted to grandstand, it was fine by me, as long as he did what I said.

'Get the saplings. Quick-like. We've got to make a travois.'

'I can ride, dwarf. Never has a Cornelian not been able to mount ...'

'Pardon me, sir, but don't be a fool. If we don't get you back within the hour, that leg will have to come off.'

'What? Devils, no! I've endured worse scratches.' The cacique had done its work, I could tell. He fumbled to get up.

'Mr Cornelius, your calf's cut totally from your leg. It's hanging by a scrap. Maybe Miss Livia can help you, but I can't do anything other than to cut it off, start a fire, and cauterize the wound.'

His breath was coming heavy, and he had a hand on my arm, squeezing tightly. Strange thing, watching him turn pale like a clear glass filling with milky fluid. No doubt he was feeling the first of the shock of the wound. A tough one, this Cornelius.

'*Soldier*!' Gnaeus called. 'Fetch some rope! We'll take this bear cub as a pet!'

One of the legionaries went to his pack horse, retrieving some length of hemp-rope. I looked about and spied the cub, still mewling, huddled by the corpse of its mother. Poor thing. The legionary approached and tossed a lasso toward the creature.

'No, give it to me, you damned fool,' Gnaeus snapped. He snatched the rope from the soldier's hands and made a toss.

There was a boom, the feeling of despair that comes with Hellfire, and the cub's head blossomed with crimson as it keeled over.

'Ia's wounds!' Gnaeus whipped around, spying Fisk on horseback, his gun in hand. 'You cur. The cub was our prize!'

'Looks like this hunt's been a bust for you, then, Mr Gnaeus. But we ain't taking no cubs back to a boat with horses and ladies. That's sheer folly.'

I had to smile at the elder Cornelian son's spluttering. Even Secundus was grinning.

'Face it, brother, today was just not your day.'

'I should have him whipped! No. Crucified!'

I didn't much care for the look in the man's eye, I can say that for certain.

Fisk stared at him, white-faced. 'If you don't want your pap to die, I suggest you get him back to the *Cornelian* pronto. We'll tend to the beasts.' He waved a hand at the dead bears.

Gnaeus stomped off to reclaim his horse but not before giving us a deadly look. Secundus approached, holding his mount's bridle, and looked up at Fisk.

'A word of caution.' Secundus slid his carbine into a leather holster on the rump of his mount, hooked his foot into a stirrup, and lifted himself onto horseback. The mare turned as he mounted. When he was of a height with Fisk, his smile faded and his young features clouded with a sombre expression.

Even though this young man showed great sense and a pleasant demeanour, he clearly was not overly distressed by his father's grievous wound. But Rumans are a strange bunch, the nobles concerned with their desires and not much else. They just don't jump the same way as normal folk.

'He's petty, my brother,' Secundus said. He sighed and rubbed at his jaw. I noticed a scar there, faint and small, but silver in the golden slanting light of endday. 'He's spiteful and selfish. But should anything happen to my father, Gnaeus will become the patriarch of the Cornelian family and he'll want to make an example of you. He doesn't like being thwarted.'

'I reckon that's something he'll need to get used to out here. It's a big, hard land with no concern for what he might desire.'

Secundus nodded, but didn't smile. 'It *is* that, Mr Fisk. But he's brought a bit of civilization with him, my father has. Be wary of Gnaeus.'

I couldn't help but ask. 'And you? What will become of you, should the worst happen to your father?'

'I shall obey my brother. He'll wed as quickly as possible, breed even faster, and by some manner get me out of the way in order to preserve his children's rights. That'll be the way of it.' He smiled then, a rogueish grin. 'Maybe I'll take up farming out here.'

I laughed.

'No, Mr Cornelius the Second,' Fisk grinned, 'you certainly ain't got the look of a sodbuster. You sit that mount too well.'

Fisk held out his freshly rolled cigarette to the young man, who took it, smelled the tobacco, and lit it from a match he took from his vest pocket.

'Shoe, you reckon Marcellus out of New Damnation could use a new scout?'

'Always need good riders, sure enough.'

'That's settled, then,' Fisk joked. 'You'll be riding with us.'

It felt good to laugh, and Secundus won me over then, when he stuck out his hand in mock agreement. Fisk and Secundus gripped forearms, as if completing a deal. Then he turned to me, and did the same.

The legionaries completed the travois with Banty sternly watching them in their labours and barking orders without deigning to sully his hands. Senator Cornelius blistered the air with curses and calls for his flask.

'Shoe, I reckon we better get to skinning this bear, looks like.'

'Looks like.'

Fisk dismounted stiffly, favouring one leg, and we set to work with our longknives. Bear meat isn't a favourite of mine, but we took great care to preserve all the sweetmeats and delicate bits of offal for the highborns to sample. And, of course, the trophy parts: the paws, the fur, the full head. The cub we slung on the back of a pony that shied and nickered at the stink of bear.

The sun disappeared behind the mountain rim, the sky and land took the washed-out colours of twilight, and it had turned cold by the time we were finished. We hied back toward the Big Rill before the mountain lions came down from their high reaches, drawn by the smell of blood.

The *Cornelian* was lit up when we returned, like a jewel shining on the waters. As its stacks pushed smoke into the sky, the whole world smelled of brimstone and blood. The lascar camped on the shore helped us with the meat and the skin, which we set to soaking.

It was only when it was fully dark that one of the soldiers asked, 'Where's Orrin?'

And when no one could answer him, all eyes turned toward Fisk and me, and then back to the darkening mountains.

SEVEN

THERE WAS NOTHING for it except to go back up the mountain in the dark. Fisk cursed, and I had to shush him, something that doesn't happen often.

'Pard, you ain't in any condition to go back up, hate to say. Go on. Get back to our horses and send me Sharbo and we'll find this Orrin fellow.'

'Shoe, we both know the damned soldier ain't lost. A stretcher done him in, most like.'

'Most like. But you just been arrow-shot yesterday. I need a partner, and you need off that leg. Send me Sharbo. I can take care of myself.'

He unslung his gun belt. 'Here. Take them. You'll need 'em.'

I laughed. 'You know my opinion on that, old friend. No.' I shook my head and held open my hands. 'Matter of fact, I'm gonna do this the opposite way.' I gestured at a legionary to give me a gunnysack.

I began unlimbering my longknives, shortknives, and various pointy things I keep on my person for occasions of need. One of the legionaries whistled, and Fisk snorted.

'Didn't know you was half porcupine.' Everybody got a good laugh at that, but by the time I'd stripped all my weapons, some of them looked at me a tad different. Maybe with more respect, maybe not.

'Hell, Shoe, I *understand* what you're doing, just not why in the blazes you'd want to do it.'

'Ain't going up the mountain with that taint on me. The stretchers would be sure to sense me.'

'You don't *know* that. And what if they sense you anyway and you ain't got shit to protect yourself?'

There wasn't much to say to that. I'd just have to trust to Ia.

Fisk left and returned shortly with Sharbo, who, once he figured out my intent, shook his head and flatly refused to go with me.

'I'm not gonna die today, dwarf. You can go on your own.'

I'd figured it would be so. Therefore, without any more jabbering, I took an unlit lantern and a box of matches, the pony, and an extra mount, in case Ia had preserved the soldier Orrin's life.

Alone, I headed back up the mountain.

It was a moonless night but the stars, like bright grains of sand, innumerable and distant, lay strewn against the inky black sky and wreathed the mountaintops. A cold wind skittered down the mountain skirts, whipped the pony's mane, and brought tears to my eyes.

It was slow going in the dark. Footholds that in the day were easy for the animals were hard to find now, and my pony kept misstepping and catching her balance. We had to stop to rest; despite the wind and cold, she was developing a froth on her shoulders and flanks. Exhaustion was close, it being the second time she'd made the mountainous trek that day.

When we neared the gulley where we took the bears, I began leading both ponies, not wanting to tax them beyond endurance. Both had made the trip up-mountain once today. I was hoping they'd each have a rider later. I didn't keep too much hope, but some.

I tied the ponies a short distance away – the bears' blood darkening the white stones near the gulley's mouth made them skittish – and, pulling my hat down and taking up the lantern, I forced my way into the bramblewrack and up the gulley.

At night, on the mountainside, subject of the stars and Ia's whims, a mind does strange things. The brush and brambles pressed close, and animals shared the space with me – there were rustles and scratches and the soft hooting of an owl. It was then that my mother's gift, that queer working in the blood, came to me. I blinked once, a long blink, my eyelids heavy and gummy. And when I opened my eyes again the gulley was just as dark, but somehow that *dvergar* part of me that I always push back, tamp away, came to the fore and I could see the night and felt at home, safe, pressed close to the bosom of the mountain. My eyes saw the inhabitants of the dark, the squirrel scurrying along the rocks, the wrangrell family roosting in the bramblewrack. I felt heavier and lighter all at once, as though my feet were rooted deep in the mountain but my spirit had expanded to fill it. As I moved up the gulley, I spied below the track made by the soldiers through the tight brush where they had beat the bears into the open.

I climbed, up and up, scrabbling from rock to rock, and it felt good to be here, untainted and with the mountains, the great expanse of air and the sigh of the trees on the breeze. But when I spotted the narrow den opening in a great cracked boulder, something made me stop, check the ground, the bramble, the sky.

I pulled a little of the brush from the opening, and it rattled like a wicker-basket seller in the market.

I entered into the den and the rich smell of bear filled my nostrils, the thick clean musk of them. But also something more. I followed the den back, into the living rock.

Folks say blood stinks of iron, and some say copper, but I've never got that from the smell of blood. Blood smells like the body that gave it up, and the mood that was on them at the time. Blood can smell like terror, pure and unadulterated.

And the den, this humble bear den, stank of it.

I was further inside, and the light of the stars filtering through the brush had disappeared. It takes light to see, even for *dvergar*.

I pulled a match, whispering a prayer to Ia that this taint not be so great as to attract attention, and filled the small cave with the smell of sulphur and brimstone while I lit the lantern. The yellow light was like a prolonged lightning flash to my light-starved eyes and I was struck blind, like a man with angelis fever, burning eyes and all.

At first it looked like the carcass of another baby bear, denuded of skin and fur, cleaned of liver and tongue and backstraps, deprived of skull and hands. But the feet told all. It was a man, bloody, raw, and more naked than the day he was born.

A flurry of bloody scraps and ripped clothing bore testament to the corpse's origin. Orrin, a man of the fifth legion out of New Damnation, had met his end here.

This was no bear mauling. This was the work of *vaettir*. Like Fisk said, they were playing with us.

I made my way back to the entrance of the bear-cave, dousing the lantern's flame. I sat on a rock and twisted a smoke, but didn't light it. I just sat in the dark, listening to the night sounds, the rustle of the gulley and the echoes of the mountain, waiting for my eyes to regain their *dvergar* dim-sight. But they didn't. They couldn't.

The night had become darker and I watched as shadows, pieces of night blacker than the darkness, moved swiftly through the bramblewrack, up the gulley, toward me, silent and swift. I had no doubt what they were. Who they were.

So I kept still, sitting on a rock, my heart hammering in my chest like a farrier at a fire, terror tucked away. And they came.

They flowed up and stopped in front of me, three shadows, as tall and willowy as aspens writhing on the heights. Try as I might, I could not make out their features. They remained parts of the sum of night, greater than the whole.

I waited.

No movement – for a long while, and I tried to keep my eyes on them, but their shadows blended with the darkness of the bramblewrack. And as I stared, I became unable to make out one figure from the other until finally I couldn't see anything other than gulley and bramble and rock.

'Come on, then, you bastards. Do it, then.' There was nothing for it but to accept what was in store. I wished I'd kept my knives on my person, instead of arriving here like some defenceless babe abandoned on the mountainside. Damnation. Me and the Ia-damned taint. It seemed I was sullied enough already that the stretchers could sniff me out.

Then I heard a sighing sound, felt the wind rattling the bramblewrack. And my eyes saw bramble and boulder. There was nothing more. No stretchers. No indigines. Just shadow.

I left the corpse in the cave and made my way back down the mountain.

EIGHT

L IVIA SCOWLED AT her father as he gestured wildly with his
cup, lolling on a divan in the stateroom on the *Cornelian*,
his wounded leg raised on a pile of bloodied pillows. She applied
raw cotton wads to the gore coming from the remains of his calf,
and I saw the vial of tersus incendia resting on the tabletop nearby.
Cornelius was as drunk as ten prancing lords, slurring his words,
foaming at the mouth, and as furious as only an intoxicated and
wounded patrician can be.

'Where is the dratted hide of that beast? I want to see it! '

'Tata. Tata. Listen to me.' Her voice was hard, cold, but not
devoid of love. 'There's no time to waste. We have to take off
your leg.'

He ignored her and, after swigging the last from his cup, peered
into its empty depths. Then he stared around the great room, be-
wildered. Blank expressions answered him.

Cimbri bristled nearby, and two lictors glowered at Fisk and me
standing in the doorway. I had descended the mountain, bearing
news of Orrin's carcass in the bear cave and remained upright and
awake long enough to inform Sharbo and Horehound of what I
found. The next morning, a contubernium of Cimbri's legion had
gathered us up. Now we were forgotten at the back of the room.
Carnelia, huddled on a nearby divan, sipped at a dainty crystal

glass of claret, while Secundus remained by his older sister, his stern face matching her own. Gnaeus stood glowering, still in his hunting clothes, six-gun at his waist. He had sneered when he saw us.

'I need something stronger. Stronger, I say!' Cornelius waved his cup around as though looking for a server or slave. Crimson drops, the dregs of his wine, spattered Livia's dress and Secundus' tunic. She didn't bat an eye.

'I need whiskey! Bring me the bottle!'

'Just let him be, sister,' Gnaeus said. 'He says it's just a scratch. So he should be fine.'

Livia whirled around to face her older brother, her expression furious. 'Are you addled? Did you fall on your head? *Tata is likely to die!* Do you not understand?'

Gnaeus looked at her, gritting his teeth.

'Oh, he knows,' Carnelia said. 'He knows very well – don't you, dear brother? Are you impatient for your fortune?'

Gnaeus spluttered. He turned first to Livia and then Carnelia before collecting his wits. 'When he *does* die, I'll have your tongue cut out and you married to a Tueton sheepherder, Carnelia.' He paused and a malicious grin spread across his features. 'Except, *dear sister*, you would probably enjoy it. The commoners spoke of a fellatrix at the whorehouse at New Damnation and you were suspiciously absent for much of our time there.'

Gnaeus poured himself some wine and bit into a slice of cheese.

Carnelia sipped at her wine and waved a hand. 'You speak of things you do not understand, Gnaeus. Remember, serving girls talk.' She pointed her index finger up and then curled it downward, as though it had gone limp.

'Gods, you children are a trial,' Livia said. 'Our father is dying. We need to act.'

'I'm fine,' Cornelius warbled. 'I'll be fine with more drink. Shape up in a trice.'

A small woman, hair pulled back in a severe bun, scuttled forward with a decanter. An obedient slave, most likely.

Hard to believe, but some folks envy slaves their positions. Far in the past the senate, mostly due to a man named Tiro, limited indenture to thirty-five years, and stipulated there should be enough money for a house and servants of their own at the end. So many folks sold themselves away, despite Ia's will, lured by the promise of future wealth.

A nice house does have its attractions, especially now that I'm longer in the tooth and still living on the plains and the face of the mountains.

But, still. They're slaves, and denied any free will. I ain't never been tempted.

In the instant Cornelius' arm was still, the mousy servant darted forward and poured the whiskey into his cup. A very deft hand, the woman.

Cornelius spotted her, and lurched left in his cushions. 'Damnation, Lupina! Don't mix whiskey with the wine!' Spittle flew from his lips, caught in the over-bright lamp-light. He drank from the cup anyway.

Livia slapped it from his hands. The liquor flew and the metal cup clattered across the wooden flooring until the same slave darted forward and snatched it up.

'I say, Livia!' Gnaeus stepped between her and Cornelius. 'He is the head of our family. Give him the respect due his station.'

Livia chilled, clearly disgusted by her brother's hypocrisy. It was an amazing transformation. Her eyes narrowed and she brought her arms to her side, hands balled into small hard fists. In even tones, she said. 'You are a *coward*, brother. If you wish our father dead, take up the Ia-damned knife and plunge it into his breast.'

She moved to Cimbri and had jerked his longknife from his belt before he could react. Turning to her brother, holding out the blade hilt first, she hissed, 'Go on, Gnaeus. One blow and you will become the pater familias.'

'He will not!' bellowed Cornelius. He tried to rise, fell back. 'As long as there's still strength in these arms, I am a match for any man!'

'Hush, father,' Carnelia said, taking another drink. 'Livvie is defending your honour.' Her words amused her and she tittered, showing teeth gone roan with wine.

'Take it!' Livia said.

'You are unhinged, woman. I'll have no part of this,' Gnaeus said, but he looked at his father, whose dissolute eyes remained focused on his son's long enough to stir whatever passed for a heart in his chest. Gnaeus turned and left the stateroom.

'He didn't want ...' Cornelius coughed and slurped his drink. 'Good lad, Gnaeus. Good lad. Don't help them!'

Livia turned back to face her father. 'You old sot. You can't ignore this.' She put her face close to his and said, very loudly and slowly, '*We must cut off your leg.*'

Fisk glanced at me and raised an eyebrow. I could tell Fisk's leg pained him as well.

'I want Beleth.' Cornelius' voice turned petulant and scared. 'He'll know what to do.'

'He's an Ia-damned engineer, father, not a medic,' said Secundus, his tone less imperious than his sister's but his exasperation clear. 'He'll tell you the exact same thing as she has.'

Livia cast her eyes around the room as though looking for help. She spied us standing near the exit next to a disgruntled legionary.

She came over to us, her bodice spattered with wine and her hair loose. She looked absolutely gorgeous. Fury became her.

'Mr Ilys, you would have done us all a great favour if you'd chopped off his damned leg when you had him on the mountain.' Though upset, she managed to give a half-smile. She turned to Fisk. 'And you, Mr Fisk. Shouldn't you be off your own leg? I seem to recall tending your ... less grievous, yet more than insignificant ... wounds yesterday.' She brushed her hair from her face and sighed. 'It seems so long ago.'

'I'm sorry, ma'am. I thought you might have been able to—'

'What? Suture my father's torn flesh back together? No. I'm no magician. That requires medical expertise far beyond my skill. Far beyond anyone's skill.'

'What about this Beleth fella? He do something?'

She arched an eyebrow and put her hands on her hips. 'Well, let's see, shall we?' She turned to me. 'Mr Ilys, will you take this lictor to Beleth's chambers and request his presence. Demand it, if necessary.'

'Beleth answering to a dwarf?' Carnelia giggled again. 'How apropos.'

'Me?' I asked Livia. 'He don't even know me. Why would he come to my call?'

'Because you are asking for me.'

I glanced at Fisk. 'You come with me?'

He shook his head. 'Sorry, pard, I've got to take a load off.'

He hobbled toward a bench on the back wall, but Livia said, 'Fisk, please. Come sit near Secundus and me. We wish to talk with you regarding the events of the day.'

'Shoestring'd be better suited to tell you 'bout what he found up in that bear den.'

'Yes, but you might help us make sense of it while we wait for Beleth.' She turned back toward Secundus and asked, 'Where's our brother gone?'

'Rutting with one of his chambermaids, most likely.'

She nodded. Both of them seemed relieved he was not present to complicate things.

I saw Fisk think it over. The man has a natural reluctance toward making connections, even when a woman as beautiful as Livia is doing the asking.

After a moment, he nodded and slowly walked to the front of the room near the divans. Not before spotting Banty sitting in the corner, half obscured by an urn. Banty jumped up, then sat back down, his blush colouring his face like a port stain.

I approached Cimbri. 'This Beleth engineer ... he ain't too frightful, is he?'

Cimbri's moustache quivered. I couldn't tell if it was anger or mirth or fleas.

'Why don't you go find out, Shoestring?'

Ia-damn him.

'Young Banty's sitting in yon corner, behind that urn,' I growled.

'What?' Cimbri turned and stomped over toward where Banty lurked, his hackles raised, jaw clenched.

I didn't stay for the rest. I motioned to the lictor, and we left the stateroom.

The silver wardwork looked much different at night. It gleamed and shimmered in light thrown from the gaslight fixtures – marvellous contraptions themselves. I'd seen them on the streets of Covenant, far east, and on the main mechanized baggage train line, but never this far west and never in a private domicile. In my worst imaginings, I'd never thought I'd find them on a boat. But as I got nearer, I realized it wasn't gas flames burning in them.

Daemonwork. Tiny *imps* battered the confines of a filigreed cage of silver wardwork, burning bright and smoking with hatred and madness. They writhed, they fumed, they incandesced.

Ia-damn this boat.

I knocked heavily on the door.

'Mr Beleth! Pardon the interruption! You're requested!' I looked at the lictor, who raised his fasces – I noticed the fronds were of holly and the axehead, buried within the bundled fronds, had a silver spike.

Dvergar, like *vaettir* and *daemons*, have an allergy to silver. That we share this trait is, I think, one of the causes of our status among mankind: the general hatred or dismissiveness we receive. In my case, the allergy is much lessened, due to the dilution of my *dvergar* blood. But being hemmed in here, caught like a fly in the lattice work of silver warding away the damnable and the immortal, my eye caught the spike in the fasces and my skin crawled with the thought of it entering my flesh.

I knocked again, harder.

For a long while I heard nothing but the light pat pat pats of the tiny bound *imps* in the light fixtures. So I banged again at the door.

I don't know what I was thinking. Maybe that this engineer would appear in a puff of smoke, with forked beard and tongue, cat's eyes and an evil stare.

Instead I heard a cough and a thump, and then a pale, plump little man, not much taller than me but twice as soft, opened the door and stood blinking in the hallway light.

'Wha … what's all this banging?'

'Mr Beleth?' Hard to believe this fella had the forces of damnation and more in his hands. His thick brown hair looked like a wind-shaped scrub-brush. He stood in his long nightgown, showing pasty white legs.

'Hold on a moment,' he said and disappeared in his cabin to return with a pair of spectacles perched on the end of his nose. He glanced at the lictor, sniffed, and then gave me a once-over.

'Ah, a *dvergar*! Why would a dwarf make such a clatter at my door after sundown? Hmm?'

He seemed surprisingly genial in spite of being disturbed from his rest. Fisk would have answered the door with a pistol in hand or not even bothered.

'Mr Beleth, you've been requested in the great room. Mr Cornelius is grievously wounded.'

He frowned and looked up and down the hall. 'What do you think I can do? Livia is an accomplished medico.'

'She wants to cut off his leg, and he won't—'

'Wait. What?'

He had a straightforward, uninflected accent, and I could tell he had spent many years in the colonies, maybe even the Imperial Protectorate, where I'd banged around for a few decades as a pup, watching the immigrants flow in and the shoal aurochs move west. But he was a Ruman, through and through.

'Bear stripped his leg yesterday on the hunt. It needs to come off, below the knee. He's drunk as a skunk and won't let anyone touch it until he sees you. Seems to think you can fix it.'

'Damnation.'

'Yes.'

'Give me a moment, will you, and I'll put on some suitable clothes?'

He ducked back into the room, quickly re-emerging in a brown suit without a necktie. As he tucked in his shirt and adjusted his jacket he said, 'Bear? Truly? I'd imagine the rifle I crafted him would keep the creatures at bay.'

'You made that gun, sir?' I whistled. 'It sure is a Hell of a rifle. What're all those doohickeys for? – the glasswork?'

'Sighting. The combination of any two lenses will provide a magnified view of whatever stands before the shooter.'

'You mean you can see far off, then?'

'Yes. That, coupled with the longer barrel, allows the shooter to hit targets at a greater range than someone firing a normal pistol, carbine, or rifle.'

'Pardon me for asking, but how much further are we talking about here?'

'Oh, two hundred to three hundred strides, I should think. Depending on windspeed and atmospheric occlusion.'

I stayed quiet. I wished he could talk normal.

He walked down the hall, and I jumped to follow. The lictor came behind us.

'Drunk, did you say? Damn that man and his appetites.'

I looked at the paunch he carried but said nothing. He noticed.

'Eh? Well observed, Mister ...?'

I debated whether to tell him Shoetring or my Ia-given name.

'Ilys, sir. Dveng Ilys.'

'We don't see many *dvergar* folks around here.' He waved a hand, gesturing to all the silver wardwork. 'Not the most comfortable of spaces for them.'

'No, I reckon not, sir. But there's some has got more resistance than others, depending on blood.'

He smiled. 'True, of course. But I'm thinking your resistance isn't that strong, is it?'

I nodded. 'That's right. I fall more on the *dvergar* side of the fence, I do.'

'You come from the tinkers? Or diggers?'

To the eastern-born and the Rumans, there's only two kinds of *dvergar*: tinkers – the smiths and farriers, the wheelwrights and carpenters, the folk with clever fingers and cunning tools – or the diggers, those *dvergar* suitable for only brute labour, digging and mining, burrowing and excavating. I'll admit there's mighty few others of *my* kind more than that. Haven't yet figured out just where I fit in, though.

'My mother was what you'd call a tinker, sir. She worked metal.

Had a real knack for it too. Still does, I guess. Haven't seen her nigh on fifty years.'

'You have the look of a tinker, Mr Ilys.' He placed a finger against his nose, winked at me, and said, 'Raw intelligence, moderated deference, and tact. Definitely tinker.'

Don't know how I felt about that, some engineer making personal judgments about me, filing me into his tidy little classification system that didn't even take into account all walks of life.

It's a miserable world we live in that places one man above another by virtue of birth. I'd like to see Beleth manage on the plains or the mountains for a fortnight and then see his judgments.

However, he *was* an engineer, so I nodded again and smiled. For a moment, I felt a great need to be off the boat and on the shore, by a fire, watching the camp smoke stir the stars and listening to the horses nicker and stamp.

Cornelius seemed even drunker than before. Livia, tense and pale, her lips tight and bloodless, sat watching her father thrash about. He attempted to rise on his good leg, waving a tumbler of whiskey in his hand.

'Ah, Beleth. Beleth, tell them.' He gestured with his glass, sloshing whiskey onto the floor. 'Tell them you'll have me patched—' He fell back onto the pillows and slurped at his drink. 'Have me patched up in a trice?'

Beleth walked around Cornelius' divan. He stopped, put his hands on his waist, and then looked from the gore of his employer's leg to Livia.

'Looks bad.'

'How very observant of you.'

I thought he might get ruffled, the little engineer, but he smiled. Didn't go all the way to his eyes, though.

'I'm no doctor—' He paused, waiting to see if Livia would interject again. She didn't. 'But I think right here should suffice.'

He leaned forward and touched Cornelius right below the knee. Then he touched him again higher, on the lower thigh. 'Or maybe here, if you can't get that leg off soon.'

Cornelius' tumbler shattered on the floor. How someone could lurch and wobble while reclining, I'll never know, but the old senator managed it.

'What?' His voice was thick and slurred. 'Can't you ... can't you summon up ...'

'A *daemon*? Of course. And it can bite off your leg, if you'd like.'

'No! No, to heal it. To fix it!'

Beleth laughed. Livia can mock and laugh, yet still convey love – I had learned this even in the short time I'd known her. But not Beleth. His mirth just sounded mocking.

'*Daemons* do no healing, sir. They can only corrupt and weaken. But the fire of their hatred can keep you warm – heat water to cleanse the wound.'

'No.' Cornelius shook his head. He lay gasping, defeated. 'No. No.'

Livia took charge. 'Mr Fisk? Mr Ilys? Will you assist?'

I stepped forward. Blood and bone don't bother me. Nor Fisk.

Secundus asked, 'And me? Where should I ... what should I do?'

'Hold his head. Roll up that napkin, thick, and put it in his mouth. He'll gnash his teeth.'

Fisk grabbed Cornelius' uninjured leg. I took an arm; Cimbri moved forward to grasp his other. The man struggled, but only feebly.

I pulled out my flask of cacique, put it to his lips, and said, 'Go on, Mr Cornelius. Drink it all down, now. All of it.' Then I tilted it up and he opened his mouth and sucked at it like a calf at a teat.

When he drew away, I watched his eyes dissolve into watery pools, unknowing, brimming with oblivion. Livia withdrew from her medical kit the steel saw I had noticed earlier. She held it up to the yellow *daemonlight*, put it back down, poured acetum down its length.

She looked at us all, thought for a moment, and gestured at a nearby lictor and slave to come closer. She jabbed a finger at the lictor. 'You hold his thigh. You—' She looked at the half-*dvergar* woman. 'You stand ready.'

'Now that he's bound and gagged, I'll take his purse,' Carnelia giggled. 'For safekeeping, I swear.'

'Sister, you think you'll have free reign when Gnaeus is head of our house?' Livia glared at her until Carnelia, still grasping her wineglass, turned and walked out of the stateroom in the overly precise way drunks have.

Not much more to say, really, unless you want to hear about the blood and gristle, how the Senator howled through the gag, how, even though he was as drunk as I've seen any man, he twisted and strained with surprising strength.

It was done. Miss Livia, spattered in her father's blood, drenched the stump in tersus incendia – sending Cornelius into another writhing fit – and then wrapped it with as much linen as she could.

Two lictors, under Miss Livia's watchful direction, placed him on a stretcher and took him back to his quarters. She followed them but paused briefly to address both Fisk and me, 'Thank you, gentlemen. I cannot express how much I appreciate your help.' She seemed about to say more, but then turned and left. The engineer nodded in our direction, adjusted his glasses, and stifled a yawn. After a moment, he followed in her wake. It was then I realized he was holding Cornelius' amputated leg, raw side down and dripping.

I looked at Fisk. He wore an expression totally new to me: his face at once softer and harder than I'd ever seen it before. He wasn't paying any attention to the engineer, that's for damned sure.

We turned to leave, but Secundus held out a crystal decanter of whiskey.

'Join me? We won't be moving upriver for the next couple of days, so there's no need for undue "spiritual" restraint, Mr Fisk, Mr Ilys.' His solemn expression was broken by a quick smile, but I could see the tiredness lining his young face.

So we sat with the young highborn, and he asked questions about the land we were in, about the river, about the mountains, while I twisted smokes and Fisk poured the whiskey. It was early morning by the time we left and a bleary-eyed lascar took us back to the eastern shore.

No sign of Banty when we arrived. But his horse was still there, so I felt confident he'd turn up, much as I wished he wouldn't.

It was cold and crisp, and my breath made crystal plumes in the air as I lay in my blankets by the fire, under the moon. A thin cloud passed across its face. Then I closed my eyes and I slept.

NINE

Fisk spent most of the next day, and the day after that, sleeping. I took Banty outriding and tried to dry the wet behind his ears. We scouted the eastern arc, a half circle starting a mile upstream the *Cornelian* and ending a mile down, out in the prairie, big sky above us, rippling grass all around.

'Mr Bantam, a word of advice.'

He acted like he couldn't hear. It *was* a mite windy.

'You're like to get ventilated if you keep squaring off with Mr Fisk, I reckon.'

He glanced at me, scowling.

I went on. 'We like you fine, Mr Bantam. But respect ain't just given, willy nilly. It takes time, needs to be earned. You keep your head down, do what Mr Fisk says—'

He kicked his horse off into a gallop and rode on ahead. I didn't follow.

A pair of roosting quail, startled by his approach, burst from the ground in an explosion of sound and feathers.

Banty whipped out his gun, fast as lightning, sighted down his arm, and fired.

He fired again. I was far enough away not to feel the blast of the infernal. But *he* must have.

One bird dropped.

When I joined him, he sat still, holding his smoking pistol, looking down at the small body of the quail, brown, speckled, and almost invisible in the grass. He didn't look at me.

'That was some nice shooting, son.' I stopped myself. 'I mean, Mr Bantam. You've got a right talent there.'

He looked at me, and his eyes narrowed. Not a normal squint into the sun, or in anger. But like he was in pain or washed in remorse. His face, normally unlined and youthful – handsome, even – looked gaunt and pale. Gunplay does that to some men. And the boy was upset.

'Let Fisk know I won't be talked down to no more.' He swallowed. 'He talks down to me again, I'll—'

'Yessir, gotta say, that was some good shooting.' I turned Bess and moved off, into the taller grasses. 'Mr Fisk wouldn't have wasted a shot, though. When he pulls his gun, what he's aiming at—'

'What?'

'Dies. Never seen him miss.'

'He missed them stretchers. I heard you say it yourself.'

'That's ...' I shook my head. There was just no talking to this boy. 'That's right. But the *vaettir*'re something else entirely.'

He snorted. 'Tell him. I ain't gonna be talked down to.'

I nodded. 'All right, Mr Bantam. I'll tell him what I saw.'

I took time to set a couple snares on the smooth, grooved entrance of a game trail dipping over the lip of an old creekbed. I'd ride back through in the morning, early, to collect whatever I'd snared. We'd gone through the tongue and livers and could use some more meat. Rabbit, I hoped. Or maybe something fatter. Coon ain't half bad, if you know how to clean it right, which I do. I ain't much for bragging, but there it is: I know how to clean coon.

Banty had a hard, angry slope to his shoulders, and he settled into his saddle like a tick digging into the soft white flesh of nether regions.

Nothing good would come of that one.

The damnedest thing is, everyone is born into this world on the edge of a knife. From the time you're wet and squalling – the slightest tip of the balance and you go sliding away, consumed by remorse, or guilt. Or revenge. Or even love. Only Ia knows how it will turn out, and he's not telling.

Faith is just believing he cares.

Livia was sitting by the fire with Fisk when I returned. Cimbri and a single lascar, too, sat on the logs next to it. Fisk had a pot of coffee stinking over the flames – he always burned it – and looked uncomfortable in the lady's presence. He kept tugging the hem of his Imperial blues, trying to straighten his jacket. Cimbri looked pained, as though he thought she should be back on the boat. His whiskers seemed to bristle with impatience.

'You've been requested at the palace,' Cimbri said, jerking a thumb at the *Cornelian*. 'Seems the Senator wants a dinner party.'

'Ain't that a little premature?'

'You obviously don't know the Senator. He wants what he wants.'

'When?'

'Tomorrow.' He shifted, and then sighed. 'Seems he's quite taken with young Mr Bantam.'

'Banty?' I couldn't help myself. It just popped right out there, like the words had a life of their own.

'I know. Damned foolish …' He coughed and looked at Livia. 'Sorry, ma'am. Didn't mean no disrespect.'

'None taken.'

He coughed again and said, 'Mr Cornelius seems to remember

Banty "saving" him. Or at least being instrumental in his ... er ... his rescue and medical treatment.'

I laughed. Ia-damn that boy. He was gonna get into serious trouble one of these days. Between the patrician and Fisk, Banty's days were numbered. Some folks just can't help themselves.

Fire calls to fire, they say. I believe it.

Cimbri pulled a machine-rolled Medieran cheroot from his brushed vest, and popped it into his mouth through his copious whiskers.

'Er. Yes. And he'll be seated as the guest of honour.'

Fisk spat, and I laughed even harder. I raised an eyebrow at Livia. 'How's your father? His leg?'

'Remarkably well, all things considered. He'd gone through quite a bit of liquor until one of the slaves found some poppy extract and we drugged his brandy. He slept for ten hours. And then was bellowing for red meat, eggs, and more spirits. Raw, preferably.'

'Which?'

'All of them. Raw.'

Fisk whistled.

'Mr Cornelius must have the constitution of a bear,' I said.

'It's Ia-damned impressive, the man's will. He's a monster, he is. The wound hasn't even slowed him down.' Cimbri stood up. 'We're gonna need more meat. And since Miss Livia asked if she could see a shoal auroch ... I thought since you're acquainted ... she, and her sister, and Isabelle, the Medieran lass, might ...'

'You think that's wise, Cimbri? Miss Livia? A hunt? With the ladies?' Fisk squinted at Livia as though trying to see what she was thinking. She blinked slowly, deliberately, and stared back. A steady, cool gaze – fearless.

'Your concern is?' she said, after a while.

'The womenfolk. I'm sure *you* know how to comport yourself, but those other ladies ...' He shook his head. 'I'll be frank.'

'Please. It is what I wish from you.'

'Those ladies are too damned foolish for a hunt. One of 'em will ride away and a *vaettir* will have her stripped way beyond her knickers before we know she's even gone missing.'

'We have faith in your abilities, Mr Fisk.' She smiled and placed a fine hand upon his rough, tanned one. It was like I could see, right there, his brains getting scrambled.

'Going out there, on the plains? Your father lost his leg. Just three days ago, a stretcher put an arrow through my leg. And there's what happened to Orrin to think about.'

'True. But we would have Secundus ... and Gnaeus ... and as many legionaries and lascars as you deem fit, Mr Fisk, each one bearing holly and silver.' She inclined her beautiful head to me. 'And you, Mr Ilys.'

'I'm afraid I don't carry much of either, but I wouldn't miss this folderol for a sack of gold.'

Livia patted Fisk's hand and smiled. 'So, that's settled. Tomorrow morning? We'll assemble here?'

'Looks like.' Fisk glanced at Cimbri. 'Have the lascars unlimber the Ia-damned wagon and port it over. We're gonna need it.'

'For the auroch?'

'Or the corpses.'

No one laughed.

And so it was I rode east again that day, until I found signs of shoal auroch. I stripped myself of all weapons and even unsaddled Bess, riding her bridleless and with only a blanket, trusting to her good sense and the balance and ability Ia had given me.

There was a moment, when the sun, grown long in the sky, passed behind a grey cloud and the world went dim. In that moment I knew I wasn't alone out on the great sea of the plains.

I felt a diminishment. I was a flea, a spark, an infinitesimal mote on the face of the earth, but I *was not alone.*

My mother would have said it was the old gods, the numen. I had half an inclination that it was a mite taller and toothier than them.

And then the cloud passed, and I scanned the horizon for indigene stretcher and shoal beast alike.

I didn't find either. I was considerably relieved, I must admit – if I'm to go to my maker without a liar's stain on my soul.

I looked at the mule, and she shivered her shoulder muscles and stamped the ground.

I wasn't going to work myself into an Ia-damned tizzy if *she* wasn't.

'I'll be skinned if you don't have better sense than I do myself.'

Bess chucked her head, turned her neck to look at me, and bared her pink and black gums.

'I know, girl. Ia help me, I know.'

Seeing that I agreed, she turned back to the plains, the mountains at our back, and walked on.

TEN

WE GATHERED BY the river in the half-light of dawn, the legionaries huddled in thick woollen paenulae with the hoods drawn over their heads, the cloaks' lead-weighted hems stirring in the wind. They clutched stock carbines in nervous fingers and the wind whipping down off the mountains sent their plumed breath skirling into the early morning mists. The lictors – always prouder than the soldiers, made haughty by their vaunted position closer to the patrician class and their religious ordination – held their fasces high, showing the silver axes bound with holly fronds. One carried a carmine brag-rag mounted on a pole, legion-style.

They'd brought over the wagon in the night, loading it and a couple of draft horses onto a raft made from planks and cleverly inflated auroch bladders and manoeuvred her in the dark across the Big Rill with paddles and poles. I harnessed the horses to the wagon and told the soldiers to climb aboard. The quartet of lictors could ride, and I indicated for them to find mounts. We had enough to spare.

'First sign of trouble,' Fisk said to the legionaries as a group, 'you boys bail out of that wagon.'

Half of them blinked and stared stupidly, not understanding.

Fisk snapped his fingers, a bright, hard sound even with the wind.

'Understood? We see one sign of stretchers, you hit the ground and flip this wagon on its side. Got me?'

There was a muttered assent and nodding of heads. Fisk looked at me and then the soldiers in the wagon, indicating they were my charge now.

Gnaeus sat on his charger, carbine in hand, chatting with the ladies of the *Cornelian*. Hard to tell if he was already drunk or if he'd just stayed that way all night.

'You'll see, Isabelle. You'll witness these brute animals. They're great stupid woolly creatures, and they stay grouped together even when they're being slaughtered.' He waved clumsily at the dark plains.

The fine-featured Medieran girl listened to Gnaeus, nodding. She had a long neck and a fine figure, and sat the horse well, decked in suede riding leathers, nicely cut, and a dainty riding cabassette perched atop her beautiful, dark curls.

She was certainly easy on the eyes.

'Brutish beasts that match the brutish inhabitants of these colonies.' Gnaeus turned slowly and looked at Fisk. 'These protectorates are filled with the most base and aberrant of all men, Isabelle. Remember that! Always keep this in mind. They'll have at you in a trice if you give them an opportunity.'

'Have at me?' She smiled and hid a giggle behind a gloved hand.

'They're scurrilous, randy dogs. They'll hump their own mothers given half the chance.'

I've spent the last ten years with Fisk. Seen him called everything. He's like stone, he is. But I could see in the set of his jaw, the cant of his shoulders, the muscle popping in his cheek, that he was exercising vast restraint.

Any other man. Any other . . .

Fisk is my partner, but I have no illusions on the destination of his immortal soul. He's damned as surely as the sun rises, as sure as the grass continues to grow. He loves the Hellfire. He loves his gun. He's a hard, unyielding man, with a long memory and impervious to regret. But there's kindness there, too, under all that. There's love and remorse. He's destined for perdition's flames, but there's good in him too. I believe that, otherwise I wouldn't have ridden with him these past long years. At least that's my view.

Banty moved his horse closer to the Medieran lass. The beasts chuffed their heads and champed in the dust. Isabelle greeted Banty, with a dazzling smile that suffused her face with a radiance to match the rising sun.

And looking at Banty now, I thought how little difference there was between him and Fisk except for the years and experience of hardship. Banty could almost have been his son, his younger brother.

He'd be as hard, too, recalcitrant and cold. If he lived that long.

The legionaries in the wagon had donned thick Tueton tunics – some more than one – and dyed leather britches. Some had focales twisted around their necks to preserve them from the cold mountain wind; others had their sagum wrapped tight around their bodies. From their belts hung longknives and pistols and utility aprons – no longer wearing lappets, instead, stained cloth hung from the belt in front – useful for wiping hands and cleaning blades during long marches or bloodwork. Only Banty bestride his horse was decked out in full Ruman uniform, although his Imperial blue jacket was devoid of phalerae. Even his boots were gleaming – he sure had dudded himself up.

Gnaeus noticed Isabelle's smile and kneed his great charger forward, between Banty and the girl.

Banty, showing some sense for once, tipped his hat and moved his horse away.

Gnaeus beamed. He pulled a silver flask from a pocket and drank, his carbine held loosely in hand.

Livia sat mounted beside Isabelle on a grey gelding, sensibly dressed in a thick furred vest with high collar, burnished grey riding skirt, and a fine pistol at her waist. Her sister, Carnelia, was similarly arrayed – and yawning.

Fisk drew near Gnaeus and Secundus. He held himself tight, his shoulders high and his reinless hand free but ready, near his six-guns. His hat was pulled down low on his brow, so that it was hard to see his eyes and, I imagine, whatever emotions lived there. Fisk was doing a job he really didn't want to do, but damned if he wasn't going to do it to the best of his ability.

'Mr Gnaeus, Shoestring sighted the auroch about two hours ride from here. Should still be in that area. But we need to get moving. And there's a stream to ford.'

Gnaeus, hearing Fisk, scowled, his face twisting in disgust as though, unbuttoning to piss, he'd discovered a leech in his britches. His expressions warred between sourness at Fisk's presence and excitement of the hunt – not that it was going to be much of one, unless you counted what was most likely hunting *us*. Auroch are big, stupid creatures; Mr Gnaeus was right on that count. It's a wonder they've lasted as long as they have.

I kicked Bess into a trot, and headed east. A lictor lost control of his mount; it wheeled and reared, and he hit the ground in a cloud of dust. Gnaeus snarled, 'You. Get on the wagon with the legionaries.'

Blushing a deep crimson, the man dusted himself off and climbed among the men in the wagon.

I've been at the head, rear, and middle of a string of horses in my time, and they make a terrible ruckus. But once you get going, all those horses moving together, the wagon creaking, it's a feeling like no other. All this life, Ia-given life, moving together with a single purpose. Damn shame, sometimes, when all that life comes together to take life. I'd hate to be a part of an army on the hoof, carrying damnation with them. I figure it would feel wonderful and terrible all at once.

Just as the sun crested the horizon, sending pink and purple streamers into the sky, Fisk rode over and matched Bess's pace.

'You think that Gnaeus will get up to his antics?'

'If he doesn't, Banty will.'

He spat. 'Shit.'

'Mr Bantam showed me some of his shooting yesterday on the plains.'

'How's that?'

'He bagged some quail.' I kept an eye on the horizon as we talked. 'He drew faster than shit through a goose. Missed his first shot, though.'

Fisk looked at me close, checking I wasn't pulling his leg. Then he nodded. 'Think he'll cause trouble?'

'Well, the boy's aggrieved, that's for damn sure. You snipped his prick a few notches when you backhanded him. He ain't gonna forget that anytime soon.'

'And Gnaeus. Damnation.'

I waited, letting that last bit hang. 'Hell, Fisk. We've been in far worse spots than this.'

He looked at Miss Livia, and then away, quick-like. 'Yeah. I reckon so.'

'Maybe there are some complications.' The woman. The *vaettir*. The Cornelians. 'Not much we can do other than cut and run. That what you want to do?' I already knew the answer.

He glared at me. 'You can be cruel, Shoe, when you have a mind. But I've always known that about you.'

'Not cruel. Just trying to get you to buck up, pard.'

He spat again. 'That right?'

I grinned. 'That's right.'

Secundus reined in, dropping back to us. 'Everything all right?'

Fisk nodded. 'Gonna ride our backtrail for a bit. Shoe, you watch the women and wagon.' He turned his horse. 'Mr Secundus, I'd be much obliged to you if you would…' The black turned again underneath him, ready for movement. 'If you'd do your best to restrain your brother. At least during the hunt.'

'I'll do what I can.'

Fisk paused for a moment, his gaze flicking toward the women, and I could have swore he was about to say, 'And look after Miss Livia,' but he shut his mouth and rode west, back toward the mountains.

'He's a strange man, that Mr Fisk.' Secundus' words suggested puzzlement, rather than condemnation.

'I once knew a man who had one of those intestinal eels from far Tchinee. Rode with him for a year. Been a lascar in his youth and fallen overboard in eel-infested waters. Didn't look like nothing was wrong with him, either, having that eel living in his belly. At night, after the fire had died down and he started to snoring, that eel would get curious, stick its head out of the man's mouth, and chitter at whoever noticed it.'

Secundus said, 'You're joking, surely.'

I smiled. 'Not about this. Saw it myself.'

'What happened to the man?'

'We were outriding the far reaches of the Big Empty. All our meat was gone, we'd been living on hardtack for a month, and it was bitter cold. Foot of snow. So we stoked the fire high, gave Jimbo an extra ration of whiskey, and waited for him to sleep.'

'And…'

'Eel peeks its head out around midnight. Starts a'chittering away. We grab it, pull it out. It's screaming at us like an infant, but vicious and hateful.' I shook my head. 'I'll swear on my mother's life it was cursing us.'

'I find this hard to believe, Mr Ilys.'

'Believe what you will. There's strange like Mr Fisk. And then there's *strange*.'

'But what happened?'

'Jimson died before daybreak. We cut up the eel and cooked it. Tasted just like you'd think. Like bile and shit.'

'That's vile.'

'Yep.' I scanned the horizon again, and then looked back along the length of the hunting party. 'Moral of the story? Don't go swimming in far Tchinee.'

'I'll remember that.'

'Could you do me a great service, Mr Secundus?'

'What do you need? I will help if I can.'

'Rejoin your brother and sisters. Keep that Hellfire at the ready. Don't drink any of your brother's whiskey. And watch the plains.'

'You're worried about the possibility of indigenes?'

Had to admit it. 'Yep. That's a hand I wouldn't bet against.'

'A certainty, then?'

I looked at the young patrician. He was good looking, honest, lively. A face as wholesome and open as the plains – before either man or *dvergar* came along and befouled them.

'If there's anything I'm sure of, Mr Secundus, trouble is waiting. Just don't know where it's gonna come from.'

'I'll stay alert.'

'My thanks, sir. And, please, if you would, have a word with Miss Livia.'

He raised his eyebrows.

I liked the lad, but he just confirmed that these Ia-damned patricians didn't seem to understand the nature of the stretchers. If we were in the deepest tracts of Aegypt, they'd watch out for the lion. But they couldn't seem to understand that these indigenes were a thousand times more dangerous.

Or maybe he *did* understand. Maybe.

I stopped my mule and waited for the highborns to come abreast me so that I might speak to Livia.

As they neared, I heard Gnaeus say, 'If this hunt comes up short, I'll have the surly one crucified.'

'I'm sure you'll find something to shoot, brother.' Carnelia looked tired in the morning light, as though she'd rather be sleeping. There was no giggling now. Her vitriol was all by rote. 'You wear your bloodlust like father wears his toga – messily, and stained with red.'

'Ia's beard, Carnelia, I need to have you bridled just to shut your mouth. But that might lower morale on the ship. The fellows would miss their fellator.'

'That again?' Carnelia laughed. 'You'd know more about cocks than I, brother. I am but a lowly, cunning daughter, but you're a great *cunnus* of a Cornelian.'

Secundus snorted, checked himself, and looked at his brother, who was glaring about, looking for someone to shoot. His gaze fastened on me.

'Ah, the dwarf is here,' he said. 'Tell me, half-man, how far to the sport?'

'When I scouted yesterday, the auroch were not more than two miles from this point. But the herd could have moved since then.' I scratched my cheek. 'Or come closer. Never know.'

Gnaeus sat silent, looking at me as though I was some dung served up steaming on a platter. He sucked his teeth and put his free hand on his hip.

'You see his lack of deference?' he said. 'These colonists have no respect for their betters.' He shifted in his saddle, and his eyes became little pebbles in his face. 'Tell me, *dvergar*, is it true your kind rut in the mud?'

It was an old joke, and a poor one. *Dvergar* have always been close to the earth, children of the mountain, children of the stone.

We work metal, we dig mines. And great brutes like this Gnaeus love our ore while ridiculing us for getting it.

In a lightly accented musical voice, Isabelle said, 'Is that necessary, Gnaeus? Does he deserve such scorn?'

'He deserves whatever I see fit to give, Isabelle. I am Ruman.'

She lowered her head so that her face was hidden and said, 'Pardon this observation, but, if your issue is his manners, it seems he has more than a Ruman, if your treatment of him is any indication of the general demeanour of Rumans.'

Blood rushed to the highborn lad's face, and veins stood out in his neck. 'Are you intimating that we have not treated you well, Isabelle?'

Carnelia erupted into peals of laughter. Forced laughter, intended to goad.

'Truly, brother,' Livia said, looking him up and down. 'These games were fine when you were a boy teasing the guards at home in Rume, but these are freemen. And proud.'

'They're dirty, lowly curs and deserve nothing but a boot in their arses.' Gnaeus spat. 'I've seen nothing in this entire shitty continent to rival the fortitude of the lowest-born Ruman, or the beauty and majesty of Latinum.'

Secundus said, 'Brother, look around you. The world is filled with wonders and new things. These White Mountains are higher and more precipitous than any in Latinum. The game in the shoallands is fat and massive. Even the bear was as fierce as any in the Gaellands, Gall, or Tueton.' He waved a gloved hand at the horizon. 'All you have to do is open your eyes and you'll see marvellous things.'

'Do not mention the bear to me, Secundus. You stole my rightful kill.'

Secundus shook his head and shrugged.

'There's no appealing to Gnaeus' sense of wonder,' Carnelia

said. 'For him to take notice of anything, you'd need to dress it up in fur and have it grunt so he can either fuck it or shoot it.'

Gnaeus twitched, and his hand went to his six-gun. But then he stopped and with great effort unclenched his fists. He spat again, tugged his reins, putting spur to flank, and rode ahead. Carnelia smiled at his retreating back.

Livia grimaced. 'God, I hope father marries you off before he dies.'

'Marriage is overrated. Or so I've heard, sister,' Carnelia quipped.

Livia coloured at the remark. The cords on her neck stood out, and she gripped the reins tighter.

'I should remind you,' Livia said, 'that if Gnaeus becomes pater familias of the Cornelian household, at best, he'll marry you to some withered old senator to curry favour in the forum. At worst, he'll crucify you. Remember the Numidian slave?'

Carnelia paused, looked away toward the mountains. 'She was his lapnurse, that's all.'

'He loved her, I think, if he's ever loved anyone in this life other than himself.'

'It's true, sissy,' said Secundus. 'And remember what he did to her when she asked for manumission?'

'Just a slave,' Carnelia said, shaking her head. 'She was just a slave.'

Livia, sensing a weakness in her sister, carried on. 'It matters not. She was his lapnurse and took his first seed. He was sweet on her. He was just a boy, maybe thirteen. He brought her flowers that time – Secundus and I caught him picking them in the garden and teased him unmercifully. But when she wanted to be freed, he had her crucified.' She sniffed. 'Think what you will, but he loved that Numidian slave far more than he's ever cared for you.'

Secundus said, 'He will be head of the household. And that

means he has the say of life or death over all of us.' He smiled at his sister, trying to comfort her. 'Just leave him be. Let him have his hunts and bed down with the serving girls, and don't argue.'

'He's a fool and an arse,' Carnelia said, her face turning sour. But after that, she fell silent and stared at the whipping grasses and the distant mountains.

I reined in near Livia.

'Ma'am, if I may be so bold ...'

'Of course, Mr Ilys. Speak.'

'Keep an eye on Mr Gnaeus, will you? Hunts are unpredictable in the Territories. It's not that Gnaeus'll get hurt ... but others, too. And there might be stretchers about.'

She glanced at me, and then inclined her head as though she understood. From beneath a flounce of her riding skirt she withdrew what looked to be a club, thick and deadly.

But when she raised it, breeched the chamber, and fed two thick warded shells into its open maw, I knew she was holding a sawn-off blunderbuss. Silver and holly shot, most likely.

'Of course, Mr Ilys. I shall be on my guard.'

Damnation. What a woman.

We moved out of the shadow of the mountains, over rises and into soft valleys ringed by shallow hills rippling with shoal grasses as the sun rose. The air grew a bit warmer, though it was still very cold.

Having to stare into the sun, once he returned, did not help Fisk's disposition.

We'd seen green slicks of auroch droppings at the stream I'd scouted earlier, and the stream ran fast, though no deeper than girth height. The herd's passing had ripped the shore up to Hell and back, and even the dullest lictor or lascar knew we were getting closer to our quarry.

Watching Gnaeus was like watching a child on New Year's Day waiting for his presents. He trotted his charger into the front – occasionally, like a boy with a pop-gun, raising his carbine as though he had spotted something and needed to take aim quickly. And then he'd swig from his wine bladder.

The ladies watched him too. Livia glanced at me, shifted the weight of her sawn-off, and winked. Carnelia, her moment of thoughtfulness over, laughed and asked bright, biting questions of Isabelle and Banty, Livia and Secundus.

I concentrated on the horizon, the brim of hill.

Fisk returned from our front-trail, and, holding up his clenched hand, indicated for us to stop.

'They're just over the next rise. A big mess of auroch. Thousands strong.' He glanced at Gnaeus. 'Congratulations, Mr Gnaeus, you're going to get your hunt.'

Gnaeus suddenly became all business, checking his bandoliers and fiddling with his carbine. 'I shall proceed first.' The eldest Cornelian looked at Secundus and Livia. 'You will follow after, as is your place. Understood?'

They inclined their heads.

Gnaeus wheeled his horse and flew off, over the hills. Fisk waved a hand at the legionaries perched in the wagon. 'Get out, you damned fools. Get ready. Shoe! Make sure these idiots watch the horizon, not the slaughter.'

I nodded. Past the waiting patricians Fisk swung the big black, who was in a high dander, her flanks frothy with sweat. They all were accustomed to sitting on a horse, but Isabelle was a real natural. They followed Fisk over the rise, and I waved to the legionaries and lictors to follow.

A thousand shoal aurochs on the hoof kick up a lot of dust. As a rule, like most animals with any sense, they don't like Hell-fire. But the noise confuses them, and somewhere back along the innumerable line of cow and bull lineage, they figured standing still was better than running if they couldn't see anything, which, most likely, they couldn't.

Gnaeus had a high, wild air to him as he raced along, firing shots into the herd. Auroch fell, left and right, and seeing the young nobleman so euphoric somehow put the damper on the other nobles' thirst for the hunt. Carnelia rode down, pulled her little pistol, and fired once into the mess of aurochs, whose lowings filled the air with a constant basso rumble. But then the patrician lass hung back, dust pluming from her horse's hooves. The rest of us watched from the top of the hillock as the eldest Cornelian son yelped and cursed and loosed *daemon* after *daemon* into the animals. His horse was nearing panic from the constant Hellfire. Carnelia turned and slowly rode back to join us. I imagine that brief taste of gunplay and damnation was enough for her.

Then Gnaeus' horse stopped. He didn't go wild, didn't rear, didn't thrash. He merely drooped his big head, tugging the reins away from Gnaeus. The Cornelian boy leaned forward and grabbed at them, but couldn't reach. So he dismounted and, the second Gnaeus' foot touched earth and he reached for the reins, the charger danced sideways and then slowly began walking away, back up the hill to us.

It was most likely the continued Hellfire – its constant unloosing of *imps* – that dispirited the horse. I know horses. They're smart, loyal creatures. But this one had probably been tried beyond all endurance by his master.

I think we all were, some.

It was a slaughter.

It hadn't rained since the night of Fisk taking the *vaettir* arrow in the leg. The ground was dry and the thousands of aurochs, now stirred by gunfire and the thinning of the herd, stirred and moved and we kicked the horses down the hill, into the massive clouds of dust thrown into the air.

Gnaeus continued to fire into the herd, screaming and laughing with Hellfire dementia, his hair tumbled forward into an oily mess, his fine riding clothes caked in dust.

The air filled with the haze of plain dirt, and it was hard to see them as they came toward us, darting, flipping, racing forward like lightning. Leaping from auroch back, rising into the air, and landing on auroch haunch – like some Minoan youth vaulting bulls.

They moved like light on water. Like wind over grass.

Vaettir.

Fisk gave a hard, bright whistle, cutting through the lowing of the aurochs and the noise of the horses.

He raised his rifle, tracked a fleet *vaettir* racing across the tops of aurochs, and fired once, just as the stretcher dropped out of sight.

'Arms! To arms, Ia-dammit!' Fisk reined his horse near the patrician women and hefted his rifle, eyes scanning the herd.

More dust filled the sky. Gnaeus still fired into the herd, but it had stopped moving away and seemed to be bunching.

A herd of auroch is like a great tide of flesh, and controlling its flow is an art for cowboys and sodbusters. I've never had the knack for cow, sheep or auroch wrangling. I take meat when I need it, never more than I need. But these auroch, these shoal beasts, hadn't fled the noisy Hellfire-bearing man shouting at them. They had drifted away, yes, but they were great stupid beasts, truly. Now they bunched together, and even pushed toward Gnaeus – among all of us the closest to the beasts, and the indigenes.

The lictors gathered close and the lascars, so far from the waters of the Big Rill, gripped rifles with white-knuckled hands. At least they had sense. They were wise enough to be afraid.

I brought Bess in closer to Fisk. Close enough to hear Miss

Livia say, 'Why are the aurochs getting so close? You'd think that they'd be fleeing ...'

'Ia-damn your brother.' Fisk wheeled his horse around and grabbed the wild lordling's rebellious mount. 'Shoe, it's time to run, pard. Them stretchers are pushing them at us.'

As he said it, a *vaettir* appeared on the back of the herd, racing across it, a great spear clutched in its massive hand. I'd been in the hot southern lands in my youth, and I spent days indolent on the beaches there, sipping booze in the company of ladies of negotiable virtue. The sharks, coming in with the tide, would patrol the waters, dorsal fins cutting into the air like knives, black against the blue of the water and sky. This *vaettir* seemed no different, swimming through the waters of the herd.

Berith was there.

I'll be damned if he wasn't grinning, showing his mouthful of sharp teeth, leaping from auroch withers to skull to rump, bounding fifteen feet with each leap and then disappearing into the herd. His red mane whipped behind him and his clothes, a colourful mishmash of fabrics, ruffled with the wind of his speed.

'Ia-dammit,' Fisk said. 'Get 'em moving, Shoestring. The stretchers are gonna work the herd into a stampede.'

He wheeled again and rode quickly down the hill, carbine in one hand and his reins and Gnaeus' mount's in the other.

Before he was halfway there, the herd broke.

They were coming. And *vaettir* – more than one – raced along with them, leaping from back to back. Hard to tell how many, through the dust haze. The *vaettir* were blurs, indistinct except for their speed and the flashes of teeth and spears and naked blades.

Fisk whipped up his gun, full gallop, and busted loose a shot, then twirled the rifle in his big hand, working the lever-action, and fired again.

Gnaeus had finally stopped his wild, stupid loosing of Hellfire.

Discovering his dire situation, he showed the only bit of sense he'd done in my acquaintance with him. He ran. Toward Fisk, toward his horse. The herd wasn't far behind. The look of terror on his face would have been more pleasing if the same expression hadn't been plastered on my own.

The lictors and legionaries had more sense than their master, young Gnaeus, and had already turned to hie it home when the first arrow took a horse in the neck and it screamed, reared, and tilted. The lictor hit the ground, hard, and didn't get up. Everything slowed and I lost track of where Fisk was, or Gnaeus' progress to safety.

'Ride! Ride to the wagon!' I yelled, hearing how shrill my voice was. But Livia was a smart lady and she'd already muscled her gelding into Isabelle's, snatched up her reins and galloped full-bore away. Young Banty was on the other side. He had out his pistol and seemed quite concerned with the Medieran lass's safety. Carnelia was close behind. To my surprise, even in my panic and terror, I registered that the three ladies were lovely to behold – their dresses like the petals of flowers caught in the first breezes of an oncoming storm.

Most of the legionaries – afoot, one and all – were doing a passable job of keeping up with the mounted folks.

'Ride!' I screamed at the lictors and Secundus. One of the honour guards had trouble with his horse and the others seemed to feel they needed to make a stand, protecting the patrician women fleeing toward the wagon. One took an arrow in his throat; as for the other, his horse's flank sprouted an arrow shaft. Secundus sighted his rifle, fired, and levered another round into the breech. The nearness of the Hellfire made my heart lurch and despair.

The women dismounted and the legionaries flipped the wagon onto its side. Livia, with horses in tow, disappeared around the far side of the wagon to huddle behind the slatted floorboards.

Bess barked once, braying, and tugged the reins from me – her way of saying, 'It's time to *go!*' – and began galloping over the lip of the hill toward the wagon. I couldn't see Fisk anymore, or Gnaeus. I could only watch now as enraged and terrified shoal auroch came over the lip of the hill, racing past the small clutch of lictors remaining there, like brown floodwaters overtaking a last hillock. The lictors – I'll give them their bravery – swung their holly and silver fasces wildly, but in vain. They were trodden underfoot.

Secundus was riding beside me, Hell for leather and firing behind him without much care for aim. The red-haired *vaettir* was coming. He was big, sharp-fanged, and fast. Like lightning dancing from gable to treetop he hopped from auroch to auroch, spinning in the air, somersaulting. In a blur he darted over the lictors, his hands lancing out, one glinting bright. And as Berith passed he left a slowly falling lictor spurting a bright spray of blood into the air, his scalp, separated from his skull, now swinging crazily from the *vaettir*'s clawed fist.

Another pass, this time a blond blur, and a second lictor, his skull suddenly raw and exposed, tilted and fell.

I looked no longer, but launched my boots into Bess's haunches, hoping to Hell and praying to Ia that her sure feet would make the next twenty paces to the wagon before the stretchers took my scalp. Secundus was there before me, and, as I neared, he fired at something behind me, so close I could feel the wind of the bullet and the heat of Hell passing. For once I was glad of the sensation.

'Arms! Get your damned guns ready!' I nearly fell off Bess and found my feet next to a terrified legionary. Never knew his name.

'Anything that moves, shoot it.'

'What about them lictors? Mister Cornelius?'

'They're dead. Got that? You see it move, bust it with that Ia-damned holemaker.'

A moment of distaste curdled the man's face as he looked at me and realized a dwarf was giving him orders. But this look of disgust turned to one of surprise as the stampede of auroch swept past us and he was drawn upwards, a knife glinting like the flash of sun on water. For a moment I thought the man was hopping up to see beyond the wagon, but when he fell his gun fell with him and his head was bloody and raw. He was screaming like a scalded dog.

Livia shoved Isabelle and Carnelia back against the axle of the wagon, and hefted her shotgun. Secundus stood nearby, and for a moment I thought it strange that both Secundus and Livia seemed dead set on protecting the young Medieran girl, even above their own blood, Carnelia. But then another shadow passed above and I felt something snatch at my head, followed by an excruciating pain as a hunk of my hair was ripped bodily from my skull. My *dvergar* blood saved me from being scalped by dint of my short stature. Banty, eyes wild, fired into the swirling, churning dust of the plains.

'Ia-dammit,' Banty said in the same tone as Fisk might.

Another legionary was lifted up, hair flying, and came down with his throat cut and without his scalp.

The wagon shuddered and rocked as the auroch thundered past us. The animals pressed in close, all around – if you got caught in them, you'd be pulped as fast as a stretcher could take your scalp. The legionaries began busting loose Hellfire in earnest, making it hard to think with the after-images of *daemons* scenting the air with brimstone. Arrows thunked into wood and horseflesh and auroch hide. The horses screamed in near-human voices, and the auroch lowed and trumpeted their panic and anger. The soldiers fired wildly, and more aurochs slumped and fell, making a little circle of destruction with us smack-dab in the centre.

In a flash, Fisk and his big black leapt into the circle, and he was firing his carbine. But not wildly. Gnaeus, the young lordling, was draped across Fisk's saddle-horn. His head was crimson and a great flap of scalp hung down, dripping blood.

Fisk dismounted, and I ran to him and helped the patrician boy off the black. He was as heavy and ungainly as a sack of oats. I dragged him into the lee of the wagon, and Carnelia gave a short screech as she saw him.

Fisk stood tall, his grey hat still perched on his head like a beacon. Maybe the remaining legionaries took strength from his presence, I don't know. But he fired, and fired again. He paused, ignoring the rushing tide of aurochs, took aim and fired again. The oppressive weight and despair of Hellfire hung in the air.

And then Miss Livia was rushing toward him, yelling, 'Get down, Fisk!'

He dropped to a knee, tucking his head down, and she brought the shotgun up and let go with both barrels as a shadow passed overhead.

There was a terrible screech – almost too high to hear, but the ear-pressure felt like diving too deep in a river, mixed with the cacophony of bees – and a wild thrashing thing fell, slamming into the wagon, bouncing off the wheel and landing in front of a dazed Secundus.

A *vaettir*.

It thrashed and whipped about like a fish plucked from the sea, its brown hair making a mess of its face. It ripped at its chest and shoulder with clawed hands and spat jagged and unfathomable curses from bloodless lips framing a saw-toothed maw. Secundus stepped forward and shot it again, once, and the spasms ceased. It stilled.

The stampede thinned, and the aurochs passed and the world was silent.

The dust swirled and settled. Beyond the ring of dead aurochs and horses and strewn bodies of lascars, thirty or forty paces distant, stood four *vaettir*. From their hands dangled bloody scalps. They stood like statues, or the bare bones of trees husked by fire.

Fisk, closest to the creatures, took aim, paused, and then lowered his rifle. He went to the downed stretcher, whipping out his longknife.

'What're you doing?' I asked.

His face was dark, unlike I'd ever seen before. He didn't even glance at me.

He knelt on the *vaettir*'s arm and hacked at it hard, three, four times – before the thing fell away. It was so much larger than his own, spanning fifteen or twenty inches. The stump spurted blood, once, twice; then the blood pulsed weakly before stopping altogether. I had the distinct impression that, though grievously wounded, the thing was not dead. After Fisk cut the hand free he turned, walked to the edge of the circle, and faced the watching *vaettir*.

He raised the severed hand above his head.

It was an angry silhouette he made, the set of his jaw and the cant of his shoulders. It was fury, pure and simple.

Livia, still holding the shotgun, reached out with one tremulous hand, touched Fisk's shoulder and looked into his dark face.

He ignored her.

Finally, he threw the severed hand into the dust and spat on it.

The *vaettir* watched, implacable and cold.

And then, as one, they made a noise between a scream of rage and a dirge – a terrible feeling distilled into one sound, ineffable, cruel, miserable. Like birds they turned, hair and clothing flapping like wings, and disappeared into the tall shoal grasses and the still-swirling dust.

We loaded the dead, wounded, and as much auroch meat as we could onto the wagon.

When Fisk ordered the remaining legionaries to port the

haunches of auroch he'd butchered, bloody and raw, over to the wagon-bed, Secundus held up a hand and asked, 'Do you really think this necessary?'

'Your pa still gonna want his feast?'

Secundus looked over at the bound figure of the fallen *vaettir* and remained silent. The lascar continued to load the meat.

Fisk dealt with the *vaettir* himself. He bound it again, at the elbows, at the ankles, at the knees. He tied it to his horse and he gagged it, stuffing a dirty shirt halfway down its throat. Then he wrapped its jaw with rope.

Short on horses now, I hitched Bess to the wagon braces and we hied homeward, back to the *Cornelian*. A damned long ride, accompanied by the bleats of the injured and the agitation of the horses. The womenfolk rode two to a horse whilst Secundus transported his scalped brother. Fisk was beyond reckoning, filled with an intense fury, his body taut, his face pained and fierce, his gun ready to hand, his eyes always roving. The poor legionaries looked as though they'd never leave the safety of the boat again. Who'd blame them. I'd be lying if I told you the *Cornelian* wasn't a welcome sight when it came into view.

It was a brilliant afternoon, sun-filled and temperate, marred only by the moans of dying men.

ELEVEN

'HE WANTS US to *what*?' Fisk asked. It had been three days since the stampede and *vaettir* attack. His leg had healed up some, but his disposition was still on the mend.

Cimbri's moustache twitched, and he snatched the cheroot out of his mouth, jabbing the smoking cherry at Fisk. 'He wants you,' he jabbed again, 'Shoestring,' and then he pointed the burning tip toward the horses where Banty was brushing them down, 'and yon Mr Bantam, to be present at the feast to regale the assembled with the tale of the stampede and the capture of the *vaettir*.'

Fisk cursed.

'Surely you're joking, Cimbri.' I normally don't get too involved with legion matters. Cimbri, technically, was in command of the scouts, since we'd signed up for the job with his boss, the Dux Marcellus out of New Damnation, and had both blooded the contract. Cimbri also had authority over Banty and the twenty or so legionaries left on the *Cornelian*. Captain Skraeling, a good chap with an easy riverman's disposition, commanded the lascars, and the Senator had direct command over his lictors. However, Senator Cornelius, with proconsular imperium, was really in charge of us all.

Cimbri looked at me closely, down the length of that long Ruman nose that disappeared into his massive and expressive whiskers.

'What do you think, Mr Ilys? Do I look like I'm kidding?'

Now that he mentioned it, no.

He shook his head again, looked off at the mountains gleaming in the morning light, and gave a sigh. He turned back to Fisk, glanced back and forth between us as though we were miscreant schoolboys, and spoke under his breath. 'Mr Cornelius ... he's been affected. That bear got more than his leg, if you understand what I'm saying.'

'Shithouse rat is what you're saying.'

'No, not that bad, Mr Fisk. Just ...' He popped his cheroot back in his mouth and clamped it in his teeth. 'Fey. Addled a tad. Childish.'

'He's a lush. Get him off the booze and he'll dry out.'

Cimbri blinked. 'Ia's blood, man, how the hell do I do that? He's an Ia-damned proconsular emissary of the Ia-damned Ruman Empire. He's got his lictors who would just love to chop me into little pieces and his private engineer who would love to feed me to that great fucking *daemon* bound in the engine room.'

Spit dribbled down his chin, and I started to worry some about *his* mental state.

'So get your arses presentable, and get over to the Ia-damned riverboat before dark. If you're not there, I'll have a contubernium crucify your arses. Understood?'

Understood.

Shaven heads were suddenly quite fashionable among the *Cornelian*'s male passengers. Lictors, lascars, and legionaries were all shorn, their craniums glistening, oiled and unmarred except for a few nicks and scrapes from razors.

A pall hung over the ship, despite the impending celebration. It had been a lark, and a boring one, steaming upriver and shooting at seagulls in the *Cornelian*'s wake. But now men had died and the darkness held rumours of *vaettir* bearing human scalps. We had buried the dead in shallow graves within sight of the Big Rill, and the men of the fifth – while accustomed to death – never let it pass so easily as to be unaffected by it. The Hardscrabble Territories had blooded the men of the fifth and the *Cornelian*.

Before, the *Cornelian*, twinkling merrily with *daemonlight* on the waters of the river, had seemed brilliant and proud, a marvellous bit of Ruman engineering and cunning, a beacon in the darkness of the Hardscrabble Territories. But now the boat – even illuminated like a great, three-tiered birthday cake – looked small and huddled. The light shone to keep the shoal beasties and stretchers at bay. It was a frontier home – a grand and ornate one, but a frontier home nonetheless – with lanterns hanging from hooks and simple wards scratched in paint above the doorways and windows in hopes of pushing back the night.

Cimbri met us at the rear boarding mechanism, grunted when he saw us, and then pointed inside at the *daemonlight*-filled confines of the boat. We could hear the chatter from the stateroom already. Cimbri followed us like a mother goose shepherding her brood.

When we walked in, all eyes turned to us, ladies and gents all, but my eyes were drawn to the *vaettir*. It was sitting upright in the centre of an elaborately patterned parquet flooring – maybe it had once been a dance-floor – etched with winding and intricate scorch marks radiating in circular patterns outward from where it sat. Chains fastened the creature's one good wrist to the floor. Manacles bound its feet. It held its handless arm still in its lap. A trellis-work of holly caged it.

The stretcher watched Fisk with the intensity of a viper drawn to strike. Its eyes never left him.

Fisk glanced at the two bald legionaries hefting shotguns on either side of the *vaettir* and then knelt and touched the scorched marks on the floor.

He looked to me and said, 'Molten silver. The engineer's bound it like a *daemon*.'

Strange.

Fisk rose, looked at the creature whose lidded eyes met his steadily, and then spat on the thing. He turned away and went to the banquet table. His shoulders looked tight and his hands, I noticed, were balled at his sides.

For a moment, the *vaettir* remained absolutely still, more still than any human or *dvergar* could manage – the stillness of statuary. And then its eyes shifted in their sockets, so very slowly, like massive gears sliding and locking into place, and it was staring at me.

I felt a pressure beating at my ears, my cheeks flushed with blood. But the sensation quickly passed and then I was taking in the thing's features. Long hair and skin as pale and unmarked as alabaster. Large almond-shaped eyes, tapering slightly at the edges like the Tchinee but bigger in proportion to its face. Long slender neck and pointed ears. Bloodless lips. It was beautiful, really. But beautiful like a big cat or the sleek finned shark, perfectly grown for killing.

It did not love me.

I tore my gaze away from its face and looked at its body. Its clothes were simple and almost elegant, except for the bloodstains. The tunic was cut to provide ease of movement, and the leggings were loose and reminded me of the garments of an acrobat. It was barefooted and the pads of its feet were snarls of callouses, rough and weathered.

It had small, high breasts and I realized, with a start, that this was a female *vaettir*. Bizarre, but my heart hammered in my chest and I felt uncomfortable and embarrassed all at once, remembering our fireside chat with Banty.

I turned back to the banquet table, but I could still feel her presence behind me. There were quite a few new faces and suddenly I was the only one in front of the stretcher's cage, being watched by far too many people, both human and indigene. I made a bow as best I could and Carnelia laughed, making a mean, petty sound. She *was* patrician, after all. Livia glared at her, and the laugh died.

'Mr Ilys, please sit here, with me, at a place of honour.' Miss Livia, beaming and beautiful, patted an empty seat. She was decked out in a carmine dress with an open bodice displaying her feminine features to great effect. Her hair was up but two delicate curls descended to frame her face. At her neck was a bright jewel on a chain. Fisk sat on her far side, his hat gone and his hair as wild as a brake of bramblewrack. His face was as red as Livia's dress.

The table was full but I couldn't see Gnaeus anywhere – I imagined he was soaking his scalp in alcohol and acetum under the attentions of chambermaids. Mr Cornelius, however, reclined at the head of table on a wide chair with massive padded arms, his face as crimson as a carnation, his leg propped up and wrapped in fresh bandages, white as yarrow petals. The Hardscrabble Territories had certainly not been kind to the Cornelian family so far.

Everyone remained silent until Cornelius said, 'Well, for fuck's sake, people. Pour drinks. This is a celebration.'

Carnelia laughed at her father's proclamation. Other men, unknown to me, added rough guffaws and reached for decanters of spirits on the table.

But it was hard for me to smile with the *vaettir* watching. I wanted to ask if a cloth could be thrown over its cage. But Cornelius viewed it as a trophy, this stretcher.

Livia took a crystal glass in her hand, filled it with red liquid from a decanter, and handed it to me. As it took the light from the table-lanterns, it glowed. I took a closer look at the lanterns.

Ia-damn. *Daemonwork*, even at the dinner table.

'Mr Fisk,' Cornelius said, his voice sounding thick and liquor-smoothed, like a skipping stone worn perfectly round by the flow of the river. 'We're all looking forward to hearing your version of the incident at the auroch hunt. Indeed, after drink and confections, we will feast on the spoils.'

'Spoils? I imagine they are that,' said Fisk, and accepted the glass from Livia. He took a big gulp. 'We lost enough men getting that bit of auroch flesh. It cost dear.' He took another swallow. I raised my own glass to my lips and tasted it. It was warm and spicy, comforting as a blazing beach-fire surrounded by drunken ladies from the southern lands. 'I hope your cook oiled the meat, and well. We slather auroch cuts with lard or oil. Ain't got much fat on them, normally.'

I heard a small titter down the table and saw Isabelle cover her mouth. Banty smiled, pouring some of the claret into her glass. He leaned into her, close. Smiling. Whispering.

He was a handsome lad, I'll give him that. And his equite parents taught him table manners at least, if none of the other kind.

Miss Livia, in a voice loud and carrying, said, 'Mr Fisk, Mr Ilys.' She swept an elegant arm down the table toward some of the unknown gentlemen. 'I'd like to present you with Captain August Skraeling of the *Cornelian* and Mr Samwell Kliment, his pilot. Beyond them sits Carnelia Cornelius, my sister, and Isabelle Modeci Santelli Diegal of Mediera, whom you've met but not officially. And of course Mr Titus Bantam, whom you all know.'

She sipped her own claret and motioned past me. 'You also have the acquaintance of Gaius Cimbri and Paterna Corianus, second in command, I believe. And there, at the end of the table, opposite my father, is Mr Linneus Gaius Beleth.' The engineer seemed totally uninterested in the proceedings and remained speaking to his companion. Livia continued, 'Seated next to him, his junior engineer,

Samantha Decius.' Another strangely humdrum name – a colonist like the rest of us, then.

She was a big girl, with a moon face and ruddy cheeks. Bright carrot-top. Eyes green and intelligent, if a little wary. I imagine anyone who's apprenticed herself to learn the summoning and binding of the infernal better be smart. Better be calm. *Better* be wary.

'And of course, last but not least, is my brother Gaius Secundus Cornelius, and my pater Gnaeus Saturnalius Cornelius, Senator of Rume, former consul, emissary and acting governor of the western Imperial Protectorate, ambassador to Mediera, hero of the Cantaline Rebellion, and laurelled champion of Rume.'

That was a mouthful. She wasn't even breathing heavy when she finished. She took another delicate sip of wine and continued.

'And finally, to all of our guests, allow me to introduce Mr Dveng Ilys, scout of Mr Cimbri's unit, and Mr Hieronymous Fisk of the same.'

Fisk nodded to the assembled gentlefolk.

'Nice to meet you all,' Fisk said. I just inclined my head. These folk didn't want to hear from a dwarf, anyway.

The same half-*dvergar* woman approached the table, bearing a large tray of honeyed confections. She first presented the tray to Carnelia and Isabelle, and each took a dainty portion.

'Normally, we wouldn't eat in such a base manner,' Carnelia said, placing the confection on her plate. She'd changed in the days since the auroch hunt. She was a dark-haired woman, pale as the *vaettir*, but now had deep circles under her eyes and was so very thin I felt I might cut myself just by looking at her. She had been prettier when she'd had some meat on her and some colour in her cheeks, when she'd filled out her bodice more. Now you could see her ribs in her chest.

She went on: 'Barbaric, really, all of us huddled round this table.

We should be dining like Rumans.' She sniffed, glanced at Fisk and me, then back to Isabelle and Banty, who grinned. I was having trouble understanding why she didn't include Banty in her disdain, but he did cut a dashing figure in his legion blues. I peeked at Fisk, but he was either oblivious or didn't give a damn. Carnelia continued, 'But maybe this is more appropriate, after all, considering our mixed company. Besides, this ship doesn't have a proper triclinium, and there's far too little space to accommodate us all at lecti. So necessity dictates we eat our food like hogs at a trough.'

Cornelius took a great swallow from his glass, covered his mouth, and gave a demur belch. ''Nelia, you could use some fattening up. You're as scrawny as a Dolian whore and half as fun.'

Finally, some colour came to Cornelius' younger daughter's face. It didn't do much for her features; mottled and furious doesn't sit well on many women and Carnelia was no exception.

'I see you got your ears lowered, Mr Secundus,' said Fisk. 'But you didn't go all the way to the scalp.'

'Ah, you don't miss much, do you?' Secundus blushed. 'I've been helping Livia tend Gnaeus. He's in terrible pain and we fear the flesh of his scalp may have become infected. And our stores of the tersus incendia have run low.' He ran a hand over his short-cropped hair. 'A shearing seemed prudent. It wouldn't do for both of the Cornelian sons be missing their lids.'

We laughed, and other conversations cropped up around the table; Carnelia, Isabelle and Banty murmured together, drinking wine, and Beleth and Samantha chatted amiably with Paterna and Cimbri.

'Mr Fisk.' Captain Skraeling possessed a rich, deep voice, like boulders rumbling down a mountainside. He had a thick barrel chest pulling tight the grey Ruman navy uniform, buttons bright and gleaming in the *daemonlight*. A rich shock of thick alabaster hair – no haircut for him – and thick white beard, well groomed, with a massive moustache, all gave him the appearance of a large brushy hillock covered with snow. 'You have a familiarity with these parts, have you not?'

'I imagine as well as the next man.'

'How lies the river further west?'

'Wide. Passing deep. Sticks to the plains with no rills to speak of. I doubt the *Cornelian* will have any trouble unless we steam further than Passasuego. We packing it in?'

'Not immediately. But we must reach the Medieran holdfast before the freeze settles on the plains. Otherwise, we'll be moored in ice for winter. Undefended and at the mercy of these loutish stretchers.'

Fisk said nothing, but Livia snorted. 'Captain, the *vaettir* are many things, but loutish isn't one of them.'

'I must agree with my sister, Captain Skraeling.' For once, Carnelia's voice wasn't biting or filled with bile. She raised a hand to her hair, as if to adjust it, then stopped, her fingers motionless near her cheek. 'They are more than louts. More than brutes or savages.' She dropped her hand and reached for her glass.

From the far end of the table Beleth said, 'And we're not quite undefended, sir.' He held up a soft, lotioned palm, like one of Ia's priests giving a benediction. 'Should the worst occur, I will unslave the *daemon* driving the engine and set it to patrol.'

'Ain't that a bit risky?'

He laughed – a dry, humourless sound. 'It is decidedly less risky than sitting unprotected on the stretcher-inhabited plains.'

'I should wonder how the indigenes might fare, facing a *daemon*, especially one so great as Gooseberry.'

I coughed. 'Excuse me, Miss Isabelle. Did you say, Gooseberry?'

She cocked her head, as though noticing me for the first time. 'Why, yes, I did.'

'A pet name, Gooseberry,' said Samantha Decius. She had nice eyes, and who knew the other blessings Ia might have bestowed on her? Intelligence. Wisdom, maybe. No way to tell until she showed her mettle. 'Master Beleth came up with it. Much better than Ebru Labadon, don't you think?'

There was a rattle. The deck pitched underneath us, and the massive crystal chandelier hanging above our heads sounded like the breaking of the world. Shouts came from the hall as the boat shifted and glasses toppled and fell.

'Samantha,' Beleth said sharply but not unkindly. 'While you *can* use Gooseberry's true name, it doesn't mean you *should*. Show some respect for the damned thing.'

She laughed and said, 'Respect? Why? It's a *thing*, after all. No better than a draft horse or a mule.' The ease with which her words came made me think this was an ongoing debate between master and student.

He sighed. Patted her hand. 'It's more than a thing, and less, all at once. Much like our guest here.' For a moment I thought he might be speaking of me. He tossed his head in the direction of the stretcher and righted his wine glass, which had spilled in the shifting of the boat. He poured another measure of claret, lifted it, drank. 'It's learning as we speak. I wouldn't be surprised if it's understood everything we've said.'

'Is that a warning?' Alarm and curiosity mixed in Livia's tone. 'Are we to guard our tongues?'

'That, madam, is up to you. We have yet to discover how much intelligence the creature possesses.'

A figure appeared at the far end of the stateroom, near the stairwell to the patrician quarters. He came forward slowly, his steps measured as though he bore a great weight or carried something easily broken. As he came closer, I recognized him by his build.

Gnaeus.

He tottered when he neared the table. He was dressed in a simple linen tunic of the Gallish cut, with long sleeves and matching cotton trousers. The clothes were dyed a royal blue so deep it was almost black. But the saturated clothes accentuated the pallor of his skin. He was parchment white.

'Where am I to sit?' he said, and his normally piercing voice was weaker but still unpleasant. 'We've seated the plebs at our table and now I cannot be seated?' He turned and looked about slowly. He had to move his whole torso; his neck remained immobile.

He approached Fisk's chair.

'You, sir. Give up your seat.'

Fisk stood up and pushed back his chair. He looked from Cornelius to Beleth and then at Livia. 'Of course.' He stepped away from the seat.

'Gnaeus,' Livia said softly. 'Do you think you should be up? Shouldn't you be in bed?'

'I am as fit as I ever was, sissy.'

As he sat down next to Livia, she motioned to a slave to bring another chair. I moved aside, allowing it to be placed next to her. Fisk would deny he wished to be seated near Livia, but I knew better.

As I rose, I caught a good look at Gnaeus. Drops of sweat glistened on his upper lip. His face seemed waxy, as if formed from warm tallow. I looked to his hair and stopped.

Thin runnels of white liquid, emerging from beneath his bangs, beaded his forehead. His hair appeared normal, if a little messy. But the more I looked, the more it appeared he had some hide perched atop his skull, seams hidden.

Ia help me, I wanted to peek underneath that scrap of hair and see what remained up top.

Gnaeus bellowed for whiskey and Lupina filled his glass. He occupied his mouth with the drinking of it.

A grunt came from Cimbri. 'I just can't figure out what the Hell these bastards want. What in damnation drives the infernal things? Why are they here attacking?' He glanced at Livia. 'Pardon, the language, ma'am.'

'Maybe they're the genius loci of this massive land. It's harsh and wild, as are they.' Cornelius managed not to slur.

'I'm sorry, Mr Cornelius. What do you mean by that?' I queried.

'Why is the dwarf even allowed to speak at this table?' Gnaeus asked loudly. He tilted sloppily in his seat, then righted himself. 'Or the other cowherd?'

'Brother, I think it would be best if you—'

'Nay, woman,' he said and gulped from his glass. 'I would not miss dining on my kill.'

Carnelia snorted into her glass. Gnaeus did not bestow on her even the smallest of glances, and I wondered if he could not move his head abruptly for fear of dislodging his 'hair'.

'Brother, I might remind you that without Mr Fisk's actions, you would surely have been trampled underfoot by the stampede.'

Gnaeus lolled in his seat. I would have wagered a gold talent that neither of the two elder Cornelian men could have sat upright unaided. A sodden pair, both grievously wounded and in much pain.

'Bah. A glancing wound. I would have been fine in a trice.'

'Brother, your horse had—' Secundus searched for the words, 'rebelled—'

'I'll have the beast slaughtered and boiled down to grease our wagon-wheels.'

'I'm sure our Gnaeus would have been fine,' Carnelia said, smirking. 'Just might have taken him time to find his hat.'

Livia signalled disapproval of her younger sister's comments.

But Carnelia ignored her. 'Or the top of his head.' She looked contemptuously at her brother. 'Maybe you should start hunting hares, Gnaeus. Brown ones. They will match your shade quite nicely.'

'As I was saying—' Cornelius broke in loudly, gesturing with his glass, petulant at being ignored. 'Genius loci. The protective spirit of a place. Much like the lares at crossroads. Or household gods. Numina. The old spirits we Rumans did away with when Ia came to the land. In this case, the stretchers are the genius loci of the Hardscrabble Territories.'

All eyes turned to Gnaeus to see if he would respond, but he sat silently, loosely holding his glass and staring somewhere between the brass buttons on Skraeling's uniform and the lands beyond the Whites. His eyes were unfocused and watery.

I said, 'I don't know about that. For many years, the *vaettir* raided in the Imperial Protectorate. They were known to appear in the Thousand Acre Wood, far to the east, though that might have been old-wives' tales.'

Cornelius frowned at me, and shifted his bandaged stump on the pillow.

'Half-man, don't ask questions if you don't want to hear the answers.'

Fisk stiffened. Livia, too. They didn't need to worry about me. I like living, uncrucified. So I bowed my head in acceptance and occupied my mouth with wine.

'No matter,' Cornelius continued. 'The *vaettir* are no match for the ingenuity and resolve of Rume.' Cornelius laughed then and emptied his glass. 'See there? She watches us. She's bound! We are her masters.'

Fisk said, 'She is bound by wardwork?'

'A strange coincidence indeed that both *daemons* and *vaettir* show an abhorrence of silver,' replied Beleth. 'She's bound by silver-threaded shackles, caged in holly wickerwork, and set at the centre of a warding circle, the *orbis argenta*. That was Samantha's idea, and I think it's a good one. But we'll see how effective it is.'

'She remains under guard?'

'Of course. Two legionaries at all times.'

'That's good. Very good.'

'What's that?' Gnaeus said, as though waking from a dream. 'A stretcher here?' His hand went to his side where a six-gun would have ridden. I was reminded of Carnelia mocking him for impotence.

Gnaeus tried to stand, pushing up from table. 'I would kill it and take it back to Rume as a trophy.'

Livia, surprisingly gentle, placed her hand on her brother's shoulder. 'We will make sure you have ample time with the creature. After dinner.'

'She's mine, lad.' Cornelius motioned for another drink. 'Getting too big for your britches, you are.'

Carnelia clapped her hands together lightly. 'Ooh, goody. Father and Gnaeus will have a spat!' She turned to where Banty and Isabelle were murmuring to each other. 'They'll have their usual individual tantrums until they're exhausted and the slaves come to fetch them to dinner.'

Both Cornelian men ignored her.

'What need for all these guards? They are mere indigenes,' Gnaeus said, trying valiantly to twist at the waist far enough to look down the length of the table. 'Wogs. Slap them in chains and be done with it.'

'You spent the latter part of the hunt dangling from Mr Fisk's saddlehorn, Gnaeus.' Carnelia grinned. 'So you missed the *vaettir*.' But her grin faltered as she looked down the length of the table at the stretcher caged there. I'll be damned if a shudder didn't pass through her frame. She was far less venomous when she continued, 'They are fearsome, brother. I have never seen the like.'

'You're mewling babes, afraid of your own shadows,' Cornelius said, grabbing a honeycake from the platter. He popped it into his mouth, talking around the food. 'Fearsome warriors, I can believe it. But you children are ascribing ... I don't know ... supernatural abilities to these wogs.' He chuckled. 'There's no creature that some fast gunwork won't take care of.'

It was Livia's turn to snort. 'Is that right, father? Including a bear?'

He spluttered, spewing wine. 'I say, Livvie, that was uncalled for.'

'I disagree. It was very called for. Look at Gnaeus. Visit the riverside graves, if you can stand and walk on your own. The *vaettir* are beyond fierce.'

'And yet we have one here bound.'

Fisk said, 'Thanks to Livia. She downed the creature.'

Gnaeus tried to turn to look at his sister sitting next to him, but turning his whole torso was too much effort.

Livia glanced at Fisk. She gave him a smile and placed a hand on his, squeezing. Ia help them if Gnaeus spied them playing pattycakes.

Then Fisk did a thing I hadn't seen in many years. He smiled. It softened the hard edges of his jaw and loosened the tight flesh around his eyes and for a moment another man sat there, a young man, his life before him, a thousand roads untaken, a thousand hardships yet to be encountered. I was struck again by how closely Banty and Fisk resembled each other.

But the moment passed. Fisk realized Livia held his hand, and he pulled his away, took another drink, raised his arm as though to wipe his mouth on the sleeve, stopped. He picked up the linen napkin, dabbed his lips.

Ia save us from love-addled boys and men.

The honeycakes were gone and the half-breed slavewoman tidied the table while another slave brought in a massive tureen of soup and began ladling it into bowls. It smelled amazing, of sweetgrass and mushrooms, onions and garlic, and was delicious.

Gnaeus ate nothing, but sat very still – as still as he was able – and drank whiskey, uncut with water.

'Soup isn't quite the course you want on a sea-going vessel,' said Samwell Kliment, smiling. He seemed a good-natured man, ginger as all get out but at ease around the high-born and ladies. 'High seas and you'd wear more of it than you'd eat.'

'Give me a horse to ride and enough Hellfire for a thousand foes. Ia save me from long sea voyages,' Gnaeus said and then stared into his glass.

The table was silent for a moment.

Skraeling slurped his soup and said, 'Long sea voyage, Mr Kliment, you have to make your rations last. You'd know that if you'd spent more time off the river and on the ocean. Soup's more common than you'd think. But served in mugs rather than fine bowls like these.'

'As you know, Captain, I'm a river pilot. And content to be.'

Beleth gave a little laugh and said, 'Whatever you do, Samantha, don't mention Gooseberry's real name now!'

There were few chuckles and general murmured assent. The party remained silent except for the sounds of spoons clacking on bone china and the slurps of the men.

The next course was buttered trout, rolling in onions and pepper and bristling with tiny bones. Not too fond of trout, myself, since that winter I spent snowbound in the Smokey Mountains above Dvergar. That stream held nothing but the colourful fish, and I spent too much time chest-deep in that Ia-damned freezing water trying to get a hold of their slippery skins.

Between Gnaeus' presence on my left and the stretcher at the far end of the stateroom, I could not rest easy. But these were

Rumans. They lit their tables and bedrooms with *daemons*. The party paid no special heed to the near-demented scalped man and the otherworldly creature in our midst.

When they brought out the roasted haunches of auroch, the great room filled with the smell of savory meat and coals and garlic. A slave with a massive carving knife hewed great chunks of meat from the leg and speared the daintier bits – liver and tongues – from an accompanying platter piled with more onions and potatoes.

Cornelius was served first and began to tuck in at once. The slaves served Gnaeus next, and began to move about the table.

Gnaeus ate slowly, taking morsels from the plate with his fingers and placing them in his mouth like a man placing stones in the mouth of a statue. After a short while he stopped and sat, somewhat dazed, staring into his plate.

Carnelia guzzled wine and pushed her food around her plate, making interesting configurations and pretending to have eaten. She was looking like death in a lukewarm bath. Unpleasant and mocking as she was, I had a moment of sympathy for the girl – spoiled rotten by birth and then absolutely terrified by *vaettir*.

Amid the clutter and clank of carving knives and cutlery, Cornelius said, 'And now, Mr Fisk, Mr Ilys, regale us with the story of the hunt! We shall dine on your story!'

Fisk looked tense and uncomfortable. Livia winced at her father's strange use of 'dine'. Under the table, she placed a hand on Fisk's knee.

I waited for an outburst from Gnaeus but he remained blessedly silent.

I said, 'Fisk ain't much of a talker, for sure. But I've told my share of stories around many a fire across this new land. Please allow me.' I set down my glass and looked down the length of the table. 'Many of you know the story, having witnessed the carnage with your own eyes. But I will try to give full account of what happened.'

I spoke of the early morning darkness, the wind on the plains, the collection of hunters. Fording the creek and the size of the herd. Ia forgive me, but I made Gnaeus seem a formidable hunter rather than the blood-thirsty child he was.

When I came to the stretchers, I pointed at the bound one who sat utterly still, watching.

'She and her brethren came, forcing the herd of auroch toward us, rousing them into stampede. They danced on the beasts' backs, like acrobats. Graceful, yes. But deadly. When the stampede overtook us – and Mr Fisk retrieved the grievously wounded Mr Gnaeus – they flew and pranced overhead like they walked on air.

'They snatched at our hair, lifting men up and cutting free their scalps. Your brave lictors fell defending us, Mr Cornelius, and many lascars. Mr Secundus showed true bravery defending the womenfolk.' I nodded at Banty. 'And Mr Bantam as well.'

I took a sip of wine to wet my mouth and finish the tale. Carnelia watched me with lowered eyes, unsmiling, as though again experiencing the furore, the dust and blood of the day. Secundus frowned and shook his head. Skraeling looked astounded and grim, while Kliment stared at me with a bemused half-smile upon his face, as though he were listening to a song or fanciful tale told in a tavern by some travelling bard.

'With our shooting and the *vaettir*'s bloodshed, we became encircled by dead aurochs and the bodies of men. And then Fisk leapt amongst us, into the circle's centre, on his big black, carrying Gnaeus. Mad with anger, he was, more than I've ever seen, and I've known him now for an age. But now I must pay tribute to Miss Livia. It was she who saw the danger coming for Fisk, dashing overhead. She called out, leapt into the centre of the circle of dead, and raised her own deadly hand. It was she who brought the *vaettir* down.'

I stood up and raised my glass. I was taller than the table but not much. 'So, if I may, I'd like to offer a toast to Miss Livia, as beautiful and deadly as the *vaettir* themselves. All honour to the woman whose bravery averted total calamity at that hunt.'

Everyone save Gnaeus stood up, pushing back chairs with a clatter, and raised a glass.

She was blushing when she said, 'You are too kind, Mr Ilys. I haven't the words to thank you.'

'Nothing to thank me for, ma'am. What you did was brave for man or woman.'

She smiled a little sadly. 'I am flattered, but there is no honour in killing.'

It was then that Gnaeus pitched forward, face-down onto the table.

Gnaeus' head struck the plate, still containing auroch liver and tongue, and his remaining flap of hair pitched forward to reveal a ragged bloody circlet and a half dome of bone white skull threaded with streaks of blood-tinged yellow pus.

Two lictors lunged forward to lift Gnaeus away bodily as Livia tried, vainly, to cover his wound with his dangling flap of scalp.

'Carnelia!' she barked, livid. 'Stop that bloody giggling.'

But Carnelia, hysterical, could not. Secundus watched his brother being carried away under Livia's supervision. He seemed stunned, thoughtful and maybe a little unsure.

'That was damned unfortunate,' said Cornelius finally. 'Almost put me off my food, it did. I had no idea.'

'It appears your eldest son has been scalped, Cornelius,' said Beleth. 'Did they not tell you?'

Cornelius harrumphed. 'Of course they did, Linneus, of course.

But there's hearing about it—' He paused and searched ineffectually for his glass. It turned out it was already in his hand. 'And then there's seeing it.' His bloodshot gaze travelled down the table. To the *vaettir*.

Fisk said, 'He's got a fever. And from what I can tell, quite an infection.' He wrinkled his nose and muttered. 'No smell worse than a wound turning bad.'

'Nonsense,' Cornelius said, but without conviction. He looked at Secundus as though seeing him for the first time. 'He'll be right as rain, you'll see. You'll all see.'

'What's got me puzzled,' said Secundus, clearly changing the subject, 'is where you learned to spin a tale like that, Mr Ilys? The hunt didn't seem half as fine a story when I told it to myself.'

There was laughter down the table, some of it still uneasy after Gnaeus' exit.

'I learned to spin tales to compensate for own stature, Mr Secundus. A story-teller is always welcome around a fire,' I said. 'And far less likely to get shot.'

More laughter.

Livia returned, looking strained but forcing a smile. She took her seat and said, 'Pardon me for that interruption, but Gnaeus was not feeling well.'

Samwell Kliment, his face straight, said, 'He seems to be in need of some tailoring.'

Livia shook her head. 'I worry that if we sutured his wound, it wouldn't be able to breathe. I have applied tersus incendia and acetum, liberally. All of the legionaries who've been scalped, save one, have died from infections or some sort of brain fever.'

I said, as gently as I could, 'It's a hard land here, ma'am. Sometimes all you can do is hope.'

When the dishes were cleared away, Cornelius clapped his hands and a slave came, bearing a carved wooden sceptre truncating in a bear's foot. It smelled raw and gamey and my stomach did a little turn as she walked past.

'I quite fancy a smoke,' said Cornelius. The slave began strapping the sceptre to Cornelius' thigh, and I realized then it was a false leg. Cornelius noticed Fisk and me staring and declared, 'She took my leg, so I'll use hers.'

Secundus glanced at Livia, since it was she, and not the bear, who had actually amputated her father's foot.

The slave used a small wrench to tighten the straps until Cornelius winced. Looking closer, I saw the wood of the leg was cleverly fashioned. It was intricately decorated, with carvings and traced skeins of silver and finely stamped leather. It had a small skean affixed to one side, such as the Ruman Northmen use, and what looked like a flask on the other side. The hinged foot itself was wooden but covered over with the bear's paw, its great claws stretching five, six inches long. Once the leg was attached, Cornelius touched the foot to the floor and the claws clacked on the floorboards.

He stood up. Everyone at the table watched as Cornelius, a senator of Rume, attempted a drunken, limping jig at the end of the table, clapping his hands and throwing his bear-leg into the air in feeble little kicks. The numbing effects of booze had done its work. After the rich foods and copious drink, most of the guests at the table could only stare upon him with expressions of muted discomfort and unease.

Cornelius sang:

'Oh ho, we're the fighting fifth with bragging sticks
Swinging swords and mighty dicks
A million virgins heard this song
We filled their bellies, every one!
A hey! A hoy! A hey!'

Carnelia clapped her hands in time with her father's dance. She was the only one. Cimbri looked a bit stunned and his second, Paterna, blinked at the Senator's gyrations. Beleth chuckled.

'Whiskey for the guests! Come, Lupina! Pour the whiskey!' Cornelius panted, and then stumped unsteadily away from the table. He stopped, turned in a circle quickly, moving his bear foot clack repeatedly, as if he were showing off his agility.

'It's fierce! Is it not? Should I take the praenomen Ursa?' The half-*dvergar* slave – Lupina – darted forward and grabbed Cornelius' arm just as he began to teeter and fall. He steadied himself on her shoulder.

'No whiskey? Come, Lupina, fetch some. And my cigars. To share with my guests.'

Lupina gently pushed Cornelius back onto his seat. He chuffed out an explosion of alcohol-scented air, still humming the tune to his marching song. Moving swiftly, the slave disappeared through the servant's entrance to the kitchens and reappeared bearing a leaded-crystal bottle of whiskey, a set of tumblers, and a wooden box.

Setting down the tray, she poured drinks with a deft economy of movement while another slave delivered them to the dinner guests. Then she opened the cigar box and presented it to Cornelius. He took a cigar, bit off the end, and Lupina lit it with a match.

We all took cigars and whiskeys, even the ladies – scandalous by New Damnation or Harbor Town standards – and wandered about the great room and out onto the rear gallery beyond the paddleboxes, over silvered water.

It was colder now, and my breath was mingled with cigar smoke and the fumes of good whiskey in my glass.

Banty, Carnelia, and Isabelle huddled at the rear rail, laughing and wreathed in smoke, the moonlight broken into a million facets beyond them on the thin ribbon of the Big Rill that dashed away to the south and east to New Damnation.

Miss Livia, arm and arm with Fisk, who looked simultaneously uncomfortable and ecstatic, strolled the length of the gallery, Fisk favouring his uninjured leg. The engineers stood near the Senator while he clomped around on his bear-leg. Below us, on the lower gallery, sounded catcalls and shouts, the clatter and tromp of legionaries without whores, fighting, or gambling to entertain themselves.

With Fisk occupied, I wandered back into the great room. Lupina glared at me, but poured more whiskey into my tumbler.

The *vaettir* remained unmoved as I stood in front of her. The two shotgun-wielding legionaries, men of the fifth, did not have that loose, casual stance of men on blockade or watch. Exposure to the stretcher for long periods had them spooked.

I swirled the whiskey in my glass and glanced at the soldiers. 'She move much?' It was possible they would ignore me or take offence that a *dvergar* would question them. But I was old when these boys' parents were born.

'No ... sir.' The last word came reluctantly. 'She's like a statue, she is, little miss Agrippina.'

I raised an eyebrow. 'Agrippina?'

'Oh, just the fellows' name for her. Vibenus came up with it. Something about his mother.'

Soldiers love their nick-names, and Agrippina – it suited her.

I looked at her. Her eyes stared beyond me. As I moved, they did not track my motion. I walked around the holly cage. It was hard to tell if she even drew breath.

'They live for aeons, it's said.'

The guard shifted, almost startled. 'That right, sir?'

'Yes.' I sipped my booze and smoked my cigar. 'The *vaettir* used to trade with the *dvergar*, when they wanted fabric, beads, steel. My mother told me that they were all naked before we came to this land.'

Someone whistled, and I realized Mr Secundus had joined me.

'Naked, you say?' He looked a bit woppy-jawed, standing unsteadily. Maybe he'd been jarred by his brother's state. Maybe he was scared of what his future might hold. Whatever the case, the whiskey had not missed him. 'Like babes in a garden, then, were they?' He laughed, looking quizzically at Agrippina. 'Give her her hand back, brush out the hair, put her in something nice, red maybe, she might look presentable. Not so savage.'

That talk sounded too similar to Banty's whorehouse rumours.

'I wouldn't try getting her into a dress, Secundus. She might scratch you like she scratched Gnaeus.'

His face clouded, thinking. But then he had another drink and laughed. 'True. She was fearsome on the plains, hopping to and fro, taking those scalps.'

I'd seen this before. Men, when finally confronting their fears somewhere safe, will try to find some humour to make the threat smaller. It doesn't work in the end. If Agrippina even moved, this poor highborn lad would piss himself.

'Mr Secundus, the *vaettir* truly are a terrifying race. But I'm curious as to whether there's more to them than blood and misery and games.'

'Are you suggesting they might overcome their natures? Rise above their savagery? They might have some modicum of civility?'

I thought for a moment. 'I'm one hundred and fifty-three years old, Mr Secundus. My *dvergar* blood gives long life – it changes perspective somewhat. Sometimes it's hard for me to get worked up over anything.'

I walked around the *orbis argenta*, looking at Agrippina, at the wardwork, the cage. And then at Secundus.

'But the stretchers, their flesh is undying, if all the tales told about them are true.' I pointed at her with my cigar. 'She'll be here for a thousand years after I'm gone. And *I'll* outlive you by a lifetime, unless I get ventilated by some pistolero.'

Secundus' face darkened at that.

'So, there's no telling how they'll act or respond. To her, she might as well have been captured by flies, our lives are so short. But mark my words, the *vaettir* have some sort of code, or culture, or ... *something*. We've never been beyond the White Mountains, and they could have whole cities over there.'

'You sound like my father with his talk of dragons.'

'I can't speak with any authority on the great wyrms. But one of the *vaettir* sits before you. We have to figure out what that will mean.'

'Means they aren't as tough as they seem, maybe.'

I sighed. Commoners like me can't just wallop a highborn lad upside the head without getting crucified. It's debatable if you can deliver sense like that, anyway.

'No,' I said slowly. 'It means we got extremely lucky.'

He tilted his glass to his mouth, noticed it was empty, smiled at me, and turned to find Lupina.

I stopped him, putting a hand on his arm before he could leave. I gestured to the open Gallish doors and the river beyond. 'Mr Secundus, I know it was a hard thing. But don't change how you remember what happened out there,' I nodded at Agrippina, 'just because we've got her caged in here. Remember how bad it was.'

He frowned, brows furrowing like dark stormclouds on the virgin plain. The expression didn't sit well on his young and as yet unlined face. He had more and more to deal with now. His father. What was left of his brother. But he loosened some, reminding me why I liked him so much.

'Understood, Mr Ilys. You are correct, but I believe I'll indulge myself in a few more moments of fantasy – and another whiskey – before retiring. Can I send Lupina round to you?'

'Much obliged, if you did.'

He smiled then. A remarkable young man, altogether. 'Would you check on Livia for me? Obviously, she doesn't need my protection, yet there are stretchers about...'

I nodded and toddled off.

I could feel the cold air coming in through the open doors. Soon Captain Skraeling and Sam Kliment wandered in, followed by the engineers. Banty walked on the deck, arm and arm with Isabelle, passing in and out of the shadows thrown by the *daemonlight*. Carnelia was watching, her arms crossed over her breasts and face caught between scorn and maybe, truth be told, a little jealousy. Cimbri stood on the threshold of one door, hands on his waist, staring out into the night, smoking like one of the smokestacks that rose above us.

I walked out on the deck, shivered with the cold, and spotted Fisk and Livia standing in the shadows cast by the hindmost stack. He was leaning against the outer rail, his head down, listening.

They did not notice me approaching. She was saying, 'So, when Metellus learned he could marry the Amelianus woman, and take all of her lands and income for his own, he divorced me with no compunction.'

Fisk was slow to speak, but when he did it was with rage, barely subdued. 'That man is an ignorant jackass.'

'It was difficult for a while. I had never loved him ...' She paused, tucked a strand of hair behind her ear. 'It was a political marriage. The plebs have it so much better in that sense. Their women are not bound by convention. But going from a matron of a household to a divorced woman in Rume, it is not something I'd like to endure again. Metellus, not content to divorce me, put about the forum and to his cronies that I was deviant, and could not conceive a child due to strange ... proclivities.' She bowed her head. 'He besmirched my name, along with ending our marriage.'

'Ia-damn that man. I would—' He stopped and gritted his teeth. 'I would kill him, if he weren't a half a world away.'

Livia placed a hand on his cheek, only for a moment, and he raised his hand to grasp hers.

'I knew you, of all people, would understand.' Her voice, measured and soft.

'Been years since I thought about the dishonour to my name.' Gruff and rumbling, his voice.

'Surely it bothers you? I don't know if I agree with what your father did, but you are of patrician birth, and by rights should be in the senate.'

He laughed, lowered his voice again.

'I was just a boy when we came here to exile. This land was like a wonderful adventure. Though a cloud hung over Father, I loved it. But he turned mean and desperate. Exile didn't suit him. It wasn't until ...'

'Until?'

'I lost *my* family ... that my feelings changed.'

'I'm so sorry.' She paused. So they stood, facing each other, her two hands holding his. I coughed.

I felt horrible interrupting, but would have felt worse if I'd continued to eavesdrop on their conversation.

'Shoe,' Fisk said.

'Pard.'

Livia let go of his hands and he remained staring at her, raising his eyebrows in a look that asked something. Miss Livia straightened her shoulders and turned to me, looking beautiful, if a little pale and cold.

'Hello, Mr Ilys. I hope you've been enjoying your evening.'

'Of course, ma'am. I'm sorry to interrupt you.'

The smile she gave me lit up her face. 'Not to worry, Mr Ilys, you are always welcome here.'

'I thought I might check on you two. It's getting colder.'

'Indeed.' She smoothed her dress, held out her arm. 'Would you be so kind?'

I took her arm and walked her back into the *daemonlight*. I caught a glance of Fisk's face as I did it, and though he seemed dark and especially thoughtful, he winked at me as I turned.

Inside we passed Samantha Decius, who was speaking rather loudly to Cimbri, Paterna, and Banty. She had a loud voice and bright ruddy cheeks.

'Gooseberry's cage is threaded with silver pipes. We pump water through them. It becomes incredibly hot and pushes the turbines, the paddle wheels, then circulates through the ship, increasing the temperature and giving us some power for other things, like the swing stages, the fans, and running water.'

'How do you bind such a massive *daemon* to begin with?' asked Paterna, shaking his head in wonder.

'There's no size to Gooseberry. Indeed, there's no size to any of the infernal. They can occupy whatever space they like. Right now, he's about,' she spread her arms and indicated a few feet, 'yay big. I daresay he'd grow titanic and consume the world if we gave him half the chance. But binding him ... well ... that's the hard bit.'

'Hold up, miss.' Cimbri shifted his cigar around in his mouth. 'You mean to tell me that our ... our Ia-damned engine could eat the world?' He puffed, making the cherry burn bright, and tucked his hands into his uniform's belt. 'Hogwash.'

'You could be correct, Mr Cimbri. There's no way to tell except to let him loose. Hardly a good idea.'

Cimbri snorted. 'I imagine. Gunplay is bad enough. Hate to see one loosed into the world.'

'That begs a question,' Kliment said. He was sitting at the table next to Cornelius and Skraeling, one leg tossed casually over the arm of his chair, glass held loosely in hand. 'I understand, quite well, how Hellfire pistols get their names. An *imp* is bound inside a shell casing, the trigger releases the hammer, which mars the binding, releasing the devil, which escapes down the length of the barrel, pushing the bullet before it with fire and anger. However, why does the *imp* not then exit the barrel and become free to cause all sorts of havoc in the world?'

'That's a prescient question, sir.' Samantha drank from a glass – water it seemed – and looked excited at her chance to hold forth on subjects relating to engineering. I searched the great room for Beleth, but he seemed to have disappeared. Cornelius took a noisy slurp from his tumbler. Lupina, standing by the Senator, pointedly ignored my empty glass. So I toddled over to the table and poured one for myself.

'The reason we're not bedevilled from thousands of loosed *imps* lies in what's called the *diavolus pellum* ward. Look there.'

She pointed to the main doorway. From our distance, the silver wardwork around it looked dark, dim, and barely noticeable from tarnish. But it was festooned with intaglios and glyphwork and arcane symbols I could not make out.

'*Pellum* warding will send any *daemon* that passes through it back to the pit it came from. There's a smaller one etched around the lip of each Hellfire barrel. The *imps* flee down the barrel, pass through the *pellum*, and then find themselves back in Hell before they know it.'

'Meanwhile, the speeding bullets are a last little reminder of their recent presence.' My voice was not kind, but they ignored me.

'That why you get after-images of the nasties after firing?'

'Yes. For an instant, they remain in our world.'

Fisk was aware of my stance on Hellfire. Cimbri, too. So there were some eyebrows raised when I asked, 'So, what happens if the warding inside the barrel becomes marred or scratched from exiting bullets?'

Decius smiled, and the smile was an honest if homely one.

'You'll have a hoppin' mad little devil on your hands then.' She laughed, but I found it hard to see the humour. The corruption done to one's immortal soul is bad enough, but freeing *daemons* into the world to work their mischief, to cause such misery? The bullets are evil enough. 'Word of warning, don't rest your guns on their muzzles.' She smiled.

Fire and oil burns. A piece of wood will burn hot, too, if you use a bellows. I've heard tell the Tchinee peoples have essences and powders that flame brighter than the sun, but no one seeks these out. There *are* alternatives. But instead we have *daemons* – everywhere. It's not right. But I was too much of a coward to say it aloud.

Everyone fell silent until Cornelius belched and lurched sideways in his chair. Lupina, coming to his side, took his arm and lifted him up. He looked even more dissolute and bleary than the day following the bear hunt, when we sawed off his leg. But that was days ago.

Livia smiled, held out her hands out like you might see in statues of Fortuna, and said, 'I believe it might be time to retire. Father. Shall I see our guests to their boats?'

He looked at us all with watery, grey eyes and blinked heavily. Then he tapped his bear's foot on the floor three times and said with a voice thick with phlegm, 'You ate at my table, drank my fire, spun me a story, avoided my ire. Go with my good will. For now.'

Carnelia said in a mock stage whisper, 'Tata likes to rhyme when he's drunk.'

No one laughed. There was silence for a moment, with an uncomfortable shuffling of feet. Lupina glared at Carnelia. Livia looked none too happy herself.

Then, like the ringing of a bell, a sound came.

'*Dverg! Chondlar a diete. Tul. Chondlar a diete!*'

It was not pitched as high as the fierce ululations of the hunt. But it was clear beyond simple sound – each syllable felt like the strike of a farrier's hammer, or the sinking sensation of a Hellfire shot.

Agrippina had decided to join the conversation.

They bustled me out of the great room, into a smaller dining area I'd never seen before, and gathered around me with questioning stares.

'She said "*Dverg*". You talk to this thing, dwarf? When you were alone with it in the hall?' Cimbri had a hand on his Hellfire and looked ready to use it.

'No. Secundus and the guards can vouch for me.'

'But it was it talking to you just now?'

'Yes.'

'Why?'

'She knew I could deliver a message.'

'All right.' He looked at Cornelius and the others. Fisk stared at me evenly, and winked again. Carnelia wrung her hands.

'Go on then,' said Cornelius. 'Tell us.'

'It was *dvergar*, wasn't it?' The junior engineer seemed excited. Kliment sucked his teeth.

'Yes, it was the *dvergar* tongue. My mother's tongue. Agrippina must have learned it, years ago, when our peoples were more friendly.'

'I couldn't give a shit about this Ia-damned history lesson.' Cimbri was as outraged as I've ever seen him, and he was regularly in a state of indignation. 'What did the damned thing *say*?'

I took a deep breath. 'It said, "Dwarf. You will die. All of you. You will die."'

Carnelia gasped and Miss Livia put her arm around the sallow girl's shoulder, pulling her in close and comforting her.

'It's insupportable, the wog making threats,' said Skraeling.

'They'll do more than threaten.' Fisk's tone was flat, emotionless.

Secundus sniffed. 'Bah. It's trying to get in our heads.'

Fisk looked at the lad silently for a moment. He turned to the Senator and said, 'Mr Cornelius, much obliged at your hospitality. A fine meal.' He nodded his thanks and turned to Livia. 'Ma'am. Always a pleasure.'

She took his hand and held it.

I bowed to Cornelius and the group, then to Livia. I didn't have to say anything, but I followed Fisk out. Cimbri looked like he didn't want to let us leave.

'Wait a moment,' I said. 'Where's Banty?'

'More important,' growled Cimbri, 'where's the Medieran girl?'

TWELVE

THE HORSES STEAMED in the night air as the boat dropped us back at camp, tired, half-drunk and exhausted. I don't know about Fisk, but *my* head was spinning with drink and the events of the evening. The legionaries who'd been stationed on the eastern bank in our absence shivered, grunted, and boarded without bothering to give us details of the watch. The fire was low, and they hadn't collected any more brushwood.

We settled down into sleeping bags by the embers of the fire. Fisk said, 'What the hell were you thinking, Banty?'

'Don't call me that. I'm not some damned child.' Back to being sullen.

'All right. Mr Bantam, what the hell were you thinking?'

'Don't see a problem, not that it's any of your Ia-damned business. We went up to the hurricane deck to look at the stars.'

'You're lucky you didn't spend the rest of the night looking at stars from atop a cross.'

I said, 'It's true, Cornelius and Cimbri looked like they wanted to kill someone when you two were discovered missing.' I scratched my head. 'Think the Mlederan lass is nobility, or something.'

Banty stayed quiet, arms behind his head, still looking up at the stars.

I said, quietly, 'She *is* pretty, son.'

'Shut up, dwarf,' he said, and rolled over.

Time was, you could walk thousands of miles in this land without seeing another soul. The stretchers kept to themselves in their high reaches, dreaming their unfathomable dreams, and only came out to trade with us once in a blue moon.

Humankind, like my pappy, had their little villages far, far, to the east. The elder *dvergar* would take a group of boys, green as grass every one, and walk us for months on end east, always east, pulling a wagon and watching the treeline for bear or boar, cougar or wolf. Sometimes there was road, but mostly not. Until the small encampments of the east came into view. We would trade and marvel at the tall folk and their strange gods and rough wares. Their liquors and their wines.

But the Smokey Mountains – the *Eldvatch* – were ours to plumb and mine and live upon, with the rest of the wide land to hunt and lay down roots. All the world was new then, eye-sweet and dappled with dew.

But the Rumans came from across the Eastern Sea. Took the far villages with sword and fire and built their forums and barracks and granaries and aqueducts. Pulled down the old temples and put up the crossroad shrines, the churches, bringing Ia, and his mercy and forgiveness, to this land.

I can barely remember the old gods.

But the Rumans brought their *daemonfire*, too, their steamers and mechanized baggage trains. They brought their Hellfire with them.

They brought a young legionary named Septus Speke. My pappy. Or at least that's what he said his name was, the few times he stopped by. He was tall, blond. Had rough hands and a low voice.

A child of two worlds, I am. Got mixed feelings about all of it, my pappy and mam, Rume and this land, Ia and the multitude of *daemons*.

My blood is tainted. Like all things, the older it gets, the more likely it'll get dirty.

My pappy never stuck around. I remember the old ways because that's how I was raised by my mam. I was born in the spring of a year, and since that day, I've seen hundreds more springs – so many I've lost count – each one blushing and full of life , from the moment the wetnurse spanked my arse to right now, where I sit, telling you this story.

A long time, and I've seen the world change.

But that day, the day we started the long steam up the Big Rill out of the Hardscrabble Territories toward Passasuego, the world seemed young again.

Gone, for the moment, was the oppressive presence of Agrippina in her cage. Gone was the constant worry and fret over Cornelius' absent leg or Gnaeus' grievous wound.

The plains beckoned.

We'd steamed for three days, riding escort by day, pacing the big riverboat, camping shoreside at night. Fisk's leg had healed, and he seemed lighter in heart than I'd ever seen him before.

By day, the gulls came to join the *Cornelian*, even this far from the sea. They wheeled and banked and dived into the bright waters churned by the boat's paddles. The bells clanged, echoing across the surface of the Big Rill while both legionaries and lictors idled on the main deck. Black smoke billowed from the stacks and somewhere, bound deep in the machine, Gooseberry burned bright, full of hate and pain and anger.

The sun was full and warm on my skin, even though the wind was cold and I had brought out my second jacket that morning.

The air smelled clean, but with the dry, faintest hint of powder. Snow would not be far off.

We began seeing livestock tracks cutting through the shoal grasses, small paths hemmed by brushwood fencing. Soon, small hutches and clay houses hove into view. Tired, raw-boned women with thick hips and muscled arms scrubbed threadbare clothing at the shore. Scraggly children screamed and chased mongrels through muddy streets, hungry looks on their faces. Somewhere ahead I heard the pinging telltale of a blacksmith, or farrier, plying his craft.

The *Cornelian* clanged and turned toward our shore. A stevedore scuttled halfway up the jack staff and unhitched the swing stages to unfurl and meet the village's sole dock. Lascars made fast the *Cornelian*, and from where I sat on Bess's back I watched as Cornelius, wearing his bear leg, Cimbri, and Beleth disembarked. A grey-haired settler in overalls and a straw hat greeted them with a feeble wave of his arm. Women watched from the doorways and children stopped chasing dogs, sticks held loosely in rough hands.

Cimbri gestured – he was dickering over something. Cornelius drew on his cigar and looked smug – an expression I could see even from this distance – while white smoke curled around his head and whisked downriver. After a while, more stevedores walked up the swing stages and began rolling casks to the *Cornelian*'s hold, followed by bushels of maize and sacks of corn and oats. Shirtless legionaries stacked and sorted and hollered and cursed, as soldiers always do when faced with work that doesn't require bloodshed. Then Livia, arm in arm with Carnelia and Isabelle, sauntered into the village.

Banty, without asking, swung his horse around and rode down to the hutches and houses.

Fisk sucked his teeth.

'You want to go?' I asked him.

'Hell, no.'

'You do. Ain't no shame in it. Miss Livia's mighty pretty.'

'I *will* shoot you, Shoe.'

Cimbri walked back onto the dock, looked around, saw us sitting on the rise at the village's edge, and waved us down. We rode down the slope, through an unfenced goat pasture with a billy glaring at us and wetting his nose with a green tongue. As we neared the village, the ground became more sodden and sucked at Bess's hooves with messy, noisy sounds.

We came within earshot. Cimbri yelled, 'Over here! Want you to listen to this!'

I found a place to tether the horses, and Fisk and I moseyed over to where an old settler sat on a stump in the sun, smoking a corncob pipe.

'Go on, old timer. Tell them what you told me.'

The old man's wattles shook. But he popped his pipe out of toothless gums and said, 'Airy much to tell, young sirs. Them things come during the night and slaughtered our cows, drank their blood. Danced in the moonlight.'

Fisk crossed his arms. Rubbed his chin.

'That all?' he asked.

'Plucked a girl's baby from the crib, through the window, and ate it.'

I whistled.

Fisk looked at Cimbri. 'You check out his story?' He put a hand on the old man's shoulder. 'How do you know this? You see it? You've got a body?'

'Naw, sir. They spirited the baby away, ate her on the mountaintops.'

'Bah.'

Fisk turned away and sucked his teeth. He motioned for us to join him.

'Don't doubt that the stretchers are causing all sorts of trouble, but I'll wager my eye-teeth they ain't taken no babies in the dark of night with no one to see.' Fisk spat. 'If I know one thing about the stretchers, they love a spectacle. Some girl smothered a bastard child, most like, and buried it.'

I don't know if I agreed. The image of Orrin's body in the bear cave came to me then; I thought the *vaettir* capable of almost anything.

Cimbri snorted, walked over to the old man, handed him a coin, and patted his back.

'Our thanks, old timer. You might want to ring your windows in holly, if you can find any around here. Lock it down at night.'

The old man blinked owlishly and gaped.

We returned to our horses, but not before Cimbri stopped us.

'Boys, Miss Carnelia asked if she and Isabelle could ride with you today.'

Fisk scowled.

'You don't have to say nothing. I told her it wasn't a good idea. And, just like a Cornelian, she didn't listen.' He laughed. 'I reminded her that the damned stretchers are on the warpath and that she herself saw what they could do, but she said no *vaettir* was going to prevent her from doing what she would. "We are Ruman!" Carnelia said. Like that was gonna keep them from scalping her.'

Fisk cursed.

'But I'll make sure you've got some legionaries at your disposal,' Cimbri finished lamely. 'And Miss Livia will accompany them, as well.'

A couple of soldiers came from the *Cornelian*, carrying the ladies' tack. I fetched mounts for them and saddled the horses.

We waited by the docks, watching the stevedores roll the casks down swing stages into the hold with hollow rattles, grunting and swearing. Eventually the ladies finished their tour of the hamlet and returned, Banty escorting Isabelle while Miss Livia and Carnelia strode arm in arm.

'Hello, boys. Lovely day for a jaunt.' Carnelia looked better than she had the night of the dinner. She'd recovered her dander. 'Dwarf, is my horse saddled?'

Livia frowned. 'Mr Ilys is a favoured friend of our family, Carnelia. Be civil, if you can find a shred of humanity in your shrivelled soul. He was there at the *vaettir* attack, too, as you well know.'

'I don't recall him hefting a gun.'

Livia cocked her head and looked at me. 'No matter. We're all armed, aren't we, ladies?' She patted her thigh, ruffling her riding dress.

Carnelia laughed. 'He's just a *dvergar*, sissy. Don't be so damned huffy.'

I interrupted. 'It's fine, Miss Livia. I *am* a dwarf. Ain't no shame in it, as far as I can see. And yes, ma'am. Got your horse right over here.'

Carnelia snorted. Fisk glared at her, and I felt glad he was my partner.

The legionaries came toddling up the swing stages, across the dock, each man wearing a knit hat and carrying his own tack. They picked out ponies, and saddled up and rode out on the plain, following the noble women riding close to the scouts, me and Fisk and Banty. Carnelia did not look at me as she rode.

Can't be certain of anything in this life but I'm thinking this is how it went: The sun's bright and hammering the earth, the wind is fresh, whipping over the Whites, and the horses naturally pair up and he rides next to her. He wants to smile and reach out, take her hand like they did on the promenade of the *Cornelian*, but there's folks watching, the other man, the other woman, the dwarf and Carnelia, the trailing legionaries fiddling with their carbines.

So they ride, the pair of them, slowly. But the horses, feeling the wide-open plains tugging, the horses want their heads.

So their walk becomes a trot becomes a canter and soon, looking back, the other man and woman are gone, they've left the dwarf and Carnelia behind, and there are only a few legionaries struggling to keep up. She's laughing now, throwing back her head, flashing teeth and smiling happily at him. And the smile is what does it, what ends it all for him, something so delicate and personal, something he never thought he'd see again. So he's lost right then, when she smiles.

He forgets about the possibility of *vaettir*.

They top the rise. The legionaries, struggling to stay atop their mounts, see the two figures, man and woman, leaning toward each other, framed by blue sky. Then they're gone.

The two keep riding until their escorts, their chaperones, are far behind. They take a gulley to track north, and then west toward the Big Rill. In a copse of birch trees near a spring that feeds the river, they dismount and tie the horses, then walk between the white-barked trunks, in the dappled glade, now in darkness, now caught in a shaft of light, holding hands.

He's awkward at first. There could be stretchers about, you can never know, even in this warm sun. She holds his hand, and he doesn't know what to do. His hand lies as dumb as a stone in her warm palm, rougher than he thought it would be, until she tugs him toward her. Then they're standing close with the perfumed scent of her breath on his face, her eyes searching his, looking past the wear of the range, past the lines of hurt from the loss of family and the exile of the Hardscrabble life.

She kisses him, and her lips are so soft he can forget the threat of *vaettir* catching them in the glade. Everything in this life is hard,

hard as stone – you fight the recalcitrant earth, you face the wind and sleet and harsh winds and plains-dust while every morsel of food is competed for and hard won – but her lips are soft, soft and sweet. Softer than anything in this life – and given freely.

His hands move to her hips and hers to his face to cup his stubbled cheek, and then to his shirt and later to his gunbelt. When the clasp is undone, the weight of the gun drags his britches to the ground, which is covered in leaves and soft enough for them to lie down. She's like a fallen flower, the flounces of her dress splayed out, wide, while his hands are on her bodice. He's bringing his mouth to her breasts, and she's laughing and trying to shuck herself out of the frilled layers of dress. They settle in the petals of her flounces and her hand finds him while he discovers the curve of her hip, runs his hand up her thigh where her gun is strapped, to the sweet centre between her legs.

And then he's over her, kissing her lips, everything abandoned, everything lost, except her scent and the warmth of her flesh, pinioned in a shaft of light in the ever-moving dappled glade. Her hands are at the small of his back, and she's whispering in his ears – what, neither could say later. She shudders and searches his body for a piece of it she can keep with her forever, and he arches his back, rising on his arms, and the motion of his body becomes frantic against her. He feels massive and infinitesimal, all at once, adrift on the sea of her body, rolling on the waves of pleasure coursing through them both and thinking, *What did I do to deserve this?*

Later, she lies there shivering, not from cold, but from tremors still wracking her body. And he looks at her face, so fine, so far beyond him and his rough life, and with the sight of her smooth skin – that delicate skin that comes with a lifetime of good food and the sunless hours of a privileged education and the steady drone of tutors– it all comes crashing in. She's a noble and he's what he is: a scout, a man living off the dried teat of this harsh land.

She kisses his eyelids, and slides her body against him once more. He responds. She shuts her eyes as she rides him, her face caught in the sun, her hair around his face, cords standing out on her neck.

Later, they're too spent for words and neither wants to think upon the consequences of this tryst. It could be death for him, she knows.

She takes a long time restoring her clothing and her hair, but it's still mussed. Beautifully mussed, he says, gloriously mussed, and she smiles, but she takes the time to right it all the same. She holds his hand as they walk back to the horses, and when they remount, he feels a desperate loneliness again, until she winks at him from horseback.

They ride back to the legionaries, returning to the world they left behind, the cruel hard one with nothing soft in it.

The legionaries dilly-dallied after they lost Fisk and Livia. *And* Banty and Isabelle. The couples had made headed off in opposite directions, splitting the escort detail and outriding the poor soldiers.

Fisk and Livia returned first, and I knew in a moment, just looking into his face – the way he looked at me and then away to the prairie, quick-like – that there had been something more than horseback riding. Banty and Isabelle took a mite longer, so much longer that I'd told Fisk he'd better remount so we could go find their bodies. But then they came riding in, sun behind them, her dress all a mess and the damned greenhorn all grins and shy batting of eyes.

Back in the village Cimbri, glowering and chomping on his cigar, waited until the ladies had dismounted and taken the swing stage back to the *Cornelian* before he said, 'Took you Ia-damned long enough for your joy ride. You missed all the hubbub. Young master Gnaeus did us all a favour and died.'

THIRTEEN

A PATRICIAN'S SON – a patrician with proconsular imperium – demands a lavish funeral. And Cornelius wasn't cutting any corners.

See, the Rumans have hedged their bets. While they recognize Ia as the one true god, on the sly they still make obeisance to the old Prodigium gods – those old titans and the ill brood of capricious gods that came before. Ia did us all a favour by wiping the heavens clean of their taint, but they lurk still in the shadows of Ruman ceremony. The nine days of sorrow are still observed – the unwashed grief, the vestes pullae, the lamentations and funeral procession. All the collected grief was the foodstuff of those gods. Ia just inherited the trappings.

Cornelius directed the boat upstream to the western shore beyond the village, a full hour's steam north, in good sight of the Whites. I took Bess and a brace of ponies, dragging a sledge up to a brake of gambels and gathered the laurel of perfect leaves for Gnaeus, and we felled enough trees for the pyre. We spent the day there, dragging logs back to the *Cornelian*, me, Fisk, Banty, Sharbo, Horehound and Jimson plus a team of legionaries and lascars. In two days, we had the pyre as high as a hillock and steeped in pitch.

Livia and Isabelle visited us to inspect the funeral pyre. Livia looked tired and pale. With one exception, her time since the auroch hunt had been spent ministering to her scalped brother, watching what little humanity the man had seep from his head as pus and burn from his body in fever. As he died, so all the Cornelian children's positions and allegiances shifted. It was as though their world had cracked and tilted on end. I would not mourn Gnaeus. But I could see that Livia, at least, would.

'My condolences, Miss Livia,' I said.

Fisk stood unmoving and looked at her.

'How's your pa?' he said, low and not without feeling.

'He's lost, as you'd expect. What with his leg and now Gnaeus. He's making a big show of—' She waved her hands at the pyre. 'All this. His grief. He's donned the vestes pullae and blotted out any decent emotions with alcohol, as usual, and generally made an arse of himself clomping around the stateroom, glaring at the *vaettir*. Most of us declined to join him.'

There was a different timbre now on the *Cornelian*. The legionaries had become dour and silent. Many sported new tattoos of bulls or skulls. To a man, their heads were shorn and fierce looking. The lascars could be seen touching their heads, lips, and hearts constantly, genuflecting to Ia.

I heard mutterings among the men, that the stretcher whore in the stateroom had killed Gnaeus, just by her presence. That she could draw men's thoughts out of their heads and reveal their deepest secrets. That if you lay with her, you would surely die.

And that more were coming. More *vaettir*. To rescue her.

On hearing of Cornelius' state, Cimbri snorted and then murmured, 'Sorry, ma'am.'

'I'm not in the mood, Mr Cimbri. My brother is being anointed by the libitinarii right now, and my tolerance for nonsense is very low.' She watched Cimbri for a moment, eyes narrow. He shifted his cigar in his mouth nervously and lowered his head. She looked back to where two bald lictors, in priestly robes, directed men to make sure each of the pyre's sides were in the right proportion – being equal in length and pleasing to Ia – and haranguing the men to arrange fragrant rosemary and sagebrush against the pile. The pleasing scent of it might lull Ia into a sense of complacency so that Gnaeus' spirit might be allowed past the trials of the shadowlands and to the great feast where all noble souls are brought before their lord, Ia. Here he sits at the head of a great and massive table, laden with food and drink and the withered bones of the old gods. Here every noble is rejoined with his or her maker and allowed into Heaven.

For the rest of us, death is much like life: we have to work to get where we're going. Pay the ferryman, cross the river, drink the lethal dregs from the cup of forgetfulness, and there the Pater Dis, the nameless hand of Ia, judges the taint done in life to our souls – our genius or iuno – and sends them to their final disposition.

It might not be the most equitable of arrangements, but it seems to work. And it's better than those old Ruman gods, what with their eternal wheels of pain, nameless dreads, capricious whims, and whatnot. I'm with Ia.

I wandered over to slather more logs with pitch and let both Fisk and Banty talk with the ladies.

Banty, dirty with the day's labours, tried desperately not to sully Isabelle's dress as he passed her the note.

I don't know what was more surprising to me, the fact that he had the gall to start private conversation with a noble or that he could write at all, though it made sense due to his equite parentage. Scouts don't need to have their letters. They need to be able to read the ground and air, ride a horse.

I rejoined Fisk and Miss Livia and cleared my throat.

'Young Banty's passed a schoolyard note to the Medieran lass.'

I didn't mention her disarrayed clothing and his stupid grins after their ride on the plain.

'What?' Livia sounded a tad shrill.

Fisk said, 'Looks like the boy's sweet on her. He's a damned silly pup, treading where he doesn't belong.'

'No, he's a damned deadly nuisance, is what he is. Isabelle is more than noble. She's the eldest daughter of King Diegal of Mediera. She's Princess Isabelle, the one who's sung about in taverns.'

Fisk whistled and shook his head.

'You mean, "The White Rose of Cordova"? *That* Isabelle?' I asked.

'Precisely.'

'But—'

'Holy shit …' Fisk removed his hat and dusted his pant leg. 'I'm as thick as a brick. Hell, Shoe, it was right in front of us the whole damned time.'

Livia smiled wearily – I was reminded that we were preparing her brother's funeral.

'But you introduced her at that dinner. Can't figure out why none of us picked up on it,' I said.

'Some did, of course. Miss Decius, she figured it out right away. And possibly Sam Kliment – that man doesn't miss a thing. Of course Beleth already knew. But if you didn't know the name that went with the royal title, it's understandable that you didn't realise.' She put her hands on her waist, and stared hard at Banty. A little bit of the fierce Livia, the *vaettir*-shooting Livia, shone through. 'Once this funeral is over, I'm going to have to sort out the pretty equite boy. He's fair to look at, with passable manners, but I believe he might need reassignment. Mr Cimbri?'

He harrumphed and looked pained. 'His folks are influential knights out of Harbor Town. Might be Marcellus is into them for a piece.'

'We can sort out Marcellus, I'm sure. He's in command of the fifth, but the fifth answers to Rume and Rume's governor.'

'Yes, ma'am.'

We were silent for a moment until a lictor began screaming at one of the sailors who'd let slip a log that tumbled downslope toward the Big Rill and managed to agitate the brace of ponies.

When Fisk and I had the leisure to return, the ladies were gone.

Despite the objections and alarm of Cimbri and us scouts, Cornelius insisted on the full nine days of sorrow heading up to the pompa funebris. We bought cattle from the hamlet downriver for the funerary feast. We kept watch for *vaettir* and the ever-hungry mountain lions that came down from the heights at night to prowl about, now that the days were shortening and winter coming on.

The day of the funeral we woke to a dusting of snow on the ground. The *Cornelian* steamed in the hard, cold air, and our breath came in crystal plumes in front of our faces.

A bell from the riverboat clanged and echoed across the Big Rill midday, when the sun was directly overhead. We gathered at the river's shore – all the scouts, the legionaries, and lascars – and waited as the slaves carried Gnaeus' body across the hurricane deck and then made procession on each lower deck of the *Cornelian*. The Senator followed behind, head covered, togated, clomping on his bear leg and ringed by lictors wearing black and hefting fasces with silver-pronged axes. Behind him came Secundus, his head covered by his toga minima – the small, more modern toga the Rumans wore occasionally like a shawl as an accent over their garb – and at his side walked Carnelia and Livia, both with their hair wild and mussed, as Ruman tradition dictated. With each step, they brought clenched fists to their breasts, as though beating their heart.

As for the husk of Gnaeus himself, he'd been oiled and dressed in his best military garb – Imperial blues and golden phalerae gleaming in the cold air – while his hair was tastefully arranged so that the horrible wound was not as apparent. But it was hard not to focus on it and think it a scrap of dead raccoon skin perched on his head.

As far as corpses went, it seemed Gnaeus' outside finally resembled his inside. He was as grey as old meat, and despite his closed eyes he looked like he had died in agony and enraged.

He'd been quite the soldier, judging from the medals affixed to his uniform. I can't imagine how much money Cornelius spent to get the boy those trinkets.

They walked his body out on the swing stages, borne on the wicker lectica, and brought him to the pyre.

They raised him up on ladders and set him at the top, fifteen feet above us.

A remarkably dry-eyed funeral, I must admit.

Cornelius said a few words I couldn't hear, and then a lictor intoned, 'We consign this soul to the tattered path through the shadowlands and up to the great triclinium of Ia, where he shall feast forever in the Lord's presence. Ia, Ia! Ia, vast and mighty, heed these offerings.' He looked around and waved a lictor to bring forward the cow, withdrew a longknife from his belt, and held it up to the sky. 'We offer them to you so that you sway the hand of the Pater Dis, the nameless, who sits in judgement on this one's soul.' Holding the knife, he led the cow over to where two lictors had a tin tub and jabbed the knife in its neck. The animal lowed and thrashed, and lictors gathered around it and forced the blood to fall in the tub until the creature was too weak to do anything other than pant and then die.

They brought the tub full of sloshing crimson back to where Gnaeus' body rested on the pyre, and with an undramatic heave ho they splashed the blood on the pitched logs. Then Cornelius himself took a torch and lit the pyre.

It caught quick and burned hot and high. The heat pushed back the gathered people. Wineskins and flasks were passed about.

Slaves passed out pewter mugs with spirits, and the legionaries handed out wineskins full to bursting. Bread was distributed freely and later, once it grew dark and the beef had been salted and basted in its own juices, hunks of steaming meat were slapped on the loaves that served as trenchers and tasted like ambrosia. I'd been feeding on shoal auroch too long.

Under hard cold stars, we drank and broke bread together. The constant threat of *vaettir* fell away, and the dark mood that had beset the *Cornelian* and the men of the fifth dissipated. For a moment at least, smiles split craggy legion faces. Soldiers and sailors and lictors slapped forearms and gripped each other in rough bear-hugs, suffused by alcohol and the reminder of death burning nearby. For one evening, they didn't cast fearful glances at the mountains looming above or whisper rumours of bloodshed or stretcher atrocity.

All this, considering Gnaeus' reputation, it wasn't a bad send off, after all. All of us, from senator to slave, coming together to share drink and food.

All except two.

By the time the booze gave out, Banty had already stolen a johnboat, cut loose the ponies on the eastern shore, and was riding hard away from the *Cornelian*, the funeral congregation just a small flame in the distance behind him.

Isabelle rode with him.

FOURTEEN

W E WERE TWO days on Banty's trail when the air turned bitterly cold. I began to fall behind, leaving Fisk the only rider left to pursue. Hate to admit it, but us *dvergar* ain't cut out for long spells on horseback. And Bess, she was born for the long haul, but not for speed.

Fisk pulled up, his black horse lathered and blasting air from its nostrils, and said, 'Go on back, Shoe. You can't keep up this pace and I can't wait for you. Go back. Tell them where I've gone. Banty can't be more than two days ahead of me. I'll take him.'

'You know what's at stake.'

'I need reminding?'

'Hell, it couldn't hurt.'

'Damn kind of you, Shoe.'

'Go on with you, then. I'll tell them.'

'Looks like he's headed toward Broken Tooth. I can get there before him if I take the Salt Flats.'

'Ain't safe this time of year, pard, you know that. And we got company, anyway.'

The Salt Flats is a high plateau between here and Broken Tooth that in winter becomes treacherous, windswept and eroded. Game flees the scrub of the steppe – moving down among the shoal grasses – and before they take the hint and follow, the wolves, the

142

bears and coyotes that prowl the edges get hungry and lose all inhibition about human flesh. Never all that finicky to begin with.

'What else to do?'

'You seen 'em?' I continued. He had to have.

He looked at me for a long time and then nodded, once.

A pair of stretchers had been pacing us for the past day, letting themselves be seen, rangy, wild, like wolves pacing a shoal auroch herd and then melting into the plains. The land had turned drier, more dust-swept and cold, with more frequent scrub-brush, wilted patches of honeymallow, and stands of organpipes. And occasionally a stretcher could be seen, taking long, loping strides with what looked like scalps dangling from clawed hands.

'Yeah. I've seen 'em.' His grey eyes scanned the horizon and then came back to me; they looked washed out. 'Ain't worried about the stretchers.' He patted his pistol, tried to smile, failed. 'Them *vaettir* only understand threat and spectacle. They won't bother you none when you turn back. You ain't got any Hellfire, anyway. They'll aim for me, I figure.'

'Thought you didn't hold with my opinion of the taint.'

'You made it up and down the mountain. My eyes have been opened.' He sniffed, shifted in his saddle.' You need to head toward Pilgrimage. Better cover, smoother trails. Them stretchers won't bother you in that direction.'

'Yep. I hope, at least.'

'Once you're gone, I'll give black her head. The stretchers'll be winded keeping up with her, however tall they be.'

I nodded.

He stuck out his arm, and we clasped forearms.

'Ride fast.'

'You, too.'

He turned and was gone.

*

As I headed back, I relived the night of the funeral. When it became clear that *this time*, Banty and the Medieran princess weren't hiding on the hurricane deck, Secundus called us all to the great room – his father being too drunk and wracked with grief to take control.

Agrippina watched as Fisk and myself, Livia, Carnelia, Secundus, Cimbri, Beleth, and Samantha gathered in the great room. The ship was still except for the sounds of the drunken funeral-goers chanting and calling from the riverside. Gnaeus' pyre still burned.

Secundus, looking much older and very grave, said, 'We have to get her back, and quickly.'

'I can see the need, what with all the stretchers about,' I said.

'There's that. But that's not all,' Livia said. Carnelia, sitting next to her, looked petulant and angry that a handsome equite scout had not stolen *her* away.

Miss Livia looked tight, intense, worried. Thin-lipped and pale.

'What did you think we are doing, steaming upriver to Passasuego?' Secundus asked.

I shrugged.

Fisk said, 'No telling with patricians, beggin' your pardon.'

Secundus looked irritated, but Livia smiled.

I looked at Agrippina. She sat immovable, inactive. But her eyes were open, and what looked like a half-smile sat on her lips. Never can tell with Rumans or *vaettir*.

Livia put her hands in her lap, looked at Fisk, and then the tight lines at the corners of her eyes softened and she gave a sad smile. She tilted her head toward him, and for a moment something passed between them – maybe a regret it wasn't them running, fleeing the *Cornelian*. If *they* had fled for love, no one would have followed, I'm thinking.

'As you all know, Mediera and Rume have an uneasy truce here in the west,' said Livia. 'The Emperor's goals for the Protectorate are often contrary to King Diegal's, and we vie for resources and territory. There was a knife-fight between two cartographers in New Damnation before we left.'

Cimbri guffawed and she allowed him his laughter, though when he stopped, he glanced at her, checking her temperament in the face of his humour.

Secundus poured a glass of wine before speaking again. 'The Protectorate, while important, hasn't been as pressing to the Emperor as the trade routes to Tchinee, and this past year, there've been quite a few sea skirmishes between Rume and Mediera regarding them. In one of the most recent, Isabelle was captured.

'Of course, we are not barbarians. Through diplomacy, we have managed to secure important mineral rights and resolve territorial disputes in return for ending our custody—'

'Possession, Secundus,' said Livia.

'Our *benevolent* custody of Isabelle—'

'See,' said Carnelia. 'He's already playing the part of senator. Aren't you, little brother? When will you change your name to Primus?'

'Hold up,' Fisk said. 'You caught her in a sea battle? What was she doing on a boat?' Fisk looked steadily at Livia. He leaned slightly toward her, his hands on the table as though none of us were present.

'Shouldn't a princess be at home?' I said. 'Protected?'

Livia said, 'We think she was en route to Tchinee, betrothed to the Emperor's heir in a masterstroke to outflank the Empire's efforts to secure a monopoly on Tchinee trade. With the discovery of the westward sea route, many Mederian ships have circumvented the blockade. Understandably, they have much to gain and very little to lose.' She sniffed. 'The Tchinee aren't above playing favourites, and the Shang Tzu incident did not help our cause with the Autumn Lords.'

Not much is known about the Autumn Lords other than they're powerful, they rule most of Tchinee – also known as Kithai – with an iron hand, and fiercely protect the Tchinee trade routes. But everyone had heard of the Shang Tzu incident, all the papers in Harbor Town and New Damnation had featured the incident. Autumnal port authorities confiscated a Ruman trade ship for 'unassessed taxes.' A nearby *equestris* class destroyer running escort to the trade flotilla razed half the dockyards in answer. If there were coffin-nails to peace with the Autumn Lords, the Shang Tzu incident was surely one.

'You're telling me that three nations are basing their foreign policies on the virtue of this girl?' Fisk asked.

'Well, virtue might be too strong a word.' Livia looked disapproving. 'Should the White Rose of Cordova already have been plucked, I imagine it will be overlooked, unless she's with child. Even *that* might be overlooked. But the goals of three nations have focused on the girl. So, yes.'

'And we were delivering her back to the Medieran Embassy in Passasuego, weren't we? But why the hell Passasuego?' I asked. 'It's pretty isolated and halfway to Aegypt.'

Secundus said, 'I think you might have answered your own question.' He straightened his tunic – hemmed in Imperial blue and bearing the crossed pilum brooch on his breast – and moved to the table. He leaned on the wood, hands balled into fists and knuckles down, so that his shoulders stood out, giving him a most warlike aspect. 'The official missives insisted that Isabelle be returned to the nearest Medieran fiefdom. We chose to interpret that loosely.'

I laughed. 'You're putting her as far away from the knightboard as possible.'

'Indeed. Passasuego is the last and most remote holdout of Medieran strength here in the Territories. In recent years, it's been mostly cut off from the rest of Medieran territory, what with the Occidens fifth at New Damnation and the third at Fort Brust.'

'Not to mention our shipyards in Harbor Town,' added Livia. 'The Ruman fleet grows larger every day, though we are still only just a match for Mediera on the high seas.'

'Once she is turned over, they will sign this treaty.' Secundus pulled a sheaf of yellowed parchment and splayed the pages in front of Fisk and me. 'It grants us sole silver mining rights from the Whites all the way to the eastern shore of the Imperial Protectorate. Essentially relinquishing the rights to this land. A land we've already won, in truth, by force of arms. But it would be an official acknowledgement of the loss. All because of a girl.'

I whistled.

'The Ia-damned idiot,' Fisk said. I wondered if he was cursing Banty or himself. 'Hard to believe you let her out of her room.'

Livia blinked, and Carnelia said, 'She was *not* a prisoner!'

Beleth, who had been sitting silently, listening intently and sipping his claret, said, 'The most important thing in the world right now is recovering the girl. If the silver rights are lost ...'

'You won't be summoning many *daemons* this year, will you? No more mechanized baggage trains, or steamers. No fancy lights or hot water on the *Cornelian*,' I said.

'No. You miss the point. Silver will continue to be mined. It's the key to our infernal industry. The nations of the world won't give up the infernal combustion Ruman engineers have been spreading for the last century. The price of silver will go up for us, and the College of Engineers and Augurs will mandate a spike in the price of our work. Unfortunate, but necessary. I imagine the Rumans will be unwilling just to acquiesce with that.'

There was a silence around the table and I watched the *vaettir*. When she blinked, it was like she was moving in amber, so slow, her eyes closing as though she was falling asleep, ineffably bored with the tiny machinations of humans. And *dvergar*.

'You are right. If Isabelle cannot be recovered,' said Livia, glancing from Beleth to Fisk then me, 'there will be war.'

FIFTEEN

FIVE DAYS AFTER setting out in pursuit of Isabelle and Banty I returned to the *Cornelian* on a bedraggled Bess, hoping that Fisk proved successful in his hunt. I had made for Pilgrimage and lodged there for a night. I was not harried by *vaettir* or beast but there were times under the blank face of sky when my heart felt it would seize up, caught with fear. Every bird on the wing, leaping buck or doe, every lonely tree held intimations of *vaettir*. Yet none assailed me.

The next day, Bess was much rested and we rode hard for the Big Rill and the *Cornelian*.

When we came into sight of the boat, Bess hawed and picked up her pace. The boat hadn't steamed any further upstream. A bitter cold had filled the sky and settled about the *Cornelian* like a shroud, bringing with it heavy snows.

Two legionaries called for identification through the flurry of snow, and I gave it. In my absence, the legionaries had constructed a windbreak for the animals and a corral to keep them. The ponies huddled together in the cold air, steaming.

The two legionaries were wary and tense, huddled against the weather and watching the plains with hard eyes, carbines in hand.

'Stretchers sighted?' I asked.

One of the men – I recognized him from the auroch hunt – shook his head but didn't look at me, keeping his eyes on the horizon. What he could see of it.

'How are things on the *Cornelian*?'

'She ain't et no one else.'

'Who?'

'The elf.'

'What?!'

'Pilinus came up missing on watch. Found some scraps of clothing and a mess of blood.'

'On the boat?'

'Naw,' the legionary said. 'Shore.'

'Well, how could she have eaten him? She's bound and trapped on the ship.'

'Might be so. Might be ain't. Them patricians seem mighty friendly with it. Maybe she's their tame devil.'

'What's your name, soldier?'

'Ain't my job to answer to no dwarf.'

'You were at the hunt, were you not?'

Finally, the man looked at me. He nodded slowly.

'You saw what happened to the highborn lad. You drank at his funeral.'

He remained still, staring at me. His face was wrapped with a scarf and the hood of his paenula was up, so he looked halfway like some far Bedoun raider from a story book or mural.

'They do not love the *vaettir*. Understand? If anything, she's held as hostage for protection.'

'There's talk that she'll draw more of 'em. She should be gutted and left for the coyotes.'

'I can't argue with you there.'

He turned back to the plains, searching.

The edges of the Big Rill were beginning to freeze, despite the current. Once I'd rubbed down Bess and draped her in a woollen blanket to keep the bitter cold at bay, a lascar broke ice and ferried me over to the *Cornelian* in a johnboat. On the *Cornelian* the filigreed woodwork of the galleries was rimed in frost.

Cimbri escorted me to the private triclinium where they'd questioned me after Agrippina's outburst. A tight, close room – though well appointed. The table was laden with crystal decanters. Lupina stared disapprovingly, her arms crossed and her hair pulled back severely from her pale face, as I helped myself to some cheese, bread, and a tumbler of whiskey, and put my arse to the fire and breathed into my glass, glad for the warmth of the room.

Cornelius himself was there, lolling on a divan, his good leg propped up. Livia and Carnelia wore their hair in artful messes, still in mourning, dressed in black to appease Gnaeus' spirit as he came before the Pater Dis.

The Cornelian clan had received a dramatic lesson on life in the Hardscrabble Territories. Short a son, deprived of the better portion of a leg. And possibly misplaced a heart.

Secundus seemed older now, the weight of becoming heir settling upon him more like a yoke than a mantle, lines of worry etched into the corners of his eyes. Carnelia seemed transparent, a ghost of her former self, and couldn't manage a sneer as she looked upon me. Livia clasped her hands tightly together.

'What news?' Secundus asked.

I told them what had happened, Bess faltering, Fisk's risky path through the winter Salt Flats.

Secundus looked tense, but nodded. Livia's expression became distressed.

'If there's anyone who can track Banty and get back the girl, it's Fisk.'

They nodded, not looking happy.

'We need your help, Mr Ilys,' stated Secundus.

'Of course. At your service.'

'We need to know more about the *vaettir*. Captain Skraeling fears we'll be frozen on the Big Rill for the winter, still some seventy miles south of Passasuego. Which means, unless we want to lose the *Cornelian* to the stretchers this winter, she'll have to remain staffed and defended.' He paused. 'And it gets pretty cold come Winter's Heart.'

'Yep. Damn cold. But she's *daemonfired*, ain't she? What you need most is meat. Meat and staples.' I drank the whiskey, set down the glass in front of Lupina. Cornelius nodded to her, and she refilled my glass with a scowl.

'Let's get down to brass tacks, Mr Ilys,' Cornelius said. Strangely, he wasn't drunk. Without the slurring and tottering, he was quite an intense man. 'You can speak the creature's language. We want to put some questions to her.'

I have no love lost for the indigenes, but I didn't like the way that sounded.

I nodded my understanding, which Cornelius took for agreement.

'You're a credit to your race, Mr Ilys. Have some more whiskey. Fetch food.' Lupina jumped at her master's voice. 'Beleth will conduct the interrogation with the assistance of Miss Decius. You will be at their disposal.'

'When're we gonna have this rodeo?'

'I imagine you'd like to rest. Is tomorrow too soon?'

'Just fine.'

'I've taken the liberty of arranging a room here on the *Cornelian* for you. Cimbri has covered your duties as scout, and we've sent a rider to Marcellus in New Damnation requesting replacements for you and Fisk.' He spoke as a man used to being in charge. So different from the sodden patrician we'd known before.

He stopped, peered at me. 'This pistolero will retrieve Isabelle? You are sure?'

I swallowed. 'Can't be sure of anything in this world, Mr Cornelius. But if anyone can, it's Fisk.'

'I hope so. For his sake,' he said, and he gave Livia a considered look.

I think I liked the Senator more when he was drunk.

SIXTEEN

I T'S STRANGE SLEEPING on a steamer. My dreams were liquid and the phantom ground never remained still, even when I saw myself on a mountainside beneath a drunken sky, climbing back to my mother's workshop. The mountain gambels hid stretchers, and legionaries bore a black body through the trees to be fed to a massive fire, *daemons* prancing amidst the flames. With great horror I realized I was trapped in the centre of an *orbis argenta*, captive and burning with the touch of silver.

When I woke, I found a tray of food and a note.

Meet us in the great room, hora secunda – Beleth

The food was plain, if plentiful, and accompanied by strong ale, which did much to settle my nerves about the proposed interrogation.

In the great room, Cimbri, Beleth, Samantha, and Secundus waited in front of Agrippina, flanked by shotgun-toting legionaries.

'We should strip it,' said Samantha.

'Strip it? How do you suggest we do that?' Cimbri replied, working a cheroot in his teeth.

'It's chained to the floor. Not like it'll hop up and dance a jig,' said Samantha.

Secundus put his hands on his hips and considered. 'Get two more legionaries in here, would you, Cimbri?'

Cimbri tromped off and returned with two additional soldiers.

'You seem fearful of it, Secundus,' Beleth said.

'You haven't seen the *vaettir* in action like I have,' he replied. 'You'd think a devil-handler like you might have a little reasonable fear yourself.'

'Fear is a taint that corrupts resolution, Secundus. In my profession, it is a liability.'

I cleared my throat. 'In my line of business, it's a necessity.'

'Ah, Mr Ilys. Glad you're here. Tell the creature to lie down on the ground, face down.'

In *dvergar* I told the stretcher to get down.

She remained sitting, cross-legged. I couldn't be sure she even registered our presence. Maybe we *did* resemble flies to her.

'Ma'am, I suggest you get on the floor.' It had been a long while since I'd thought in *dvergar* and there was calmness there – in the cadence and rhythms of the words from my mother's people – a feeling I'd long forgotten. For an instant I remembered Mam calling me to dinner, her voice high-pitched and irritated because I was so late.

Agrippina remained still.

Beleth said gleefully, 'This promises to be fun! Samantha? The brand?'

On the great table was a canvas kit, four feet long. Samantha opened it, revealing tarnished metal rods, skewers with leather-wrapped hafts. And what looked suspiciously like cattle brands.

'The *dolor* glyph, Samantha, I should think.' Samantha withdrew one of the brands and handed it to him, haft first.

A legionary went to the wall and cranked a handle. The wicker-work cage lifted, and Agrippina was free of the holly mesh. Beleth smiled and without ceremony jabbed the glyph into the *vaettir*'s stomach.

She hissed an insectile sound, thrashing, cringing away from the point of contact with the glyph as much as her bindings would allow. Which wasn't much.

'Have the Gossip's Bridle ready, Sam.'

Samantha withdrew a metal contraption, steel with a leather harness.

Beleth nodded at the legionary, who raised his shotgun and trained it on Agrippina. 'Go ahead.'

Samantha, with steady hands, slipped the bridle over the *vaettir*'s face and then shoved her onto her side. The silver-threaded chain clanked and drew tight; Agrippina's good arm straightened and she rolled onto her back.

The legionary, keeping his shotgun pointed at her face, stepped hard on the stretcher's handless arm.

Her face resumed the blank stare, as though whatever intelligence living behind her eyes had fled far away and what was left was pure resistance.

Beleth chuckled. 'This *will* be fun. It'll be obstinate, I believe.'

Samantha looked at him with curiosity.

He blinked and said, 'I've been coercing and suborning *daemons*, from *imps* to *archdaemons*, for the last thirty years.' He swung the brand and placed its end on Agrippina's stump. Her arm jumped and twisted and smoked, but the legionary's boot kept it in place. 'This damned wog should present no problem. It just needs softening up.'

I looked at the engineer. A short man, a soft man, doughy around the middle. Delicate hands. Nicely dressed in a tweed suit with a watch fob running into a vest pocket. Groomed whiskers, slicked hair thinning on top.

A gentleman.

Not a patrician, but one of the new class of equites who'd risen far on ability, intellect. You see them in New Damnation and Harbor Town, these bright, avaricious men, faithless and sharp and rich – on their way to market or counting houses. Men of industry, men of intelligence.

I'm not sure they don't scare me more than the *vaettir*.

The stretchers now, they're inscrutable, opaque, and beyond the ken of man. Some ways, they're like the bear, the shoal auroch, the mountain lion, the killing frost. They have desires, but they are natural, the instinctive habits of their species. But Beleth? He was driven solely by ambition and appetite.

'Secundus, have I ever told you of my time among the Autumn Lords? I was young, and my master had taken up rooms in the Howling Quarter in the city of Kwanti. We would spend the days in the great libraries, among the scrolls and collected knowledge of three thousand years of Kithai civilization.'

Secundus shook his head, wary yet polite.

'The Autumn Lords don't look at the infernal the way we do. The Tchinee, in general, see things different from us Rumans. In some ways they are hopelessly backward. In others, you'd be surprised at their insight. *Daemons* are considered raw forces to be harnessed, thought to be without malevolence. Or beneficence.' He moved to the kit and picked up a particularly jagged and evil-looking blade. It was serrated and long and possessed of a deep tarnished patina. He thumbed the edge, whistled. 'But *we* know better. Do we not, Samantha?'

Her moon-shaped face displayed no emotion, neither excitement nor disgust. I hoped mine remained equally inscrutable. For a long moment, we all focused on Beleth and that knife.

Under Beleth's direction, the legionaries manoeuvred the *vaettir* onto a wide sluice-board fitted with various hasps and straps. They swiftly bound Agrippina to the board and then refastened the silver-threaded chains to it. With a grunt, they lifted the whole contraption and placed it on the long dining table, underneath *daemonlight* fixtures. Trussed up like a hog, she was. And Beleth's eyes shone like a butcher's.

'Now the thing is in position, please remove the Gossip's Bridle. She'll need to be able to speak. To cry out.'

Samantha approached the *vaettir*'s head, unclasped the buckle to the evil looking mask, and stepped back with remarkable swiftness once the bridle was in hand. Beleth withdrew a thick leather strap, whipped it over Agrippina's head, and pulled it taut so that the *vaettir*'s head was flush against the sluice-board.

'Remarkable constitutions, these elves. They can take as much pain as a corporeal *inferis* or *daemon*.' He tsked, and moved to stand above the *vaettir*. 'I learned many things, though, in far Tchinee. Not just their curious opinions on *daemons*. An elder August One took my master into his confidence, and it was at his hands that we became initiates into the art of Lingchi, which means "slow slicing".' He bent, pinched the *vaettir*'s ear between thumb and index finger, and drew the knife down its length, a light, shallow cut. 'The Autumn Lords, and all of the Tchinee, have such artful names for everything. *Daemonwork* they call "Fire Gardening". Gravedigging is "gatekeeping". But Lingchi is called "Death by A Thousand Cuts". For the Tchinee, Lingchi destroys their afterlife … it doesn't preclude it, but they enter their heaven with their rich integument of flesh corrupted and flayed. The thousand cuts destroy their souls as well as their bodies.' He patted the *vaettir*'s cheek. She snapped at him. He jerked his hand back faster than I would have thought possible, given his podge. It seemed the prospect of bloodshed made him spry. Agrippina blinked slowly, and her lips pulled back to reveal jagged, triangular teeth. 'Yes, my dear. Your deathless flesh shall see such pain – a thousand cuts is only a small taste of what I shall visit upon you. And that was just the first.'

He looked at me and waved the knife in my direction, beckoning me to move closer. I did, reluctantly.

'Ask her where her kind sleep.' He kneeled and began cutting away her clothing.

'Where they sleep?'

'Yes, Mr Ilys? Where they sleep.'

I put the question to her in *dvergar*.

She remained unmoving and silent. Beleth had cut away her clothes and now she lay before us, naked and pale, a foreign creature splayed before captors, her arms stretched away from her body, her legs parted.

They were beautiful, the *vaettir*. Her skin shone milk white and unblemished except for the mark on her stomach and stump where the *dolor* glyph had burned her. Blood oozed from her pointed ear. She had high, small breasts, each tipped by a rose-colored nipple. Her sex was tufted with white hair, and once she was totally bare I watched the legionaries' reaction to her body so I wouldn't have to think about my own. They shifted their weight and gripped their weapons tighter. There was magnetism there, even for me, and I could see how the rumour of the *vaettir* whore in New Damnation could have gotten its start.

Beleth made a long, slow cut on the palm of her good hand in parody of the wedding wound, the nuptis sectum. Not very deep but deep enough.

'Repeat the question, Mr Ilys.'

I did. Silence.

He smiled and chuckled in the back of his throat. It was a sound I was to become all too familiar with. And one I soon wished to never hear again.

He instructed a legionary to hold her head, grabbed her upper lip, and ran the knife point across the length of the soft tissue. It split and poured blood.

'It's important, during Lingchi, to alternate focus from the sensitive areas to those with less sensitivity. Should you focus too much on only the hyper-sensory areas – the lips, the fingers, the pubis – that pain will block out the rest of the injuries.'

I shuddered. Ia save me from the hands of gentlemen.

There weren't a thousands cuts, not that day. But many more than I'd like to think about. By the time we were through, Agrippina looked like a blood covered statue. Immobile and silent and covered in bloody rivulets. The sluice-board gutters were a thick, crimson-clotted mess.

Secundus and Cimbri, giving me guilty glances, had left after the first few wounds began to flow freely.

Eventually, it was just Beleth, Samantha, four legionaries, and me. Beleth instructed me to keep asking the same questions, going back and forth between, 'Where do your kind sleep?' and 'Where is your home?' And one other. 'Have you seen the great wyrms?'

Ia help us, the Senator must want another hunt.

Agrippina answered nothing.

When we neared the end of the day, and Beleth had begun exploring her privates with the knife – something I wish I could scour from my mind's eye with lye – he looked up at me from his ghoulish crouch above her and with a grin he said, 'Ask it when it was born.'

Holding back my gorge, I said, '*Drae gnell vae ferth*?' which translates loosely into 'When/where did you come forth?' which is the *dvergar* way of asking birth, or parentage, or origin. A common phrase.

This question, she answered.

'*Ya gnell vis teine!* Vis teine!'

And then her mouth opened and closed, swimming in blood, and a sound came from the ruin of her chest up and out past flayed lips. It was a cough, a bark. A strange low-pitched ululation choked with phlegm. A laugh.

Beleth hopped up, knife dripping. 'What did it say?'

'She said—'

'She?' He laughed, making a bright, jolly sound – lively in contrast to the noise coming from the *vaettir*. He pointed to the stretcher, now just a mass of white flesh streaked with red. 'There's no woman there. Don't be coy, dwarf. What did it say?'

He came closer to me and the crimson knife was very near my chest. I looked at its tip. He saw where I was staring, grinned again, and gave two small jabs in jest. ' "Now, sir, before I prick thee." '

What a great comedian, this engineer, quoting from the master wordsmith, Willem Bless, and his play *Our Heavenly War*.

'She ...' I paused as his smile faded. '*It* said, "I came with the fire." '

He raised the bloody knife high, and for a moment I was frightened her words had angered him and he intended to strike me with the already soiled blade. But he just scratched his head with a bloody hand, still holding the knife.

' "I came with the fire"? That's it? Exactly?'

'Yes. It could be said as "I emerged from fire", I guess.'

For a moment, he looked stunned. His face went slack and the fierce intelligence that usually informed his features fled, and he looked just like any well-dressed, ageing man. A butcher. An engraver. A clerk, possibly, or a wheelwright. But Beleth quickly composed himself. His eyebrow arched, and he said, 'Hmm. Interesting. Very interesting.'

I couldn't see it. But I'd have liked to know what surprised him so.

He wiped the blade on the clothes he'd cut from Agrippina and then tossed them in a bin.

'We'll keep her like this. Naked to all eyes.' He returned to the table and replaced the bloody knife. 'A good day's work, all said and done.' He waved his hand, crusted brown to his elbow, at the legionaries. 'Clean up the blood on the floor, on the stretcher. Sponge her off. I'll want a clean … canvas … for tomorrow.' He turned to leave, stopped, and looked back at them. 'Feel free to take any liberties you might want with her body.'

Beleth actually *winked* at the men and then walked from the room. I looked at Samantha, and her face remained blank, waxen. She ignored my stare and followed her master.

Neither of them noticed the looks of absolute horror on the faces of the soldiers.

Later, in my room, I sat on the bed and watched the flickering yellow light of an *imp* batting its tattered wings against the fine silver cage. I felt more worn than after a week of riding in stretcher territory.

I opened the window and let the frigid air in. I wanted a drink but didn't know how to go about getting one on the *Cornelian*, and right then I couldn't move to save my tainted soul.

I don't know how long I sat like that, staring into the wood panelling. Eventually, a soft knock came at the door. I opened it. Livia stood there, holding a bottle.

She said, 'Secundus told me what Beleth is doing to the *vaettir*.' She put the bottle on the writing desk and took my hand in hers. She looked at me, close, but I couldn't meet her eyes. 'You want to tell me about it?'

I shook my head. What was there to say? It's a monster of a world, and we make our way through it as best we can.

She released my hand and poured two glasses of liquor, I don't know what kind. She put the tumbler in my palm and I drank – sweet, fiery liquor I'd never tasted before, amber-coloured, full of spices and the hint of citrus.

When I had finished, she poured me another, patted my shoulder.

'Shoestring,' she said, and I realized this was the first time she'd called me by my nickname. 'I'm sorry for what we've done to you.'

I looked at her, and she stood there, nervous, pale, and beautiful. I realized she truly was sorry. I nodded. She smiled sadly, making the crow's feet at the corners of her eyes crease, and went to the door.

'I'll have Lupina come around, bring food.'

I nodded again, watching the *imp* throw itself against its silver cage. Livia left.

I lay down on my bed and thought about Agrippina for a long time. Eventually I rose, pulled on my boots, pulled on gloves, and put a gilded silver longknife in my belt. I went back to the great hall.

The legionaries guarding Agrippina nodded to me as I entered. She was naked still, and most of the injuries from her interrogation had become angry red scars – a fine lattice-work crisscrossing her face, her breasts, her stomach and legs.

Vaettir heal fast.

Her head pivoted toward me on a long, gimballed neck. Her lips, flaked with dried blood, pulled back to reveal her jagged teeth in a horrible parody of a smile.

I put a gloved hand on the haft of my longknife.

'I can end this for you,' I said in *dvergar* and watched her face. It was like stone, and her watery eyes remained still as a mountain pool untouched by man or wind. 'You say the word, and I'll end it.'

She remained motionless for a long while, staring at me, her eyes like pools gathering light. She glanced at the nearest guard. Then back to me.

'They might not kill me,' I said.

Her smile grew. She moved her shackled arm, and the chains gave a faint rattle.

'That I can't do, ma'am.'

Agrippina opened and snapped shut her mouth like a beaver-trap. Fast. Her teeth clacked together.

'That's what I'm afraid of.' I sighed. 'It will get worse, you know. You're unbowed now. But that man ... he won't let you die before you break.'

She smiled again, her newly healed lips pulling away from teeth.

On my way out, a burly legionary hefting a shotgun said, 'Hey, what'd you say to her? The engineer's ordered us to report all activity.'

'I asked her the same questions we asked today.'

'Huh.' He looked puzzled. 'Why?'

'Thought she might be more talkative without someone cuttin' on her.'

'That was a wash out, then.'

'Bullseye.'

SEVENTEEN

FISK IS STINGY with words. It's in his nature. But when he returned without the girl, carrying another gunshot wound, and accompanied by a fierce-faced, tawny-haired Northman aedile, we didn't need telling to know that there'd be trouble without a full accounting.

Again, we gathered in the small stateroom. The faces of the Cornelian brood, and of Beleth, Samantha and Cimbri, were like stone, mirroring Fisk's, as he told what happened after he left the *Cornelian*. Later, many years later, I passed through Broken Tooth and got the rest of the story from the townsfolk there.

What I heard then was piece-meal. What I know now is still patchwork. Fisk can be as miserly with his words as he wants, gods rest his soul, but it's a story that wants telling. And I am growing old now, and need to tell it.

After my departure, Fisk had ridden on.

He rode North, to the very edge of the Hardscrabble Territories where the land plateaus up to a salt desert and the sky grows brittle, the big black restless beneath him, steady and uncowed by the wind in the moisture-less, freezing air.

Wild shadows – always at the corner of his eye – moved with him. They did not follow me.

The Salt Flats are rippled and rough and specked with strange rock formations that look like huge, gnarled fingers pushing up through the earth, twisted and veined and white with lime. Fisk rode the black, frothed and foaming even in the chill, through the strange protrusions, up a rocky escarpment and back down into a crevasse where he hobbled the horse, withdrew his carbine, and scrambled back up to the escarpment's ridge. He wrapped himself in his oilcoat, took out his pouch of tobacco, and, instead of rolling a cigarette, put a pinch in his lean, hard jaw and worked it into a mash.

Fisk's gaze never stopped roaming.

Through the night he waited, as the moon rose in the crystalline sky and hard pinpricks of stars gleamed and wheeled in the heavens above the gnarled stone fingers. His breath in the cold air came in white plumes. Inside the oilcoat, his body ached from days in the saddle with only a few hours here and there for rest. His thigh itched where the stretcher arrow had transfixed it only a fortnight before.

He waited. The coyotes began yipping in the distance, and the moon, near full, fell westerly in the starlit vault of sky.

Fisk, weary from days on the trail, closed his eyes.

The shadows were almost on top of him when he awoke. The moon was gone, and the land had grown dark. Two impossibly tall figures darted from shadow to shadow, up the escarpment, sticking to the gnarled stone fingers.

Fisk gripped his carbine and waited.

In the starlight, the lead *vaettir*'s hair looked grey, dark. But Fisk knew it was red. Berith. The one who'd shot him on the plains.

Berith crept closer, his long legs propelling him over the earth, toward Fisk's position.

Fisk waited.

Berith paused mid-footfall, almost in parody of a sneak-thief. His face remained in shadow, and Fisk peered hard at the stretcher. The *vaettir* remained still.

The second *vaettir* came forward, and the one Fisk called Berith raised his hand to stop him.

'Oh, shit,' Fisk murmured. He threw off the oilcoat as he rose and began to fire, filling the night air with burning silver, holly, and the stench of brimstone.

He hit Berith twice, once in the chest, and again in the arm. The shots knocked him backward, tumbling over and over, arse over head, down the escarpment.

The other *vaettir* gave a high screech of pure rage and somersaulted forward, hands suddenly holding two wicked-curved longknives, its head wreathed in wild flying hair.

Time stretched like molasses, and Fisk's body thrummed with action. He clenched his teeth and levered another *imp* round into the chamber in a lightning-fast and smooth movement, took aim at the flying *vaettir*, and squeezed the trigger.

At the apex of its leap, it jerked and twisted, rolling in the air. It hit the ground with a heavy thump, scattering loose rock and shale with a dry clatter.

Fisk jumped forward, working the action on the carbine, and put another round in the fallen *vaettir*, still struggling to rise. Again, he fired into the prostrate form. It jerked and twitched. Two steps closer and he put his boot on the stretcher's neck, jammed the carbine's barrel into the *vaettir*'s eye socket, and fired. The stretcher's head distended and went slack, blood and grey bits splattering on the dusty earth.

Carbine held in white-knuckled hands, his chest rising and falling, taking in huge draughts of air, Fisk turned back to where Berith had tumbled.

Berith was nowhere to be seen. Fisk whirled around. At the top of one of the limestone fingers, a shadow crouched, arms stretched out as though to jump. Fisk sighted and fired.

The shadow arced into the air in a blur, flipping backward and screeching a high, angry sound, falling away out of sight. Fisk ran after him, ignoring his arrow-struck leg. He ran among the gnarled white stones, firing at the blur of his adversary as it bounded from stone-top to stone-top, clawed hands scrabbling at rock and whipping through the air.

Berith gave a strange, piercing yelp and dived behind a large formation. Fisk reached the rock and went around the side, gun at the ready, waiting to shoot.

'Ia-damn you, you son of a whore. I must have nailed you,' Fisk said, furious. 'Come on, you bastard.'

Nothing.

Silence stretched out and not even the clatter of shale shifting underfoot sounded above the stir of the Salt Flats.

Fisk turned back to the downed *vaettir*, sprinting, his spurs making bright chinging sounds in the night.

The body was gone.

The dust of more than ten days hung on Fisk when the three highwaymen stepped from the bramblewrack lining the road into Broken Tooth.

The black was beyond exhaustion, shivering in the cold air after so many days on the trail. It nickered at the highwaymen's appearance.

'Long ride, looks like,' the largest of them said. He had jet-black whiskers, dark circles under his eyes, and lean, muscled arms. He hooked his thumbs on his gunbelt.

Fisk cracked a feral smile. The big man was armed, and one of the other two had a pistol, but the last had only a longknife.

'Long trail is right,' Fisk said, waiting. He held the reins loose in one hand, let the other pull back the oilcoat and expose his Hellfire. 'Looking forward to a drink in yonder Broken Tooth.'

'You'll be walking the rest of the way, mister.' The big man's voice sounded like rocks clattering down the mountainside. 'We'll be taking that fine horse and whatever money you've got.'

Fisk laughed once and the smile died on his face. 'Tell you what. Just because I don't feel like wetting the ground with your blood, I got ten denarii for you boys.' He let the reins fall to his saddlehorn and dipped his fingers into a pocket of his trousers, waiting for the big man's move. The black nickered again and shifted underneath him.

The dark-haired man tensed, drawing up his shoulders as though awaiting a blow, and began to draw.

Fisk whipped out his pistol and fired, sending a bright after-image of a winged *daemon* booming into the night. The big man grabbed at his chest, body hitching, with a surprised look on his face. His companion slapped leather and found a matching hole above his heart, burbling his lifeblood out and over his shirt and vest, steaming into the night air. Blood spattered the third man, who had been standing behind them, and he turned and fled before the gunshot pair had begun to fall.

Fisk holstered his pistol and withdrew the carbine. He levered a round into the chamber, raised the gun to his shoulder, and sighted the fleeing man as he ran. After a few moments, he squeezed the trigger and the fleeing man gave a gurgling yelp and fell.

'Ia-damned fools,' Fisk said, and he kicked his horse into movement toward the lights of Broken Tooth.

EIGHTEEN

F ISK FLICKED HIS cigarette into the street, turned away from
the stables and walked to where the sounds of laughing men
and clanking glasses grew louder. An out-of-tune piano filtered
through the sounds of the saloon. The scent of wood smoke hung
low and fragrant in the frigid air, and he could feel the warmth of
unwashed bodies and a large fire coming from the building with
a weathered and worn sign proclaiming it a saloon with rooms to
let, under the proprietorship of one Ruby.

He pushed open the doors and the noise died down but didn't
cease as the patrons turned to stare. A gust of cold air pushed past
Fisk into the warm saloon, and some of the denizens shivered.

He entered the building, saddlebags over his shoulder, carbine
in hand. At the bar, he said, 'Whiskey. Leave the bottle. And steak.
Bloody.'

The bartender, a young, hard-faced *dvergar* woman, said, 'Ain't
got no steak. There's stew. Maybe a duck.'

'Duck, then. Meat. Cheese. Whatever you got.' He dug in his
pocket for some of the money Cimbri gave him before he left the
Cornelian. 'A room. A bath.' He tossed an aureus on to the deeply
stained wood of the bar. The gold coin spun, glinting in the light
from the lanterns and hearthfire. The bartender's eyes grew wide,

and she snatched it up, bit it, and then tucked it away into her apron.

'I figure that should cover me and more.'

She retrieved a brown earthen bottle and a dark, rough ceramic cup and placed them in front of him. He pulled the cork with his teeth, spat it on the bar, poured a measure and knocked it back.

'Keep the change, ma'am.'

The bartender nodded and began mopping at the counter with a dirty rag. Fisk lifted his rifle and placed his saddlebags on the counter, looked at the bartender. Wordlessly, she took them from him and placed them behind the bar. He poured another drink and dumped it down his throat, squinting his eyes as it burned.

'There was a couple came through here before me. I was supposed to be meeting them. Young man, pretty girl. They'd have been tired.'

'Ain't seen 'em. No one through here 'cept prospectors and cartographers. And the painter.'

'The painter?'

'Some shithouse-rat crazy painter, wanting to document life out on the plains.'

'Damnation! – the man must be addled.'

'He's fucked up, that's for sure.'

'Obliged if you let me know when they get here.'

'Didn't get your name.'

'The name's Fisk.'

For a while, he just stood there at the bar, slowly pouring small amounts of whiskey into the ceramic cup, inhaling sharply after he drank each shot. The bartender brought out a plate with half a duck, swimming in grease, some potatoes and a hunk of dark, grainy bread. He took the plate into the dining area and, finding no tables empty, simply sat down at an occupied one and began to eat.

'Can't you see we're talkin' here?' A fat man in overalls and a threadbare coat said, bristling. The other man at the table raised his eyebrows.

Fisk poured some whiskey into the glass in front of the fat man. 'Happy birthday,' Fisk said, waiting until the man raised his cup and drank before settling into his meal.

Fisk ate slowly, his lean stubbled cheeks working hard as he chewed away, until the duck was gone. He soaked the fat into the bread and ate that with the potatoes. After a while, the fat man and his companion continued their conversation.

'Coming through from Fort Brust, maybe we can get on at Bonaventure.'

'Might be. I served as a supply aedile during the first expansion, when them beaners were a'raiding.'

'Think they'll run the rails through Broken Tooth?'

'Might be. We're close to the Snake so they can take on water. And it's a straight shot to Passasuego, heading west.'

'This fucking town could sure use it.'

The fat man nodded his head and focused on his drink. 'Hard to believe they've got a monster pushing them wheels.'

'Hell, they're Rumans – they'd strap their mothers to an axle if they thought they could move goods.'

Fisk paused eating and said, 'That's for damned sure.'

The men went silent.

When Fisk was through, the plate scraped clean except for a pile of duck bones, he poured the fat man another drink. He followed that by pouring one for his friend, and leaned back from the table, his own cup in hand.

'Let me ask you a question, now that we're all chummy,' Fisk said. He knocked back his whiskey and continued, 'You seen a young man, dark hair, probably dusty and cold from a long haul on the trail? He might be in a Ruman cavalry outfit. But he'd be packing Hellfire.' Hellfire pistols were expensive and Fisk looked pointedly at the fat man's bare waist. He sipped his whiskey. 'He'd have a young dark girl with him, Medieran. Long hair, brown eyes? Pretty?'

'You a bounty hunter?'

'You could say that.'

'Let's have some more of that whiskey so I can collect my memory.'

The man had two glasses before he admitted he had not seen the pair.

Fisk stood up, holding the bottle. 'Gentlemen, thank you for the company. You see a pair matching that description, and I'll stand you to more than just a couple of drinks.'

There was an upright-piano player, a thin, jaundiced Gallish man, drunkenly playing and begging for tips and drinks in a lilting, slurry accent. Fisk, warm and loose now that he'd eaten and most of the whiskey had made its way inside of him, ignored his natural distaste of Galls and strolled across the room, spurs making bright sounds in the barroom.

He stood by the player, rested his elbow on the piano top. The piano-player looked up at him.

'You know "The White Rose of Cordova"?'

The men spread his index finger and thumb down the length of his moustache, plastering it to his bloodless upper lip. 'Of course, monsieur. I know many popular songs.'

Fisk flipped a sesterius at the man. He snatched it out of the air, smiling.

'Very generous, sir.'

'Play that every half-hour. Starting now.'

'I will, kind sir.'

'Let's hear it.'

The piano player worked through the intro of the song and began singing the words in a warbling voice:

'*A stone wall, high and proud,*
Surrounds the garden grounds ...'

Fisk stared at the common room, watching the tables of threadbare men, drinking everything they could afford in hopes of forgetting their pains and incessant labours. A hard life, out on the plains, here in the Hardscrabble Territories.

No one looked up, no one noticed Fisk watching. A couple of trampled, run-down whores worked a table of men playing cards.

His smoke hadn't chased out any vermin.

Fisk went to the bartender, bought another bottle, took a drink, and asked, 'You got an aedile in this town?'

'He's a Northman, so he fancies himself a sheriff. Name's Reeve.'

'A sheriff? Like a chieftain or something?'

'Somewhat. He wears a hand-forged Northstar brooch on his chest, like the rest of them star-worshipping pagans.'

'Damnation, how'd he get appointed?'

'Word is he saved a nobleborn in a skirmish against the bean-ers,' she said, covering her mouth as she said the last word. 'The patrician had some pull with the governor.'

'Cornelius?'

'Shit, no. Marcellus.'

'Marcellus ain't the governor.'

'Hell he ain't.'

'Marcellus is a legate.'

'Same damned thing.'

'Right,' Fisk said, shrugging at the woman's ignorance. 'Where's he at?'

She chucked her head at the front door. 'He'll be down the

street at the jail, sleeping, most like. Either that or at the whore-house.'

Fisk thanked her, retrieved his carbine, and went back into the cold.

Lucious Reeve was asleep in a hammock, cradling a bottle, when Fisk entered the jail. The *daemonfire* lighting – a luxury in a town such as Broken Tooth – showed three small cells, the largest acting as an office for the aedile with two benches near the barred windows, and a desk littered with papers.

Fisk strode to the desk, his spurs ringing in the close quarters, and rifled through the papers. Mostly edicts and policy changes from Fort Brust or New Damnation. Some signed by Marcellus and others by Lucullus the Younger.

Reeve stirred, shifted, and began snoring.

Fisk approached the cell, grabbed the iron door, and swung it shut with a clatter. Reeve shot up, fumbling for his Hellfire.

'What in the blazes?' He nearly flipped the hammock trying to get out, gun in hand. 'What the hell ye think yer doing?'

Fisk looked at the man, now behind bars. 'I thought I was looking for an aedile. Instead I found a sot, napping.' He sucked his teeth and looked around the jail. 'You know where I can find aedile Reeve?'

'Stand a'fore ye.' He tapped a tin star affixed to his chest. 'I'm sheriff in these parts.'

'Huh. The dwarf at the bar said you fancied yourself a chieftain.'

The man's face purpled, and his thick moustache twitched. 'Ain't no chieftain, citizen. Sheriff's the lawman in the Gaellands shires, blessed by the stars.'

'This here's the Hardscrabble Territories.'

'Same stars overhead.'

Fisk opened the cell door, and motioned the man to exit.

Reeve holstered his pistol, uncorked the bottle and took a swig. 'So, what's so Ia-damned important that ye had to rouse me from my winter's nap?'

'I'm on orders from Senator Cornelius, the governor.' Fisk withdrew a silver eagle from his vest pocket.

Reeve's eyes widened. 'A centurion, then.'

'Acting.' Fisk held out his hand.

Instead of taking it, Reeve slapped the bottle into his palm. 'It's mescal, from the maguey.'

Fisk unstoppered the bottle, took a long pull, inhaled sharply, then said, 'Passing acquainted. Looking for a couple. A boy – a man who ran off with a person of importance.'

'Person of importance?'

'Imperial importance.'

'Well, what do ye want from me?'

'You seen anyone like that?'

'A boyish man and a person of Imperial importance? Nay, haven't seen 'em.'

'He's a man, my height, looks a bit like me, maybe half my age. Dark hair. Packing Hellfire. Might be in cavalry uniform, might not. The girl—'

'Girl?' Reeve laughed. 'Ye said person of Imperial importance.'

'Yeah, a girl. Pretty. Long neck, fine features. Olive skin.'

'Sounds dee-lightful.'

'Seen 'em?'

'Nay, I've not.'

Fisk cursed, placed his hand on his Hellfire pistol, shifted his weight – thinking. 'I need you to keep an eye out, then. They'll be riding from the south, Big Rill way.'

'Trouble always comes from Big Rill way. North? There's only the Big Empty.'

'I'm staying at Ruby's. Gonna sleep off the trail.' Fisk took another pull off the bottle and then handed it back to Reeve. 'You'll need to watch the street.'

'Aye. Go, centurion. I can give ye some respite.'

Fisk put out his hand, and the men gripped forearms.

Fisk rolled out of bed and had already levered an *imp* into the chamber of the carbine when the banging on his door stopped.

'It's Reeve.'

'Ia-dammit, man. Come in.'

Reeve entered the small bedroom. It was late, now, very late, but the sounds from the barroom had only increased in the few hours Fisk had been asleep. Fisk tossed the carbine onto the room's single, mussed bed. He sat down on the mattress and pulled on his boots.

'Couple rode in from the south. Followed them to the saloon. Might be the birds you're looking for.'

Fisk rubbed his face. 'Man and woman? Good lookers, the both of them?'

'Cloaked heavily, but they come matching ye description, as far as me old eyes can see.'

'From the south?'

'Aye, just as you said, centurion.'

'Have the piano player do "The White Rose of Cordova" and see how they react. I'll be waiting out front.'

'Ye going through the bar? They'll see ye.'

'There's the window.'

Reeve looked from Fisk, to the window, and back.

'Gods save ye from madness.'

Fisk moved to the dresser, threw water on his face from the basin, towelled off. He grabbed his gunbelt and strapped on the Hellfire. He chucked his head at the door. 'You might want to mosey on back down, don't let them get out of your sight.'

'There was something else.'

'Something else?'

'Aye. The birds rode in and made a beeline for Ruby's. I'm on watch in the shadows of the mercantile porch. Once they were inside, I hung back, just to let them get a'settled.'

Fisk withdrew a pistol from the holster, emptied the *imp* rounds into his hand, and ran a calloused thumb over each warding. He thumbed the rounds back into the pistol's fixed cylinder. His hands moved quickly, making short work of both guns.

'I caught it only from the corner of me eye. A blur.' Reeve shook his head as though clearing it. 'Like a spirit following behind the pair. Couldn't get a bead on it.'

'Big thing. Moving fast?'

'Aye. Fast and tall, it was.'

Fisk stood looking out the window, cursing, rolling the words in his mouth, slow and deliberate. Spitting the words. 'Ia-dammit.'

He went to his saddlebags and withdrew a small box. 'If you've got any extra men, get them now. If they have Hellfire pistols, load up with these.'

'Special rounds?'

Fisk nodded. 'Silver. Holly tipped. Made special by Cornelius' tame engineer.'

The sheriff's eyes widened. 'What're ye saying, man? We facing unbound *daemons* like roam in the Northern Protectorate?'

'Worse. *Vaettir.*'

'Damnation. I thought they remained content to stay in the Whites.' Reeve popped open the box, removed the bullets from his pistol, and replaced them with the holly-tipped rounds, cursing. 'Ye bring trouble with ye, centurion.'

'Seems I've a knack for it.' Fisk levered a round into the carbine, shrugged on his oilcoat. He held his hat in his hands, ran his fingers around the grey brim's edge, and placed it on his head. 'Remember,

"The White Rose of Cordova". Let them see you looking at them. The boy—' He put his boot over the window casement, stopped, and looked back at Reeve. 'The *man*, he's deadly. Stay out of his way. Once he sees me, he won't be focused on the girl as much. That's when you should try to grab her.'

'Let me see that eagle again.'

Fisk withdrew it from his pocket and tossed it to Reeve. 'Keep it until this is over. And if I'm not around to collect it, you can pack it off to Livia Cornelius, daughter of the Senator.'

Reeve had sense enough not to remark on that.

'Ye believe it'll get that bad?'

'There's stretchers about. It's already that bad,' Fisk said, and he disappeared out the window, leaving Reeve holding a still-warm silver eagle in his hand.

NINETEEN

THE NEXT DAY, Beleth had no questions at all for Agrippina. He had only a straight razor, a large, dark tome, a quill, and an oversized inkwell.

We breakfasted in the great room with the *vaettir* looking on. Fried fish, nuts and small brown limes, eggs and pickles, and crusty bread with butter, coffee, brandy. I must admit, I did not do the victuals honour. I couldn't manage to eat while Agrippina watched from her cage.

'You do not approve of me,' Beleth said, popping a bit of fish into his mouth and chewing.

'Wouldn't say that, sir. Ain't my place.'

'Nevertheless, you do not approve.'

'I ain't one to approve or disapprove of anything, sir.'

'Why do you not carry Hellfire, Mr Ilys?'

'Don't need it.'

'Really? You're a cavalryman in service to the Empire in a fierce, untamed land. And you carry no gun.'

'Don't mean I'm unarmed.'

Beleth smiled but it did not touch his eyes. 'I find it peculiar that you don't carry one. Is it due to some pacifistic philosophy?'

I chuckled. 'Like them what the Autumn Lords massacred?'

'Exactly.'

'I'm half-*dvergar*, sir. We're a peaceful people, but we're fine with some bloodshed if there's a reason to it. Defending our own. Protecting ourselves.'

'I see. Then there must be something else.' He cracked a boiled quail egg on the table and carefully peeled it, took a pinch from the salt-well and applied it liberally, and then placed the egg in his mouth and chewed thoughtfully. Swallowed. He had the mechanics of eating down, that's for sure. 'Is it a religious fastidiousness?'

I looked at my plate, and then back at Beleth. 'I was born a *long* time ago, sir, before there was six-gun damnation everywhere. I've made it this far without one. Don't see why I can't live out the rest of my days without having one, either.'

'Damnation? Interesting choice of words. So it *is* a religious fastidiousness. The usage of the infernal is sanctioned by the Emperor himself, as head of the church and high pontifex. As Ia uses the infernal to punish the wicked, so shall we harness its power to drive the interests of the Empire.' He wiped his mouth and threw the napkin onto his plate. 'Nevertheless. This is good. Religious beliefs are mutable and weak in the face of true adversity. Despite all the evidence of the infernal around them, there are non-believers, yet they pray when girded for war. Saints will forget their own teachings when confronted by fleshy temptation. Peaceful idealists will kill when their children are threatened.'

I had the feeling he might have forced those issues a few times in his life. He looked at me, and I'll be damned – it was like I was a specimen to be collected, a butterfly to be pinned to a board or an insect to be judged and catalogued by some natural philosopher. I was less than nothing to this man, just a creature that he now knew more of.

He said, 'So, in the end, you've just not been pushed far enough to take up a gun. A piece of damnation, as you say.'

I stayed quiet but held his gaze until he broke it by pushing away from the table and standing up.

'Let's hope you never are.' He clapped his hands, all business. 'I won't need you much today, as it will be an afternoon of experimentation. However, please remain on hand to ask any question I might want to put to the thing.' He looked at the legionaries guarding Agrippina. 'Gentlemen?'

Once the legionaries had uncaged and bound the *vaettir* appropriately, Beleth approached her still-naked form.

'Hmm. When we are done I will require, from now on, that the beast be washed each morning.'

I don't know what was more frightening to me, the implication of his words – that this would be an ongoing ordeal for Agrippina and thus myself – or what followed.

'This will be your job, Mr Ilys. Perhaps the intimacy with the thing will give you insight as to its nature.'

With that, he flicked open the straight razor, took a strop to it, and whisked it back and forth until it met with some fantastical ideal of sharpness that existed only in Beleth's own mind.

'Make sure it's bound well, gentlemen. Today I get up close and personal with the beast.'

And that he did. But he started slow.

When the blood was flowing well enough to collect, he unstoppered the inkwell. He filled the rest of it, catching the drops streaking down her arm and dripping from her fingers.

Replacing the lid, he held the bottle tight and shook it vigorously, mixing the blood with the ink. He turned to the massive black book, opened it, and removed some loose scraps of paper from between the pages.

He spent a good long while trimming his quill with a pocket-knife. Looking at no one, he said, 'It's important to have an extra large reservoir cut into the quill when dealing with blood.

Coagulation, you know. So, the ratio of blood to ink needs to be around one to two.' He thumbed the quill's nib and then blew on it. 'That'll do nicely, I think.'

He dipped it into the blood-ink mixture and scratched at a scrap of paper. 'Yes, that will do quite nicely. Let's see how well it works on flesh. Mr Ilys, if you'll be so kind as to bring the *Opusculus Noctis* over here so I might view it as I work?'

I don't know about being kind, but I did what he said, Ia save my soul. I did what he said.

He spent a long time that day painting glyphs on Agrippina's skin. She remained as still as stone. At one point, she closed her eyes and I saw them move slightly under her lids, as though she were dreaming.

The wounds he'd made on her to get the blood had healed by the late afternoon, and her body was an intricate map of glyphs and indecipherable marks.

Beleth called for brandy, and when no one responded he looked at me and said, 'Is your hearing deficient?'

I nearly lost my temper. I'm not too proud to admit it. But I kept my tongue. So I'm still breathing today.

I poured him a brandy, which he drank as he smoked.

'I've worked through the Vesalian lexicon, each glyph, and none had any effect,' he mused aloud. He sipped his brandy, puffed his cigar, and blew smoke rings at the ceiling of the stateroom. 'I'm wondering if I should try to make some symbolic binding between the *primori orbis* and the body of the *vaettir* and then complete the glyph …' He rubbed his chin, holding the cigar in his mouth. Then he waved his hand at no one. 'No matter. We have all the time in the world for experimentation.'

Later, after he'd left, and we'd moved her back to the centre of the *orbis argenta*, I washed the blood and drawings from her body with warm soapy water and a rag. Around her forehead, throat, elbows, knees, and ankles were strong leather straps holding her tight against the wooden sluice-board, now soiled with black blood and the ink mixture. Two legionaries watched with troubled expressions.

I said, 'Do you eat? Have they fed you?'

Agrippina kept her eyes closed. I cleaned her chest and moved down her arm. The blood was tacky in places and took some scrubbing to get off. They're tall, the *vaettir*, and I imagine I'm the only living person in the world who's ever been as close to a live one in the whole history of stretcher, man, and *dvergar*.

'*Do* you eat?'

Her eyes shot open and fixed on me. In them I saw pain, hatred. Which only made sense. Would she ever capitulate?

She opened her mouth as though to speak, and I noticed how cracked her lips were. I went to the table and retrieved a pitcher of fresh water and poured her a glass. When I tipped the glass to her mouth, water spilled over her lips and down her chin, but she worked a thick tongue around in her mouth, moistening it. After a moment, she accepted some more, swallowing heavily and panting afterward like a massive dog.

'Do you eat?' I asked again, keeping my voice hushed.

I went back to the table and made a small plate of fish, bread, eggs. I poured two tumblers of brandy. Placing it all on a small tray, I brought it back to Agrippina, laid out flat on the sluiceway in the centre of the stateroom's parquet flooring, at the exact centre of the *orbis argenta* burnt into the tiles.

I took a piece of bread, buttered it, and brought it to her lips, pushing it into her mouth.

She closed her lips, worked her jaws, and then spat the saliva-softened bread into my face.

The legionaries erupted into laughter, elbowing each other.

I had children once. You didn't know that, did you? I spent thirty years raising a family: a boy, two daughters. I had a wife who loved me, but I was young and stupid and had the wanderlust. When our oldest was born, something went wrong and she was never whole. It was as though two children lived within the same skin. One was kind and loving, the other impulsive and mean-spirited. I've had food spat in my face before.

When you're bound by love, you can work through it.

But this thing wasn't my child. I wiped off the gobbet of moistened bread hanging in my whiskers. I knocked back first the brandy I had poured for her, and then the brandy I had poured for myself.

I dumped the bucket of bloody water on Agrippina, then left, looking for Cimbri and a boat to the eastern shore. I needed to ride.

TWENTY

WHILE FISK WAS sleeping, it had begun to snow. The cold had settled in and made brittle the mud of Broken Tooth's main street. The wagon ruts and footprints had frozen in hard, treacherous dips and valleys and crunched underneath Fisk's boots as he walked. Snowflakes drifted through the air like bits of eiderdown from a busted pillow, and his breath was crystalline in the early morning air.

Fisk scanned the rooftops and galleys and frozen opaline alleyways for the stretcher. Reeve hadn't been specific, and there could be more than one. There can always be more than one stretcher.

He moved into the street. Other men might have tried to keep their back to a wall, get some cover, but not Fisk. He was as blunt and forward in gunplay as he was in everything else in life, except maybe women. He held the carbine loosely in his big, rawboned hands, and he composed himself, searching for the calm needed for killing.

From inside Ruby's, he heard the first strains of "The White Rose of Cordova", the sad lilting minor of the verse to major lift of the chorus. The sound of the Gallish piano player's voice carried through the desperate wooden slats of the frontier saloon, out into the street, fraught with wood smoke, love, and blood.

'*The virgin bloom is on the white rose.*

Dare I climb that garden wall ...'

There came a clattering commotion from inside, and the doors flew open.

'And when I pluck it at night's close,
Into her breast I'll fall, into her breast I'll fall.'

From inside, someone yelled 'Blazes!' and cursed and two cloaked figures burst into the frigid night, the larger tugging the smaller along by the hand.

He let them get halfway across the street before Fisk called out, 'Mr Bantam! I've come to get the girl.'

Banty hunched his shoulders as though he'd been shot and turned, still holding Isabelle's hand. Banty pushed her behind him, and said, 'Go. Go get the horses.'

She hesitated. Even from where he stood, thirty feet away, Fisk could see the confusion on her face, the doubt and the terror. Maybe the honeymoon wasn't working out as either of them had planned.

'Go!'

Reeve clomped out onto the wooden platform in front of Ruby's, watched the girl flee toward the stables. He walked slowly down the wooden sidewalk, keeping his body facing Banty and his hand tight on the pearl grip of his six-gun until he was behind Banty and moving across the street to the stables.

Banty squared himself and threw his cloak over his shoulder, freeing his gun hand.

'Don't have to come to this, Mr Bantam,' Fisk said, and was surprised to find himself meaning it. Now, when the moment was on him to shoot the boy, he found himself strangely reluctant to do so. 'We take the girl back to the *Cornelian*, and I'm fine with letting you go on your own way. No harm done.'

Banty laughed – a hard, desperate sound. 'You gonna plug me

with that rifle when I turn to leave? Don't look like you'd let me go.'

Fisk dropped the carbine and held up his hands. 'You can just ride away, son,' he said. 'There's too much at stake for us to let the girl run off with the likes of you.'

'Ain't your son, goatfucker.' Banty spat each word.

Fisk tensed, and he eased his oilcoat behind him to better get at his six-gun.

'Hold on. You don't want to leave here in a box.' Fisk's tone was placating.

Banty laughed again, a little wild and jittery around the edges. 'We'll see about that. Ain't like the Ia-damned Senator's gonna let me wander wherever I want if I give her back. Prickly sonofabitch'll send out bounty hunters.' He swallowed. 'And we're lawful wed.' He held up his left hand. A cut crossed his palm, angry and red. The girl, no doubt, would have a matching one.

Fisk nodded. 'Figured as much. Sure you said the vows, took the oath, and gave each other the wedding wound before the *Cornelian* was out of sight. You bedded her soon after. If not before.' He shifted his weight, hand near his six-gun. 'Enough bickering. The girl. I'm taking her back, wedded or no. We ain't going to war just because you played house with a noblewoman. You throw down your piece, I'll let you get a horse and leave.'

Banty telegraphed everything. His shoulders went up, his face scrunched into an ugly, petulant grimace, and he drew. Fast as shit, Fisk told me later. Banty drew and fired.

Before Fisk's hand slapped his pistol-grip, there was a great boom and the phantom image of a *daemon* ghosting the air as something tugged hard at Fisk's shoulder and a piercing heat spread across his chest. Ignoring the pain, Fisk cleared his pistol from the holster, steadied himself, and let loose the Hellfire.

Smoke and brimstone covered the men, each in his own little

cloud of damnation, until the winter wind whipped down the street and ripped the smoke away.

Both men remained standing, but Banty's gun was at his feet and he held his gut in an unmistakable pose. Like some supplicant come before the Emperor, he slowly sank to his knees and looked at the blood on his hands.

Fisk holstered his pistol and approached Banty, who by now had begun to cry, making a high painful keening sound like a coyote in a trap. It held all sorts of pain: the physical agony of the gut shot, the realization that nothing had worked out the way he'd planned, the desperate sting of the loss of the girl, the loss of the world that held her.

Fisk grabbed Banty and eased him into a supine position. The boy's legs weren't working right, and his arms and hands had tremors running through them like an axe-struck tree.

'Oh my,' the boy said, staring. 'Oh my.'

'Shhh, now, Mr Bantam. Shh.' Fisk held the boy's head but turned to the door of the saloon. 'Doctor! We need a doctor out here!' Strange – there were no faces at the door of the saloon watching the gunfight.

A commotion sounded from inside Ruby's, the shuffle of feet, a yell, breaking pots and glassware, the clatter of a chair falling to the floor, the tumble of a body. The doors remained shut but shadows played across the window-front. A man bellowed, another screamed.

Banty hissed in pain, and Fisk turned his attention back to the boy.

'Mam. I want ...' Banty was having trouble breathing then. He spoke in gasps, like a child in his pain. 'I want my mam ...'

'We're gonna patch you up, Mr Bantam.'

'I got you, though,' the boy said, looking at Fisk's shoulder.

'Yep. You sure did. Hold on, now.'

Another scream came from the saloon. There was a bright flash in the small leaded windows, then something heavy slammed into the wall with a thud, and then a terrible screech and more thumps. Another blast of Hellfire.

Silence then except for Banty's crying. It came in short gasps now, his weeping.

'Mam ... I want ...'

'Reeve! Get over here!' Fisk screamed, looking at the stables.

'I want ...'

His words failed. He scrabbled at Fisk's chest with numb, uncoordinated fingers, trying to find something to hold on to, to tether him to life.

The blood was coming hard and fast, pooling in the wound and steaming in the cold air. Snow fell onto the boy's upturned face and quickly melted into the gut wound. Banty's tremors stopped and his arms sagged, losing strength.

He looked up into Fisk's face and Fisk looked back, watching the boy's eyes widen – as though suddenly seeing new plains and vistas open up before him as he topped a rise, sun at his back, on a spring mare. His soul, whatever taint it might have on it, had begun its passage through the shadowlands to await judgement by the Pater Dis – that he be seated in the hall of Ia at his feasting table. Or to be cast into the fiery abyss.

For the boy's sake, I hope Dis held his finger on the scales pointing toward Ia.

Banty exhaled. He didn't draw breath again.

Head bowed, Fisk sat in the centre of the main street for a long while, holding the boy's body. Fisk brought two bloody fingers to Banty's face and closed his eyes.

'Ia-dammit,' he spat.

Dazed, Reeve stumbled across the opening of the main street to where Fisk sat. Reeve bled from a deep, furious gash on his forehead. Blood streamed down the man's face and clotted in black bolls in his tawny beard.

'Came outta nowhere.'

'The stretcher?'

'Aye. Whipped above me like a bat or something, with big pale arms. Snatched at my hair and cut me. Took the girl. I couldn't stop it.' The blood ran into his eyes.

'Ain't this all gone to shit,' Fisk said. He narrowed his eyes, looking at Reeve who was touching his scalp, tentatively. 'Be thankful you still have a head of hair.' He paused. 'Or a head to grow it on.'

Fisk freed himself from Banty's corpse, pushing the body away and unfolding each leg as though the joints were hinges, creaky and frozen stiff with the cold.

'Help me pull the boy out of the street. I won't leave him like this.'

Each man took an arm and began dragging Banty's body to the plank sidewalk that lined the street. When they were through, they arrayed the boy's limbs as best they could and Fisk removed Banty's gunbelt, slinging it over his shoulder.

'After he and the girl came out of Ruby's, there was a commotion inside. Gunshots.'

Reeve's face remained blank. But he said, 'There's a darkness on ye, centurion. It follows ye.'

'Might be, sheriff,' Fisk said. He pulled his pistol, turned the chamber, pulled bullets from his own belt, and thumbed the fresh *imp* rounds into the cylinder.

'Let's check out the damage,' said Fisk, and he chucked his head at the saloon doors.

They turned to go in, but there came a great screech and then a rising sound that was pitched higher than the wind, higher than the thrum and surge of their own heartbeats.

The two men looked up.

Upon the apex of the saloon stood a *vaettir*, long red hair unfurled in the wind.

It made a harsh barking sound, the likes of which neither the Northman nor Fisk had ever heard before. Over its shoulder was slung a dark object. Cloak-wrapped and delicate.

Fisk had his pistol drawn in an instant and took a bead before Reeve even had time to react. But the stretcher leaped, lancing through the air in a blur, landing on a nearby roof and leaping again skyward, not in the least hindered by the bundle on his shoulder. Fisk tracked the creature with his pistol, but did not fire for fear of hitting what, or who, was wrapped in the cloak.

The *vaettir* plunged toward the stable, hit the weathered wooden shingles and rolled, coming to his feet, his teeth blazing in the early morning darkness, sharp and bright.

Snow flurried around him. He hefted the bundle easily. In the wind, the wrappings of what the *vaettir* held came undone, revealing dark hair, an olive-toned cheek.

It was indeed Isabelle.

The stretcher laughed again, that same barking sound they'd heard before. The *vaettir* thrust an arm upward in a fierce, defiant gesture. Victorious and savage, mean and full of mirth, but a familiar gesture all the same.

At first it was hard to tell what the creature held aloft, it was so dwarfed by his massive hand. But when Fisk saw, his stomach sank in his belly and he cursed. He cursed both himself and the gigantic, terrifying *thing* perched on the stable's roof.

The *vaettir* held a severed hand. White as alabaster and bloody at the wrist.

The stretcher flung the hand at the men in the street below, winging it at them as if tossing a bone to a pack of dogs. Then he erupted into the air with a great leap, his garments ruffling with the speed of his passage. He barked his laughter, bounding from rooftop to rooftop down the main street westward, taking the girl with him.

'Ho-lee shit,' Reeve said, blood pouring down his face, into his beard. 'Yonder son of a bitch wants killing. Truly.'

'*Damnation.*' Fisk turned and picked up the severed white hand. 'Help me find a bag for this.'

It was a slaughterhouse, walls painted red, blood splashed across the bar, the bottles, the tables, the rough slats of floor.

While Fisk was slipping out, Berith was slipping in.

The *vaettir* had come in through the rear of the building, using a door facing the scrub and shale and bramblewrack of Broken Tooth, into the relative warmth of Broken Tooth's saloon.

He'd had a blade on him. A big blade, flat steel. There was no way all the heads could have been severed otherwise.

Everyone. The fat man and his companion, the *dvergar* bartender, the whores, the men playing trumps in the corner, the Gallish piano player, the field hands and labourers.

All dead.

They built a pyre. The frontier-chapped, ruddy-faced women came out of their mud-spackled huts to help Fisk and Reeve pile the bodies and their parts in a great heap behind the row of main street buildings.

The few children old enough to understand what had occurred, grieved. The others latched onto their mothers, dazed and scarcely comprehending the news that their fathers and brothers and uncles would never return home.

Fisk found a bucket of pitch in the stable and drenched the planks and wood beneath the bodies.

Reeve chanted words of blessing in a strange northern tongue, holding his hands up to the gunmetal sky and beseeching the old gods, the prodigal ones, for the souls of the dead's protection and their forgiveness.

When it was all done, and the pyre as high as a cottonwood was aflame, Fisk brought Reeve a bottle from the blood-spattered interior of Ruby's, uncorked it, and handed it to the sheriff.

'My new friend, ye carry damnation with ye.' Reeve took a long drink from the bottle. 'What we do in life dictates out afterlife. It's a slow corruption of the soul, this Hellfire we carry. Ye will regret it. And so will I.'

'You sound like my partner.' Fisk took the bottle and drank, staring into the fire. 'You tell me some other way to protect myself without corrupting my soul.'

'I carry it as well, centurion. I don't fault you.'

'Then that's enough Ia-damned talk of damnation.'

'As ye say,' Reeve murmured. A pause, then he declared, 'I'll be coming with ye.'

'You should stay here. These folk need you.'

'They're loading the wagons in the morning and heading to Fort Brust, or so Velda informs me.' He snorted. 'She seemed to think it was my fault.'

'Nothing you could do to stop that stretcher.'

'Aye. So ye say.' He waved a hand at the huddled folk warming their hands at their kinsman's funeral pyre. 'But these people will ne'er trust me again. So, I'll ride with ye tomorrow.'

'You said you reported to Fort Brust.'

'Aye, 'tis true. But yer a centurion.'

Fisk nodded. 'I'll stamp some papers with the eagle before we leave.'

'Thank ye.'

They clasped forearms as they had once before. And drank.

TWENTY-ONE

N<small>O ONE POURED</small> drinks. No one laughed. The Cornelian brood had stared hard at Fisk, waiting for him to begin his story. They had studied him and the wild-haired Northman he had brought with him through the snow to the *Cornelian*.

It had turned bitter cold, and the Big Rill had iced solid at the edges, making it hard for the lascar to ferry the men. Eventually, Skraeling turned the boat and lowered the swing stages in preparation for the winter, bringing the ponies into the hold. The season would be spent far from Passaseugo, out on the plains, beneath the White Mountains. Sharbo and the other hunters had ridden for miles east and found no sign of shoal aurochs, nor geese, nor deer.

Livia tried to smile, but it didn't touch her eyes. Carnelia, sitting in a wide reading chair, was flipping her foot nonchalantly, and chewing a bit of hair. Secundus kept his arms crossed and looked grave. Beleth sat very still, with Samantha and Cimbri behind him.

Cornelius himself was sober and pale, dressed in a clean tunic unblemished by wine or whiskey stains. He tapped a forefinger on the triclinium's table and said, 'Now, if you please, Mr Fisk.'

Fisk told his story, speaking slowly and without embellishment. When he came to Broken Tooth, Reeve interrupted and took up the tale, and then Fisk finished it with the death of Banty and the *vaettir* bounding away with Isabelle.

When he was done, Fisk produced a sack, reached in gingerly, and withdrew a slightly desiccated, severed hand. It was grey and small and smelled of corruption. He placed it lightly on the table.

'It's Isabelle's. Done in retribution for the stretcher out in the stateroom.'

There were gasps and choking sounds. But Beleth said, 'And you are sure this is hers? And how do you know the creature hasn't killed her and then dumped her body?'

Fisk was quiet for a while but his gaze, steady and grave, remained unblinking. 'I don't know that. Always a possibility, I reckon.'

Carnelia, looking wild around the eyes, leaned forward, peered at the hand, and began to cry. 'It *is* hers.'

'How can you be sure?' Cornelius barked. 'How?'

'Just look at it. Think of her eating breakfast, or holding a glass, or writing. It's *hers!*'

Cornelius cursed heavily. 'You, Fisk. You are dismissed. We no longer require your services here. You are hereby ordered to return to Marcellus in New Damn—'

'It occurs to me,' interrupted Beleth, looking keenly at the severed hand, 'that with a little help from our neighbours below,' He put two fingers at either side of his head like horns before continuing, 'Mr Fisk has provided us with the means of discovering Isabelle's – or her corpse's – whereabouts.'

Livia said, 'Speak plain, engineer. What are you talking about?'

He sat back, a sly look spreading across his face like an oil-stain, and raised a finger. 'There are three ways to summon and bind the infernal. One is to raise a *daemon* from Hell and bind it with wards to utilize its power. This is the simplest and safest. Relatively safest.' He took the crystal decanter of port and poured himself a measure, grinning. 'The second is to force a *daemon* into an object.

Give the bound *inferi* a goal – in this case, locating Isabelle – before it can be released.'

'Locating her? What happens when we – er, it – finds her?'

'The binding no longer holds the creature and it is free.'

'Not banished back to Hell?'

'Unfortunately, no.'

'What about the bearer of the item?' I asked.

Beleth tsked. 'Depends. It's possible to fend off a *daemon*. But the bearer is inextricably linked to the object until its goal is acheived. And the object must be part of the person or thing that must be found.'

'Fend off?' Livia asked. 'How would you go about that?'

'First, you'd need a full engineer to perform the necessary ward-work. You'd require some knowledge of how and when the object would be reunited with the infernal vestment. Both of which are unlikely. But it is possible.'

Fisk stood up. 'How long does it take?'

'A matter of a day or so.'

'What do I need to do?'

Miss Livia placed her hand on his arm. 'Is this necessary? Can we not suborn some rank soldier to this task?'

Cornelius looked at his daughter, frowning. 'This man is willing. He wishes to atone for his failure to recover Isabelle.'

'No,' Livia said, and her face looked contorted, as though two emotions warred within her. 'He failed once in reclaiming Isabelle. What's to say he won't fail again?'

Cornelius, Secundus, and Carnelia looked back and forth between Fisk and Livia. Carnelia's eyes widened as she understood. Secundus' gaze softened, and he smiled sadly and then glanced at me. I shrugged my shoulders. What the hell was I supposed to do?

Fisk looked at Livia, and damned if the man's eyes didn't soften too. But he straightened his back and took a deep breath. He stood as tall as he could, undaunted in front of the nobility.

'My name is Hieronymous Cantalus Fiscelion Iulii. I will recover Isabelle or die trying.'

Silence then, until Cornelius began guffawing. He reached for a decanter.

'You're telling us you are the son of the exiled Senator Cantalus?' Cornelius asked.

Fisk nodded, once.

'Well, why should you give a damn about this?' Cornelius posed, drinking a large glass of port. Yet he was suddenly very interested in Fisk. 'Your family is in disgrace, its name damaged beyond repair. You're lucky the Emperor didn't have the Praetorians dash your brains out on the ground when you were an infant.'

'I barely remember Rume, and my father was an arsehole.' He turned, his eyes fixed on Livia. 'But I had a wife once, long ago. And a daughter. We lived out on the plains, in the shadow of the Whites. I—' He stopped and swallowed. Livia's hands trembled. She looked like she wanted to touch him. 'I loved them. We had a life.'

The two stared at each other as though no one else was there.

'We'd see the stretchers moving, but we never had no truck with them. They didn't bother us. They were like phantoms slipping through the grasses and the trees down by the river. Until that Berith came. Until that red-haired son of a bitch came.'

Fisk's Adam's apple moved up and down painfully in his throat. We all watched him. Livia's eyes were as large as pools and nearly as wet.

'At first it was the dog. He killed it and strung it up for us to see.' He breathed deep, his big, rawboned hands clenched.

I can't imagine how hard it must have been for him to reveal all this in front of so many hostile listeners. But he kept on. 'And then it was the livestock. The bastard took my goats and busted down my corral, setting my ponies loose. I'd chase them down, and he'd let me see him. Smiling big on the rise above the valley, all teeth, a gutted goat slung over his shoulder.

'So I took up all my possessions, all the gold and silver I had taken with me when I fled my father, and I rode to New Damnation and bought this six-gun and my carbine from an engineer there. Came back home, ready to kill that son of a bitch.'

Secundus poured some port for Fisk but he waved it away and continued, all the while looking at Livia.

'But he disappeared, for a year or more. And we went back to life as usual and didn't spend any time counting our blessings.' He passed a hand over his eyes, and a weariness settled on him like the snow that blanketed the *Cornelian*. His body shifted and the defiance in him that I knew so well, the hard core of the man that never relented, it was gone. And he just looked hurt, and tired, and full of loss in that infinitesimal shift of his body.

'She was growing, shooting up like a weed, my Kallie. She had hair the colour of sun on wheat and a laugh like a bell. She loved the animals, feeding and watering them.

'I was busting sod behind the mule when Lenora started screaming. And there was Berith, holding Kallie like a porcelain doll. She wasn't crying. She was scared and amazed and confused, but she wasn't crying. I took up my guns but that son of a bitch just stood there, out beyond the corrals, grinning like a devil and holding Kallie in his hands.

'When I came near, he danced away. She started crying then.'

Now Fisk accepted the drink Secundus offered, and knocked it back.

'Ain't much left to say. He ran the way stretchers do, bounding all around. I chased him. For hours. Farther and farther away from the house while Kallie called out for me, crying. I could never get close enough to him to know I wouldn't hit my baby girl when I shot.

'He must have grown bored with the game. He disappeared. I never found her body.' His eyes were too dry, his voice too steady. If only his voice could break, or if he could cry. Ia pity the man who grows so hard. 'We tried to have another, but Lenora had trouble with Kallie to begin with, bleeding and the like—'

He looked dreadful, the hollows of his cheeks deep and his eyes sunken. Every cord on his neck stood out, and his arms were tense. His hair had frosted in the time since he had left to reclaim Isabelle; there was more white than black now.

'I left one morning to hunt and when I returned, she … she was swinging from the rafters. Without Kallie—' He unclenched his hands and finally looked away from Livia, staring at his palms. 'I wasn't enough to make life worthwhile.'

He balled his fists again and stood seething. A more dangerous and pitiable man I've never seen.

'So I will take this Ia-damned hand and do whatever the summoner wants me to do, whatever stain it might leave on my immortal soul. And I'll hunt for Isabelle until I'm dead. Or she is.' He shook his head slowly. 'Can't back out of this, Livia.'

'It's an old wound, Fisk. Can't you—?' She looked at him, her eyes welling, and the rest of the room fell away, her father, her siblings, the engineer. Everyone and everything. And it was just the two of them. 'If you go, I go with you.'

'No.'

'If you can go and bind yourself to that—' She gestured toward the severed hand that remained on the table. The grey thing pointed an accusing finger at Fisk. 'Then I can come too, and there's no man or woman who will stop me.' She looked around the room with such a fierce stare not even her father dared speak. 'And Isabelle will need me when we find her.'

No one said anything.

The silence drew out and I could see Secundus frowning. I almost felt pity for the boy, who now had to put duty to family before his own inclinations. Cornelius looked at his daughter with surprisingly moist eyes, wanting to say something but not finding the words.

Eventually Lupina entered carrying a half-bottle of whiskey – winter rations were in effect – and filled small glasses for everyone.

'What happened to your father after he left Rume, Hieronymous?' Cornelius asked, voice catching. He looked a bit embarrassed at the hitch in his throat, so he busied his hands trimming a cigar and lighting it from a match.

Fisk shifted again, slumped, and then sat heavily in one of the cushioned chairs in the small stateroom. 'He got rich, trading with the Medierans, living in New Cartena.' Fisk looked washed-out, exhausted. 'After his exile, he didn't care much for Ruman influence.'

'Why should he? He managed to flee Rume with three talents of gold.' Cornelius gave a sallow grin. 'The Emperor was absolutely *furious*.'

'Sounds like you enjoyed the scene.'

'Of course. Every senator in Rume loves it when Tamberlaine gets egg on his face, the old goat.'

'How's that?'

Secundus said, 'While the Emperor is feared and obeyed, there's not a senator, knight, or man in the cursus honorem who hasn't found himself poorer due to Imperial edicts.'

Carnelia sniped, 'He's a greedy old lech, Tamberlaine. Thank Ia he adopted Marcus Claudius, who's reputed to be as temperate as he is handsome.'

'Marcus Claudius is a gibbering moron,' Cornelius said. 'He can fuck and get children on highborn and servants, but not much else. Another reason this damned abduction complicates things. If I could return Isabelle to the Medieran Embassy at Passasuego, we could spend the remainder of my governorship in Harbor Town or some other cultured city, raking in taxes, and then I could arrange your marriage to him, Carnelia.'

She gasped and clapped her hands, her earlier frustration at being a pawn in Ruman familial games now forgotten. 'Oh, really, Tata?'

'Shut up, both of you,' Livia said, her eyes blazing. 'This is no time for your frivolities. With Isabelle lost, we are at the brink of war. I'm sorry your whiskey-sodden brain can't keep that hard reality front and centre.'

'I say, Livia, you can spend your days running mad among the colonists due to your special circumstance—'

Carnelia gasped. Secundus looked pained. Beleth and Samantha carefully inspected their glasses of alcohol. 'My sullied name, you mean?' Livia asked. There was no shrillness, no rise and fall of outraged inflection. Her voice was deathly quiet. But it was as though one of the Gallish double doors to the hurricane deck had blown open and a spill of snow had frozen the room.

Cornelius harrumphed and cleared his throat. 'Your special *circumstance*. But don't presume to stop the normal flow of—'

'Father,' she said, her voice clear. 'Despite all the love I bear you, stop speaking now. I was once a useful political piece for you to play on the board. You did, even though I begged you not to. And now I am no longer a useful piece for you. My name has been sullied irrevocably. In the forum and the senate hall and the finest tricliniums in Rume, when they speak my name they whisper – matron macula. I will never marry again. I will never be able to appear in any public familial function for fear of shaming the Cornelian name. And why? Because as a strategist, you played me poorly! So do not refer to my downfall as a *special circumstance* or I swear to Ia and all the old gods that I will chop off your other foot and feed it to the dogs.'

Carnelia clasped her hands to her throat as if choking back some dire exclamation. Cornelius sat back in his chair, his jaw loose and quavering. Before, his whiskers had seemed fierce, but now he looked an unkempt old man. Secundus scowled at his sister and crossed his arms. I tried to keep very still and not draw any attention to myself.

Livia tucked a wild hair behind her ear and took a deep breath. 'I am sullied beyond repair. But I do not need *you*, Father. I have my own fortune – my mother made sure of that before you divorced her – and I can make my way in the world just fine. From now on, I shall steer my own course.'

Tears gathered in Carnelia's eyes as she watched her sister, and I felt a moment of sadness for the younger woman – still bound within the familial games. Still a viable pawn on the board.

'I ... I never knew you felt this way, Livia.' Cornelius said. He ran his free hand through his grey hair. 'I want you to be ...'

'Happy? Then you will not hinder me now.'

Cornelius nodded.

Livia sighed. 'Tata, I love you dearly. But both you and I know there's no real public life for me back home. And here ...' She gestured to the stateroom, and the movement encompassed more than just the dull wood and silver of the *Cornelian* hull and planks – it encompassed the vastness of the Big Rill, the White Mountains, the Hardscrabble Territories, and massiveness of this new land. And somewhere in there, I imagine, it encompassed Fisk, too. 'Here I can discover my destiny.'

Secundus cleared his throat. 'I'm afraid I can't allow that, sister.'

Livia turned to him, giving him a cool look that would have made most men tremble. 'Indeed?'

'You are still a member of the Cornelian family, despite the unfortunate slanders against your name. I assure you, now that I am ...' He stopped, took a breath. 'Now that Gnaeus is gone, I have been thinking and planning. I will address the slanders against you by taking Metellus to court.'

Carnelia snickered. 'For what? Spreading rumours?'

The young patrician shook his head. 'During your wedding feast I overheard Metellus speaking to one of his cronies about the purchase of a silver mine in Dolia.'

Cornelius shook his head. 'While it's frowned upon, senators have been able to join in industry ever since Justininus sat on the stone chair. Anyway, the Dolia silver mines have been exhausted, or so Imperial missives tell me.' He tapped a finger on the table. 'Which is why we're here, at the edge of the Ia-damned world. Silver.'

Secundus nodded. 'I believe Metellus knew of the impending failure of the silverlode in Dolia and inflated the price of the mine in the last census,' he said, holding up his hands as if weighing a talent of silver. 'By a thousandfold.'

Cornelius' eyes widened, and he whistled. 'Defrauding the College of the Indemnities! You'll win no friends in the senate if you don a wolf's head and nip at one of their own.' He laughed. 'Oh, but what a way to enter into the rolls, son! A fantastic way to start a career.'

Secundus narrowed his eyes. 'I will prosecute him far enough that he fears me. But I would never be able to win. I have not enough clout nor gravitas, and the backbenchers would not support me. I can, however, make a big enough clamour that he might accede to my demands.'

'Which would be?'

'A formal declaration that Livia was a good wife, and true, and that all of the slanders against her name were false and propagated by his political enemies.'

Carnelia clapped her hands together. 'Bravo!'

'I won't be there to see it,' Livia said simply.

'What do you mean?' Secundus said.

'I do not plan on leaving this land for you, little brother. You'll make no marriage arrangements for me.'

'Livvie, this way we can arrange a suitable match—'

'Do what you will, but I'll not return to Rume.'

'You will if I tell you, sister.' He had forced some steel into his voice.

Livia's eyes blazed and she placed her hands on her waist. I had the distinct impression that she was thinking of pulling her sawn-off from wherever she kept it in her dress.

'Then I renounce the Cornelian name.'

Carnelia's glass dropped, shattering on the table. Secundus' mouth opened and then shut.

But Cornelius, now that he'd had enough whiskey, laughed. 'You will do no such thing.' He raised his glass. 'I am immensely fond of the two of you at the moment, and I would see no ill-will between you.' He slurped his drink. 'You, Livia, are free to do as you like. Provided that you remain a Cornelian and do not get killed. For the love I bear you. You, Secundus, will do exactly as you said and bring suit against Metellus.'

'Why, if you'll not keep her with us, father?'

'The Cornelian family can trace its name back three thousand years.' Cornelius looked serious for a moment, thinking. Then he said, 'Because *no one* drags us through the mud and gets away with it.'

'What about me, Tata?' Carnelia asked.

'What about you?'

'What great plans do you have for me?'

'It is a shame my blameless child was labelled a whore and deviant, while my – let us say – more amorous one is what I'm left to work with. Be that as it may, I will still try to arrange some sort of union for you with Marcus Claudius.'

Carnelia's expression became sly and she picked at her fingernails as she said, 'Say I want to renounce the Cornelian name myself, and find my way in this new land?'

Cornelius laughed until tears streamed from his eyes. Livia kept a straight face but Secundus could not hide a smile.

When he could breathe again, Cornelius said, 'Ah ... daughter, I will miss your charming conversation very, very much. I'm sure we can all visit you at whatever whorehouse you end up in.'

Carnelia blanched. She stood up and left the triclinium.

The laughter lasted longer than you would have expected, coming from a father and brother. Rumans just don't act like regular folk.

Finally, having regained his composure, Secundus said, 'Beleth, you stopped speaking too soon.'

'Uh, yes, er – whatever do you mean, Secundus?'

'The third way to summon and bind a *daemon*. Please go on.'

'Well, er, the third way to summon and bind a *daemon* is to direct it to possess a human.' He popped a handful of almonds into his mouth. 'Very painful stuff and it ends, usually, in death. But a simple enough process – it's the containment of the infernal that is complex. Marking a vessel for possession only requires a bit of inkwork on the subject—'

'Do you know these markings?' Livia asked.

'Of course.'

'Fascinating. Did you learn them during your time in far Tchinee, studying with the Autumn Lords?'

He nodded slowly, one eyebrow arching.

'Might we see them?'

'Now?' Beleth was resting his glass of whiskey on the top of his belly. He brushed his hand on his trousers then dipped it into his shirt pocket to withdraw a thin cheroot, which he lit from a match. All the while ignoring Livia's stare. Finally, after he was puffing merrily, his head wreathed in dark smoke, he said, 'It seems my hands are occupied. Samantha?'

Samantha had remained quiet during the whole length of the conversation but now sat forward and pulled a piece of paper from her breeches, laying it flat upon the stateroom table. She scratched an intricate circle with a sharp charcoal pencil. When she was through, she passed it to Secundus, who glanced at it and then passed it around the table. When it came to Livia, she looked at it, and then folded the paper.

'Interesting. Thank you for the lesson. I hate unfinished subjects. Are there words that go with the process?'

Beleth squinted at her. 'Why do you wish to know this?'

'I am curious.'

'Of course there are words,' Samantha said. 'None that should be spoken here.'

'Ah. I understand.'

Fisk cocked his head. 'What's all this about, Livia?'

'It is nothing.'

Then Livia stepped forward, and despite the eyes of family upon her, she took Fisk's hand in hers, brought it to her cheek, and said, 'I go with you.'

He was silent, the muscles working back and forth in his cheek, grinding his teeth. Finally he said, 'Of course.'

It was only later I realized that Livia had kept the piece of paper.

TWENTY-TWO

'You really gonna go through with this?' I asked Fisk and Livia as we lingered in the small stateroom after Fisk's debriefing. Cimbri had taken Reeve to get accoutred for scout duty – he was replacing Banty for the time being – and we had time before Beleth was ready for the binding.

There was a lot going through my mind then, more than just the consequences of having a *daemon* invade Isabelle's hand. The events of the last week living on the *Cornelian* among the patricians and – worse – performing the grisly interrogator's duties for Beleth had really disturbed my normal demeanour; I felt desperate and raw. It is easy to tamp away feeling from a remove of many years, but at this point, my chest was a roil of emotion, of guilt and anger.

And adding to this, a haggard and trail-beaten Fisk had now returned to us. Empty-handed.

Fisk looked at me, inclined his head slightly, and said, 'Shoe, you *know* me.'

I slowly nodded my head. 'Yep, I sure do.' I lowered my voice and looked around, wary that Lupina or Samantha might re-enter the small stateroom unannounced. 'But *you* don't know that man, Beleth.' I pointed to my temple, and said, 'He's shithouse-rat crazy, that one. He don't care about you. He don't care about the Senator or Miss Livia or this boat. He don't care about nothing. I know him now, more than I ever wanted.' I looked helplessly at Livia; maybe she would back me up. 'We're all entertainment for him. He'll bind something horrible to you. He'll fill that hand with the foulest rot from the depths of Hell just to see how it affects you. You don't have to do this.'

'You know I do.'

'Livia? Talk to him. He'll listen to you.'

'To what end? So he can be even more disgraced and sent away, back to the garrison at New Damnation? So the person most able to help Isabelle is banished? So I can't be near him in such brief time life gives us?' She took Fisk's hand, held it in her lap. 'I have not known him as long as you, Mr Ilys, but I know that he won't be deterred.' She brought his hand to her lips, kissed it. 'We are both barred from our original society. For that I am grateful. The stain on my name gives me a freedom I'd never have been allowed otherwise.' She kissed his hand again, and they looked at each other with soft eyes.

I watched the lovers. A strange pair they made, both fallen from their birthright. Both with names besmirched. Both strong in different ways. Their love for each other was obvious, writ large on their features.

It's a strange thing, love. It is a great gift Ia gives us, beyond name or family or honour. A gift we give ourselves? Hell, I don't know.

'Well,' I said, slumping back into my chair. 'Shit fire. I guess I'm gonna have to go too. Gimme some of that whiskey, will you? I'll be damned if I'm going to watch this dog and pony show sober.'

Beleth's quarters were large, the size of the small stateroom, and as I examined them I realized his rooms could very well sit directly above the stateroom we had just left. A large *orbis argenta* was burned into the floorboards and at the centre point was a terrible scorch-mark, witness to some dire combustion. A great table stood littered with sketches of wards and intaglios, inkwells and spare parchment, sandwells, wax blocks, knives and stoppered bottles with dark currents swirling in their smoked glass. There were bullet moulds, a stack of small silver ingots – a fortune large enough to buy another *Cornelian* sitting there as pretty as you please – a scrawl of holly, a smelting brazier, and the empty casings of Hell-fire shells. This, all along with the tools of every firearm-inclined engineer – numerous engraver's tools, vices, awls, V-shaped burins, needles, hammers, tongs, and a great mounted eyeglass I could only assume was for finer wardwork. There were dark wooden cabinets and podiums holding thick books. Skeins of open pipe-work came through the wall and snaked across the ceiling, held tight with brackets, to a large basin. Behind a small enamelled bamboo partition – a relic, I surmised, from Beleth's days in far Tchinee – stood a modest bed. No wild cavorting with *succubi* here. A wall of Gallish doors was mostly hid behind heavy drapes. Beyond the bed towered an imposing wardrobe, doors negligently left open, stuffed with suits, jackets, hats, and patent leather shoes. It seemed that Beleth was quite the clotheshorse.

But more noticeable than the clutter was the stink of sulphur and the acrid odour of silver smelting and burnt flesh.

Samantha led Livia, Fisk, and me into the room. Beleth who sat at the great table, affixing a silver hasp onto the ragged stump of Isabelle's severed hand, frowned at our entrance. He shook his head and said, 'As much as I appreciate the audience, this is a rather delicate procedure. My pardons, Miss Livia, but you and the dwarf will have to leave.'

Beleth scared me. But I had no intentions of letting him have Fisk to experiment on.

'We shouldn't be any problem,' I said, holding up my hands.

'No, Beleth,' said Livia. 'I think we'll stay.'

Beleth put down his utensils. The smoke from a pot of something near his elbow, made him whip off his glasses and rub his eyes.

He sighed. 'Are we going to have this now? This contest of will?'

'No contest,' Fisk said. 'They're just concerned for my person.'

'It isn't your body we're worried about,' I said.

Beleth's eyes narrowed, and he looked at me sharply. His lips pursed. He thought for a moment, then stood up, walking to the centre of the *orbis argenta*.

'In a little while, a *daemon minima* will occupy this space. Those wards will bind and contain him, for a while.' He walked outside of the *orbis argenta*, and I noticed two smaller, denser, circular intaglios of wardwork. 'As the summoner, I shall stand here. Mr Fisk shall stand here.' He let his hands fall to his sides, and he looked very exasperated and resigned. 'Where will you stand?'

'We'll be fine right where we are,' Livia said. And suddenly she was holding the same pistol grip sawn-off with which she'd brought down Agrippina. I hadn't seen her take it out from beneath her dress. She thumbed back the hammers and said, 'You're not the only person with a little mechanical knowledge, Beleth. I filed down the hammer catch. I'm holding it back with my thumb. Should anything happen to Mr Ilys, Fisk, or myself, it'll release and you'll share our fate.'

Beleth laughed. 'You'd doom all these people on the boat, and possibly this whole region, just to keep an eye on me?'

'Doom? Hardly.'

He laughed again and shook his head. 'You, madam, are an idiot. Should something go wrong in this room, you having a gun pointed at me will be a blessing. The alternative would be –' he smiled, showing teeth – 'unpleasant, to say the least. Quick death by that gun would be welcome.' He pointed to a bench. 'Stay out of the way and remain absolutely silent, and you might live through this.' He beckoned. 'Mr Fisk, if you'll please come forward and stand here.'

Fisk moved to where Beleth indicated, his back stiff and the faintest hint of a limp marring his stride. He hadn't changed from the ride back from Broken Tooth, and his clothes were discoloured with blood and the dirt of the trail. He kept his hand on the six-gun. He looked utterly weary.

Beleth nodded to Samantha and she left, shutting the door carefully.

'Where's she going?' asked Fisk.

'Somewhere near, but safe. Her quarters are warded.'

'Why?'

'All procedures like this involve great danger. What did you think we do here?'

'Always figured you raised devils,' drawled Fisk.

Beleth walked to the worktable, opened a leather kit all too familiar to me, and withdrew a knife. He turned to a large book, opened it, and removed a small piece of paper from its pages. Turning back to Fisk, he said, 'Yes, we do that. But in a larger sense, we contain and direct raw energy. In this way, we are like gods.' He gestured to me with his knife. 'Your pious friend is no doubt offended by that, but it is true. Mankind can assume the power, even the aspect, of the divine.'

'And the infernal,' I said.

He said, 'Remain absolutely silent. Once blood has been sacrificed and placed within the circle, attentions beyond your understanding are focused on this space and any word ... any *sound* that passes through the air above the *orbis argenta* ... can be construed as part of a binding covenant.' He looked at us. 'Nod your head if you understand.'

We nodded.

Beleth chuckled and picked up the severed hand, turned, and approached Fisk once more. 'Put out your hand, Mr Fisk.'

Fisk stuck out his hand, palm up. The knife flashed out and Fisk's palm gained a long mark, a parody of the wedding wound. Blood began to drip from his cupped palm. Fisk winced but nothing more.

'On Isabelle's hand, if you please.' Holding out the silver-hasped limb, Beleth waited as Fisk's blood dripped onto the grisly thing, streaking the skin. Beleth put it in the centre of the *orbis argenta* and took his allotted position just outside.

The room, already dim, seemed to grow darker at the edges and corners and the thrum and hiss of the *daemon*-heated water surging throughout the ship quieted. The scorched silver intaglios of the *orbis argenta* radiated with a cold, hard light.

Beleth said, 'In girum imus nocte et consumimur igni.' His voice was pitched low, and it deepened as he went on. 'In girum imus nocte et consumimur igni. *In girum imus nocte et consumimur igni.*' Over and over, he repeated his incantation. As his voice deepened and the lights dimmed, I thought about the phrase. It meant either "we wander in the night, and are consumed by fire" in the tongue of Rumans. Or it could mean "we enter the circle in the dark and are consumed by fire".

I heard a strange cadence to the words, and soon little arcs of yellow light, like miniature falling stars, dashed about within the *orbis argenta* and a darkness pressed in all around us, a palpable darkness, a darkness spun from hatred and damnation and sin. I felt it creeping toward me, and it pulsed and throbbed. Or maybe that was my terrified blood pumping through my body, tensed and ready to flee. I could not see the room's walls. All my attention was drawn to Beleth's voice and the darkness coalescing now in the centre of the circle, laced with golden flashes as though someone had tossed in a shower of golden coins, flashing and winking in some unknown light.

'In girum imus nocte et consumimur igni,' Beleth said again, low and sonorous.

I heard a ringing like the tolling of a great bell, and in my mind's eye I saw the words Beleth spoke and realized they made a horrible burning circle, moving forward and then curling back on themselves, like a snake devouring its own tail.

The darkness swelled inside the *orbis argenta*, and I felt a popping in my ears as though I was descending a cliff. My breath steamed in the now bitterly-cold air and rose in front of my face, and I watched as the darkness, like ink settling at the bottom of a glass, shifted and became sediment in the silver circle of wardwork on Beleth's chamber floor.

I felt a great distance then, as though we all stood on the edge of a great chasm above a darkling plain where *devils* and *imps* sodomized penitents, *daemons* desecrated flesh, and the *inferis* capered and pranced and gibbered in tongues that no man, no *dvergar*, had ever heard, but all could understand. On every tongue a malediction, in every action an atrocity.

I was going to run. Something was coming, something massive and unstoppable, wicked and full of glee. I was going to scream, scream into the impregnated air, scream into my hands, scream and scratch and tear at the door to be let out.

I glanced at Livia. Her face was utterly white, as though a *vaettir* or *vorduluk* had cut her sanguiducts and drained her of all life. Her lips pulled back in a grimace, her eyes wide. She shuddered in absolute terror.

The bell tolled again across the darkling plain spread beneath us. The darkness swirled and centred itself like some mad whirlpool caught in oil, slowly turning, narrowing, laced with lighting and golden arcs.

The darkness at the edges of my vision pushed past us, and now all that we could see were strange shapes contained inside the black ink of the summoned abomination. It mocked us with inky visages, like frescoes cut from obsidian. There Fisk was locked in embrace with Livia. There he strangled her. Here I stood naked with a blade. There I had cut open Beleth and spooled his guts into a noose that I wrapped around Livia's neck. And more images, flashing, *flashing*. There a *vaettir* held a child. There its gutted body roasted on a spit over a fire. Faster and faster the images came, each one more horrible than the last.

I couldn't see Livia, but I could hear her gasping.

I blinked, and it was as though, in the instant my eyes closed, the room filled with flames and the screams of the doomed and damned and above us all sat a Crimson Man on a throne, dripping with blood and grinning, grinning with terrible ferocity. The Crimson Man held out his arms like he was gathering wayward children unto himself. Drenched in blood, he held a sceptre and wore a crown and under his chair – his throne – was a mountain of living damned. And he smiled. A smile that could devour the world.

When I opened my eyes once more, the room returned and now the darkness was almost welcome. Anything to keep the Crimson Man at bay. Anything.

I told myself to flee, but my body was not mine to command. I could not move.

The surge of blood hammered in my ears and I felt an unbearable pressure behind my eyes and then I was screaming, truly screaming in a high-pitched, tortured wail. I was joined by Livia.

Our wails made strange infernal harmonies and the *orbis argenta* glowed, very bright, sending white light into the room and illuminating Beleth and Fisk at the edge.

Beleth raised his hand and spoke a word very clearly. 'Invado!'

And suddenly the pressure was gone. The room was different, yet it hadn't changed at all. The *orbis argenta* still glowed but the viscous black had vanished, and the darkness in the room had reverted to the wholly ordinary darkness of the *Cornelian* at night.

Beleth stepped forward, out of his own circle, and glanced at Fisk. Fisk had his pistol drawn and was blinking rapidly.

'The danger is, if not gone, relocated for the moment, Mr Fisk.' He motioned to the six-gun. 'You can put that away. Be thankful you showed enough restraint not to fire it.'

When Fisk spoke, his voice was raw. 'Why's that?' he said.

Beleth sighed and shook his head. 'Just be glad, Mr Fisk.' He turned and knelt near the hand. It was no longer the grey of decaying flesh. It had turned glossy and obsidian, as though dipped in ink. It didn't take an engineer to figure what the hand possessed.

'Mr Fisk, I believe your new friend is waiting for you now. You must pick it up.'

'That red man. He the one in the hand now?'

'Yes.'

'And when we find Isabelle, he'll be released?'

'Yes. That is his impetus to assist you. The promise of release. And help you he will. He will do anything to be freed.'

'Once he's unbound, he'll be loosed?'

Beleth nodded gravely. 'The *daemon* in the hand is a minor one—'

I laughed, and even I could hear the panic in my voice. 'Nothing minor about that son of a whore ...' I stopped, looked at Livia.

She was still pale but she let a smile touch her lips and said, 'Do not worry about my sensibilities, Shoestring. He's an abomination.'

Beleth stared avidly at the hand. 'Nice work there, I must say. The *daemonic* vestment is almost fully transmuted.' He stood up, stepped away. 'As I was saying, the *daemon* in the hand is a minor one. The red man is to Gooseberry as a candle flame is to an inferno.'

'Ia help us,' said Fisk. 'You're shitting me.'

'I shit you not.'

Fisk walked to the centre of the *orbis argenta*. He looked from me to Livia to Beleth. Then he slowly reached down and picked up the hand.

For a moment pain and despair washed over his face. He gasped, and looked at the room as though he was seeing other things, other vistas than what stood before him. His body twisted as though from invisible blows. And then I saw a thing I'd seen many, many times before.

Fisk set his jaw.

It was a small thing. A nothing in the face of the infernal. But he gritted his teeth, locked his jaw, and straightened his shoulders. It might have been a terrible weight he bore, but – Ia damn it – he would bear it.

It made me smile. Fisk and me sure weren't simple scouts no more. We'd experienced so much, so quickly – Livia loving Fisk, this cursed boat carrying the cursed engineer, Banty's death, the warpath *vaettir*. He was a centurion now and I was – what was I? A torturer's assistant? – an evil man?

Fisk caught my stare, nodded to me. And then, in utter seriousness, winked.

It was as though he said, *Shoe, I got this damned thing*.

I looked at the blackened *daemon* hand he held.

I thought, *You sure do*.

TWENTY-THREE

THE MORNING THAT a lascar walked from the west to the east shore of the Big Rill both crew and passengers on the *Cornelian* felt a sinking despair, akin to the feeling of Hellfire.

Full winter had come, bringing with it the baying of wolves and the promise of stretchers.

The morning of our departure, lascars lowered the swing stages over the icy surface of the Big Rill. It had stopped snowing but the sky loured slate grey. Clouds raced across the face of the heavens, and the wind cut through the legionaries and lictors like a *daemon*-driven wheel-saw from a lumberyard. Men sank into their cloaks and jackets and huddled around braziers and in the lee of stacked johnboats, gripping carbines in numb fingers.

We had been long hours in preparation, the urge toward haste was fierce. Beleth and Samantha spent their time in his quarters, making the ship reek of brimstone and smelted silver and scorched holly. The stinks of an ammunitionist.

I spent my time tacking out the ponies while Fisk and Livia spent the daylight hours in discussion with Cornelius and Secundus. Fisk looked both wan and washed out, restless and antsy. As though he could never be comfortable – even though he bedded down with Livia each night. He wore the *daemon* hand around his neck on a silver chain – given him by Carnelia, strangely – and it became obvious to me that it had a weight that was only apparent to those of us who had been in Beleth's chamber that night.

The night before our departure, Cornelius had feted us in the stateroom. Lupina served fresh bread and auroch swimming in thick ale-based gravy, honeyed cakes and many bottles of claret and glasses of whiskey.

But it was sombre, the dinner. Carnelia was subdued, and while Secundus scowled and looked askance at Fisk sitting so near and affectionately to Livia – either worried for her upcoming journey or disapproving of Livia and Fisk's affection, I could not tell – he said nothing. Even Cornelius stayed sober. Skraeling, stroking his whiskers, offered to take up Hellfire and accompany us. Kliment told us of the river's route, should we care to follow it wherever Fisk's *daemon* hand led, and offered a pilot's map of the Big Rill, all the way to Passasuego.

We all stood in the greatroom where Livia had removed Cornelius' leg, smoking cigars and drinking last glasses of whiskey, discussing the final disposition of Agrippina when the senator made a last bid to keep his daughter on the *Cornelian*.

'I will have Secundus bring Metellus to trial for slandering your name. We can repair the damage done. Just stay with us.'

'Yes, Livvie. Please stay.' Carnelia, who seemed even more skittish and nervous recently, licked her lips and glanced at Fisk.

Cornelius also looked at Fisk, convinced he was the only reason his daughter was leaving.

Livia must have appropriated Gnaeus' winter wear, because Fisk stood accoutred quite finely in new shirt, britches, leathers. But however finely he was dressed, the *daemon* hand hanging from the silver chain around his neck reminded us all that he was cursed.

Livia, who had ceased wearing the frills and flounces of Ruman society and taken up a wardrobe of thick leather riding skirts, knee boots, and wool vests over tunics, put her hand on the grip of the sawn-off shotgun strapped to her hip and shook her head sadly. 'No,' she said. 'I love you both, but there must be a Cornelian present. And we'll be taking the *vaettir.*'

Beleth coughed. 'I think not. I still have certain procedures I'd like to pursue regarding—'

'No, Beleth.' She made a chopping gesture with her hand. 'You'll have to slake your bloodlust in other ways. If there's a chance the stretchers will trade Isabelle for the creature, we are going to take it.' She turned to face him wholly, and her hand remained on the shotgun's grip. 'Samantha will be joining us as well.'

Beleth pushed his glasses back on his nose. 'You can't— Absolutely not! She is my apprentice!' He paused, tugged at the bottom of his vest, and placed his hands in his pockets. 'I apologize, Miss Livia, but Samantha must remain with me. I require her presence.'

Livia, face hard, shook her head. 'No, Beleth. She *will* come with us and deal with the thing you put in the hand, when it is rejoined with Isabelle.'

'She won't be able to protect Fisk. He's bound to this fate just as—'

'Master,' said Samantha, 'there *are* things I can do to protect him.' She stopped and then softly added, 'As well you know.'

'Mr Cornelius,' Beleth said, his face flushed. 'Samantha is my ward and apprentice.' He pointed with his cigar at Livia. 'I ask you to stop this nonsense.'

Cornelius looked from Livia to Beleth and then to Fisk. 'Ah, then you would go in her place?'

'Don't be ridiculous, Cornelius.'

Maybe it was the tug of familial blood. Maybe it was the challenge inherent in the word "ridiculous". Maybe it was a moment's realization that he just plain didn't like Beleth – found him a scurrilous and distasteful little shit of a man. Cornelius' whiskers quivered, his mouth set in a hard line. He said, 'Surely you wouldn't put your own comfort and interests before the welfare of the Empire? Because were you to think of doing so, I might have to consider that as treason.'

Beleth laughed. 'You can't be serious. All we're talking about is the welfare of a scout.'

'A centurion,' I said.

Cornelius said, 'We're talking about the welfare of an asset valuable to the Empire. There's getting there, reclaiming Isabelle. And then there's getting back with her alive.'

Beleth's face went tight and angry. 'I have always served you faithfully, Cornelius. To meet such treatment now—' He set down his whiskey and dropped the cigar cherry down in the glass. It hissed as the liquor extinguished it. 'To be stripped of my apprentice, one whom I've supported and guided over the years *at great expense*! Once we are near a settlement of any reasonable size, I will take my leave of you and search for another patron.'

Cornelius laughed. 'You've never served anyone but yourself, Beleth. And you've done that amply.' Cornelius poked Beleth in the stomach and then turned to Livia. 'Feel free to shoot him, daughter.'

Livia said, 'It is tempting.'

Beleth turned to leave. 'I am serious, Cornelius. I have never been treated in this manner in my—'

'Get used to it. Cimbri!' He looked around until he found the tribune. 'Escort Beleth to the vacant chambers at the end of this hall. Make sure he hasn't a scrap of silver or sharp object on him. Then keep him there, under guard, until he learns his station.'

Cimbri nodded, and took Beleth's arm roughly. 'But how would I recognise that?'

Eyes rolling, Cornelius said, 'I will alert you, Cimbri.'

Samantha cleared her throat. 'Mr Cornelius, leaving my master unwarded for long periods might be unwise.'

'Why is that, miss?'

'He has enemies. Not all of whom are corporeal. Botched negotiations.'

The Senator laughed. 'All the better.'

Beleth's expression was blank, placid, if a little red. 'Gooseberry will eat you all alive,' he said calmly.

If he had seemed upset at Samantha's reassignment and his treatment by Cornelius before, he showed no inkling of it now. There's an old *dvergar* saying: "Fury gathers in stillness." Two legionaries escorted him from the room.

That night I awoke to a great roar and the groaning of the ship's hull. My water basin had overturned and as I went out into the hall I found Cimbri, Reeve, and Kliment looking about blearily in various states of undress, for was very early morn. I went back to my single shuttered window and unbolted it, getting a hard blast of cold air in my face. I stood and looked out upon the vista there. The moon shone bright and blue upon the snowy landscape. A webwork of cracks haloed the *Cornelian*, radiating out and away from the ship.

'He's banging at his walls again.' The voice came from behind me, and I jumped. It was Kliment. He'd followed me back into my own room.

'How do you mean?'

'Oh, the old devil's bound tight as a tick in our boat's belly, he is. But he's a feisty one, our Gooseberry. I've served on quite a few steamers and never seen a *daemon* as restless.'

'You've seen him?'

''Course. I'm a pilot. Need to know every bit of my vessel. I take a peek at the bastard before every watch.'

'What does he look like?'

Kliment tugged at his long johns, scratching his balls, and turned to leave.

'Black fire,' he said, going out into the hall. 'Like a small column of black fire. Oily smoke and flames all tamped down into a little-bitty container. But when you close you eyes near him …' He stopped at his door, yawned, shook his head. 'He spans stars. And he ain't pretty.' He looked about with his lips puckered as though he wanted to spit in disgust, but there was no spittoon in sight. He swallowed. Then Kliment gave a little salute and said, 'You're lightin' out of here in the mornin', Mr Ilys. Get some rest.' He disappeared into his room.

I wandered down the hall to check on Fisk and Livia. When I rapped on the door to their room, Livia greeted me in a nightgown. Her hair was wild, and she wore a worried expression.

'Miss Livia, just wanted to check on you, make sure everything was all right.'

She tried to smile, but failed. 'My thanks, but it is late and we have—'

'That Shoe?' came a voice from behind her.

She turned, looked back into the room. 'Yes, he's checking on us.'

'Let him in.'

She did nothing for a long moment, and I couldn't see her face. But eventually she pulled the door wide, exposing the room.

Fisk sat on the bed, reclining against a mound of pillows, shirtless and in breeches. The gun wound had been bandaged, but Fisk was white as bleached bone and thinner than I ever imagined possible, ribs standing out. His eyes were dark, circled in what almost looked like bruises.

Around his neck, the silver chain. The *daemon* hand hung on his chest like a black claw grasping at his heart.

'He pulls me, Shoe. I can't sleep.'

'He?'

'The Crimson Man.'

Livia moved toward him, sat down on the bed, and placed a damp cloth on his cheek.

'Weren't that bad a couple of days ago. He was there, you know, but only tugging lightly. And Ia bless Livia. My heart's saviour. But tonight ...' He passed a hand over his eyes and exhaled, clearly exhausted. 'Been a long week.' He patted Livia on the leg and smiled weakly at me.

'You think some cacique might help?' I suggested.

He nodded. 'Can't hurt.'

I returned to my room, grabbed my flask of cacique. When I pushed back into the room, she was holding his face in her hands, kissing his closed eyelids.

'Excuse me, ma'am.'

'Oh ... Shoe. Didn't expect you to be quite so quick.'

Fisk's eyes popped open. 'Ah, thanks, pard.' He took the flask and upended it into his mouth. He drank for a long while, until the flask was empty.

His arm dropped to his side, loose, ungainly. He closed his eyes.

'Can't he just take it off?'

Livia shook her head. 'It would free ... *him*.'

Ia-damn.

'Know what I miss, Shoe?' Fisk kept his eyes closed, but spoke in a voice half delirious, half pained.

'What?'

'Miss the sap of spring on the plain, green shoots everywhere. The fresh winds coming down from the heights. Wood smoke on the air, the scent of meat. Even you, telling your tales by the fire. Sage and sweetgrass and winterfat.' He paused. 'Horses champing and nickering, smell of dung. Sun on my skin, wind in my hair. Those are good things.'

Livia's face collapsed, and she put her hand on Fisk's chest. She wasn't much for crying, that one. But she had a tough time hiding away the pain. Pain makes honest folk of us all.

'I too miss the range. Drinking in New Damnation. Running scout on patrol. A simple life, that,' I said, trying to follow his thoughts.

Fisk's face clouded and he said, very low, 'He pulls me, Shoe. I can't rest while he's with me.'

'We're leavin' in the morning. We'll find her.'

'And then what? I think this is the end of us, Shoe. I want you to have this.' He waved his hand at Livia, who went to his saddlebags and withdrew a large portfolio. She handed it to me.

Inside was a deed to a large farmstead, some hundred miles west of Fort Brust, on the edge of the Hardscrabble Territories on the banks of the Great Mammon River, signed by Lucullus and endorsed by numerous aediles from some office in the colony's capital of Novorum.

In addition to the deed was a bank note for a half talent of gold.

'Ia protect me, Fisk. This is a gift for a noble, not the likes of me.'

'You've been a rock, pard. Never knew better.'

'But—'

I couldn't think of anything to say. I looked at Livia and tears stood welling in her eyes. She nodded, encouraging me to take it.

I dropped the portfolio on the table. 'No. *Bullshit*. You've got this thing. *You've got it*. Never seen a tougher bastard than you, partner. We *will* get the girl, and Samantha *will* contain the Crimson Man. And then you can reclaim your land. You and Miss Livia will need somewhere to live.'

He laughed weakly. 'You always was a good storyteller. Even when you were telling them to yourself.' He rolled to his side. 'He might let me sleep now. He knows we're leaving in the morning. And he's mighty happy about it.'

Livia stood up, followed me to the door.

When I stood outside, she tilted her head down and kissed me on the cheek and whispered, 'You are a good friend, Shoe. You might not believe it, but what you said helped. You have my thanks.'

She shut the door, leaving me standing in my britches in the hall, breath coming in plumes.

My room was icy by the time I returned. I closed the window and latched it shut.

Falling asleep took a long time.

Needless to say, Beleth did not see us off. Reeve and Cimbri sat in watch over the man as he fulfilled his ammunitionist duties, and Samantha stepped in to make last inspections of the skeins of silver-threaded pipework and whatever arcane administrations the great *daemon* Gooseberry required, though she seemed very nervous to be doing so.

The legionaries were troubled – the constant threat of *vaettir* had put them on edge and in-fighting had become commonplace. Cimbri's voice was hoarse from shouting, and even his implacable second, Paterna, looked harried and sleepless as they assembled the conscripts and assigned duties.

In the *Cornelian*'s hold, they moved Agrippina into a wagon. Though a legionary had covered her nakedness with a long woollen coat and trousers, she was as I'd last seen her: strapped to the torturer's board. Her face was obscured by the Gossip's Bridle, and she was trussed so tightly, it was a wonder she could draw breath at all.

Fisk and Secundus arranged for the silver chains to be bolted to the wagon while I assisted Livia with her gear.

There's maybe two or three miles of foothills before the Whites get treacherous. We rode out from the *Cornelian* in the glaring bright of a sunny winter's day. Seven people, sixteen horses (and one mule, my sweet Bess). One *vaettir*, gift-wrapped. A wagon.

In the company rode Fisk, Livia, Reeve, Samantha – looking very uncomfortable bundled in winter wear and on horseback – and a fierce-looking tribune named Manius, a quick whip of a legionary named Titus Petro, and myself.

And Agrippina, of course, but I did not count her. Nor the Crimson Man.

The seven of us made a sacred number, riding forth, or so Reeve told us in his rough brogue. The number of the Prodigium, the number of the old gods, before Ia gained primacy. I didn't like to think about the significance of that. 'We are seven, and blessed,' Reeve intoned, his breath crystalline and sparkling in the slanting morning light. 'May we have the strength of each: the Mater, the Pater Dis, Gemini, Mithras, Veneris Magna, Nyar and Amor.' I didn't like the man, Reeve, despite Fisk's seeming fondness for him. The legionaries seemed nonplussed regarding his blessing – it's long been known that soldiers still worship Mithras in secret. They all have tattoos of the great bull on them, somewhere.

'And Ia protect this journey, help us save Isabelle, and keep us from damnation,' I added, not looking at Reeve.

He laughed and I felt my ears burn, my cheeks go ruddy.

We rode north, in the shallow rises and valleys of the White's foothills. There had been heavy snow in the preceding days, but the wind had carved it into gleaming white-blue sculptures abutting upturned boulders and snarls of bramblewrack, stands of gambels and aspens, the drifts like frozen waves on a wintry shore. The air was still. The horses' hooves whisking and crunching on the snow, the occasional nicker of a horse or Bess's intermittent brays, were the only sounds. Titus Petro became mired in a snowdrift, and it was long minutes before we could extricate his horse, which fortunately seemed none the worse for wear after the episode. It kept its head above the snowline and expelled huge draughts of air, but remained calm and didn't thrash about.

This boded well for the trip.

Fisk rode point, the *daemon* hand swinging freely on his chest, outside his oilcoat. He kept the carbine in one heavily gloved hand and the languor that had afflicted him the previous evening seemed to have vanished in the freezing, brilliant air. His eyes were bright, his movements crisp. And even though the man never normally smiled – as well I knew – at times I felt there was a smile lurking behind the rim of the heavy leather gorget he wore covering the lower half of his face. I hoped it didn't reflect the hideous grin of the Crimson Man.

Livia paced him. She had a fine hand for riding, her competence matched only by her beauty and exceeded by her intelligence. I have never encountered a more formidable and singular woman than Livia of the Cornelians.

The legionary Manius drove the wagon, pulled by two enormous draft horses and laden with supplies, tent, water, grain, extra ammunition, and of course, Agrippina. I checked her occasionally during the ride, and gave her water.

Titus looked at me strangely as I was dripping water into her mouth, past the Gossip's Bridle bit.

'Heard tell they take neither food nor water, but live off their own hatred and take comfort only in fornication,' Titus said. Reeve reined in his horse closer and watched me.

'Don't know nothing about that. But I know Isabelle, and I'll make sure this stretcher is still alive. She's no good as ransom if she's not.'

Reeve nodded, and Titus tugged on his horse's reins and slogged off through the snow.

The sheriff looked at me closely. 'Ye have religion, do ye?' he asked.

'You could say that.'

'Ye keep faith with Ia, and Ia alone?'

'That's right.'

He nodded his head. 'That's good, *dvergar*. Very good. I'd rather have men around me with allegiance to *something* than the faithless ones. Those who're too lazy to believe in anything when the evidence of the divine and infernal is all around them.' He stuck out his arm. 'Well met, Mr Ilys, and between us, we might see this mission through.'

I looked at his hand and didn't want to shake it. Always been taught not to tolerate those who revere the old religion. The *daemon* hand, Reeve, even Agrippina, made me feel rudderless, adrift, without some centre point. Before we began riding with the Cornelian brood, everything had been simple. We were soldiers then, outriding for the Empire, with Ia protecting and defending us against the taint of the infernal. And now? We'd become the preventers of war, with the weight of three great powers yoked around our necks. With the obscure goals of the *vaettir* to consider. And the nefarious designs of the Crimson Man leading us toward Isabelle.

What did I want? Did I know anymore? I'd become as lost as any mare's colt among the shoal grasses. Here, Reeve's prodigious benedictions seemed less heretical than the Shoestring of two months ago would have countenanced. Here, in the shadow of the White Mountains, the politics regarding Isabelle fell away and she was just a girl, grievous wounded, in need of rescuing from monsters.

I looked at Reeve for a long time, watching the expressions chase each other across his face. Earnestness, puzzlement, confusion, and mirth. Finally, I clasped his forearm. He grinned, the smile splitting his beard wide open and showing a bristling mouthful of teeth jutting in all directions. He released my arm, turned his horse, and returned to the front, where Fisk led.

Reeve was an adept horseman and handled himself well. With the exception of Livia and Samantha, everyone in the company had served in the either the fifth legion or the cavalry. It was strange to see Fisk leading such a group. I was used to him taciturn – just us two, riding scout under the vault of sky. And this outing was no jaunt, nor hunting expedition.

We rode all day until the sun passed over the rim of mountaintops wreathed in clouds. The whole earth took on a half-lit quality, and the air became so cold it hurt to breathe. We found a copse of thick pines and made camp in the lee side of a small clearing. Reeve, Titus, Manius and I unlimbered the large oiled canvas tent from the wagon while the rest of the company gathered wood, hunting through snow-covered timberdrifts.

Ultimately, Samantha had to draw a ward on the frozen earth and bind an *imp* in it. There we piled on the wood. Even sodden and rimed with ice, it caught and burned merrily. I flipped open my outrider's kitchen, stuffed with spices and dried herbs I'd gathered from the *Cornelian*'s kitchen under Lupina's watchful eye, and began cooking a stew in the pot I'd packed on Bess.

Water, crushed winterfat and fiddleneck and sage, peeled potatoes, chopped onions, and some salted pork went into the pot.

When it's bitter cold, like it was that night, it's important to get something hot and filling into the riders, and oats into the horses. In some ways the wagon was a great blessing, for it allowed us to pack more than we'd have been able to carry otherwise. And in winter everything is harder, takes longer.

It was dark by the time the tent was up. Titus and Reeve used a draft horse to drag a large log over to the fire, so that there'd be warmth all night, while Samantha banished the *imp* back to Hell. The flames needed its assistance no more.

We ate stew from pewter mugs. I took a few rocks and placed them in the fire for the companions to stick in their sleeping bags.

Fisk, who had a bright, impatient look about him, said to the group, 'We'll watch by twos. Shoe will take first watch with me. Best get some sleep, all of you.'

Titus lingered by the fire, along with Samantha, but Livia, Manius, and Reeve went into the tent to take their rest. Fisk stared at the trees ringing the fire, smoking a hand-rolled cigarette and pacing.

I wrapped the stones in a scrap of canvas, stood up, and took them to the wagon. Agrippina's eyes were closed and her face taut when I carefully removed the Gossip's Bridle. I uncovered her arms and legs one at a time and massaged them, bringing back warmth and restoring some circulation. Her bonds would remain until we found Isabelle. Nothing more I could risk doing for her. Just hope she didn't die.

'At night, the big mountain lions come down out of the heights to feed,' Titus said.

Samantha and Titus talked while they watched me at my ministrations.

I exposed her long leg and gripped the thigh and began abrading the skin with my rough palms, kneading the muscles underneath. I could feel her tense and then loosen as my hands worked into her flesh. Her eyes were open, gathering firelight. She observed me with the most curious of expressions.

'Are they fearless?'

'Aye. Quite fearless of man or beast. I've seen one attack a horseman sitting astride a warhorse.'

Samantha said nothing. I imagine a woman who can suborn *daemons* to her will wouldn't be too frightened by the threat of an errant mountain lion.

'So, you raise devils? That *imp* was a neat trick. Would've had to rub my fingers raw with a tinderbox.'

'Yes. I'm an engineer.'

'How do you become one?'

She was quiet for a long while before answering. 'Don't know, really. My pa was an engraver in Covenant. Put the fancy scroll-work on rich men's guns, their longknives and swords – though swords have fallen out of fashion.'

'Sounds like a good living.'

'It was. I grew up with a burin in my hand, helping my father in his workshop.' She raised a gloved hand and carved at the air. 'I learned to read early and was too much trouble for the tutors my parents found for me. So my folks scraped up enough money and sent me on a big-bellied cotton cruiser to Rume, where I was presented to the College of Engineers and Augurs.'

While Samantha spoke, I placed the hot stones on Agrippina's body and, as Ia is my witness, she sighed. Her eyes became lidded, and she looked at my face, running a tongue over cracked lips.

I gave her water, but she spat out the stew I gave her. After the bread, it didn't surprise me.

Titus said, 'Had an uncle who was an augur. Mean sonofabitch. Always cuttin' up animals.'

Samantha ignored him, staring into the fire. 'The college accepted me. And when I was old enough, Beleth took me into his service as an apprentice.'

'That old cunnus?' He took something from inside his coat and drank. He offered it to Samantha, but she shook her head.

'He's a hard master, but the best at what he does. It's a shame he's been so ... so disgraced. They warn us in the college not to become affiliated with patricians, because their influence will compromise our work.'

'Word among the boys is he enjoys cutting the stretcher.' Titus chucked his head in my direction. 'Maybe got an unnatural hankering for the wogs, if you know what I'm saying.'

I couldn't tell if a blush coloured Samantha's wide, moon-face in the dim light of the fire, but she was quiet for a long while. I was thankful the man didn't ask if she shared Beleth's bed. Or proposition her, homely as she was.

'He's a strange man, one I don't know very well despite my years in his service.' She said it with simplicity, and her tone made clear it was all she had to say on the matter. Her face remained inscrutable.

Titus stood up, cracked his back, and shook blood back into his legs.

'Been a pleasure jaw-wagging with you, ma'am, but I'm for bed.'

She nodded, staring into the fire.

I carried on placing the hot stones about Agrippina's body and massaging her limbs.

When you're holding someone's hands, kneading the flesh of the fingers, the meat of the palm, the muscles and sinew running up to the intricate collection of flesh that is the primary way we *interact* with the world, you get a sense of scale. Of the *vaettir* we encountered, Agrippina was surely the smallest. But she was ten feet tall, if she was an inch.

Holding her remaining hand in my own, I began to realize, truly, how much larger she was than me.

I moved up her forearm, kneading the flesh, working around the notched leather strap binding her to the torturer's board at the elbow, and onto her upper arm. I was working blind, my hands moving under the heavy woollen blankets and tarp covering her. But her face was exposed for now and her large eyes tracked me as I worked. Occasionally she'd draw back her lips and expose two rows of sharp teeth.

'You had some of that stretcher pussy yet?' his voice came low and soft in my ear.

I jumped and turned. My hand twisted and sprouted a blade. Fisk.

He stood beside me. Grinning.

It was a grin unlike any I'd ever seen except once before. Full of mirth and hatred. A hungry smile, showing teeth.

'I think she likes you, Shoe,' he said. Then he made a slurping sound in his mouth, in imitation of a sexual act I will not mention here. 'You make quite a pair.'

His eyes seemed uncommonly bright, and he stood hunched over, very close, his head thrust out toward me.

The *daemon* hand swung on its chain between us.

He glanced at the knife. 'You plan to prick me, dwarf? Stick me with one and the stretcher with the other? Is that it?' He chuckled, and it rose like sap and stuck in the back of his throat, phlegmy and thick.

I exhaled through my mouth, frozen breath rising up in front of my eyes. I forced the tension to ease out of my arm, my shoulders, my legs, and I replaced the knife in my sleeve.

He stood there looking at me avidly, his jaw working in and out as if he'd spent a night chewing kokoa leaves.

'Hey, pard, you remember that time we ran into Mack Lentilius out near Breentown? That mean bull auroch had him treed?'

Fisk's face fell; he looked axe-struck. He stared off into the trees, and his mouth hung open, slack.

'Uh, yeah.' He rubbed his hands on his coat. 'He was hollerin' for us like a scalded baby.'

'That's right. And when we came into the clearing, that big ole bull just blew air through its nose and then pushed off into the brush. You remember that?'

He nodded. 'Shoe, I'm—'

I turned and walked around him. 'We've had our share of good times, haven't we?' I flipped back the tarp covering Agrippina's handless arm, rolled back the wool blankets, and started working on her. 'Remember that furlough in Harbor Town? Don't think I've worked off the hangover yet, you know?'

Fisk brought his hands in front of his face, looked at them hard, as though trying to discern their intention or deeper meaning.

I stopped. 'You got a terrible burden, pard. And I'm sorry you took it up.'

He nodded.

'Think it might be best if you watch yourself around the ladies.'

Again, a single nod.

'You don't sleep anyway, do you? You can't, not with that thing.'

'No. I don't sleep. When I close my eyes—'

'Right,' I said. 'So maybe you should do some roving at night. Around camp, but not in it.' I looked at him closely. 'Scouting, right?'

He didn't respond. He walked over to the big black that stood steaming among the horses and ponies, withdrew his carbine from its long leather holster, and walked away, out of the circle of light thrown by the fire, into the trees and beyond.

When I looked down at Agrippina, she was smiling.

TWENTY-FOUR

W E PUSHED HARD north early the next day. Fisk seemed even more agitated and desperate to move. Livia did what she could to console and soothe him, but the *daemon* drove Fisk unmercifully.

At rests, when the horses took water or had their nosebags full, Fisk would smoke handrolled cigarettes and stare at us and the horses with narrowed eyes, spitting into the snow or cursing under his breath. When we rode, he seemed to unclench and his expression would lose its pained look, his shoulders would unkink, and we could pretend, for a short while, that our dour but steadfast leader, friend, partner, or lover was back. But we had to keep moving.

Two days later, we came out of the foothills and onto a high plain. In places, the land smoked and spewed great billows of steam and sulphurous stink. We'd find livid green and orange pools of standing water, liquid even in the freezing air and very hot to the touch.

One afternoon, we passed a rocky field that spewed boiling water into the air, creating strange icy formations jutting up from the snowcover. It was a strange and otherworldly landscape.

Then a single rider approached, trailing a small pack mule. Bess brayed and chucked her head as he neared.

Fisk held up his hand for the company to halt.

When the rider drew closer, Fisk hollered, 'Howdy, sir! Where you riding to?'

The horseman stopped and unwrapped a heavy scarf that kept his face from the cold. He was a middle-sized man, burly, with a thick black beard and merry eyes.

'Ain't riding to anywhere. Just riding away.'

'Away? Is there trouble behind you?'

The man began to laugh, and I watched as Fisk's face clouded and his eyes became mean.

'Trouble?' The man said, jerking a thumb at his backtrail, 'Damn, mister, *Hell* ain't a half-mile yonder.'

Fisk's hand shot to his pistol. The man's laugh died, and his horse turned in place and champed.

The rider cocked his head at Fisk, and he narrowed his eyes. But the man still smiled. 'My apologies, mister. I'm riding from Hot Springs, where a whore stole my heart and a cardsharp stole my money.'

Manius and Titus laughed, and even Livia smiled.

Fisk sat stock-still in the saddle, hand hovering by his six-gun. I couldn't see his face from my position, but I feared he was grinning a crimson smile.

I pushed Bess forward. 'Well met, mister. I can't tell you how sorry I am to hear your story. Cardsharps cheat, it's true, but whores win in the fairest way possible.'

The man shifted his gaze to me, but not before noticing the *daemon* hand hanging from Fisk's neck. 'You have a point,' he said, his mirth drying up like a watering hole in the midst of the Hardscrabble Territories at high-summer. 'Ride straight, you'll hit a gametrail that you can see even under snow. Follow it to the crick. Follow that upstream, and soon you'll either see or smell Hot Springs. Stinks like a rotten egg.' He looked at the bright sun and sniffed, raising his reins. 'Hell, just follow my backtrail.'

He touched the brim of his hat in farewell. 'Pleasure, gents and gentlewomen. I best be on my way.'

'Half-mile distant, then? Over yonder rise?'

The rider looked at Fisk for a long while. Fisk sat unmoved in his saddle, his hand hovering over his Hellfire.

The rider nodded, and kicked his horse into movement. He didn't look back.

'Looks like we're all going to Hell, then,' I said, trying to put some lightness into it. 'Either that or Hot Springs.'

It was an affluent if muddy silver-mining town perched halfway up the skirt of a peak they called Brujateton and ringed in smoking hot pools of sulphurous water. Despite its obvious Medieran heritage, Hot Springs, or Ria Kalla as it was called by the elder denizens, was a lawless town under neither Ruman nor Medieran protection or rule.

That did not mean it was unprotected.

We rode into town, Fisk in the lead, Livia close by his side. She had taken to remaining with him at all times, except during those hours we camped. The *daemon* hand would not let him rest at all then. And it ate at my heart that my friend, my partner, the most reliable man I knew, could be corrupted in such a way. But there it was. The Crimson Man was like a high mountain stream that flooded and washed over its shores, wearing away at the earth. Fisk was becoming possessed.

Great woolly beasts of men stood guarding the road leading to Hot Springs. They were dressed in makeshift uniforms emblazoned with the letter C over their bulging chests. As we rode in they stared at us, unsmiling, and fingered the grips of Hellfire pistols. Bully boys, every one. Many wore gladii or oversized longknives. A dour, unsmiling bunch to a man.

We were riding down the main thoroughfare, the snow-mulched

mud sucking at our horse's hooves with sloppy sounds, when one of the men – a big blond-headed giant who looked like two Reeves had been fused to create one gargantuan Reeve – stepped out in front of us.

He tipped his hat to us, just a formality. 'Welcome to Hot Springs,' he said, looking at each of us in turn. 'Hotel and saloon at the far end of the street. Livery stables behind them, right near that bristle of aspen tips. If you would, I'd ask you to direct your attention to yon building there.' He pointed a thick finger, bristling with coarse hair, at a white brick building nested between two wooden ones. A sign hung above two more bully boys lounging on the wooden-slatted porch. It read, 'Croesus Mining Company, William T. Croesus, Proprietor.'

The big burly man said, 'Mr Croesus welcomes all travellers to Hot Springs but bids us admonish you to shed no blood nor prevent the pursuit of industry. Otherwise …' He turned and looked down the length of the main street toward the slope of Brujateton and the wooden platform erected beneath the weight of the mountain.

A gallows.

'My thanks, travellers. Spend freely and keep yourselves indoors during the night, for there are stretchers on the move. Although we guard this settlement, we can make no guarantees regarding your safety. But you are free to enjoy all Hot Springs has to offer.' He turned and walked to the front of the Mining Company building, took the steps up to the porch. He sat on a bench and watched us until we rode off.

I drew Bess close to Livia. She had a tight, worried expression on her face. She watched Fisk cautiously.

'A word, Miss Livia?'

She nodded and stopped her horse. She was cold, pale. Her eyes were wide and worried.

'You and Samantha should room together tonight, instead of …'

She gave a terse jerk of her head and said, 'Yes. He's becoming uncontrollable. That *thing* around his neck is seeping into him.'

'Right. I'll have him bunk with me in the stables.'

She looked surprised. 'Why the stables?'

I cocked my head at the wagon and Manius. 'Agrippina. She'll want watching, and I don't think it would do to have these brutes discover our cargo.' I looked at Livia closely. 'The *hand* won't do well indoors, I don't think.'

For a long moment she looked at Fisk, riding ahead between Titus and Manius driving the wagon. She turned back to me, and for the first time I truly saw her desperation. It was all bound up with love and heartache and sorrow. A beautiful woman, Livia. And now afflicted by her love.

'I—' She stopped. 'I love him and don't know what to do about it. I've ... never felt this way before. Both of us—' Her eyes grew luminous and moist but she blinked and swallowed hard. 'Both of us are so *compromised*. And there's nothing we can do about it.'

I bowed my head.

She nodded. 'I will tell him the arrangements.'

'Maybe I should be there, too.'

We kicked our mounts forward and caught up to Fisk. Livia, her horse very close to his, reached out and softly touched his arm.

'Baby ...' she said, hushed and low.

His head pivoted, reminding me for a moment of the long necks of the *vaettir*, their inhuman, predatory grace. He fixed his eyes on her, and then me. They were cold, distant, and cruel.

'My love,' she said and his expression shifted, like a man waking from a nightmare. I was glad to see he still had that scrap of humanity left him.

Livia said, 'I will make arrangements for the rest of the company at the hotel, since I carry the purse.' She paused. 'Tonight, I think I should room with Samantha.'

Fisk looked at me and raised his eyebrow.

'I need your help, pard, watching after Agrippina. Without her, we won't be able to ransom Isabelle. I need you to *remember* Isabelle. Tonight we share a bed of hay.'

He looked at us, his face as blank as the surface of Big Rill when it hits the plains, wide and smooth and untroubled. Placid on the surface, but underneath currents deadly and terrible. After a long while Fisk tried to smile, and it looked almost genuine. Almost.

Before he took up the *daemon* hand, he had been guarded – stingy, even – with his emotions. Now he was seemingly so much freer with them, but it all meant nothing in the end.

'Right. I'll miss you, my heart,' he said. He took Livia's hand and kissed it.

I think maybe a little of her died then. Or maybe that infinitesimal part of her that was her soul alone grew larger. Expanded.

Hellfire and damnation. I don't know.

We took the horses to the stables, passing the Croesus Hotel and Saloon, where our company was to lodge. The stables were a new construction, a large, half-empty affair with two towheaded boys attending to all the travellers' mounts. The massive building was a long way away from the main street, and connected by a wooden walkway. It still smelled strongly of raw rough-cut pine lumber, half-sweet and half-rotten. Livia paid for the horses with a handful of sestertii and a wan smile. The company dispersed.

I drew Fisk aside.

'Might be you should outride a bit on one of the fresh ponies, check out our front trail.'

He looked at me, his face devoid of any expression. 'No.'

'Fisk, it's a terrible weight you bear and it will only get—'

He bowed his head, and when he raised it again his jaw was clenched, but he didn't have a murderous air about him. Maybe the Crimson Man was there, maybe not. Fisk's mouth didn't fill with flame, his eyes didn't ignite with hatred. Maybe he had whupped the *daemon*, at least for the moment.

'If I outride, I'll never turn back. *He* won't let me.' He stopped. 'You got some cacique?'

''Course.'

He held out his hand.

I went to Bess and retrieved the bottle in which I keep my supply. I handed it to him.

'You told me there was water in this.'

'Huh? Might've. It's expensive. Gotta ride west of Harbor Town to get it.'

He pulled the cork with his teeth and spat it at me. It bounced off my forehead and rolled into the hay.

He put the bottle to his mouth and drank, long pulls, his throat working up and down painfully. When he was done he went to a rough pine bench, sat, and rolled a cigarette on his knee.

'I'll keep this here with me, pard.' Then he tucked his tobacco pouch back in his vest and popped the cigarette in his mouth. He dug in his shirt pocket for a match.

I waited, watching him.

'Do I need to hobble you?' I was only partially joking.

He laughed, patting the bottle. Cigarette smoke curled around his head. 'You already have.'

'Keep an eye on the stretcher, will you?'

He nodded and hefted the bottle again.

I went in search of dinner for the both of us and some charcoal for the farrier's brazier. It was going to be a cold night.

The Croesus Hotel and Saloon was a nice place – done up in the Hellenic style with columns everywhere – with crystal chandeliers and a polished mahogany bar that spanned twenty feet if it spanned an inch. A wide-open room with tables where men and women, gentlefolk and labourers, all mingled together without strife or umbrage. The open area mirrored the bar. Grand stairs, at the rear of the building, led up toward what I could only assume were the lodging rooms. Liveried clerks and baggage boys – all bearing the Croesus crest – scampered to and fro, offering patrons assistance. Two bully boys stood to either side of the front door.

The hotel smelled of roasted meat and beer and good tobacco.

I had purchased a wheel of cheese and some bread at the bar and was sorely tempted to draw out my time with a small libation, yet I resisted. I was saddened by the fact I wouldn't be sleeping there on clean sheets and drinking whiskey in the warmth of the saloon.

I left there with great reluctance. My time on the *Cornelian* had clearly softened me.

Along the main thoroughfare, I found the general mercantile – also owned by Croesus and Company – and bought some withered apples for Bess and a sooty gunnysack full of charcoal.

It was full dark and freezing when I returned to the stables. Fisk was dead drunk, insensible in the hay. So I broke off some cheese and bread, wrapped them in cloth, and placed them by him, should he awake in the night. I filled the brazier with coals and lit it, enjoying the heat radiating off the metal. After I had warmed my extremities and eaten, I went to the wagon, removed the bag of stones, and placed them in the coals to heat.

After a moment of consideration, I walked over to Fisk and gingerly removed the bottle from the crook of his arm. He had consumed enough for four men to become drunk. There was enough left for me to take a swig or two to fend off the cold.

I felt content and as happy as possible as I placed the warm rocks on Agrippina, massaged her arms and legs, and then wrapped myself in coarse woollen blankets and fell asleep in the hay.

*

I'm sound asleep and snoring when he rises on silent legs. He stands over me for a long time, looking down at my small form wrapped in grey blankets. Had I been awake, I would have worried. He leans over me and the *daemon* hand turns on its hasp, catching on its obsidian surface the thin, sharp light seeping into the stables from the blue stars. When I shift in my sleep, he grins a terrible smile and walks out into the night, coatless, his hand on his six-gun. Still grinning.

There's no whorehouse in Hot Springs – at least no obvious one like in New Damnation – so he moseys down the main street, whipping out his pistol, twirling it, and reseating it in the holster. But *fast*. So fast it's like some sleight of hand – except this trick ends in death and damnation. He takes bead on a lantern in a window, a windvane at the top of a house, the sign of the lares crossroad college at the end of the street. He draws on the doors, the windows. He draws on a falling leaf.

He draws on the moon. He draws on the stars.

When he nears the Croesus Hotel and hears the strains of guests' voices inside – drunken and full of revelry – filtering through the chill night air, Fisk clicks his heels together like a merry partygoer and mounts the steps. He licks cracked lips, sore from the unaccustomed toothy smile and whistles the chorus of "The White Rose of Cordova".

He's framed by light as he pulls the door open and enters.

Livia shook me awake.

She fell backward and sat down hard on her arse as I came up suddenly, brandishing a naked blade.

I stood up, resheathed my knife, went to the wagon, and flipped back the tarpaulin. Agrippina was where she was supposed to be.

But Fisk wasn't.

Shaking my head, I looked around. Behind Livia stood Titus,

bloodied at the temple and holding his arm as though he'd been injured.

'Oh shit,' I said, slumping back on the hay.

'He came to the hotel,' she said. 'But there wasn't much of Fisk in there.'

Titus nodded. 'He busted in, had the piano man play "The White Rose of Cordova" over and over again and started drinking at the bar. Drinkin' heavy, like a man desperate for drink. He did that for a while, catcalling and cursing. When I came to him and tried to calm him, because the Croesus brutes were watching, he damn near ripped my arm from the socket.' He shuddered. 'I got off easy. The look in his eye... ain't never gonna forget that.'

Livia, looking more fraught with worry than ever, said, 'The Crimson Man wanted to play cards.'

'That's right. He out-cardsharped the cardsharp. Neat little man from Covenant in a three piece and carrying a hogleg. Name of Piet Mondsall, heard all the whores talkin' bout him. A ladies' man and almost as rich as Croesus himself.'

I rubbed my face. This wasn't going to be good.

'So they sat down to play, Fisk slinging around a bottle of whiskey and grinning that—' He paused, swallowed. 'That hungry grin I ain't never seen before on him except for recently. They sat down to play, and Fisk was winning. He was taking the cardsharp for a bundle, and folks were gathered around the table. The sharp pulled out that hogleg of his and put it right on the table, pointing at Fisk, and Fisk just smiled bigger and said, "Let me deal, one last time," and he started flicking them cards out on the table and each one of them landed face-up with a death's head grinning at the cardsharp.' Titus shook his head. 'Like he'd switched decks or something. And the grin on that skull was just like the grin on his face.

'So the sharp grabbed up his hogleg, put it right in Fisk's face, and pulled the trigger. But the hammer just clicked. Fisk started laughing, and I can't remember exactly what he said, because if the truth be told, I was damn near to wetting my britches right then, but he said something like, "That won't work against me," and something about Hellfire being at his command and right then all the guns in the room went off.'

'For that second, when all them guns let go, the room stank of brimstone and we was all surrounded by fire and *imps* and above it all Fisk laughing, and it was like, shit—' He blinked and swallowed again. 'Like *Hell on earth*, I guess. Lots of folks got hit then from the gunfire. But I was watching the guards, who nearly jumped out of their skins as their six-guns let go. They came a'barrelin' into the barroom, holding those smoking pistols that had just blown holes in their holsters. Started pulling the triggers immediately, aiming to gun down Fisk, but he just threw back his head and laughed more. Ain't a laugh I've ever heard before. Ain't one I want to hear again.'

I pushed myself up from the hay, grabbed the bottle of cacique, and handed it to Titus. He took a long pull and shivered with the alcohol. I offered it to Livia, but she pursed her lips and shook her head no.

'Fisk's arm shot out like it weren't even part of him, and that dead hand around his neck was a'glowin' like a coal in a fire. Fisk snatched up the cardsharp's neck. There's a cracklin' where all the sharp's bones start a'breakin, and Fisk swings the man around in one hand like he was a flail or something and beats the guards to the ground with the sharp's body and paints the room red with the blood a'pourin' from the sharp's carcass and the bodies of the guards. At some point the sharp's head was squeezed right off and rolled across the floor, and that's when the screaming really started.'

Livia said, 'I heard the shots and came downstairs, fearing the worse. The townsfolk were huddled against the wall, screaming, while Fisk was laughing and beating to death the guards who kept coming. Beating them with their own bodies. But when he saw me...'

'Miss Livia appeared in the doorway, and Fisk stopped dead and dropped what was left of the guard he had in his hands, so I roused myself and snatched up the sharp's hogleg and a'clobbered him on the back of the head. He dropped, but not without a couple of licks, and I'm afraid I might've cracked something in there.'

Titus took another messy belt from the bottle of cacique.

'The remaining guards took him and threw him in the jail.' Livia cocked her head to the stable doors that stood open. 'He's to be executed at dawn on the gallows.'

'And Manius?'

'Dead.'

'Reeve?'

'He caught a swipe from a guard, but he should be along soon. He's getting Samantha and our gear together.'

I felt poleaxed. I had known the Crimson Man was strong, but not *this* strong, able to take Fisk over completely.

'What are we gonna do?'

Livia was quiet for a long while.

'When the sun rises, I will go to the Croesus offices and plead for Fisk's life and explain the situation we're all in if we do not recover Isabelle.'

I nodded. It made sense. Croesus was a Hellene, judging from his name. And, even if he was not a Ruman, then surely he was someone who understood the security that the Ruman presence in the Hardscrabble Territories provided. The Medierans were a great power, but most of that power was vested in ships and the sea. Rumans ruled the land – the legions made sure that remained true. Croesus would see his interests lay with Rume if we explained the situation properly.

'If he doesn't listen?'

'If he doesn't listen, Fisk will die. We will never find Isabelle. If Fisk dies, there will be war.'

TWENTY-FIVE

THE WINTER SUN exploded over the plains to the east and the light filtered through the steam and smoke of Hot Springs, colouring the buildings with the orange and yellow of flame.

The sound of falling hammers on pine lumber – the industrious noise of coffins being built – resounded over the cock's crow and the braying of mules. Already, even in the half-light of dawn, people gathered around the gallows, breath steaming, their booted feet churning the ice and freeze of night.

Livia had returned from her rooms to the stables to gather me and Titus. She was dressed in her finest garb: a beautiful gown, low cut, with a long sable coat, and black leather gloves lined with fur. Jewels at her neck, her ears. Though I would wager gold she had the sawn-off on her person.

She was breathtaking.

To Samantha and Reeve, she said, 'We need you to remain here and watch the gallows, ready the horses.' She stopped as though something had just occurred to her. 'What will happen if Fisk dies? Will the Crimson Man be released?'

'No.' Samantha shook her head. 'He will remain seated in the hand, which can then be destroyed, sending him back to Hell. Or someone else could take up the object and gain his power. The conditions must be exactly right for him to gain his freedom; the hand must be rejoined to Isabelle. She doesn't need to accept it, but the hand must be joined with her in some way.'

'Hung over her neck, then, if she isn't able or willing to take it?'

'Yes.'

I didn't like thinking about what would happen then.

'You'll be able to protect her, correct?' Livia gave a frantic, desperate laugh. 'This is all pointless if you can't protect her.'

'Yes, I can. There is no animus toward her from the *daemon*. It's a strange covenant based on the wholeness of things. Once she takes the hand, she will be whole once more and the conditions of his bindings will be fulfilled and void. However, Fisk, who has served as the Crimson Man's prison and bearer, I do not know if I can protect him ...'

Livia bowed her head. She looked so lovely in the dress, the jewel shining at her throat, the diamonds sparkling at her ears. Strange she had packed such finery for this mission – how could she have known we might have any need for it? – but I was glad she had.

'We cannot concern ourselves with Fisk's welfare after we reach Isabelle.' When she looked at me, I knew she was lying. She would never stop concerning herself with his welfare.

I would save him, if I could. But we weren't going to make decisions based on that. Not anymore.

As hard as it was to come to that silent agreement with her, come to it I did. Fisk's life was a small thing in comparison with the lives that would be lost in a war between Rume and Mediera – and possibly the Autumn Lords.

The Ruman army is the largest and finest fighting force in the known world. They're hundreds of thousands strong and bring with them Hellfire in all its various forms: gun, cannon, mechanized baggage train, and steamship.

But Mediera is mighty, too. It is said that put side to side, her ships could span the seas and could put a fighting force anywhere in the world within days.

And the Autumn Lords? Should they care to make war, they would have all the might of Tchinee behind them, with three thousand years of civilization driving them on. Who knows what kind of army they could marshal?

No, I couldn't even fathom the cost to the world if we lost the girl.

'Have all prepared to leave quickly. If I can't convince Croesus ...' Livia stood straight, clasped her purse close to her breasts, and said, 'No matter. I *must* convince him or all is lost.'

She turned and left the stables, and I followed her.

We mounted the steps to the Croesus Mining Company building under the watchful gaze of two over-muscled bullyboys. They did not look happy, but opened the door for Livia and scowled at me as we passed inside.

It was a beautiful building, white stone, and the interior was accoutred like any affluent counting house or seat of industry in New Damnation or Harbor Town – even Sulla or Novo Ludnum – with dark imported woods, leather chairs, bookcases and filing cabinets filled with tomes and ledgers.

We were led into a waiting room. The bullyboys remained with us, breathing through their mouths and fingering shotguns. After a few minutes, another brute appeared in the door and waved us back into a small but well-appointed office. The guards withdrew.

A tall, studious-looking man sat at a large desk littered with papers. His suit-jacket was slung over his chair-back, and his vest looked rumpled. Ink stained his fingers, speckled his cuffs. He was as lean as a harpoon and stared over his spectacles down his long nose at us. He had the officious look of a secretary, bred in the bone.

Behind him was a large closed door, with a gilt C embossed on its front.

'Can I help you?'

'We're here to see Mr Croesus.'

He put down his pen, leaned back in his chair. 'Are you, now? I don't recall Mr Croesus having any visitors on his schedule.'

'Good.' Livia smiled 'Then he shouldn't be too busy to talk with me.'

'I don't think you understand, ma'am, but Mr Croesus isn't a man to have conversations with every passerby. It's my job to weed out the crackpots and ne'er-do-wells.'

'My message for Mr Croesus is of the utmost importance. I assure you, he will want to speak with me.'

The man held up his hands in a reasonable gesture. 'You are a person of means and high-birth, judging from your speech and manner of dress. But why should I allow you access to Mr Croesus? After all, you could have weapons stored about your person and a desire to do him harm. Will you submit to a search?'

Livia looked disdainful at this – quite an expression on her beautiful face. You never want to be on the receiving end of her scorn. She said, 'My name is Livia Saturninus Cornelius, daughter of Gnaeus Saturnalius Cornelius, and I am here on Imperial business.'

The man's eyes narrowed. 'Cornelius, eh? And why would the governor of the Hardscrabble Territories send a woman – however fetching – to our little town, accompanied only by a *dvergar* servant?'

Livia sighed and removed her gloves. 'We came here with more in our company. But one is dead, and another you have incarcerated and intend to hang.'

The man steepled his fingers and narrowed his eyes. I had the distinct impression that he was enjoying himself. Immensely.

'Ah, the possessed man who destroyed the hotel and killed the guards.'

'Yes. He bears something that is vital to the safety of this region.'

The man laughed and said, 'The black hand that we cannot remove?'

'Yes. We are on a mission of the utmost importance.'

'Tell me about it.'

'I think that information would be better suited for Mr Croesus' ears.'

He pulled an ornate watch from his vest pocket and checked the time. 'Very soon, your companion will be hanged by the neck until dead. I suggest you start talking.'

Livia hesitated only a moment before outlining our mission. She told him of Isabelle, Banty, and the *vaettir*, the *Cornelian* locked frozen in a stretch of the Big Rill, miles away from anything else.

'If we cannot reclaim her, there will be full-scale war. I must make sure Mr Croesus understands that even this little town will be drawn into it.'

The man laughed, throwing back his head and holding his stomach. A full laugh. He was vastly amused. This went on until I thought he might have lost his mind or been drinking cacique. But finally he stopped and began wiping his eyes.

'Oh, gods, that is *rich*.' He chuckled again and placed his spectacles back on his long, bladelike nose. 'You Rumans have fucked things up royally, haven't you?' He looked to the atrium. 'Mykos! Dinus!'

Two bullyboys popped their heads around the corner. 'Yes, Mr Croesus?'

The expression on Livia's face wasn't one I'd like to see again. It seems being duped wasn't high on her favourites list.

Ia-damn him.

'Take our visitors into custody.'

I don't know if you've ever heard a patrician of high intelligence and fierce motivation curse because she has been thwarted, but it is something very memorable. When she was done, Croesus' smile had faltered and he looked grim.

'Ah. There's the Ruman superiority we've come to know.'

He stood up, picked up his jacket from the chairback, and put it on. 'Fortunately, the cell we have for you has a good view of the gallows.'

Livia looked like she wanted to throttle the man, and I wondered if she truly did have the shotgun under her dress.

'But *why*? Why would you want to risk war? Surely that can't be good for business?'

He gave a tight smile, opened an ornate box on his desk, and withdrew a cigar. He trimmed the end with a pocketknife, scraped a match on his desk blotter and then stood there puffing on the cigar, getting a good cherry going and filling the room with redolent smoke.

'Well, that's an interesting speculation, ma'am, but one that's not quite on the mark.' He smiled again, but this time there were teeth involved. Seeing the smile, my stomach sank a little. I was reminded of Beleth, and his thousand cuts. 'I don't like Rumans. But that alone is not enough reason for me to execute Imperial emissaries, which I am planning to. However I'll think of something.' He pointed at Livia and me with the burning tip of the cigar. 'Once the man is dead, you'll be dangling shortly after.'

'But *why*? I demand an answer!'

'You are in no position to demand anything.' But that smile crossed his features again and he said, 'War. That's my favourite word. You know what goes with war? What goes with war in this age of the infernal?'

He walked around his desk. One of the bullyboys grabbed Livia's arm. I was wrenched around by the elbow and felt something hard jam into my side – a pistol nose.

'*Silver*. The whole world will war on – and for – silver.'

He made a great bow, hand in flourish, his head almost touching the floor. 'I thank you for the advance warning. We will be well fortified when the first shots are fired. And if I give better rates to the Medierans? Who will know?'

Livia laughed then, even though her arm being twisted behind her obviously hurt.

'You're an idiot, Croesus,' she said, and the scorn, the complete disdain for him, was like acid. 'If you think you're going to be allowed to keep this little—' She wiped the air with her free gloved hand to indicate the building, the town. 'This *pipedream*, well, there are three legions between Harbor Town and Fort Brust. And Mediera? They have *maybe* five hundred men in Passasuego, you fool. The only reason we Rumans haven't taken this whole land with Hellfire and sword are certain treaties that will mean absolutely *shit* if Isabelle cannot be recovered. You'll be overrun and the silver ours.'

Croesus nodded at his guards, and they hauled us through the waiting room and into the cold air of the street.

'We shall see, ma'am. Unfortunately, *you* won't.' He turned to her guard. 'Mykos, make sure she has a view of the gallows.'

It seemed like a long walk, back down the main street to the gallows. Strange how time can stretch when your life is coming to an end. The two guards kept our arms twisted behind our backs quite painfully, and there was no way for Livia to get to her gun, if she even had it.

I had a short blade I could get to, but to what end? Livia being killed? A bit of Hellfire ripping through my back?

The jail was built of the same white stone as the Croesus Mining Company building, but it resembled a short squat block, more reminiscent of a legion's carcer – the army holding cell – than a jail. They led us in and placed us in a cell with a barred window facing the gallows, but not before frisking us. Although they did frisk Livia, either her outraged expression – or their reticence to maul a woman – kept them away from her most private areas. It amazes me that propriety would make even brutes act so stupidly.

'Do you still have your—' I whispered, leaving the question unfinished. At the front steps of the jail two guards stood with their backs to our cell, looking toward the gathering crowd waiting for Fisk's hanging.

Livia didn't reply but I somehow I got the impression that she did. They had removed all my sharp pointy things.

We watched the gallows. A single guard accompanied by a swinging noose stood on the upraised platform, holding a shotgun.

The time stretched out and a dog barked hoarsely into the morning air. The murmur of the crowd increased, and a trio of dirty boys ran around the gallows, swinging sticks. Soon the noise grew – something was happening. But even craning my neck I couldn't see what was occurring on the street.

Soon enough, Croesus' lean figure appeared, along with a brace of guards leading a hooded figure in dusty grey garb. Fisk.

The murmur of the crowd died, and the mass of folk in front of the gallows parted. Croesus, the guards and Fisk mounted the steps up to the gallows. It was very short work whipping the hood off Fisk's head and replacing it with the noose.

Fisk looked drugged and bleary, and I remembered that Titus had brained him good with the cardsharp's pistol, to the point he feared he might have cracked Fisk's skull. Fisk was pale, and his mouth was slack.

But the *daemon* hand still hung from his neck.

Croesus walked to the front of the platform and raised his arms as though welcoming the multitude before him to a dance or a dinner.

'My friends,' he said, his voice loud. He was a politician, born and bred. He infused his tone with goodwill and understanding tinged with regret. 'I'm sorry you are all gathered here today to witness this. This has to be the worst part of my job as city founder and mayor – the execution of criminals.'

He bowed his head and appeared overcome with emotion. But when he looked again at the crowd, his face was furious.

'Friends, this man ...' Croesus pointed a finger at Fisk. 'This *monster*! He came into our loving town, our beautiful hamlet, and killed! Many of you witnessed his violence at the hotel, saw how he was possessed of some infernal madness.' He jabbed a long finger at the sky. 'But I will not allow this to stand! It is my duty to protect you all. And in the course of my investigation into his origins and companions, I discovered a terrible secret! This man has brought with him agents, agents of Rume, working toward the downfall of our beloved town!'

He looked to the crowd and held out his hands. 'We happy here. We have good jobs. The Croesus company keeps us all safe from *vaettir* and the infernal influences of the perverted Ruman Emperor and his engineers and warmongers.'

He paced the front of the gallows like an intemperate cat stalking the bars of its cage. 'But this man, this creature of Rume, came among us. To kill. To interrupt the honest flow of industry! And he brought with him conspirators!'

Croesus' long finger jabbed at us. Two hundred heads turned as one and stared at Livia and me, framed in the jail window. A woman spat and cursed in a thick tongue. A hunk of muddy ice was chucked at the jailhouse by some hidden crowd member.

'So, today we take a stand. By executing these conspirators, these—' He paused here, thinking. '– these assassins, we take a stand against Rume and all of its corruption and evilness.'

The crowd turned back to the gallows, and Croesus moved to stand beside the dazed Fisk.

Livia shook her head, and I saw the tears of rage and frustration in her eyes.

Croesus put his hand on the lever that would release the gallows trap. A guard cinched the noose to the side of Fisk's head so that his neck would snap – a small mercy.

'By the power invested in me by the good people of Hot Springs, I do condemn this man to death.' And then, without any more ceremony, he pulled the lever and Fisk dropped beneath the platform.

Livia closed her eyes and hit the window casement with her hand. I don't know what I was feeling then.

Sorrow, maybe. Anger.

Everything remained silent. I looked away from Livia and back to the gallows and the dark crowd gathered around it, steaming in the hard, cold air. The wanton boys with sticks had stopped their play, and the townsfolk, far from clapping and exuberant at the hanging, remained utterly still.

A dog gave one long, painful wail.

On the gallows, the guards and Croesus peered into the open hole of the trapdoor. Smoke rose.

I touched Livia on her arm, and with a hoarse voice, said, 'Miss Livia. Something is happening.'

She opened her tear-stained eyes and gasped.

Flames licked up the rope that held the noose and Fisk. Soon the smoke coming from the gallows billowed and the guards and Croesus began calling for water.

And then townsfolk surrounding the platform began to scream in terror.

The flaming rope around Fisk's neck went slack as he rose. Up through the trapdoor he came, rising up in the air, still tethered around the neck, his arms outstretched as though he'd been cruci-fied. Grinning.

His eyes had vanished, replaced by burning black flames stream-ing into the air, and he threw back his head and laughed, a boom-ing sound that reverberated off the buildings of Hot Springs, off the slopes of Brujateton. I could feel the vibration of that terrible sound coming through the stonework of the jail floor, shooting through my skeleton. I felt weak, feeling it – weak as though my legs might collapse or my bladder cut loose or I would run gibber-ing around the cell. It was a sound that blotted out all thought, all reason. A sound like fire, burning away your memory, your kindness, your kinship with your fellow man, and leaving nothing behind except fear and madness and desperation.

He hung in the air, grinning at the screams of the townsfolk, arms outstretched. *There's nothing left of Fisk now*, I remember thinking. He opened his mouth and it was like looking down a well, or the open bore of a shotgun, or the maw of Hell itself.

The thing that had been my friend and partner Fisk spoke a word, a word I've never heard before and I hope I'll never hear again. It was curdled with hate, twisted by cruelty.

He spoke in the language of Hell.

The horror it caused – I can't do it justice. If his laugh was bad, the sound of that one utterance was a million times worse. I watched as Croesus' eyes widened and his hair caught on fire. I think I saw the moment when sanity fled him and, even then, could feel some sympathy for the man.

Even the worst of men didn't deserve to die that way.

The guards lifted shotguns and drew six-guns but the weapons would not fire – not against Fisk and the terrible thing he carried with him, carried in him. The men threw down their guns to flee, but it was too late.

Once the word had been uttered, the flames spread like an explosion. Out from his eyes, out from the open bell of his mouth, out from the burning noose around his neck. Out from the burning *daemon* hand beneath it.

Townspeople ignited. They ran to and fro, some dropping to roll in the mud. The gallows became a pillar of fire rising to the heavens, licking at Fisk's feet as he hung in the air, still with that awful grin splitting his face. The backwash of heat hit me, stinking of brimstone and sulphur and corrupted flesh. The stench of Hell.

Fisk descended, through the flame and smoke, hovering in the air, his arms still wide in cruciform. His eyes burning incandescent with dark flame. Smoke poured off his body.

But he smiled. He smiled.

And saw us.

He swept forward, the smoke and flames trailing from him like a robe. Upon his head was a crown of fire and in his hands were a sword of fire and an obsidian sceptre of coalesced smoke.

And he was so happy.

'Don't think I've forgotten about you two,' he said. And he raised his sword, bringing it down in a fiery arc.

There was a tremendous crack, and we – Livia and I – were flung away from the jail wall as it was pulled asunder. Stonework exploded as though it were straw, and the sound was as cacophonous as the world being born into existence from the mind of Ia.

I never passed out of consciousness, not when Fisk floated through the breach in the jail wall, not when he looked down upon us with eyes so terrible, framed in flame and bearing infernal accoutrements.

And he laughed.

'We're running a tad behind schedule, *friends*,' he said. 'I must become whole.'

My body was lifted up by an unseen hand, and I felt myself moving through the superheated air, out under the sky. The pressure was unbearable and I felt the breath being pushed out of my lungs, my ribs cracking like kindling. In the air I could smell the scent of human flesh burning, hair and clothing and meat all mixed together in a charred greasy odour – fatty and rank and stinking like some charnel house that had caught flame – that clung to my nose and clothes. I opened my eyes. Livia was hanging suspended, too, awake and looking at Fisk with her eyes wide and mouth a grimace.

I thrashed and squirmed as we floated out and away, past the inferno of gallows, past the burning corpses of the townsfolk, and beyond, to the centre of the main street.

And then, as we hung ten feet above the slush of the street, Livia threw up her leg, kicking the hem of her dress high. When it fell, she held her shotgun in her hand and had it pointed at Fisk's face.

'Put us down.'

Fisk – or the Crimson Man – laughed again. He was having a high old time.

'As you wish, madam,' he said, and his eyes rolled back in his head.

We fell.

Titus and Reeve appeared in the smoke and helped Livia to her feet. It seemed the whole world was aflame, and I couldn't stop myself from coughing. It was as though some *imp* billowing soot and flame had lodged itself in my chest and would not let me stop hacking.

I felt a soothing hand on my arm and was surprised when Samantha lifted me to my feet with strong hands.

'We must get to the horses now!' she cried. 'Before the stables catch flame!'

She dragged me across the street to where the air was clear. I gained my breath long enough to look around.

There was no one left alive in Hot Springs save our small group. I shuddered.

'Come,' Titus said. 'We must hurry.'

Fisk lay unconscious on the ground. Gone were the crowning flames, the robe of smoke, the sword and sceptre of fire. Fisk looked very small lying there in the muck of the main street.

Reeve picked up Fisk as easy as hefting a sack of potatoes and slung him over his shoulder. He trotted off, and we followed after. A merry little party we made, half-running through the remains of a burning town.

When we arrived at the stables, Samantha stopped. I looked from her to the puzzled faces of Titus and Reeve.

'What's the matter?' I asked.

'The doors. They're wide open. We closed them before the hanging.' Reeve pulled his pistol. 'We were going to shoot down Croesus and his guard on the gallows but the guns wouldn't fire.' He spat on the ground. 'That *thing* didn't want 'em to.'

Livia said, 'You all would have died.'

Reeve grunted. 'Aye, ma'am. That we would have. But I weren't going to let them take a Ruman centurion without a fight.'

'Fools,' Livia said, but her smile belied her words.

'But this ain't right,' Titus said, and he withdrew his six-gun and peered into the stable.

The horses were fully tacked and agitated, nickering in their stalls. Something was wrong.

When we approached the wagon, the trouble became plain.

The bodies of the stable boys lay upon the ground. They'd been torn asunder. The hay around their bodies had soaked up their blood.

The wagon was empty.

Agrippina had found her freedom.

TWENTY-SIX

WE PUT THE burning ruin of Hot Springs behind us and followed the trail up Brujateton. Samantha had wanted to bury the dead, but Titus said, 'Ma'am, you're a kind soul, but that would take weeks. You think *he* will give us that time?' He jerked a thumb at the wagon where Fisk was being carried, unconscious.

Fisk had been unconscious since Livia had threatened him with the shotgun and he'd let us fall.

'When do you think he'll wake up?' Titus asked.

Livia, looking very weary, gritted her teeth and said, 'Let us be happy he's not awake now. And that he still breathes.'

Samantha frowned and said, 'It takes enormous energy to do what he did.' A worried look crossed her plain, wide features, and I drew Bess alongside her. We were in the shadow of Brujateton's peak, and it was cold. It would be night soon but none of us had wanted to camp among the corpse fires of Hot Springs.

'What is it, Samantha?'

'No minor *daemon* could do what Fisk did. I think Beleth might have—'

'He loaded the deck, didn't he?' I said.

She nodded, very slowly. 'I fear so.'

'This is just getting better and better,' I said. 'And Fisk?'

'The Crimson Man, as you call him, expended a lot of his power in the ... the event. He won't disappear, but it will be a while before he's back to full strength.'

'So, we'll get Fisk back for a little while?'

'Yes, I think so.'

Reeve whistled. 'Be one doozy of a hangover our man will have.' He turned his horse and rode on, up the slope.

That night we found a flat promontory rimmed in firs and made camp. Wind had whipped the ground clean of snow, and brushwood was plentiful. It was agreed that one of the five of us would keep watch at all times – that we'd sleep in turns – and we found a break in the firs where we could find some relief from the biting gusts coming down from the peak of Brujateton.

Agrippina was out there, somewhere.

I don't know how I felt about her then. Part of me thought of Agrippina and her brethren like intelligent animals – bears or cougars, even – having been trapped by man and tortured. Maybe driven mad. There's just no telling with the stretchers. Their minds work differently. Without the influence of silver or holly their incorruptible flesh never dies, so they assume the immortal aspect of nature and the land itself, as tall and unknowable as the mountain, as swift as the river, as deadly as hoarfrost. They make me feel young, by comparison, the elves. They're the teeth of the earth, come to eat the living, and they're as hungry and pure as fire.

From somewhere out there, she watched us.

Fisk awoke in the darkest hours of night.

I was on watch, and a thin, high layer of clouds wreathed the moon and obscured the stars. The firs whined and thrashed in the wind coming off Brujateton. He coughed a few times and rolled the blankets and tarp covering him away from his head and sat up.

I must say I'd seen him looking better. He rubbed his face and ran a tongue over cracked lips.

'Water.'

I gave him a canteen and he drank until it was empty and then threw it back to me.

He sucked in a sharp pained breath, put a hand to the back of his head where his hair was matted with dried blood.

'You remember anything?'

He nodded. 'All of it.' He scooted down the wagon's bed until his legs dangled off the end. 'Except for after the fall – when he let me go.'

Fisk sniffed and looked at the wagon bed, then glanced at me questioningly.

'While we were in jail and the others were trying to figure out some way to prevent your death, the stable boys decided to take a peek under the tarp.'

Fisk cursed and wrapped his arms around his body.

'They think they were rescuing a princess or something?' He spat again and shivered. 'It's cold as shit on a shingle, Shoe.'

He sat that way for a long while, staring into the darkness, his arms wrapped around his chest, covering the *daemon* hand resting above his heart.

'Oh, damn, pard. I'm in over my head,' he said at last.

'He pushing on you now?'

'Some. I can feel him.' He uncrossed his arms and took up the *daemon* hand in his own. He was quiet for so long I thought he'd fallen back asleep or passed into a trance. He looked up and said, 'He's tugging on me, Shoe, ready to go. North. North and west.'

He pointed into the black firs ringing in the camp. 'That way. She's that way,' he said and dropped his arm.

I sat by him on the wagon bed. It was cold, and the wind didn't help anything.

'Listen, pard. Come first light, we head out. Leave this wagon, take the horses and ride hard as we can.' I patted his knee. 'We'll get to Isabelle and do what we need to do.'

He cocked his head back at the empty wagon. 'You don't have your girlfriend no more.'

'Right. Not much we can do about that now.'

He looked around. 'Livia? How is she?'

'She's had it bad, fearing for you, truth be told. You two never really had it easy, did you?'

From inside his jacket, he withdrew a tobacco pouch and a paper and began to roll a smoke. But his hands shook so badly, I took the pouch from him and twisted the tabac for us both.

'I'll get Livia,' I said. I moved to the embers of the fire, pulled a burning branch, and lit my cigarette. 'I think she's got some heavier clothes for you.'

He nodded.

When I scratched at the tent Livia was instantly awake. She rolled upright, and I heard Reeve and Samantha shift in their bedding. She appeared in the flap and said, 'He's up?'

A few moments later she reappeared in full winter garb, holding a large heavily furred coat and gloves.

'He's over there.'

I smoked my cigarette near the fire and couldn't help but see their wordless reunion. She went to him, coat in hand. He sat on the wagon bed, his head down. She stopped and stood before him and waited like that until his face came up, streaming with tears. I was amazed at that – seeing tears on Fisk. He was a killer, born and bred. But whether he wept, for himself, or what he'd done, or where he found himself, I didn't know.

She placed the heavy coat in his lap and put her hand to his face and he latched onto it like a drowning man to a line. He put it to his cheek and kissed the palm.

She pressed in, kissed him, and the look on her face was as inscrutable as I've ever seen.

My cigarette was down to the butt, so I flicked it away into the night, and went into the tent to get what sleep I could before the break of dawn.

We scuttled the wagon the next morning and packed the tent and the rest of the oats and ammo on Bess. I took a pony, even though I didn't want to, and we rode hard north for the next three days.

It was overcast and had began to snow again. In the day, Fisk was back to normal, calm – silent, even. But at night the Crimson Man would turn the screws on him, and Fisk would become restless and antsy, prone to cursing, or worse – laughter. None of us wanted to be reminded of the events in Hot Springs.

Finally, we came into a shallow valley before ascending the other side up and up into a forest of gambels, and I spied what looked like smoke tracing a faint path through the air, coming from high up in the V where two peaks met.

'Look there,' I said to Fisk, pointing. 'That pass.'

His eye rolled and began to smoke, as though matching whatever fire burned on the heights. 'We must go. She is there,' he said, his voice not human.

I was frightened to see how fast he had changed. He was gone, and the Crimson Man seethed and burned.

Fisk rode ahead, and Livia kicked her horse to catch up.

I waited for Samantha. With the events of Hot Springs and the rigours of the trail, I had remembered something that I needed to ask. 'You were saying Beleth duped us,' I said once she pulled next to my horse.

'I think so.'

'Then if it ain't some minor *daemon* kicking around in there, who is it?'

Samantha scowled the majority of her time in the saddle, but the look on her face this moment was different. Thoughtful. Maybe a little preoccupied.

'There's a whole miserable cast of *devils* and *daemons* that we, as engineers, can draw up.' She sighed. 'It's hard to explain.'

We rode on for a while, following the path in the snow that Fisk and the black had carved out for us.

'Everything has a counterpart. Many counterparts.' She waved one gloved hand at the mountains. 'All of what you know is seen as if through a veil that's been drawn over your eyes, and if you could just go a little … *sideways* … you could see everything, all of nature and mankind – you could see it differently. There are infinite worlds stacked like parchment upon one another.'

I nodded even if I might not have understood.

'But things cross over,' she said.

'*Devils. Imps.*'

She shook her head. 'Not originally. Think bigger.'

'What? Elephants? Shoal aurochs?'

She laughed, but it was short and bitter. 'You are *dvergar* and have lived for countless years, right?'

'I wouldn't say *countless*. But I am older than anyone here.'

'When your mother was young, had she heard of Hellfire and raising devils?'

I thought about it for a long while. Shaking my head, I said, 'No. That came with the Rumans, she always told me. Mam used to talk about when the world was new and there were no guns – no way for any man nor beast to force a *dvergar* from our mountain. She always kept with the old gods, the gods of tree and stone.'

Samantha looked toward the mountaintop for a long while, as though thinking, choosing her words. Finally she said, 'Not here, but very far away on the other side of the world, the first engineer came into the world by piercing the veil.'

'What's that?'

'Before then there were the old gods – Mithras, the Pater Dis, Veneris, the twins. The others. And even older spirits, the numem that drove life, the gods of the house. The gods of rock and stone.'

I was having a hard time following. I tugged on the pony's reins, drawing myself to a stop. After a bit of trouble, Samantha reined in her horse.

'What are you telling me here, miss?'

'You need to know the truth, at least. Of the *daemons*. Because they have your friend in thrall.'

'You know about all this? How it came about?'

She nodded. 'I was schooled at the College of Engineers and Augurs in Rume. I have much knowledge.'

I didn't know what to say to that so I said nothing and waited for her to continue.

'His name was Emrys and not much is known about him, but he managed to marshal the numen and put a pinprick in the fabric of worlds. And something came through.'

'What came through, Samantha?'

'Ia, the Stranger.'

'No.'

It was lies she told.

'There's no doubt. Emrys had apprentices. I've read their journals. They went insane, to a man, but their accounting was thorough, if garbled and crazed. Ia came through, a creature of darkness.'

'No.' I slapped my leg. 'Ia is light. Ia is the good lord who welcomes us into the afterlife and judges our souls with the Pater Dis at his side. He might be hard but he is fair.'

She looked at me sadly. 'I'm sorry, Mr Ilys. But that is not true. Ia came through and scourged the land, caused a century of disease and despair and darkness.'

'Scourged?' I laughed. 'Then where is he? Why isn't he known? Where is this scourge?'

She sighed again. 'This happened nearly two thousand years ago. And on the other side of the world.'

'No.'

'He came through and laid all the countries of the world to waste for ten years. No army could stand before him, no weapon hurt him. By all accounts, Ia was a creature of unbelievable scale. He caused the interregnum mundus. The dark age.'

Shit, was all I could think then. *Shitfire. Ia damn this heifer straight to Hell.* I felt like I rose and sank all at once. I wanted to punch the woman's fat moon-face. I wanted to knock her to the ground and have my horse prance upon her bones until she breathed no more.

But I didn't. I breathed deep and tried to take it all in.

'And then, after deaths innumerable and corpse-fires as high as the sun, he withdrew upon himself, becoming smaller and smaller. Some said to sleep. Others said to wait like a fisherman with a net, between mankind and the stars, fishing for our souls when we die.' She shivered. 'East, far east, in a blasted land called Ombra Terra, he lies sleeping. That is Ia.'

'It don't make sense, woman. None at all. Why do the Rumans bring temples to him from overseas? They come from Latinum with their priests and temples and preach goodness. Good deeds and kindness.'

'Somewhere in history, it all got mixed up. Once engineers learned how to summon *daemons* through the fabric of worlds through the pinprick Emrys created, it was easy to recast Ia into a benevolent force, if only for political reasons. And to set all the *daemons* in opposition to Ia.'

'Don't make sense, woman. None.'

'It's hard to come to grips with, and it's knowledge the College of Augurs and Engineers are privy to and not many others. Maybe the royal family.'

'Okay, say it's true. You're telling me that the Ruman royals would get into bed with something that damned evil?'

She threw back her head and laughed, a rich throaty sound. I could see Sam's back teeth in her wide mouth.

When she got a hold of herself, she said, 'I'm sorry, Shoestring, but you obviously have never been to Rume. Your opinion of patricians is influenced by Cornelius, who is among the best of them. Rumans getting in bed with *evil*?' She chuckled again. 'I don't think there's any doubt about that. Consider the westward expansion.'

'What about it?'

'It's dependent on Hellfire.'

She had a point, but I couldn't leave it there. 'If Hellfire is so bad, how come you're training to be an engineer? If Rume is so corrupt, why are you working with the Rumans?'

Her jaw tightened, and she turned away to look at the other riders, who had now stopped and were looking at us.

When she turned back, her face was hard, tight. Unforgiving.

'It's a fallen world we live in, Mr Ilys, full of evil men and people wanting to take what you have and kill the people you love.' She shook her head as though fending off something terrible. 'I've taken the path best suited to me. And there's no Ia waiting to judge me at the end of it, so ...'

It was all nonsense, I thought. Godless, amoral nonsense. The events at Hot Springs had driven all reason from her. I wouldn't listen to any more of it.

'Why in Ia's name—' I stopped. 'Why the Hell are you telling me this?'

She tugged at her scarf, her breath white and whipping away on the air. 'Emrys, beyond all imaginings, survived Ia's crossing.

He managed to close the pinhole between worlds, but imperfectly. Or so it is said, and I have to believe that it has been closed, otherwise this whole world would be ruin.' She removed her glove, and then blew on her fingers. 'But there were other worlds beyond the one that brought Ia through. And Emrys spent his remaining days learning – and teaching others – how to summon and bind the creatures of what we call Hell into our world.'

'Why? You'd think he would have had enough with Ia if what you say is true.'

'He hoped we could harness these *devils* and *daemons* so that, when Ia awoke, we would be able to do battle.'

I laughed. I wasn't buying it, no sir. Lots of hearsay and nothing that could be proven.

Something occurred to me. 'But this whole talk started when I asked who Fisk is toting around his neck.'

Samantha slipped her hand back into the glove and looked at me closely. Snow fell in large flakes, and my pony began to become restless.

'Judging from his crown, sword, and sceptre, I think Beleth put the King of Hell in Isabelle's hand.'

'The King of Hell?'

'The Fiend. Belial. Whatever you want to call him.'

'Holy shit.'

'Exactly.'

'What in tarnation was Beleth thinking?'

'I don't know. I would guess he wanted the mission to reclaim Isabelle to fail.'

I shook my head. 'How will you stop the Crimson Man?'

'There's no way, except one.'

She leaned to the side and withdrew a knife from her boot. It was tarnished and black but the blade was long and the edges gleamed.

Silver.

'When we get close enough to Isabelle, and we know her exact location, I have to kill Fisk and send Belial back to Hell.' She watched the expressions cross my face. 'It's the only way.'

TWENTY-SEVEN

WE PUSHED OUT of the valley by midmorning, up and over a small ridge. The smoke on the peaks had diminished and faded away so completely, I almost questioned whether it had been there in the first place. The trail we followed became more rugged and rocky, and the horses struggled to keep their footing as we passed over the shimmering, frost-bound mountainside. The land was frozen as hard as iron, and the streams were gripped with bitter cold, making breaking through to the water for our mounts hard going and laborious. Whoever dismounted to do the job was sweating by the end, and then, afterward, shivering with cold.

Everyone was tired and chilled to the bone.

Each step forward, toward the peak, took us closer to the release of the *daemon* in the hand. What might happen gnawed at me like floodwaters at a loamy riverbank. It seemed less and less likely Fisk could be spared, and I could see, by the constant stormcloud over Livia's fine features, that she was thinking the same. I felt like I was being drawn and quartered, each possible outcome a torture to itself.

And the Crimson Man made it no easier.

He was grinning now. Fisk covered his face with a heavy wool gorget but the smile was there, full of teeth and the promise of blood and fire.

Only late in the afternoon, after the sun had passed over the rim of the world and plunged the party into the half-lit blue-grey of twilight, did we call a halt. Fisk looked annoyed and agitated.

'You need to simmer down, pard. Why don't you take a fresh horse and see if you can rustle some meat. Saw a lot of deer tracks 'bout a mile back. Large game trail cutting through, even with the snow.'

His eyes blazed like embers but they didn't start smoking. After a moment, the ornery cant to his shoulders reappeared and Fisk dismounted, untacked, and picked out the freshest pony to ride. His jaw worked furiously, his lean stubbled cheek popping. I could hear his teeth grind.

We made camp in the lee of a rocky overhang where the snow had not touched the earth. On the way up to the shelter I had seen some brushwood, either from an old avalanche or a rockslide, so I took the draft horse and led him downslope a fair piece and dragged the largest fallen tree back to where the rest were setting up camp. Titus and I started to work on the brushwood with axes. Soon we had a pile of wood and a fire burning bright and high.

We all huddled close to the fire, warming our chilled bones; even the horses pressed in tight around us, their nickers echoing eerily off the rock walls of our camp. After five nights on the trail, we all knew our duties. Soon, after each of us had eaten some hardtack and drunk from the meagre stores of coffee we had, the others went to bed, leaving me watching the dark and listening for Fisk's return.

Livia sat with me.

'Did you ever have children, Shoe?' she asked.

'Had a few, but haven't seen them for fifty years or more.'

'You ever think they might be more trouble than they're worth?'

I thought about my eldest – the troublesome one. 'Yes. But you love them anyway. Don't matter if they're a handful.'

She was quiet for a long while. 'I've always wanted a family but never had someone I wanted to have it with. And now...'

She was crying, unreservedly. Livia was the strongest woman I'd ever met, but the world and the Crimson Man had beat her down pretty good. I wasn't feeling too good about things myself.

The fire popped loudly, and she wiped away the tears.

'Miss Livia, this will all work out, I know. It might look bleak now, but you have to have faith—'

'In Ia?' She smiled and patted my hand, not realizing what she said felt like a knife turning inside me.

Everything was falling apart.

Livia suddenly looked shocked, and she rose from her seat. I turned to see what had agitated her.

The Crimson Man walked into the firelight, drenched in blood. He had lost his hat somewhere, and his face, shoulders, arms, and hands were covered in gore. All was red except for the white of his smile and the black orbs of his eyes.

'Hungry?' he said in a voice thick with blood or phlegm.

He slung the carcass of a boar from his shoulders and tossed it at our feet.

Putting everything I had into it, I barked, 'Fisk! Get a hold of yourself!'

He recoiled as though from a blow. The fiendish smile left, and he cursed loudly. Fisk, again.

'Ia-damn me, Ia-damn me to Hell,' he said. He walked over to the nearest snow drift, scooped up a handful, and began rubbing clean his face, his hands.

The next morning I had the boar cooked, some stew on the fire, and enough meat to fill everyone's stomachs with hot food.

We rode out early and made good time up the mountainside, past gambels and aspens, firs and snarls of bramblewrack all covered in snow. Higher and higher we rode, horses chuffing and nickering and tossing their heads. The world was quiet and no one spoke, following the path up to the pass.

The ground became clear of snow, maybe due to mountain currents, maybe because, for some reason, snow couldn't fall here. We were hemmed in on both sides by steep, rock walls, and our mounts' hooves clattered and echoed loudly. There were no trees and bramble now, no scrub brush nor any sign of living things.

Even Fisk's crimson grin had died on his face, and he looked back nervously at the riders following. Reeve and Livia kept close behind while Titus rode escort to Samantha, still a novice, unsteady in her saddle and in constant jeopardy of toppling over.

I brought up the rear. I hesitated before advancing into the shadow of the pass and looked back on our trail.

The whole world lay shimmering behind us in blues and whites, and I could see, far out and away, a patch of sunlight streaking across the face of the land as fast as a dream.

Then, I followed Fisk and the others into pass – into the dark.

'We're close!' Fisk called back. His voice was rough, excited. That night he'd spent a long time rubbing his face clean of blood and even longer finding his hat, the grey weathered outrider's brim that he'd worn for years.

We rode for what seemed like hours on that winding path, and with each step my heart grew heavier and wearier. I grew tired of watching Samantha. Don't know whether she guessed my reason for keeping so close to her – to keep her safe from Fisk and the thing he carried – or if she put it down to the vagaries of the trail.

The obsidian walls of the pass had closed in tight until I thought we might be forced to turn back. But after a mile of riding single file in a narrow passage in which I could almost reach out with both hands and touch the black, wet rock walls, suddenly the trail opened up and made a slow dip away from the heavens.

The horses were skittish, and the air became more dense and warm. The fog, at first just a hazy occlusion of the light, intensified until I had trouble seeing Samantha or Titus riding only a few paces in front of me.

I called for a halt and dismounted so that I could link the horses with some hemp rope.

While I unbundled the rope from Bess, Reeve said, 'Strange the ice and snow have disappeared so suddenly.' His voice bounced around and came from a strange direction in the fog.

I looked around and, on impulse, pulled off my glove and put my hand to the ground.

'It's hot! The rock and the ground!'

'Aye,' said Reeve, who on dismounting had discovered the same.

I heard, faintly, Livia say, 'Hot Springs was surrounded by pools of boiling water. We must be in some place where the crust of the earth has worn thin.'

'Near Hell, you mean?' said Titus.

'No. There are mountains of fire in Latinum that spew molten rock and ash. Hellish, yes, but occurring naturally. We must be near such a place.'

Samantha, just visible in the fog, glanced at me.

'We are close,' said Fisk.

Not much to say after that. I linked up the horses and remounted.

Another hour, now riding blind in the fog, and we came into a long-dead caldera, the wide opening more discernible using my ears than my eyes. The echoes changed, lengthened.

'If ye have Hellfire,' Reeve said. 'I suggest ye draw it now.'

We passed large, upright black stones in the mist, and the air became utterly still. Fisk reined in the black and dismounted, and the rest of us followed suit.

Titus and Reeve had pistols drawn, and Livia held her sawn-off comfortably, as though it was an extension of her arm. Samantha produced a carbine from somewhere.

I approached Titus asking quietly, 'Manius' guns. Where are they?'

He raised his eyebrows, then turning to his horse removed Manius' pistols from a saddlebag.

'You know how to use one?'

'I think I can figure it out.'

As I turned and began cinching the belt around my waist, Livia stepped in front of me and said, 'What are you doing, Shoe?'

'Puttin' on this gunbelt.'

'Why? I thought you were against Hellfire.'

'What does it matter now? We're at the end of the trail and I don't know what's gonna happen.' I stopped and looked at her closely, seeing the noble desperation there, her beauty. Her love. 'I don't want to die just yet. And I don't want you or Fisk or any of these others to die, either. So if that means a little taint done to my soul, that's just how it's gotta be.'

From ahead, in the fog, Fisk shouted again, 'We are close.'

His voice was tight, excited, and not entirely human.

'We three should investigate. Titus! Reeve! Stay with Fisk,' Livia said.

We moved between the towering black stones that stood like sentinels in the fog.

'Think there's stretchers about?' Titus whispered.

'Has to be. Otherwise, who's guarding Isabelle?' I said.

I was thinking about the girl, her beauty and grace. Her doomed love for Banty. To remind myself why we were there.

There's a million reasons to do anything. Most folks – human, *dvergar*, or perhaps stretcher, even – don't know the reason deep down inside. If you'd asked Livia, or me, why we were cold and hungry and terrified on some haunted mountaintop, we'd have said: to prevent a war between Rume and Mediera. But deep down, we were doing this for a girl, vulnerable, alone, surrounded by monsters and terrified. There's reasons and then there's reasons.

'Look.'

Reeve pointed to a large empty fire pit surrounded by smaller black rocks. Titus walked over and nudged the coals with his foot, turning over ash and exposing a cherry hot ember, still smoking.

'Ain't been gone too long, if they're gone at all.'

Samantha said, 'Look here.' She stood near one of the tall black rocks. It stood twenty feet high, easy.

The obsidian obelisk looked porous, riddled with wormworks, until you got close enough.

'Flames,' she said, and she ran a gloved hand down the face of the stone. 'Intricately carved. Fire carved into the living stone.'

It was true. Layer upon layer traced the stone from the base to as far up as I could see. The craft was chillingly beautiful, stylized if a bit rough – it would never sell in a Harbor Town market except as a novelty. The sheer amount of it on the obelisk made me marvel.

I walked to another stone.

'My god,' I said, touching the stone. 'Here too.'

Titus went to another obelisk. 'And here.'

Over thirty stones stood in the rocky clearing. Each one inscribed over and over with flames.

I shuddered, thinking about the *vaettir* spending countless years scratching these images of fire into the almost impenetrable stone.

'Maybe it's their way of writing,' Samantha said. 'And it just resembles flames.'

'No,' Livia replied, 'That is *fire*. Over and over. Fire.'

'Dis' ballsack! That's a harrowing thought,' Titus said.

'We are close,' Fisk stated again. His voice was from farther away now, echoing off the stones.

'Fisk!' Livia cried. 'Fisk, wait!'

The etched stones were forgotten in an instant. We turned as a group and raced around the clearing. The space we were in was shaped like a bowl with the monuments and fire pit in the centre, the ground sloping upward toward higher, blank-faced walls.

'He's here!' Reeve called, and we ran toward the sound of his voice.

Two more pillars of flame-etched stone framed the entrance to a cavern, low and dark. As quickly as I could, I raced back to Bess and found the silver-rimed lantern we'd moved from the wagon onto the mule and brought it to Samantha. It was only a moment's work for Samantha to inscribe a ward onto the stone ground with chalk, prick a finger – dripping blood into the reservoir on the lantern's lid – and say soft words under her breath. I knelt close beside her as she did. It was easy enough to slip the silver blade from her boot. Fisk may need it by the end, but it won't be her that gives him that release. It will be me.

The bright light cast from the *imp* – silently screaming and batting at the silver tracery of its cage – reduced our sense of foreboding at entering the dark cave. But I already had a bad feeling, and the *daemon* summoning and binding didn't help,

Samantha handed the lantern to Reeve, the tallest of us all, and we slowly walked forward.

There were bones. Countless bones in piles. The light from the *imp* lantern flickered, and shadows danced on the jet-black walls in strange recursive patterns. The cavern walls were close and tight. I felt sweat prickle under my heavy coat and gloves in the still, hot air.

Titus picked up a large bone and looked at it.

'Leg bone from an auroch.' He stopped, waved Reeve over with the lantern. After brief further observation, he said, 'Teeth marks. The stretchers did a good job gnawing on it.'

Livia picked up another bone and held it up to the light.

'Oh, no.'

It was a jawbone. The jawbone of a man.

'Teeth marks here as well.'

'Are ye saying those creatures eat men?' Reeve's voice, usually full of mirth, sounded dead and dull in the hollow, bone-filled expanse of the cave.

'We need to find Fisk,' said Livia.

Reeve led us farther into the interior of the cave, past heaps of bones, most gone grey. A fine powder dusted the ground, and I realized it was the grinds of a millennium of bones stored in this horrible place.

We came around a bend and there stood Fisk, the *daemon* hand glowing red at his neck, and in his own hand, a skull. He stared into its empty eyes. The integument of flesh had been stripped away, but there were still long locks of dark lustrous hair affixed to the skull in patches.

And the Crimson Man was there, too, in him, eyes smoking.

He laughed, and it wasn't the hate-filled, mocking laugh we'd grown used to. It was a softer, self-loathing laugh, full of anger and despair.

'Too late,' he said. 'Too fucking late.'

'Isabelle,' Livia gasped, hands going to her mouth.

Samantha bent over, scrabbling for the knife in her boot that was no longer there. Her face widened further in shock, and part of me felt regret at taking it from her. The Crimson Man was terrible to behold, and the only thing to improve his appearance would be a silver knife in his chest.

Fisk's hair caught flame in a burning circlet around his brow. Gone forever was my friend, my partner. Gone forever was Livia's lover, the pistolero out of New Damnation. Gone was the

Centurion of Rume, son of an exile, once destined to be a senator of the Empire.

He looked upon us as the Crimson Man, the Fiend, Belial, King of Hell. Blood dripped from his skull, covering his face.

'Bound!' He spat, and streaks of flame lanced from his brow like the first rays of the morning sun shooting through the treeline. 'Bound in this sack of meat!'

'Out!' I yelled, grabbing Livia and Reeve and pushing them back. 'Out! *Now!*'

I seem to remember shouting, '*There's no holding him back now!*' But the words may have never left my throat. Perhaps it was just an errant thought caroming around my skull.

The Crimson Man ignited like a pile of logs steeped in pitch. We fled back, but the heat pulsed from his body like the blowback from a blast furnace, tremendous and intense. I pushed Samantha ahead and hoped that Titus was keeping up. But when I looked back I saw the legionary hanging in midair, locked in an invisible grip, his back arched and his mouth open in a terrible O of agony, flames licking up his frame. His hair caught and he screamed, a high-pitched skittering sound like a pig being slaughtered.

The bones around us, brittle from the centuries left to dry inside this barrow, combusted like kindling.

We fled. Behind us the Crimson Man laughed.

'No more *fucking around*!' he bellowed. 'No more silly games!'

We ran, stumbling over the uneven cavern floor, struggling with our terror and the overwhelming heat.

Livia and Reeve spilled out of the cavern and ran toward the centre of the standing-stones and the fire pit and the horses. Samantha and I followed close behind. The air, even with the fog, felt icy-cold and fresh. I took in great draughts of it and drew the Hellfire from the gunbelt.

'I come for thee, humans!'

The maw of the cavern looked like the gullet of Hell, full of flame and the scent of burning bones. Oily black smoke poured from the opening and clung to the face of the stone wall, rising upward.

'Get in the fire pit!' Samantha said. She huffed like a mare coming off a long gallop, yet was strangely calm. I felt a sudden overwhelming admiration for the homely woman.

She glared at me. 'A knife! I need one! Mine is missing.'

I whipped out my longknife and put it in her hand. As slick as a mink's prick, she'd drawn it across her palm and now gripped it in her bloody hand. With the point of the dagger, she began scratching wards into the hard stone. The blade screeched on the earth, and her blood spattered over the wards.

Reeve seemed ready to vomit, but had his gun out. Livia looked crazed, her hair in a tangled spill over her face, but she gripped her sawn-off in her hand. Samantha scratched and bled on the stone, moving in a circle around the fire pit.

'Subsisto. Vos non obduco,' Samantha said, hushed and urgent. But the sound travelled clean and clear through the air. 'Ego prohibeo vos ut ultra progredi, Belial, ego prohibeo vos ut ultra progredi, *daemonis.*'

The air brightened and streamers of steam rose from the ground and pushed away from the mouth of the cavern as the Crimson Man came forth, riding the boiling air, crowned in fire and robed in flame and bearing the sword and sceptre of the King of Hell.

The Crimson Man floated over the black rock of the caldera toward us. Livia raised her sawn-off, and Reeve did similarly with his six-gun. Samantha still scratched at the stone, speaking the words faintly, under her breath.

As the Crimson Man advanced on them, the horses screamed in human voices, rearing and pulling at their tethers, maddened by the heat and the burning figure. Even steadfast Bess was hawing and kicking at the air. Fisk's black reared mightily. The halter rope threading the horses together snapped and whipped out through the many tie-rings. The horses wheeled and ran with a great clatter of hooves on rock up and out of the caldera, back through the pass.

The Crimson Man came forward and touched down on the black rock of the caldera floor. Around him the fog burned away. There was only blazing hot air shimmering with heat.

I took hold of the pistol at my waist and pulled it free from its holster. It felt dead and dull as some stone I might have plucked from the ground. I thumbed back the hammer. But I couldn't fire on Fisk. Try as I might, I couldn't pull the trigger.

Reeve wasn't so finicky. He raised his six-gun, sighting down the barrel.

But the Crimson Man's own hand shot up, palm-up and fingers splayed, and the gun did not fire. The Fiend smiled.

Reeve threw his pistol aside and yanked his longknife from its sheath, leaping over the bloody ward etched into stone, flying at the creature that was once Fisk.

'Stay behind the ward!' Samantha cried. But Reeve, his movement smooth and deadly as a mountain lion, was already past. His hand whipping around, he slashed viciously at the Crimson Man's neck. But the Fiend was fast as flame and pulled back, out of reach.

The *daemon* twisted unmercifully and brought his sceptre of smoke down hard on Reeve, smashing into his torso and tossing the sheriff backward, where he collapsed in a crumpled heap.

Then it was just Livia and Samantha and me standing inside the warding, looking at a burning mockery of man. He grinned at us and dark flames ran up and down his frame, mottling his skin. His eyes smoked like furnaces. The *daemon* hand burned and glowed white hot and seethed at the air. But the grin was the worst.

'It's been a pleasure, but now our time has ended,' he said in a terrible voice, looking down at the warding spattered in blood. 'Ah ha! We know our glyphwork, do we? You've a fine hand. But it is hardly enough to keep me out.'

His sword sprung from his hand like an eruption of flame, and he held it high over his crowned head.

In a cold, calm voice, Livia said, 'Stop! I offer myself!'

'No!' Samantha and I screamed together. 'Livia, no!'

'*In girum imus nocte et consumimur igni*!'

The Fiend found this infinitely amusing, and he laughed, throwing back his head. 'You have nothing to bind me, little mortal! Unless you offer the life growing in your belly?'

Livia's hands went to her stomach, and her mouth opened in an O of surprise. Tears streamed down her sooty face.

He laughed again, a cruel mocking sound.

'No matter. I shall soon have all of you, every scrap and bloody ribbon.'

With the flaming sword he smote the earth, a blur on the living rock. The black stone cracked with a sound as enormous as the sky and as massive as a thunderclap. The earth shook, and Livia and Samantha fell to the ground. Standing stones split and fell into ruin with thunderous crashes.

The circle was broken. The Crimson Man came forward.

And then, with a high-pitched screech, a blur came from above like some massive bird of prey descending from the heavens, falling almost too fast for my poor tear-swollen eyes to track, and hit the Crimson Man with the force of a hammer falling on an anvil.

Agrippina.

The momentum of her leap knocked the Fiend's human form to the ground and they grappled like drunken fighters brawling in the street. The Crimson Man's flames died and his hellish accoutrements – the sword and sceptre – disappeared, back to whatever infernal limbo they were called from.

Black smoke hung near the ground, this *daemonic* cloud wreathing their forms and obscuring them from view.

Then there came a strange yelp of pure joy, and a scream of pain, and Fisk's body flew from out of the oily smoke and landed half upon a collapsed stone pillar.

The *daemon* hand was gone.

Laughter came again, this time thicker, wetter, from an alien throat.

She rose.

All her jagged teeth exposed, she smiled – she too breaking into flame, the crown searing the air. She lifted her arm, the one Fisk had so cruelly shortened, and there was a black hand. The *daemon* hand. Fused to her incorruptible flesh.

She had become whole once again.

'Run!' I yelled to Livia and Samantha, still motionless in the ashes of the fire pit. 'Flee!'

I moved to stand in front of the massive thing. The monster. The Queen of Hell.

The black hand lanced out to grip the air, and I felt my ribs crunch.

The thing that was once a *vaettir* turned her black smoking eyes toward me, and all my resolve failed. I wished then that I too had run.

My feet left the ground and I was lifted in the air to hang in front of her face, wracked with pain from the crushing pressure of her invisible grip. Heat poured off her like the blast from a smelter, and her overlarge eyes, at this close vantage, looked like two holes into the deepest abyss, boiling out streamers of thick black smoke.

She grinned and said in *dvergar*, 'Lover,' flicking her tongue in her mouth. 'You, I will let live.'

I yelled again, 'Run! Get to the horses!'

From the corner of my eye I saw Samantha try to tug Livia away, but she would not move.

'Ah, my little vermin, so selfless, so brave.' She drew me in closer, so close I could barely stay conscious in the withering heat. The stink of sulphur and brimstone was overpowering.

'I have a message for the world. And you will be my emissary.' Her grin grew, wicked and lascivious. 'You are mine. For the lust you bore for this creature. This flesh. You will tell them I am coming.'

Turning her head she looked to the western rim of the caldera, to the peaks of the highest of the White Mountains. 'This vessel is so much more commodious than the other meatsack. Her millennium of knowledge is now mine.'

Her head snapped back to face me. 'Go. Tell the world I am coming, and when I do, I will be at the head of an army of these children of fire. These deathless ones. I shall gather them to me from the lands beyond these mountains.'

She laughed and I could see down her black gullet, her dark tongue. 'I will drown the world in blood. I will roast your infants on spits and feast on their flesh. I will slaughter you all. I shall bathe the land in fire.' The lascivious smile appeared again. 'And you, my messenger, shall be consecrated with a kiss.'

Her face filled my vision and her searing flesh pressed against mine, her lips pressing hard to my mouth, her tongue worming in. In all my years, it is the one thing that still haunts me, in the depths of night when I am alone and sleep will not come. I'll never be able to forget it. Such torments and pleasures were contained in that kiss, such cruelty and lust, that I nearly lost my wits.

Nearly.

I twisted my hand, and the silver blade sprouted from my fist.

I jerked my arm up and planted the knife in the underside of her chin, driving it up through her mouth and into her brain.

Then I was falling, flung away as the body of Agrippina fell to the caldera floor and thrashed, convulsing as the flames died and the blackness of the *daemon* coalesced and condensed down back into a lifeless hand threaded on a silver chain.

And I knew no more.

TWENTY-EIGHT

IT WAS A long ride back to the *Cornelian*.

Titus was beyond dead; he had returned to ash. Reeve's body was badly broken, and he was coughing blood. Fisk, though bruised, seemed otherwise unharmed – whatever Hellish power that preserved his flesh as he burned, I couldn't understand. He only seemed singed, but remained in an unconscious stupor.

I had pulled something in my shoulder after being flung away by the dying Agrippina, so digging graves for both the legionary and the *vaettir* would be a long, painful experience. Samantha was for leaving the one-handed stretcher as a warning to other *vaettir*, but it did not seem right to me. So, alone, I marched back up the pass and recollected the horses and Bess. They had fled back along our trail far enough to feel safe, and there they had stayed. I had no doubt this was due to the sense and calm demeanour of my girl, Bess. I tethered the other horses, but took the draft and Bess out of the dark pass and back down to the nearest stand of gambels, where I found and cut four long saplings suitable to make two travois for our injured. I spent the rest of the day digging and laying to rest the body of Agrippina and such ashes of Titus I could find.

In the morning, after a wretched sleepless night jumping at sounds and staring at the dull, dark walls of the caldera, Samantha and Livia sat close together, ministering to Fisk and Reeve. Reeve moaned softly, weakly thrashing his head with the pain. I had made the last of the coffee and handed out hardtack rations.

'Poor Isabelle,' said Livia.

'Damned shame, that. She was a true beauty and a fine rider. I curse the day Banty took to wooing.'

Livia waved off my words. 'They loved each other. At least she knew love in her short life.'

I could not refrain from asking. 'Will there be war?'

Livia looked unbearably sad and utterly frustrated. 'I believe so. King Diegal is unlikely to wave an olive branch after his daughter was abducted and devoured by stretchers because of Ruman negligence.' She had been gazing into space but now looked up. 'Do you think what the thing said is true?'

'What?' I said.

'That there are more *vaettir* beyond the Whites.'

I tossed the cold dregs of my coffee on the small fire I had made with the last of the charcoal from Hot Springs and – I am somewhat ashamed to admit – an armful of bones I'd collected from the cavern. I don't think any of the bones were human.

'I reckon so,' I said. 'It was cruel and loved to torture us – with the truth.'

I walked over to the *daemon* hand lying upon the ground.

'What are we gonna do with this?'

Samantha came over. 'We can't touch it. I'll get it into a sack and keep it safe until we reach the *Cornelian*. I'll see if I can convince or coerce Beleth to send its resident back to Hell.'

I nodded. We couldn't leave it lying there for the *vaettir* to find. That made me think.

'Where do you think the other stretcher went? The one who started the fire? The one Fisk calls Berith?'

Livia knitted her brows and said, 'They have focused on us for a while, but now I fear they have gone to harry the *Cornelian*.'

Samantha, lashing a tarp to two gambel saplings, said nothing. Her face looked grim.

'Damnation, I about had enough of them fucking elves.' I lifted up the travois and set to lashing it to the draft's backstrap.

When the travois were ready and both men firmly lying in their beds, Samantha took some time to choose the better fragments of the flame-inscribed stones to bring back to Cornelius.

On the ride out we stopped at the mouth of the pass and looked back at the ruin of the caldera.

Low, but with intensity, Livia said, 'Ia damn this place. I would destroy it, had I the power.'

'Don't bother calling on Ia to damn it,' I said, and the words felt strange upon my tongue. But there it was. For some reason, I truly did believe what Samantha had told me. I felt ashamed and stupid and angry all at once for having spent so much of my life trying to keep faith with what turned out to be a tall tale spun for a reason lost in the mists of history. There was Hellfire sweeping the world, and now a war was imminent too. Battle cruisers would soon be filling the seas, and legions would be on the march. Rume and all its petty lords – so far removed from the rest of the world and its concerns, the concerns of real folk – reached out its long arm to play another cruel jape at my expense. It had wiped clean the slate of my heart, my faith. I was empty inside now, without that centre, the well of strength, I'd drawn from. I felt as barren and devastated as the shattered rock that we looked down upon.

'Ia can't help,' I said. 'This place is already damned.'

We rode through fields asleep under blankets of snow. The travois carved great ruts in the ground cover. Game was few and far between, and the handful of small villages we passed on the journey back to the *Cornelian* were terrified of any strangers, having discovered the ruin of Hot Springs. Rumours differed regarding its destruction. Some thought it was the work of a secret Ruman force dispensed by the governor to destroy untaxed trade in the region and claim the silver mine for Rume. Others said that Croesus' wickedness and silverlust finally cracked the bowels of Hell and Mammon himself, the great greedy *daemon*, came up through one of the smoking pools to claim Croesus' soul and lay waste to the town.

But the most common rumour was that the *vaettir* had committed the horrendous act.

Fisk was still unconscious, even after days, and Reeve had settled into a silent drunken sulk – the results of a bottle of shine we had bought from a farmer who had let us camp in his barn. Reeve was outraged that his broken body might have betrayed him so heinously. But he would live.

Fisk was more troublesome.

Sometimes he cried out strange words in a language no one could understand. Other times he chuckled. It was not the all-encompassing evil mirth of the Crimson Man, but the sound reminded me enough that it made the hairs on the back of my neck prickle and my skin go cold.

One village claimed the *vaettir* had raided in the night and taken a young woman and her lover and devoured them on the nearby mountain top where the elders had found a spatter of blood and some scraps of flesh and clothes in the snow.

Before, we might have doubted them. Not now.

Five days after the confrontation with the Crimson Man, we were riding through the shoal plains under the wide-open frozen sky when a rider appeared over a far hill. A single soul, on a lone horse, galloping as though all the devils of Hell followed him.

We reined in and waved, but when he saw us, he changed course and rode away.

'That horse is gonna die right under him, way he's going,' I said.

'What could he be fleeing?' Samantha asked.

'*Vaettir*, maybe,' said Livia.

We watched him go. Two days later, we reached the *Cornelian*. Or what was left of it.

The *Cornelian*, still locked in the ice of the Big Rill, had seen fire gut its upper half from the roof of the boiler deck to just before the prow. It still smoked.

But somehow the fire had not devoured the whole boat, and as we rode into sight of it we saw a large camp, now on the shores of the river. Many campfires sent columns of smoke into the air to be whisked away by the wind whipping off the Whites. A veritable tent city, it looked very much like an army on the march.

'Oh my,' Samantha said. 'That could have been very bad.'

'What do you mean?'

'Gooseberry. If the fire had burned hot and high enough to melt silver—'

'Big angry *daemon* loosed upon the world,' Livia said. But even though the sentiment was dark, there was lightness to her voice. She grinned at me. 'But, blessed twins, how I'm glad to be back.'

Secundus greeted us as we rode into camp. His face fell as he counted riders and saw that we did not have Isabelle with us. Legionaries took the horses, and the Cornelian heir himself helped us move Fisk and Reeve into a tent and under blankets. All the staterooms had been gutted by fire, including Cornelius'.

Livia told him the state of things, the ruin of Hot Springs, the sad end of poor Isabelle. The confrontation in the caldera. Samantha produced some of the flame-inscribed stone. He ran his hands over the face of it.

'This does not bode well. King Diegal will see this as an outrage.'
War was inevitable.

'And the *daemon* hand?'

'Not destroyed,' Samantha said. 'I have it here. I need Beleth's assistance to destroy it and send its occupant back to Hell. Its power is too much for this world, I fear, and beyond me to banish.'

Secundus looked very troubled.

'Brother, what happened here?' Livia asked gently.

'The *vaettir* came. Attacked in force.' He shook his head. 'We fought them off, and then they returned the next night. That was when the fire started.' As though remembering something, he said, 'Father's absolutely livid that his marvellous riverboat has been so damaged.'

'How did it start? Why didn't the whole boat catch fire?' Livia asked.

Secundus shrugged and said, 'Cimbri had a good idea. With the boat locked in ice, the *daemon*-fired pumps used for replenishing the *Cornelian*'s water supply could be used to fight the fire. We lost a couple of men dousing the flames, and most of the interior of the boat is sodden now.'

I asked, 'How did it start?'

He grimaced. 'We don't know, really. But they had come. They scalped a handful of our shore guards; staved in their skulls, too. So we sounded the alarm and pulled the men back from the shore. Some of them never made it, hauled off to god knows where.'

Samantha, Livia, and I exchanged glances.

'But the fire?'

'I'm of the opinion it was Beleth. He must have managed to start a fire when the alarm sounded. When the legionaries guarding him smelled the smoke and released him from the room, he escaped in the confusion.'

'The rider,' I said.

'What's this?'

'We saw a lone man riding Hell for leather. Looked like he was gonna kill his horse. When did this all happen?'

'Five days ago.'

'He's heading toward Passasuego. I imagine to the Medieran stronghold there to ask for sanctuary.'

Secundus said, 'I never liked that Ia-damned engineer.'

I flinched at his choice of words.

'But I have some good news for you, Miss Decius.'

She raised her eyebrows. 'What's that?'

'You have now been promoted to engineer. Congratulations.'

We all laughed, except for Samantha. Her expression was pained, and I could tell that the *daemon* hand was foremost in her thoughts. It was hers to deal with now.

'Oh, and I have more good news,' said Secundus. 'Follow me.'

He led us through the camp, past legionaries at cook fires, lascars oiling weapons. The ground by the shore was frozen hard, and it crunched beneath our feet. He brought us to a large military command tent, guarded by two burly legionaries. Smoke came from a chimney that peeked from the roof.

'Father! Livia has returned.'

The flaps of the tent were thrown back, and standing there was Cornelius, still using that damned bear-leg. He beckoned us inside.

A tent that could have held twenty men was now filled with the furniture and accessories of his quarters.

Cornelius hobbled in circles around the tent's small cast-iron stove as we relayed the events of the last days. He cursed mightily in more than one language when he learned of the carnivorous nature of the *vaettir* and Isabelle's end.

When we had finished, he looked grim. 'Ia-dammit all to Hell. Summon Sharbo and that Silenus fellow. We must send word to Marcellus in New Damnation to secure the mines at Hot Springs and ready the army for war. I must write missives to the senate and the Emperor.' He stopped his lopsided pacing and rubbed his chin. 'By Ia's beard, I'm in a pickle. I'll be lucky if they don't send a replacement for me on the next ship over here once they get this damnable news.'

'Poor Isabelle. Such a dear girl,' Secundus said, shaking his head.

'We have until winter ends before Diegal will realize something is wrong and begin to marshal his forces. He expects us to arrive in Passasuego, or some other Medieran embassy, by spring, with Isabelle.'

'Do you have to tell Diegal what actually happened? It's a big, hard land here. We can say she was abducted by indigenes, which is true.'

'Yes. That's the way. When the Emperor gets the news – with luck months before Diegal begins to suspect – he'll start shipping legions over to keep the colonies. We cannot hope to stand against the Medieran navy – they are too strong. But they can never match the might of the Ruman legions in any land battle. So, it will be a race to get enough men over here before Diegal locks down all sea routes.' He cursed again, this time in Gallish.

Exhausted, he sat down and called for Lupina to bring him wine. She entered from the tent's back flap with a large decanter and many glasses. 'Well, at least we can remain civilized here in the provinces,' he said as he waited for her to pour. He grabbed his glass and gulped. Then she poured for us all.

'Father,' said Secundus, 'would you like to show them your trophy?'

Cornelius' eyes lit up, and his whiskers quivered with his excitement. 'Of course! The best thing to come from this whole sorry mess. How could I have forgotten? Back here.' He hopped up and stomped to the back of the tent, leading us outside and a fair distance away from camp.

There was a long wooden table, on top of which was a tarp-shrouded object.

'I bagged this whore's son at fifty yards while he was a-leaping and prancing about, coming at the retreating shore guards. Haven't figured out how I'm to mount him. I've sent for a taxidermist from New Damnation.'

He pulled back the tarp.

It was the *vaettir*, Berith.

An apple-sized hole was punched through his chest, directly through the heart.

I laughed out loud.

What a beautiful sight.

It was a long, hard winter and, by the end of it, when the thaw finally came, the *Cornelian* had mostly been repaired and there was a new village on the shore at the point in the river where the boat had been locked in ice. The legionaries and lascars called it Winter Camp, but the settlers who had begun to appear during the first blushes of spring called it Bear Leg. The Senator was inordinately proud of the name.

When winter released its icy grip on the Big Rill and the grasses became green once more, the trees filled the air with a thousand motes of pollen – making some of the men sneeze terribly – and a group of us gathered on the western shore of the river, in a clearing in the gambels, to perform a ceremony.

Ruman weddings are always held under the vault of sky, so that all who may wish to, can bear witness to the joining of two immortal souls. The marriage of Hieronymous Fiscelion Catalan Iulii and Livia Saturninus Cornelius would be no different.

Fisk had awoken from his dream state groggy and bruised. He never spoke of it, but I could tell he remembered everything. His eyes were haunted, and something had given when the *daemon* rode him. He'd changed, found it easier to laugh, easier to smile. I have to think that when the Crimson Man had Fisk in his terrible possession, Fisk came to understand that life is too short to be unduly stingy with affections or their display.

I was so very glad to have my friend and partner back. And so happy to lose him to Livia.

We stood in a circle, with Fisk and Livia at the centre, to witness their vows.

Livia was beautiful, dressed in a gown of white that almost concealed the growing bulge of her stomach. And Fisk was garbed in Gnaeus' finest uniform and laureled with a grass crown, Rume's highest military honour. Fisk had told me, late one night when we were in our cups, that Cornelius had drawn him aside and said, 'If you're to be the father of my first grandchild and the husband of my eldest, however independent and strong-willed she is, you're damn well not going to embarrass me by being a lowly scout. Congratulations, you now have the rank of legate and are assigned to advise on all my decisions regarding the Hardscrabble Territories. You shall be honoured for your sacrifice regarding the *daemon* hand.

'Now, wipe that look off your face and have a drink.'

The day of the wedding was perfect. As the air blew warm with only the faintest hint of the fast retreating winter, it ruffled the gambel tops and stirred the grasses.

Cornelius performed the invocation. Holding high the knife, he said, 'Above you the sky, below you the stones; as time passes, remember – like a stone should your love be firm, like a star should your love be constant. Let the blessings of Ia guide you in your marriage; let the strength of your wills bind you together inextricably. Let the strength of your dedication make you inseparable. Possess each other, yet be understanding. Have patience with each other, for storms will come, but they will pass quickly.

'Hold out your hands.'

Livia and Fisk, facing each other, held out their hands, palm up.

'Will you, Livia Saturninus Cornelius, take up the knife?' asked Cornelius.

'I will,' said Livia.

'The wound you make is the essence of all pain and hardship in life. For any two people to be joined, there must be sacrifice,' Cornelius intoned.

Livia drew the knife across her palm, cupping her hand afterward to collect the blood. Her father took the blooded blade from her.

'Will you, Hieronymous Fiscelion Catalan Iulii, take up the knife?'

'I will,' Fisk said.

Cornelius handed the knife to Fisk, who gripped it, looked from the blade to Livia's beautiful face, luminous in the spring light, and smiled as he cut his hand.

'The pain you feel is her pain, always. The joy you feel is her joy, always.' Cornelius stopped, raised his arms, and joined his own hands together. 'Let your love be incorruptible and undying. Now join hands as man and wife and go forth with the gods' blessings.'

Fisk and Livia clasped hands. The blood from their wedding wounds commingled and joined, dripping to the ground. And when they smiled at us, the cheering crowd, they did it as one.

I rode out of Bear Leg on Bess with only enough food for two days. This time I wore Manius' guns, loaded with silver and holly.

Up we rode, into the Whites, for I needed to be alone and to look upon the earth from a great height.

We were hours climbing, and the sun grew old in the heavens and fell past the lip of earth and the sky turned purple and pink like a floral explosion.

I reined in Bess, who hawed once at me and then playfully nipped at my leg, showing green teeth. I dismounted, letting the reins fall. Bess would go nowhere without me and would find me if I called.

I hiked upward for hours, even in the dark of night. Once I heard the screech of a mountain lion but it did not molest me and I hoped to all the gods that it did not find the scent of Bess appealing.

Sweat, pouring from my brow, had darkened my shirt and vest by the time I stopped and took up my vigil on a rocky promontory high above Bear Leg and the Big Rill.

Below me, far below, I could see the dying fires of the camp and the flickering yellow *daemonlight* of the revivified *Cornelian* glimmering on the waters of the Big Rill. It would be steaming south soon, with me on it.

I did not know when I would be able to return to these peaks, to feel rock under my feet, the comfort of the mountain. I am *dvergar*, and this is important.

Throughout the night I knelt, watching the lights die, listening to the wind, the breath of the world, the sigh of the mountains. The stars, shining indifferently above me, wheeled in the heavens.

I felt them then, I think. Ia was gone, dead to me, but there were the old gods, the spirits of rock and tree, of water and wind. The numen.

I needed some kind of faith.

The night grew old and everything stilled and it seemed that I was the only living person in the world awake at that moment. The *daemonlight* from the Cornelian, the smoke from Bear Leg, all gone. The world was dark, and I felt so rooted to the mountain and the sky that I couldn't tell where I left off and the others began.

I felt whole, once more.

The sky in the east lightened as the sun rose. It crept over the rim of the earth, its light streaking forward and painting the land in oranges and reds, purples and deep blues. Rocks and trees cast long shadows in the slanting light. I watched as the night gave way to day.

My thoughts turned to my friends, those I had known and loved, those far away, those near, and I felt a connection with them all. But darkness filled me too, as I sat looking out at the land from that vantage. As I rose and prepared to make my way back to Bess, I looked out and imagined countless fires on the plains, sending black smoke up to the vaults of heaven.

Fire calls to fire, they say.

I lowered my eyes from the view and made my way down the mountain. I'd had enough with flame. I wanted to see no more.

War was coming.

Acknowledgements

Big thanks go out to Stacia Decker, my agent, for her guidance regarding this industry in turmoil and to John Rector whose enthusiasm for this novel has not waned in the intervening years since he first read it. Much gratitude goes out to Mark Lawrence, Myke Cole, and Pat Rothfuss, all of whom, at the time of writing this, were kind enough to read and say nice things publicly about this work. I'd like to thank Steve Drew of Reddit for his encouraging words, Chuck Wendig for his humor and signal boosting, and all the people of the Twitters and Interwebz who have helped to get the word out about *The Incorruptibles*.

Huge ups to the team at Gollancz – especially my editor Marcus Gipps and copy editor Olivia Wood – who've been extremely supportive and a pleasure to work with. Edward Bettison created an amazing cover for this book. Somebody buy that team a drink. They deserve it. Possibly a backrub, but don't get too handsy.

Of course, I must mention my lovely wife and children who've been a constant support and source of motivation for me. And let's not forget the Cookie and Bear, my mongrel canine muses, always down for a little scratchy-scratchness to ease the heavy burden of the writer at work.

Finally, I'd like to thank you, the readers, who remain the true reason why I do this whole writing thing. I would give you a big ole kiss if that wouldn't be too creepy (or a disease vector).

No? Well, okay, then. We'll just settle for a fist bump. Thanks. Y'all rock.

Fisk and Shoe will return in

Foreign Devils